*In a last-ditch attempt to save the galaxy,
Luke Skywalker, his wife, Mara, and Jacen
Solo blaze new frontiers in uncharted
realms as the dazzling Star Wars space
epic continues. . . .*

STAR WARS®

THE NEW JEDI ORDER

FORCE HERETIC II
REFUGEE

SEAN WILLIAMS
AND
SHANE DIX

BALLANTINE BOOKS · NEW YORK

Star Wars: The New Jedi Order: *Force Heretic II: Refugee* is a work of fiction. Names, places, and incidents either are a product of the author's imagination or are used fictitiously.

A Del Rey® Book
Published by The Random House Publishing Group

Published in the United States by Del Rey Books, an imprint of The Random House Publishing Group, a division of Random House, Inc., New York, and simultaneously in Canada by Random House of Canada Limited, Toronto.

Del Rey is a regstered trademark and the Del Rey colophon is a trademark of Random House, Inc.

www.starwars.com
www.delreybooks.com

ISBN 0-345-42871-4

Manufactured in the United States of America

First Edition: May 2003

OPM   9   8   7

ACKNOWLEDGMENTS

Once again, we would like to thank many different people for their help in many different areas, among them Kirsty Brooks, Chris Cerasi, Leland Chee, Richard Curtis, Nydia Dix, Sam Dix, Nick Hess, Enrique Guerrero, Eelia Goldsmith Hendersheid, Vanessa Hobbs, Helen Keier, Greg Keyes, Mike Kogge, Jim Luceno, Christopher McElroy, Ryan Pope, Michael Potts, Sue Rostoni, Shelly Shapiro, Matt Stover, Daniel Wallace, Walter Jon Williams, Lucy Wilson, and Sebastian Yeaman. Special thanks go to the members of the Mount Lawley Mafia, for inspiration, and the SA Writers' Centre, for patience. This novel was inspired by all the people who wondered what happened to the Ssi-ruuvi Imperium after *The Truce at Bakura*, and by Kathy Tyers for bringing those big lizards to life in the first place.

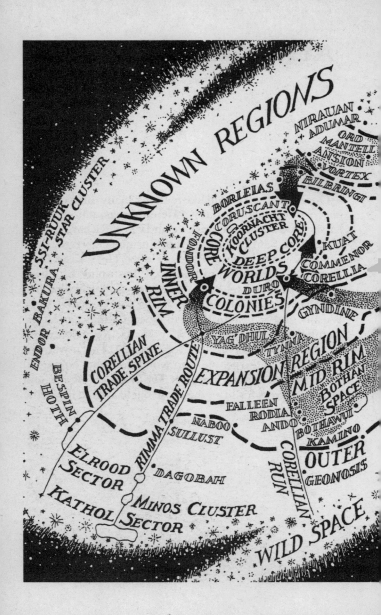

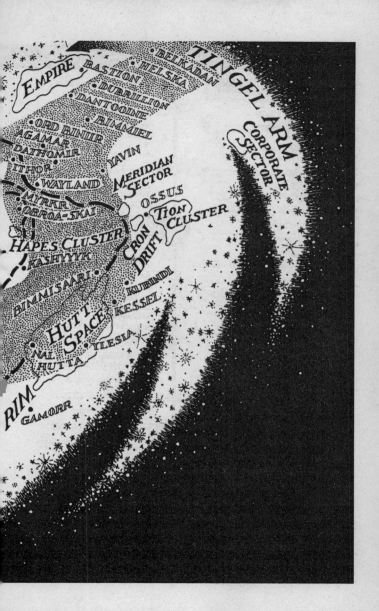

THE STAR WARS NOVELS TIMELINE

There will always be people who are strong for evil.
The stronger you become, the more you're tempted.
—LUKE SKYWALKER, Jedi Master

DRAMATIS PERSONAE

Arien Yage; captain, *Widowmaker* (female human)

Blaine Harris; Bakuran Deputy Prime Minister (male human)

Danni Quee; scientist (female human)

Goure; Bakuran worker (male Ryn)

Grell Panib; general, Bakuran Defense Fleet (male human)

Han Solo; captain, *Millennium Falcon* (male human)

Hess'irolia'nuruodo (Irolia); commander (female Chiss)

Jacen Solo; Jedi Knight (male human)

Jagged Fel; Twin Sun co-leader (male human)

Jaina Solo; Jedi Knight, co-leader of Twin Suns (female human)

Keeramak; mutant leader of the Ssi-ruuvi Imperium (genderless Ssi-ruu)

Kunra; Shamed One and heretic (male Yuuzhan Vong)

Leia Organa Solo; former New Republic diplomat (female human)

Luke Skywalker; Jedi Master (male human)

Lwothin; advance leader of the P'w'eck Emancipation Movement (male P'w'eck)

Malinza Thanas; founder of the Freedom resistance movement (female human)

Mara Jade Skywalker; Jedi Master (female human)

Molierre Cundertol; Prime Minister of Bakura (male human)

Nom Anor; former executor (male Yuuzhan Vong)

Saba Sebatyne; Jedi Knight (female Barabel)

Shimrra; Supreme Overlord (male Yuuzhan Vong)

Shoon-mi Esh; Shamed One heretic (male Yuuzhan Vong)

Soontir Fel; former Imperial Baron, now assistant syndic in the Chiss territories (male human)

Tahiri Veila; Jedi Knight (female human)

Tekli; Jedi healer (female Chadra-Fan)

Todra Mayn; captain, *Pride of Selonia* (female human)

Wynssa (Wyn) Fel; youngest daughter of Syal Antilles and Soontir Fel (female human)

PROLOGUE

The man who was no longer a man stood before an alien who was not what it seemed.

"Everything is in place," the man said.

The alien tasted the air as though sniffing for lies. "Are you certain?"

"Yes, General," he replied confidently. Nevertheless, he felt extremely self-conscious of how he was standing. The aliens he thought he was dealing with were particularly good at reading body language; the slightest gesture or twitch of a facial muscle might be misconstrued as doubt. "The population has been lulled into a false sense of security—or if not security, then certainly hope that security might one day be possible. Barring the unforeseen, all should proceed according to plan."

"I am pleased," the alien said, claws clicking on the floor as it paced restlessly before him.

Inwardly he sighed his relief. Meeting his side of the bargain was literally a matter of life and death. "Does that mean—?"

"When you return, and I am *completely* satisfied that your half of the bargain has been met," the alien said sharply, "then and only then will you receive that which you desire." The alien's tail thumped the ground once: *End of discussion.* It couldn't have been clearer if it had used words.

He shrugged, nodding his acceptance of the alien's

terms. There was no reason to believe that things wouldn't go as expected. He would get what he wanted. He had taken care of everything, after all.

"Then I shall leave you, General," he said, "with your permission."

It looked him over briefly as it concurred. "You may depart," it said in a series of tones too loud for the human ear to endure comfortably, yet possessing such subtlety that few could comprehend it. No human mouth had ever uttered so much as a single word in that tongue.

That he spoke it fluently was simply to be expected. "I shall meet you back here in a matter of days."

"Be assured that I will be waiting," the alien said, still pacing the floor. "And remember: we have what you want."

He bowed, knowing that he could never forget that. As he left the picket ship via the narrow umbilical, his body adapting to free-fall with built-in ease, he eagerly anticipated his return to claim what was rightfully his—the triumphant beginning of his new existence. It didn't matter how many lives it cost. He would happily stand by a bonfire of bodies if that's what it took for a chance to warm himself on immortality's fires.

With a smile, he set a course for destiny.

PART ONE

EXPEDITION

Luke Skywalker scrambled up the rocky slope, his lungs burning with each heavy breath he took. He was relieved to hear his nephew beside him also panting for breath, because that meant his own difficulties with the climb were in no way a reflection of his age or fitness; it was simply that the atmosphere on Munlali Mafir was thin, that was all.

Behind them came the terrible baying of the Krizlaws. The sound was high-pitched and piercing, even through the rarefied atmosphere, and sent a shiver down his spine. With their great rancorlike heads bent low, sniffing for a scent, Luke knew that the smooth- and pink-skinned aliens wouldn't be too far behind, converging from around the ruined palace to join in the hunt for the landing party.

He glanced over his shoulder, half expecting to see them snapping at his heels already. Thankfully, though, they weren't that close. But even as he looked, he saw seven of them emerge from a decorative archway at the base of the nearest wall, tripping over one another and slipping on the rubble in their haste as they headed for the ceremonial mound. Another three jump-rolled from a window, scurrying out of sight behind a statue.

Small reddish eyes, two thin arms tipped with three poisoned claws, two powerful legs designed for pouncing, mouths with jaws extendable enough to swallow a human head in one gulp . . .

The thought was a reminder for Luke that he should keep moving.

"Only ten of them," Dr. Soron Hegerty said, the surprise evident beneath her own panting. She seemed to be finding the pace more difficult than the others, barely keeping up even with Jacen's help. "There have—always been—eleven. I thought that—might have been—significant."

A second later another Krizlaw leapt through the window, shattering what little remained of the already splintered ornate frame, then dashed for the mound also.

The xenobiologist shook her head, as if to suggest she was tired of being right all the time. "Eleven," she confirmed.

"Come on, Doctor Hegerty," Jacen said. Luke felt his young nephew subtly augmenting her stamina with the Force. "We have to keep moving!"

"Ritual hunting party, you think?" Lieutenant Stalgis asked. The stocky Imperial in light combat armor turned to snap a shot back at the seven coming up the mound. The blaster bolt took one on the shoulder, provoking an earsplitting squeal of pain, but didn't slow the creature down.

"Something—like that," Hegerty gasped.

Luke and Jacen exchanged worried looks. The xenobiologist was tiring fast, and the top of the mound was still some distance away. The structure consisted of soil packed tight around a central core of stone, creating a tall, conical pseudo-pyramid with a truncated, stone summit perfect for an impromptu landing field. The shuttle was waiting for them there, engines warmed up and ready to whisk them off to safety. The only problem was that at this rate, with the doctor's endurance flagging, they weren't going to make it.

The two Jedi turned simultaneously to see the Krizlaws making their way up the slope in assured and steady bounds, digging in with their claws and using their enormous thigh muscles to propel them forward. Seeing Luke and Jacen making a stand, the creatures hurried their ascent, their howls intensifying with each leap. Luke had seen the effects these ululations could have on lower lifeforms when he'd witnessed the Krizlaws feeding. The intense vibrations of their howls stunned nerve centers, disoriented senses, and sent muscles into spasm. While their prey was thus incapacitated, the Krizlaws would eat them whole. Dr. Hegerty had said that the Krizlaws believed the still-beating heart to be essential for good digestion.

You won't be digesting this *Jedi*, Luke swore determinedly. *Whole or otherwise!*

He sent his senses deep under the surface of the mound. Packed it might be, but the soil wasn't bound like ferrocrete. There were fissures underneath the surface, numerous pressure points that, with one solid nudge, could be . . .

There. Signaling Jacen, he mentally linked up with his nephew using the Force-meld technique perfected in recent months. Together their minds pushed at the pressure point he had found beneath the surface. Dirt erupted from the slope below as though a buried machine had suddenly come to life. The shower of dirt hid the shifting forces beneath as disturbed ground found itself falling, gathered momentum, disturbed more in turn, and became an avalanche that swept over the Krizlaws, driving them back down to the base of the mound.

Stalgis cocked an eyebrow. "Impressive," he said approvingly, and with obvious relief. Slinging his blaster rifle over his shoulder, he headed back up the mound at a more leisurely pace.

"We're not out of this yet," Jacen said.

Luke silently agreed. Urging himself forward, he activated his comlink. "We're on our way," he reported. "Any sign of disturbances?"

The pilot of the Imperial shuttle didn't waste any words. "All clear. We're ready for liftoff."

Above them, he could hear the whine of engines. Relieved that they would soon be offplanet, Luke allowed himself a moment to puzzle at what had gone wrong. Everything had gone so well at first. Munlali Mafir was a planet that Hegerty had listed as one whose indigenous population told of a migratory world that had once appeared in their system, stayed briefly, and then vanished. It wasn't necessarily Zonama Sekot, but everyone agreed that the lead was worth following up.

Upon arrival, however, it had been apparent that something had changed. The Jostran natives of Munlali Mafir were, according to Hegerty's records, slow-moving centipedes barely larger than a human arm. What they'd found, though, was a colony of Krizlaws—listed as feral herd beasts with no more intelligence than a common nerf—and no sign of the Jostrans at all. Something appeared to have elevated the Krizlaws to full intelligence while at the same time wiping out the Jostrans. Either that or the Imperial probe records had simply been wrong. The language used by the Krizlaws was in fact the same as that recorded in Hegerty's files, except that it was attributed to the Jostrans.

The Krizlaws were not a starfaring species, so the arrival of the Imperial shuttle had prompted an enthusiastic welcome. Luke, Jacen, Hegerty, and a small honor guard of stormtroopers had been invited to a ceremonial banquet at which the visitors had witnessed the grisly eating habits of the planet's indigenous inhabitants. The local chief, who looked indistinguishable from the others except for a brightly colored belt wrapped around his smooth midriff, had freely passed on the legend about the "Star-World" that had appeared in the sky four decades earlier. Lacking telescopes or other optical instruments, their observations had been somewhat limited, but it seemed that this Star-World had appeared as a blue-green light in the skies of Munlali Mafir. It had stayed there for almost three of the planet's months, then—as mysteriously as it had appeared—it disappeared again.

For the time that this Star-World held its place in the sky, Munlali Mafir had undergone a period of increased seismic activity. Numerous volcanoes around the planet erupted, and the lands making up the three continents had been rent by groundquakes, all of which resulted in the deaths of many of the natives. Although the locals at the time—whether Jostrans or Krizlaws, Luke had been unable to determine—had no geologic knowledge to speak of, or indeed any understanding of the gravitational effects that astral bodies could have upon each other, they had, nonetheless, associated the spate of disasters with the arrival of the new planet. To them, the Star-World was a harbinger of death and upheaval, and Luke made every effort to reassure the chief and his people that it was unlikely the Star-World would ever return.

It was then that the trouble had started.

A hush had descended on the gathering as Luke patiently explained that the visitation of the rogue planet had been nothing more than a chance event, and it was doubtful that such an occurrence would be repeated. He assumed that Zonama Sekot was simply looking for somewhere safe to hide, and had moved on once it had become clear that Munlali Mafir was inhabited. It was very possible, he had assured the chief, that the Star-World was in fact by now on the other side of the Unknown Regions. He explained that the terrible consequences of its visit—the ruin of most of the planet's stone cities, the disruption to ocean currents, and the impact upon some vital environmental resources such as aquifers—were only temporary. These things, he promised, would soon return to normal.

Instead of being relieved by his reassurances, though, the locals had become agitated. The chief had signaled his guards, and the visitors—esteemed guests just moments earlier—had suddenly found themselves treated as captives. Luke had forbidden any form of resistance from his party, confident that he could talk their way out of a violent confrontation. It was only as he had tried to make contact with the chief through the Force, however, that he'd realized just how difficult this might prove.

These beings, it turned out, had two centers of consciousness. Where Luke might ordinarily have influenced any other creature's thoughts and convinced it simply to let them go, there was no one place to apply pressure within the chief of the Krizlaws. One thought center was bright and alert, and easily deflected his probe; the other was dull and diffuse, as slippery as a nooroop egg. He couldn't influence either as easily as he'd hoped, and the revelation threw him for a moment. He had never encountered this situation before.

During his confusion, one of their stormtrooper escorts had been forced onto the ground. A robed Krizlaw tipped the stormtrooper's head back and, bizarrely, attempted to force some sort of wriggling grub down his throat. The man gagged and tried to spit it out, but the tiny creature went down anyway.

That was enough for Luke. Giving up on direct control, he had used the Force to thrust the robed Krizlaw away from the fallen stormtrooper. The man's life-signature was still strong, despite his revulsion at the unexpected "meal." Pushing his own guards away, he had helped the stormtrooper to his feet while Jacen quickly freed himself and the others. Within no time at all, they had broken free of the Krizlaws and were running for their lives.

As they fled, Luke had heard the distinctive sound of

the chief screeching commands to those gathered around him. Soon a group of eleven "ritual hunters," as Hegerty thought of them, had formed and given pursuit.

The chase through the decaying palace had been fast and furious, with two of the stormtroopers at the rear of the group being snatched up by the jaws and claws of their pursuers within seconds. The sound of their cries as the Krizlaws fell upon them was terrible to hear, but their deaths had given the others valuable seconds. When one of the Krizlaws was successful, all of the hunting party came to a halt to devour their prey. This was the first hint that Hegerty had received of the nature of the ritualistic hunting group comprised by the eleven Krizlaws. Maybe now, Luke hoped, with most of the eleven buried beneath the rubble, they would give up the chase.

It was a nice thought, but Luke still didn't feel confident that they were out of trouble just yet. Even now, as they neared their objective at the top of the ceremonial mound, he didn't allow himself to embrace the relief that he could sense emanating from Stalgis and Hegerty. Self-confidence had a way of making one lower one's guard, and that could cost lives. He wasn't about to assume they had escaped until they *had* escaped.

Finally, the slope eased and they staggered onto the mound's wide, stone summit. The *Sentinel*-class landing shuttle rested on an eroded bas-relief depicting a mythical battle between two hideous-looking deities. At the top of the extended landing ramp stood a gray-uniformed Imperial pilot, waving for them to hurry.

"Gee, what's the rush?" Stalgis said dryly, putting an arm under the shoulder of the only other surviving stormtrooper—the one who'd been force-fed the grub. "Can't they allow us a few moments to admire the scenery?"

"Maybe that's why," Jacen said, pointing ahead and to his left.

Approaching with an ungainly but effective series of long-legged leaps were the three Krizlaws who had separated from the rest of the hunting party at the base of the mound. It was clear they were going to reach the shuttle first—which probably explained their triumphant howls and ululations.

Luke gathered the Force about himself and Jacen. By using it to increase their speed, the two of them could head off the three Krizlaws, giving the others opportunity to get to the shuttle. Three of these creatures would certainly be no match for the lightsabers of two trained Jedi.

Barely had he taken a step when matching howls sounded from off to the right. A quick glance told him that eight more of the Krizlaws had found them.

"Eleven again," Hegerty said breathlessly. There was a hint of defeat in her tone.

"They can't be the ones we buried," Jacen said. "It's not possible!"

"They aren't," Luke said. "They have different markings. These must be replacements."

"How did they *know*?" Stalgis asked.

The question became moot as the eleven howling aliens converged on the escapees. Two Krizlaws separated from the rest and headed for the shuttle, giving the Imperial waiting at the top of the ramp good reason to hastily retreat inside. Seconds later, laser cannons issued from their retractable housing and began taking potshots. The Krizlaws were too fast, however, their long leaps taking the gunner by surprise.

Luke stopped running. There was no point wasting energy on a mad dash if there was no chance of making it. Sending for the shuttle speeder bike was also pointless, since that could save only two of them at the very most. A familiar meditation damped down feelings of frustration and anger; this was no time to give in to darker emotions, he told himself. There *had* to be another way to save the landing party from the approaching aliens.

Stalgis assumed a sharpshooter's pose and snapped off a dozen rounds in quick succession. One of the Krizlaws stumbled and fell, missing one of its arms and geysering purplish blood. Luke watched in horror as the creature staggered back to its feet and continued on, limping. Stalgis's jaw clenched as if biting down on frustration, but he kept on firing.

Luke and Jacen placed themselves at two points of a defensive triangle, with Stalgis and the other stormtrooper at the other corner and the exhausted Hegerty in the middle. The xenobiologist was only slightly older than Luke, but she had no battle skills. The type of expedition she was used to, Luke imagined, would have had little cause for running like this.

Krizlaws spread out in a circle around them. Luke used the Force to discourage those who came closest, but knew it was only a matter of time before he and the others were rushed. There was no way they could possibly repel all nine at once.

As he steeled himself in preparation for the inevitable attack, and possibly a fight to the death, his thoughts went out to his son safe in the heart of the Galactic Alliance, and he sent a wordless message of apology to Mara, waiting in orbit in *Jade Shadow*.

The *Millennium Falcon*'s exit from hyperspace was anything but graceful. Leia gripped the arms of her copilot's chair, glad that Han had finally installed one that accommodated her slight build.

Behind her, she could hear C-3PO rattling.

"Oh my," the golden droid exclaimed, shifting unsteadily on his feet to try to keep his balance. "I hope we haven't hit anything!"

Han flicked a couple of switches; then, when that obviously failed, he leaned back in his seat and kicked the base of the console. A few seconds later, their trajectory flattened out.

"Sorry about that, folks," he said to no one in particular. "Normal services have been resumed."

Leia rolled her eyes and glanced back at Tahiri. The young Jedi sat stoically in her seat, her stare fixed at a point outside the cockpit canopy. Throughout the journey, she had remained quiet and unresponsive to any attempts at conversation, her thoughts focused firmly inward. Leia hadn't pressed her; she sensed that some complicated healing process was taking place in the girl, and she was reluctant to disturb it.

Nevertheless, there were times when she felt that a more direct approach might be appropriate—especially those times when Tahiri's brooding silences went on for hours at a stretch, never seeming to end. Tahiri's blackout on Galantos had been a startling setback, occurring at a time when Leia had believed that Tahiri could be on the mend. Still, there could be no faulting her reactions when she'd woken up; without her well-honed Jedi instincts, they might not have reached orbit when they did—or, indeed, made contact with the mysterious Ryn who had helped them escape.

Leia inwardly sighed. Whatever was going on inside Tahiri, it was frustratingly inconsistent.

The subspace receiver bleeped. Leia glanced at the scopes and opened the line.

Captain Mayn's voice issued from the comm speakers. "*Falcon,* I await your instructions."

"Glad you could join us, *Selonia,*" she said. "Have a nice trip?"

"As pleasant a stroll as one can expect through hyperspace."

Leia smiled at the captain's remark as she surveyed the

planet before them. Bakura was a beautiful blue-green world known for its agricultural and repulsorlift exports. Its two moons had been heavily mined for materials used in the manufacture of the second Death Star. It was also right on the edge of the galaxy, diametrically opposite the corridor of worlds that had first fallen victim to the Yuuzhan Vong invasion. "From Bonadan to Bakura via Bothawui" was an old saying that suggested it was easier to get from the Corporate Sector to Bakura via a wide detour to Bothan space than it was to go straight through the Core, with its dense overlap of mass shadows and treacherous hyperspace lanes. It also connected three high-tech but otherwise very different industrialized worlds. Where Bonadan was a desertified wasteland, Bakura was still verdant and pastoral, on the other end of the spectrum of environmental degradation.

Belkadan, the first world attacked by the Yuuzhan Vong and one of Bonadan's relative neighbors, was in a spectrum of its own, its biosphere modified to suit the aliens' introduced biological factories. Leia hoped she never saw the day when such degradation stretched from one side of the galaxy to the other, linking all the worlds she knew in a terrible web of pain and sacrifice. If the day ever arrived when Shimrra ruled over Bakura, then she would know that the end had truly come.

For now, though, it still looked peaceful enough . . .

Numerous satellites orbited the planet, and she imagined that it wouldn't be long before someone detected and hailed the *Falcon* and *Pride of Selonia*. Assuming that normal procedures were still being followed, all entries into the system were closely monitored; the Bakuran government was constantly alert for another Ssi-ruuvi invasion. After the first attempt twenty-five standard years before, four destroyers and cruisers—*Intruder*, *Watchkeeper*, *Sentinel*, and *Defender*—had been specifically constructed and installed to guard the system. Two of them—*Watchkeeper* and the task force flagship *Intruder*—had been destroyed when co-opted into service to the New Republic at Selonia and Centerpoint. That left only *Defender* and *Sentinel* to hold the fort.

"Bring back any memories, Leia?" Han asked with a crooked grin as his hand reached out to squeeze hers briefly. She returned his smile but didn't respond directly. They had visited Bakura very early in their relationship; under other circumstances, she might have let herself enjoy the reminder of those headier days.

"Stand ready, *Selonia*," she told Mayn. "See if you can raise the planetary network. Don't identify us; use *Selonia*'s registration codes." Mayn responded in the affirmative, and Leia switched to another frequency. "Twin Sun One, maintain formation unless ordered otherwise."

"Understood." Jaina's voice came briskly from the cockpit of her X-wing. The remaining fighters of Twin Suns surrounded the two command vessels in a flattened dodecahedron, missing one point.

"Do you sense anything, Jaina?" Leia asked her daughter.

"Nothing out of the ordinary."

"What about you, Tahiri?"

"Huh?" The young Jedi snapped out of some deep thought. "I'm sorry, what?"

"I asked if you were picking up anything unusual through the Force," Leia said.

"Oh, no—nothing yet, anyway." Tahiri closed her eyes as she sent her mind reaching out through space, seeking any echoes of the people on and around Bakura.

"Tahiri is looking now," Leia told Jaina.

There was a slight but meaningful pause from Jaina's end. Leia had noticed a definite reserve growing between Jaina and Tahiri, but she'd had no opportunity to discuss it with her yet. The present arrangement—with Jaina on duty more often than not, and rarely aboard the *Falcon*—

meant that there was simply no time to be alone together. If something had happened to get in the way of the friendship between the two young women, Leia had no idea what it was.

"Okay," Jaina finally said. "We'll keep our sensors peeled."

Han brought the *Millennium Falcon* around along a broad arc designed to end quite clearly in orbital insertion. Leia wanted no ambiguity that they were on a peaceful mission, despite their military escort. After the Ryn's vague hints, she wasn't taking any chances.

She opened a line to *Selonia* again: "Any word yet, Captain?"

"Nothing," Mayn replied. "We're picking up some light chatter, but not much else. There are a large number of vessels in parking orbit or in station docks. Most of them just look like freighters."

"No launches?"

"None detected."

Leia considered this for a moment. "Keep hailing them," she said shortly. "They must be ignoring us or simply not noticing us. Either way, they won't be able to keep it up much longer. Let's just stick to our course and see what happens. And be ready for anything."

"Understood."

Leia turned to Han. He sat in silence beside her, his brow pinched with worry. "You okay?"

He looked at her and cocked one eyebrow. "Do I really need to say it?" he asked.

She shook her head and sighed. He didn't need to tell her that he had a bad feeling about this; she could feel something was wrong, too. But without evidence she had no reason to act any way other than normal.

Finally the subspace channel crackled and a response came in. "*Selonia,* this is General Panib of the Bakuran Defense Fleet. Please state your intentions."

Leia remembered a Captain Grell Panib from an earlier visit to Bakura; she imagined it was probably the same person. A short, stiff-backed redhead, he'd had all the social graces of a hungry Wookiee.

Mayn ignored the request. "We're allies, Captain, looking for a docking vector—"

"I'm sorry, *Selonia*, but we're going to need more detail before we can give you one."

"Of all the . . ." Han muttered.

"It's a perfectly reasonable request," the general went on, his voice taut with a tension Leia couldn't immediately fathom. "There has been no notification of you coming—"

"General Panib, this is Leia Organa Solo," she interrupted before Han could explode. "We have come to your planet on a diplomatic mission. We would have notified you in advance but communications have been unreliable around here of late."

There was some hesitation from the general. "I appreciate what you are saying. There have indeed been problems with the communications networks. Nevertheless, I must insist that you now state your intentions for coming here."

"Hey, how about you drop the attitude," Han responded hotly. "We're the guys who saved your skins from the Ssi-ruuk a while back, remember?"

"I remember; I recognized that beat-up old freighter the moment I saw her."

Leia hid a worried smile as she watched her husband bite down on an indignant retort.

"But things aren't so simple anymore," Panib went on. "We have something of a situation here at the moment."

"What kind of situation?" Leia asked.

"You're not welcome here!" A new voice crackled over the restricted comlink frequency. "Go steal someone else's ships!"

"*What?*" Han exclaimed. It was clear this time that he didn't intend to hold back. His face reddened as he leaned forward to speak into the comm unit. "Listen, you—"

"Wait, Han," Leia cut him off. He looked at her with an incensed frown, but did as she asked. "General Panib, is this person speaking with your authority?"

"Certainly not!" the general responded, spluttering. "And whoever it is shall be court-martialed as soon as—"

"You can't court-martial everyone, General," the intruder mocked. He had distorted his voice to mask his identity. "You can't silence the truth indefinitely!"

"When I find out who is responsible for this," the general blustered, "I swear that I shall have you—"

"The truth?" Leia broke in. "And just what *is* the truth?"

"There is nothing to discuss here!" The general's voice was rising as he lost control of the situation. "We don't need you meddling in our affairs!"

"We aren't here to meddle," Leia defended quickly. "Although I will admit that we are concerned about your affairs. I believe you're in great danger, General. People masquerading as allies may have recently contacted you. I can assure you that they are not what they seem."

"Whereas you are, I suppose." This came from the person who had broken into the conversation, his voice dripping with derision. "At least they don't pay lip service to the idea of an alliance while eroding our defenses and leaving us open to attack!"

Leia bridled at this. "We have *never* abandoned our allies!"

"Like you never abandoned Dantooine and Ithor?" the stranger shot back. "Or Duro or Tynna or—"

Cold fury welled up in her. "Every planet lost cuts us deeply! Every *life* lost cuts us deeper!"

"I must apologize, Princess," Panib said anxiously. The

general's tone had changed dramatically from a few minutes earlier, and he sounded genuinely apologetic. "We are doing our best to find the source of the transmission."

"I'm sorry, too, Princess," came the distorted voice of the intruder. "But I'm afraid that the time has come to find ourselves some new allies."

"Uh-oh," Han said from Leia's side, his eyes scanning the display in front of him.

"What is it?" she asked.

"*Sentinel*'s launching bays just opened," he said, shaking his head ominously.

He pointed at the screen. Issuing from the launching bays of the cruiser *Sentinel* was a swarm of Ssi-ruuvi battle droids, coming directly for them.

"Whatever it was we came to stop, I think we might be too late."

"Uncle Luke! Look!"

Jacen guided his uncle into the double mind of one of the nearby Krizlaws. He had used the Force to cloud the brighter, more intense mind, but still the creature kept on coming. Somehow, the more doltish mind was enough to coordinate the body while the higher mind was elsewhere.

"And exactly how is this supposed to help us, Jacen?" Luke asked.

"Look closer," Jacen pressed. "We're not dealing with single creatures here; they're symbionts!"

"Two creatures combined?" Luke said dubiously. "I don't see how that—"

But then, suddenly, he *did* see. The higher, brighter mind of the creature belonged to the rider and was the directing intelligence; it gave the orders that the body then carried out, no matter how wounded. The lower mind belonged to the body, which could keep going even with the higher mind disabled. Jacen's theory certainly fit

the evidence—and he was intuitively better at understanding animals than Luke was.

But if he was right, then the lower mind should be
more easily startled by pain. And if that was the case,
why hadn't the one in which Jacen had disabled the
higher mind simply run away from Stalgis's blasterfire?

He soon found out. The riding intelligences were fero-
cious killers: crudely intelligent but not open to reason.
Trained to hunt, not to discuss differences, the pack would
keep coming as long as some of the riders remained to
keep the lower minds in check.

Following Jacen's lead, Luke sent his mind into another of the Krizlaws and clouded its controlling intelligence. It, too, continued to obey its higher mind's final
instructions, snapping hungrily at the four people along
with the rest of the pack. Luke and his nephew continued
around the circle of beasts, one by one confusing their
higher minds. It was only after they had disabled the
sixth creature that there was a noticeable change in behavior. The pack became less orderly, less focused, while
their baying became more unsettled and aggressive. Luke
could feel a note of alarm entering the remaining higher
minds as the thoughts of those around them descended
back to their natural, animalistic states.

As fascinating as it might have been to observe, though,
it wasn't helping the landing party. Two of the enraged
creatures rushed the group and were repelled by the combined blasterfire from Stalgis and the injured stormtrooper.
One of the Krizlaws collapsed with a yelp and a whimper
at their feet; the other, having taken a blaster bolt to the
throat, leapt away, spitting blood. Barely a second had
passed when another attacked from the far side. Luke
took this one out himself, stepping forward a single pace
as he brought his lightsaber up in a glowing arc, stabbing
at the beast's soft pink underside. It fell to the ground,
but he hadn't killed it—the jaws of the alien continued to

snap at Hegerty's feet as it scrambled relentlessly toward her. Stalgis brought the nozzle of his rifle around and placed a precise blaster shot into the side of the Krizlaw's head to finish it off.

Two more attacked them, uncoordinated and clumsy, and Luke felt his world contract into a furious concentration of teeth and glowing red eyes, with bright flashes of energy—blade and bolt—adding a surreal counterpoint to the proceedings.

Another Krizlaw lunged, extendable mouth open to engulf him. He swung his lightsaber again, this time with more force—using the thought of Mara and Ben to strengthen his resolve to stay alive. The blade cut through the creature's forelimbs, but it wasn't enough to halt its movement through the air. It connected solidly with Luke's chest, knocking him to the ground. Its huge, slavering jaws were suddenly centimeters from his face. Before he'd had the chance to bring his lightsaber up to defend himself, five blasts sounded from nearby, each one striking the alien's head. Mucus and blood splashed Luke's face, and the Krizlaw fell heavily to one side. He would have liked to offer his thanks to the stormtrooper who'd fired the shot, but he had already turned his attention to the other creatures attacking them. There wasn't time to be grateful.

Luke climbed to his feet, bringing his lightsaber to bear in anticipation of the next onslaught. But there was none. All of the Krizlaws suddenly recoiled, each emitting a sound that was so high-pitched it hurt his ears. He remained in a defensive stance, dumbstruck, his blade still held in front of him waiting for the attack that refused to happen.

Around him, the air was thick with confused, animal thoughts as the Krizlaws wheeled and fled, scrambling and leaping in an uncontrolled, chaotic mass for the lip of the plateau.

Mystified, Luke turned to check the others. Stalgis had a cut to his forehead; the stormtrooper was bleeding steadily from a bite to his shoulder. Hegerty was unharmed. Jacen favored his right leg as he snapped off his lightsaber and turned to face them, a look of satisfaction on his face.

"Your doing, I presume?" Luke asked.

"I managed to get a handle on the lower minds," Jacen explained. "Finally. Once we'd knocked out enough of the riders, they were unable to assert themselves. The pack was frightened of us and took the first opportunity to get away."

"Is the pack a group-mind, do you think?" Hegerty asked, clearly intrigued by the idea.

"Yes. With a fixed number of components forming a stable configuration," Jacen added.

"Of course!" Hegerty said. "There were always eleven of them! They probably evolved that way, and the creatures controlling them now simply took advantage of the configuration."

"And that's how they knew when some of their number had been killed," Jacen said. "Whenever a vacancy was created in the group, there was always another Krizlaw to fill it, with the new ones automatically knowing as much as the others in the meld."

Luke nodded in agreement. It made sense. Now was not the time to be discussing it, though. "We should get to the shuttle while we still can," he said. "I'd rather not hang around and wait for the chief to put together another group—this time with controlling intelligences intact."

They did as he suggested, with Hegerty taking the lead. Stalgis assisted his injured comrade, while Jacen and Luke brought up the rear.

"Good work," he told his nephew as they walked. "And timely, too. I don't know how much longer we could have held them off."

Jacen nodded, his expression one of simultaneous relief and pride. "I had to do something. I couldn't let us be taken down by a pack of animals."

"Never underestimate the power of the animal," Luke said soberly. "Sheer numbers can overwhelm the best of tactics. Along with not having any fear of death, it's possibly the most powerful weapon an enemy can have."

They reached the landing ramp with no further incident, although the baying of Krizlaws was a constant and eerie reminder of why they should get off this planet and never look back. Luke helped the injured stormtrooper into the shuttle and onto one of the craft's small cots. Stalgis followed close behind, grabbing a medpac on the way.

"He's going to have to be examined thoroughly," Hegerty said, speaking to the others in a hushed tone so that the stormtrooper wouldn't hear. "That force-feeding he received could be dangerous."

"He seems okay now," Jacen said. "Apart from the shoulder wound."

"I think Doctor Hegerty is more concerned about internal injuries," Luke said, glancing over to where Stalgis was administering treatment to the injured trooper. Now that the fight was over, he certainly looked paler and weaker than he had outside.

Hegerty nodded. "We'll need to warn *Widowmaker* that he might require immediate surgery—as well as decontamination."

"But why?" Jacen asked.

"You said the Krizlaws are symbionts," she explained. "But symbionts with *what*, exactly?"

"Some other species, I guess," he said.

The doctor nodded again. "Remember the missing Jostrans?"

Jacen blanched as Hegerty's point hit home. "You don't really think—?"

She shrugged. "Maybe they're not missing after all."

"We'll let Tekli know," Luke said with a sinking feeling in his stomach that was nothing compared to what the stormtrooper would feel if he learned of their suspicions. He filed through the cabin while the others took seats preparatory for launch, his thoughts turning over the whole Krizlaw/Jostran affair.

It all seemed to make sense now, as things often did in retrospect. The passage of Zonama Sekot through the system must have destabilized the local environment enough to encourage a warlike clan or subspecies of Jostrans to take over the Krizlaws, giving them a competitive edge. Zonama Sekot had been responsible for helping that particular clan, but it had been at the cost of the previous Jostran civilization.

The pilot lifted off just as Luke reached the cockpit. He strapped himself in, watching the ground scanner as he did so. Another group of Krizlaw/Jostrans was converging on the shuttle, and he silently gave thanks that they were no longer out there fighting. It would only have been a matter of time before they would have fallen to the creatures.

Luke was grateful that the shuttle offered no parting shots as it swept a comfortable distance over the heads of the eleven snapping aliens. Once upon a time the gunners aboard this craft might have strafed them as they launched, but Luke had repeatedly emphasized that their mission was a peaceful one and that there would be no unnecessary loss of life—human or otherwise. Thus far, the Imperials had accepted his terms happily enough, with Captain Yage and Lieutenant Stalgis backing him up. Many of the crew, Stalgis included, had friends or family who were still alive because of the actions of the Galactic Federation of Free Alliances around Orinda. Nevertheless, there was a definite undercurrent of resentment. To some, he would never be anything more than the Rebel boy who was responsible for the death of Emperor Palpatine. But regardless of their feelings toward him, he would never let their disrespect undermine his confidence or authority.

He turned away from the thoughts, settling back into his seat as the shuttle sped skyward, leaving Munlali Mafir behind him. He was relieved to be going home—or to the closest thing to home they had, anyway.

"Hail *Jade Shadow*," he instructed the sensor officer.

To Luke's surprise, Danni Quee took the call. "I gather you had some trouble with the locals," the young scientist said.

"An argument over dinner, that's all. Is Mara there?"

"She's tied up at the moment, but she says not to worry. Can I pass on a message?"

"No, that's okay. But tell Tekli to take a shuttle over to *Widowmaker*. We have a patient for her."

"Who's injured?" she asked quickly. Luke could tell without her having to say anything that she was worried it might be Jacen.

"A stormtrooper," he explained briefly. "It's not so much that he's injured." He fought for the right word. "He's just . . . infected, I guess."

"I'll warn Tekli to be ready. Did you learn anything useful about Zonama Sekot?"

"It's been here, as we thought—but not for many years."

"Another hit and run?"

"I'm afraid so. If we only knew what it was looking for, it would certainly improve our chances of finding it."

"It's a big galaxy," Danni agreed.

"Excuse me, sir," the pilot interrupted. "You've got a communication coming in."

"Sorry, Danni. Got to go." Luke thanked the sensor officer and moved forward to where the holodisplay rested between the two forward seats. In the display, he saw the solid figure of Arien Yage, captain of the Imperial frigate *Widowmaker*, *Jade Shadow*'s official escort through the Unknown Regions. Her hair was tied back in its usual severe bun and her expression businesslike.

"We have visitors," she said, wasting no time on pleasantries. "Fifteen minutes ago, a Chiss corvette and two full squadrons of clawcraft entered the system. They are on a high-powered approach vector, clearly intending to lock on to our orbit."

"Communications?"

"None as yet, although we hailed them as soon as they appeared on the scopes. I've put the squadron on full alert."

"How long until they come within range?"

"Approximately thirty minutes."

"I'll make sure we're back by then," Luke said. "Keep an eye on them, Captain, and keep me informed."

Yage's image nodded and fizzed out, then Luke sank wearily back into his seat. Two Chiss squadrons were more than a match for a dozen Imperial TIE fighters, but *Jade Shadow* with Mara at the controls was worth an entire squadron on its own. If it came to a fight, they would be evenly matched. He just hoped it didn't come to that. The last time he and Mara had entered Chiss space, in Thrawn's day, their dealings had been conducted amicably, if cautiously.

Fatigue washed through him, and he tapped the Force to sweep it away. He was tired of fighting, yes, but he wasn't about to give up. Besides, there was nothing yet to suggest that the Chiss were looking for a fight. For all he knew, this might be the way they normally approached unidentified vessels found wandering in the Unknown Regions. The Chiss were efficient and pragmatic, to the point of appearing cold to those unfamiliar with their ways. Until Luke was certain of their intentions, he could do little more than wait.

He moved back into the passenger cabin to check on the injured stormtrooper. The man was unconscious. The upper half of his uniform had been removed to enable Stalgis to get at the wound on his shoulder, and there was a sheen to his skin from perspiration. Stalgis was leaning over the stormtrooper, holding a stim-shot, a look of concern on his face. He straightened when he saw Luke.

"He's going down fast," Stalgis said. "I don't have the facilities here to check for new poisons, so we're going to need to get him to *Widowmaker*'s medical bay fast."

Luke motioned Jacen to come forward. "See if you can hold his vital signs stable. We're moving as quickly as we can, but it might not be enough."

His nephew bent down next to the stricken trooper and placed a hand on his forehead. Luke felt waves of healing energy pour off his nephew and into the stormtrooper. He placed one hand on Jacen's shoulder to lend him strength.

"Looks like we might have attracted attention to ourselves," Luke whispered to him.

"What sort of attention?" Jacen returned equally as softly.

"Chiss."

The trooper's condition worsened steadily as the shuttle roared up toward the orbit occupied by the mission's two central vessels. Luke could feel the man's immune system failing as the invader spread its chemical and genetic tentacles through his body, beating it into submission. Jacen didn't suggest using the Force to kill it, and Luke knew he wouldn't until the choice between it and the trooper became absolutely clear.

Hegerty watched with an expression of concern mixed with intense curiosity. Luke doubted whether the woman could ever *not* look worried; the lines in her face were permanently etched that way. For the sake of Stalgis, and in case their fear turned out to be unfounded, Luke refrained from asking the doctor if she'd ever seen anything like this before. They'd find out soon enough—or so he hoped, anyway.

The sensor officer stuck his head out of the cockpit. "Another communication, sir."

Luke returned to the cockpit, leaving Stalgis and Jacen to care for the stormtrooper. Yage's hologram was back.

"We've had a reply," she said. "Commander Irolia of the Expansionary Defense Fleet wants to speak to the person in charge. I told her you were on your way back from the surface, but she said she wanted to speak to you immediately."

"I guess you'd better put me through, then," he said.

The copilot made way for him without having to be asked. Luke straightened his robes as he took the empty seat.

Yage's face dissolved from the holofield in a flicker of static; it was replaced a few seconds later with the image of the upper body of a blue-skinned woman dressed in a burgundy-and-black uniform. Her eyes were the deep red of her species, and her expression held nothing but blunt authority. Chiss matured quickly, but still Luke was startled by the fact that she looked no older than his niece, Jaina.

"You are Master Skywalker?" Her voice had all the warmth of a droid.

Luke nodded curtly and said: "I am leader of a peaceful mission from the Galactic Federation of Free Alliances. We are in the middle of an emergency. I lost two of my crew in a ground fight with the natives of the planet below, and a third is seriously injured. If we don't get back to orbit in time, he'll die. Your arrival into this system has put my squadron on full alert, and means our docking procedures will be that much more complicated. If I should lose another because of your interference, I will be extremely—"

"Please do not threaten us, Skywalker," the Chiss woman responded calmly, staring unblinking from the flickering holofield. "Our intention is not to impede your docking procedures, or any other of your procedures. I require only that you meet with me in person at the earliest possible convenience."

"Of course," Luke said. "We'll arrange it as soon as I return to the *Widowmaker*."

"When or how you arrange it is irrelevant. Know, however, that I will not remain in this system for long. Comply with my request, or face the consequences."

The image winked out.

"Well, you heard the commander," Luke said to the pilot, who had watched the show with interest. "I guess we'd better get moving . . ."

"All X-wings," came Jaina's voice over the subspace combat channel, "lock S-foils in attack position. Clawcraft: arm and target approaching vessels. Battle plan A-seven."

"Copy that," Jag returned on behalf of Twin Suns' Chiss pilots.

Leia watched as the formation of fighters split into three groups—two pairs and a triplet, Galactic Alliance and Chiss fighters flying alongside each other with perfect precision. The calm command in her daughter's voice made her proud; no matter how surprised by the sudden attack Jaina must have been, she didn't let it show. Neither was there any suggestion of concern for the fact that her squadron hadn't had any experience in combat against Ssi-ruuvi fighters.

Any sign of composure that General Panib had displayed earlier now evaporated totally in the face of this abrupt turnabout of events.

"Please, wait," he urged frantically. "There's been a terrible misunderstanding!"

"You bet there has," Han said. "One we intend to clear up for you very shortly. Those ships belong to the enemy, and we'll knock them out of your skies if they come anywhere near us. You got that?"

"More launches," Leia said, registering fighters coming from *Defender*. "A-wings and B-wings, this time; not Ssi-ruuk."

Han glanced at the scanner board. "Those had better be coming to help us, Panib."

"*Falcon*, I beseech you not to order your ships to open fire!" All semblance of calm had left the general's voice; only panic remained. "All these ships comprise a peaceful envoy to ensure your safe passage to orbit."

"All of them?" Han snorted. "Yeah, right. If entech-ing humans and using them to fly those fighters heading our way constitutes peaceful behavior, then I don't think we're speaking the same language. Those fighters have precisely thirty seconds to turn around before we start opening fire."

"Han, look at this," Leia said, studying the display be-fore her. It showed one of the Ssi-ruuvi vessels up close. The image was fuzzy but clear enough to make out some details. "Do those engine housings look familiar to you?"

Han frowned at the image. "What about them?"

"They look an awful lot like ion jets to me."

"So?"

"Since when did the Ssi-ruuk start using standard en-gines on their fighters?"

"What are you saying, Leia?"

"That there's more here than meets the eye," she said. "You'll note also that our transmissions are not being jammed."

Han's frown deepened as his instincts conflicted with what Leia was suggesting. "It has to be a trick," he said, shaking his head. "They want us to drop our guard."

Leia wasn't convinced. "It doesn't add up, Han. If they really wanted to do that, then why not just let us land first and *then* attack us?"

She could almost see the thoughts behind his eyes racing through his mind. What if Panib *was* telling the truth? A mistake could be extremely costly.

Then there was the matter of the mysterious intruder on the secure comm channels. He had been silent since the Ssi-ruuvi vessels had launched. If their intentions had been to stir things up between Panib and the visitors, in order to ensure the worst possible reception of the alien fighters, then they had certainly succeeded.

"The pilots of those ships aren't human," Tahiri said, breaking into the discussion softly. Leia turned to face the young Jedi; the girl's eyes were still closed, as though meditating. "They're definitely alien. And—" She hesitated for a second, then her eyes flickered open. "Everyone's heard the stories about the Ssi-ruuk and how awful entechment is. It's supposed to be agony, right?"

Leia nodded, still remembering the look on Luke's face when he had been rescued from the mighty Ssi-ruuvi vessel in which he'd been held captive, years ago. Exposure to the perverted entechment technology, and to the life energy forcibly removed from those taken captive in battle with Bakura, had touched him profoundly.

"Well, these minds aren't suffering," Tahiri said. "They're clean."

"What are they, then?" Han asked.

"I don't know," Tahiri said. "I've never touched minds like these before."

When Leia stretched out her senses, she, too, could detect no trace of anything malevolent in the approaching fighters.

"I don't care if their minds are as serene as Alder-aanian snow," Han growled. "They're still attacking us!"

"Are they?" Leia asked. It was all too easy to assume. "We don't want to start a war by accident—not if there's an alternative."

"And what if you're wrong, Leia? I don't want them to end up using Jaina as target practice out there."

"Nor do I, Han." She touched his hand in reassurance, then spoke on the secure subspace comlink to the squadron: "Twin Suns, fall back to flank *Selonia* and *Falcon*. You are instructed not to fire unless we are fired upon. Understood?"

"Understood, *Falcon*." Apart from the slight hesitation in Jaina's voice, the order was accepted and acted upon immediately. In the face of the rapidly approaching swarm of Ssi-ruuvi fighters, the combined Chiss and Galactic Alliance squadron peeled away and swooped back to cover their command vessels.

Han squirmed in his seat but didn't say anything more. Leia shifted uneasily in her seat also. She felt reasonably confident that she was doing the right thing, but she couldn't help feeling nervous at the same time. The last time she had come face to face with Ssi-ruuvi fighters had been on a war footing. She remembered the strength of the fighters' shields and their maneuverability in dogfights—and perhaps more vividly she remembered how the alien capital vessels would collect survivors with their "trooper scoopers" in order to suck out their life energies and hurl them back at their former allies . . .

"Gunners standing by," announced Captain Mayn on *Selonia* as the fighters came within range.

Leia held her breath.

On the scanner board, she saw the alien fighters break formation and scatter to adopt a defensive wall around the incoming vessels, just as an escort would do. No shots were fired, and they stayed a discreet distance from both

Falcon and *Selonia*. When the second contingent of ships arrived, the A-wings and B-wings slotted into the existing pattern with only a small amount of jostling.

She exhaled with a heavy sigh.

"Thank the maker," C-3PO said from behind her.

"You can say that again, Goldenrod." Han leaned forward to trim the *Falcon*'s course slightly, a motion designed to disguise the relief he was feeling, Leia knew. "We're not out of the woods yet. In case nobody has noticed, we're now effectively caught."

"But at least we didn't start a war," Leia said. "And this way, we just might get some answers."

"What if we don't like what we hear?" her husband asked wryly.

Leia shrugged. "We'll deal with that as it happens."

Han turned to the comm. Panib, who had been frantically trying to attract their attention over the subspace channel, sounded like he was going to sob with relief.

"Thank you, *Falcon*. You won't regret this."

"We'll reserve judgment on that until we hear what's going on," Han said.

"I understand," the general responded. "But first I must once again ask that you state your intentions."

Han put a weary hand to his forehead. Leia gave in.

"We'd like to set down at Salis D'aar," she said, "and meet with Prime Minister Cundertol."

"I'm afraid that won't be possible," Panib said. "The Prime Minister is unable to meet with anyone at the moment."

"I don't understand, General," Leia said. "Why—"

"Bakura is currently operating under martial law," he explained without allowing her to finish her question. "I shall be in charge until the crisis is over."

"Then perhaps we should meet with you," Leia said. "Whatever this crisis is, I'm sure we can do something to help you out of it."

"Your help would indeed be welcome," the general said, although he didn't sound overly enthusiastic. "However, Salis D'aar is unsafe for you at the moment. Dock with *Sentinel* and I shall take a shuttle to meet you within the hour. I'll explain everything then."

"Understood," Han said. Leia noted the look of skepticism on his face. "Just don't try and tell us that the Ssi-ruuk are now the good guys, though, because I can tell you now we won't believe you."

"Not the Ssi-ruuk," Panib said. "The P'w'eck."

Realization dawned, then, for Leia—and from Han's face, she could tell it had for him, too.

"Okay, General," she said. "We'll see you within the hour."

The comm went dead.

"The P'w'eck?" Tahiri repeated. "Weren't they the slaves of the Ssi-ruuk?"

"They were indeed," Leia said.

"But how—?"

"I guess that's what we're about to learn," Han said, the tension in his posture already easing. He reached forward to punch a new course into the *Falcon*'s command board. "In the meantime, let's show these reptoids how to fly."

Leia relayed the situation to Captain Mayn as Han sent the *Falcon* streaking toward *Sentinel*. While she could understand his readiness to accept the immediately obvious explanation, she preferred to reserve judgment until she'd heard what Panib had to say. Nothing, she knew, was ever quite as simple as it seemed.

Only by force of will was Jacen able to hold on to the contents of his stomach as he watched Tekli operate on the injured stormtrooper. The man lay facedown on the operating table, naked to the waist and fed by numerous intravenous drips and tubes. They had barely reached the *Widowmaker*'s medical bay in time. Had it not been for Luke and himself propping up the trooper's defenses with large amounts of the Force, the alien invader would have probably overtaken his immune system completely and effectively killed him. As it was, Saba Sebatyne still had to strengthen the stormtrooper while Tekli tried to isolate the organism, carefully cutting through and around delicate tissues with her vibroscalpel. It was difficult and dangerous work, but after almost forty-five minutes of painstaking surgery, Tekli seemed to have finally exposed the problem.

The centipedelike creature the stormtrooper had been force-fed on Munlali Mafir had turned out not to be a "meal" at all, but rather, as Hegerty had suspected, an uninvited guest. The juvenile Jostran had survived the acids in the man's stomach long enough to burrow its way into his abdominal cavity and locate his spine. Once there, it had used the tips of its many legs to infiltrate nerves and tunnel into his spinal column. It had been working its way up to his skull, gradually taking over his body as it went. Tekli had caught it at the very top of the man's spine, just as it was about to invade his brainpan. Its central body had already sent dozens of hairlike tendrils snaking into delicate neural tissues, and these were making extraction exceedingly difficult. Tekli didn't doubt that the creature had numerous defense mechanisms designed to discourage removal. The filaments could physically damage nerve cells during extraction, or they could excrete any number of chemicals designed to kill as much tissue as possible around themselves. Only with the help of Jacen was she able, strand by strand, to finally save the stormtrooper from a horrible fate. Jacen attuned his mind to that of the Jostran and kept it docile while Tekli worked, finding it much easier when it was on its own rather than in a pack of eleven.

Jacen couldn't shake the ghastly thought of what might

have happened as Tekli scooped up the wriggling body of the alien and dropped it into a tissue sample container. Hair-thin tendrils trailed it like roots from a plant.

"Well done, my friend," he said. "Master Cilghal would be proud of you."

"Thank you, Jacen," Tekli said, stepping back from the table and removing her gloves, leaving a medical droid to suture the patient's wound. "But perhaps we should save congratulations until the anesthetic wears off."

The Chadra-Fan's ears were limp with fatigue and her fur appeared dull. It was clear that the intense concentration required for the operation had taken a lot out of her.

"You're exhausted," Jacen said.

She nodded. "I feel as tired as you look."

Jacen acknowledged the comment with a tight smile. He hadn't had time to change from the gear he'd worn on Munlali Mafir. He'd only had time to wash the dirt and sweat off his face and hands. In all, he suspected he looked as exhausted as he felt.

They left the patient in the care of Imperial meditechs. Outside the surgery, they met Lieutenant Stalgis waiting in the narrow corridor. He had removed his helmet—revealing a long, lined face that suggested an age much older than his thirty or so years—but like Jacen, he hadn't had time to fully refresh himself yet.

"How is he?"

"He's fine," Jacen reassured him. "He just needs time to recover from the surgery."

"The thing—the Jostran—" Stalgis's face contorted into a look of revulsion. "Has it? . . ."

"It's been removed."

Relief rolled off the lieutenant in waves. "I can't tell you how grateful I am, to both of you. Tarl is a friend, as well as a member of my ground team. If he had died—if we hadn't made it back in time—" Stalgis gesticulated for lack of words.

Jacen placed a hand on the armor plating of the man's upper arm. "We were glad to help. But I suggest you get some rest, now. Your friend is going to need you when he wakes."

Stalgis nodded almost formally and strode off up the hallway.

"Perhaps you should listen to your own advice, Solo."

Jacen turned to find Danni Quee standing behind him. She was smiling, but there was no mistaking the concern underlying it.

"I'm okay."

"You're tired," she said, her green eyes flashing at him. "And don't even try to deny it."

A touch on the back of his hand signaled Tekli's departure. He sent a wave of gratitude to the Chadra-Fan through the Force, then devoted all his attention to Danni. She stood before him wearing a standard Jedi expeditionary suit with her arms folded across her breasts. Her blond, curly hair had been cut to her shoulders.

"It's true," he admitted, stepping closer. "I *am* tired. In fact, I'd give anything right now to be able to curl up on my bunk and sleep for a day or two."

"Not even an attempted denial," she said. "I'm impressed, Jacen. Unfortunately, there won't be time for you to sleep. You're wanted on the bridge now."

Momentary alarm welled up in him, but he pushed it back down. "Is anything wrong?"

"Nothing that can't wait ten minutes for you to clean up."

"Is it the Chiss?" he pressed.

"In ten minutes you'll have all the answers you need. But if you were to meet Commander Irolia looking like this, it would probably be taken as a declaration of war."

"She's not letting us proceed?"

Danni continued to evade his questions. ". . . illegal use of biological weapons or something . . ."

"At least give me a hint!"

". . . cruel and unusual punishment . . ."

"All right, all right!" Smiling, and feeling energized by the brief exchange, they walked along the narrow corridors of the Imperial frigate to the cabin he'd been assigned. "Tell Uncle Luke I'll be there shortly."

"That's what comlinks are for." Her expression was mock indignant, but turned into a smile as she turned and headed off for the bridge.

"The planet is a legend," Commander Irolia said. Her youthful features were set in stubborn, self-assured lines. "I cannot believe that finding it is your true objective."

"I assure you that it's much more than a legend," Master Skywalker said. Saba was amazed at his self-control. She knew that he was exhausted and irritated, but all he allowed his face to display was calm and patience. "We have evidence that it once existed; the only question is whether it still exists today."

"What evidence is this?"

"We were told about Zonama Sekot by Vergere, a Jedi Knight from—"

"Vergere?" Irolia's eyebrows shot up at the name. "The same Vergere who sabotaged the Alpha Red initiative?"

Master Skywalker didn't flinch from the truth. "The Vergere who prevented genocide the likes of which this galaxy has never seen, yes."

The commander's exhalation had a mocking bite. "You expect me to trust her testimony?"

"No one is forcing you to accept anything," Captain Yage said, clearly annoyed by the Chiss commander's mockery. "We only want to go about our business. That's all."

"But what *is* your business? That's what I am attempting to determine."

The meeting was being conducted on *Widowmaker*'s bridge in full view of the crew. Irolia carried herself as though it was her own ship and her own crew. Her tone and poise displayed nothing but self-assurance. Saba knew that, should anything happen to the Chiss officer or the small contingent of guards that had escorted her across, then there would be dire consequences for Master Skywalker and his expedition. What's more, Irolia knew that *they* knew—and that, presumably, was why she was so confident.

Saba wasn't an expert on humanoid appearances, but she imagined that the Chiss commander would have been regarded as quite striking among her own people. Her face was narrow and angular, her blue skin smooth and soft looking. Her wide red eyes contained both character and intelligence, and upon entering the meeting, had quickly scanned everyone on the bridge. She didn't doubt that the woman's evaluation of them would have been equally as brisk.

"All we ask," Luke said, "is for the freedom to look."

Irolia paced three steps to her left, contemplating his words. "This is our territory," she said. "You do realize that."

"We recognize your authority over regions near here, yes. But we weren't aware that the Expansionary Defense Fleet had specifically annexed this system."

"If I were to tell you that we have, would you leave?"

"We are a peaceful expedition," Luke said. "Would you bar a trading mission from your territory, or a scientific team?"

The commander laughed. "Don't try to fool me, Skywalker! You're no more a trader than I am. And as for your motives being scientific, I ask this of you: Were you to find this planet, what exactly would you do with it?"

A new voice spoke up from behind them when Luke

hesitated: "It is our hope that Zonama Sekot will help us in our war effort, and in doing so save trillions of lives—including your own."

Commander Irolia turned her attention to Jacen Solo, who had just entered the room. "Then your intentions are clearly *not* scientific, but rather military. So why should we allow you to pursue such objectives when you so readily interfere with our own?"

"Alpha Red wouldn't have won the war," Luke said calmly. "It would have turned us all into monsters."

"That's the war I'm talking about," Jacen said, stepping down into the center of the circular bridge to join the others. "The war against ourselves."

Irolia took a long moment to consider this. "It surprises me to see Imperials and the New Republic working alongside each other," she said finally.

"We are no longer referred to as the New Republic," Luke said. "We have a new name now: the Galactic Federation of Free Alliances."

"And the Empire has freely joined this Alliance?" Irolia asked, glancing at Yage.

"It has," the captain said.

"I suppose the Chiss are welcome to join, too."

Luke seemed unfazed by the commander's sarcasm. "The decision would be yours. But yes, you would indeed be welcome to join in due course."

Irolia snorted derisively but didn't address the Jedi Master's comment. Instead she said, "What concerns me the most here, I think, is the makeup of your senior crew."

Master Skywalker shrugged. "I have already explained that the military contingent is purely defensive."

"That might indeed be true. But the intention lies in its leaders. Mara Jade Skywalker, Luke Skywalker, Jacen Solo—all renowned Jedi warriors."

"Danni Quee is an accomplished scientist," Jacen pointed out.

"Yes, I recognize that name. And Soron Hegerty we know, of course. They fit in with your stated aims."

Danni looked both startled and flattered to be recognized; Hegerty, on the other hand, showed no reaction at all.

"But you also have a Barabel among you," Irolia continued. "How does it fit in?"

Saba stiffened.

"*She* is a Jedi Knight," Luke said.

"Another warrior, then?"

"Not in the sense that you mean."

"Really? Most reptilian species I've ever met have been aggressive and predatory."

Saba's tail thumped the floor. She couldn't help it.

Captain Yage took a step forward at this. "Tell me, Commander, how would you feel if I were to tell you that most Chiss *I've* met have been arrogant and condescending."

Luke signaled for patience. "Saba is life-sensitive. We hope that she will detect Zonama Sekot by its Force emissions when we are near it."

"Have you had any luck so far in this?"

"Not yet. That's why we need to keep searching."

Irolia nodded after some thought. "Very well, Master Skywalker. I will agree to this only because we, too, would like to see this war brought to an end." She signaled to her bodyguards, who handed her a flat, rectangular package about the same size as her outstretched hand. "This memory disk contains authority codes and routes sufficient to get you to Csilla. They will remain active for one week. In that time, you must present yourself in person to obtain permission to travel within our boundaries. Without that permission, any trespass will be regarded as an act of aggression, upon which you will be expelled or destroyed. Do I make myself clear?"

Luke accepted the disk with a resigned look. "Abundantly clear."

"Then my mission here is complete." Commander Irolia's gaze briefly swept the room. "Perhaps we shall all meet again on Csilla."

"That's all you came here for?" Captain Yage asked. "To tell us to report to your superiors?"

"Not quite," Irolia answered. "I was ordered to give you the disk only if I thought you trustworthy."

"And if we weren't?"

The Chiss commander smiled at this, but said nothing in reply. She simply nodded farewell and, with an imperious gesture, ordered her bodyguards to follow her as she strolled from the bridge.

"Why that trumped-up little—"

Again, Luke silenced Captain Yage with a gesture. "She's just doing her job, Arien. We can't blame her for that."

"Nevertheless, I'll be happier when she's off my ship." She turned away to coordinate the disembarkation of the Chiss shuttle.

"I can understand perfectly where you're coming from, Captain Yage." The hologram broke into static, then cleared to reveal the face of Mara Jade Skywalker at the controls of *Jade Shadow*. "I don't even want that woman on my *scopes*."

"You caught all that, Mara?" Luke asked, facing the image of his wife in the holofield.

"Loud and clear."

"What gets up my jets," Yage said, "is the assumption that we're answerable to them at all. The Empire has been collaborating with the Chiss for years, ever since Thrawn's day. But there's no treaty—we don't *owe* them anything. Just the idea of having to report our every movement to them makes my hair stand on end."

"We have to respect that we're in their territory now, Arien," Luke said. "And they do things differently than we do."

"Assuming we *are* in their territory," Mara said. "How about looking at that disk?"

Jacen took it from his uncle and put it into a reader. As Irolia had promised, it contained routes and security codes, but nothing else. The Chiss were tight-lipped when it came to doling out information. They were lucky to get this much.

"Thoughts, anyone?" Luke asked. "Do we plow on regardless, or should we comply with their request and report in?"

"It's your decision," Yage said.

"Yes, but to reach that decision I would like to hear everyone's opinion."

"I don't think there's any great harm in doing what they say," Mara said. "Even though it does irk me."

"I say to the Maw with them," Yage put in. "They can't tell us what to do."

Luke nodded quietly to both women's comments. "Jacen?"

"We'll need access to their information," his nephew replied. "It would make things much simpler. Soron's data is accurate but doesn't cover more than ten percent of the Unknown Regions."

The xenobiologist had looked slightly bored throughout the political exchange, but seemed to perk up now that she'd been brought into the conversation. "The Chiss have been expanding through this section of the galaxy for decades. Irolia clearly knew of the legend of the wandering planet, so it must be common knowledge among her people. I believe access to their data would be invaluable."

"But would it actually make the difference, do you think?" Luke folded his hands in front of him, as he so often did when pondering weighty matters.

"It certainly might." Hegerty nodded at the map. "This small amount of data has already told us something interesting. Note the outer edge of their territory. See how it has held firm against the Yuuzhan Vong incursion? They have either developed similar jamming and combat techniques as your own fighters, or the enemy has withdrawn its offensive in order to concentrate on other areas. I would imagine that the answer to this mystery would be of interest to your tacticians back home."

There was a general murmur of agreement following that observation. The heads of the Galactic Alliance seemed an awfully long way from the Unknown Regions, but Hegerty—and Irolia—was quite right. Luke's mission was military at least in the sense that any information of military value would immediately be added to the war effort. Even though galaxywide communications didn't reach into the Unknown Regions, subspace transmissions could be relayed through an isolated holocomm on the edge of Galactic Alliance space. All communications from the mission were relayed to Cal Omas immediately.

Luke nodded. "You might be right. But tell me, Saba: have you detected any sign of Zonama Sekot in this vicinity? If we are hot on its scent, then we might not need to contact the Chiss at all."

Saba straightened, her nostrils flaring involuntarily. "I sense nothing. If Zonama Sekot iz here, it iz well hidden."

"I thought as much. It's like looking for a droid in a desert: something's more likely to find us before we find it." He nodded again. "I'm of the opinion that we should do as Irolia says and check in with the local authorities. As Soron said, it couldn't hurt. And who knows; it might actually help." He glanced around to everyone, as though waiting to see if there were any objections to his decision.

When no one spoke up, he said, "Okay, then. I'll leave the details of the course with Mara and Arien to prepare. Those of us who just came back from Munlali Mafir will need a break before we take on anything else."

Captain Yage smiled. "I'm sure you won't get any argument from Doctor Hegerty on that score."

The meeting broke up, then, leaving Mara Jade Skywalker and Captain Yage to discuss the finer points of the Chiss map. Luke motioned to Saba, Jacen, and Hegerty, and they joined him for a quiet discussion near the bridge's exit.

"How did Tekli get on with the Jostran?" was the first thing he asked his nephew.

"It was touch and go for a while," the young Jedi replied. "Another centimeter and it would have been too late. But she caught it."

"That's good," the Jedi Master said with a solemn expression. "I would have hated to lose someone else."

The reminder of the two stormtroopers killed on Munlali Mafir was sobering. "This one has examined the data you gathered, Master," Saba said. "There iz a correlation with the other regionz through which Zonama Sekot iz recorded to have passed. The Jostran/Krizlaw symbionts are not technologically advanced, so they do not pose an immediate threat. But they are aggressive by nature. The living planet seems to have exhibited similar avoidance tacticz elsewhere."

"The Krizlaws are certainly aggressive," Luke agreed. "That the Jostrans gave them intelligence only made them worse. I wonder, then, could this be what it's running from? After all, we know Zonama Sekot has a strong presence in the Force. It might be simply trying to hide itself from anything it associates with violence."

"It iz possible," Saba said.

There followed a moment of pensive silence. Saba suspected the silence was due more to weariness than anything else. Her sensitive nostrils could smell the exhaustion emanating from the three humans around her—especially Master Skywalker and his nephew.

"You must rest," she said to them. "You will be no good to anyone if you do not."

"You're quite right, Saba," Luke said. "I was just thinking about Dif Scaur. He's obviously told his side of the story to the Chiss."

Saba nodded. Scaur was the head of New Republic Intelligence; he had worked extensively with the Chiss scientists on the virus Alpha Red, which would have completely wiped out the Yuuzhan Vong and all their biotechnology had it been brought into play. That the Jedi had put a stop to the plan irked Scaur. He might not be above taking steps to thwart the Master's own plans in return.

"We'll see what's waiting for us at Csilla," Jacen said, his gaze drifting to where Danni Quee stood on the far side of the bridge. "Forewarned is forearmed."

"But forearmed can lead to a foregone conclusion," Luke pointed out. "We shouldn't jump ahead of ourselves. The last thing we need now is a self-fulfilling prophecy."

"Just the usual sort," Saba said, hissing with amusement.

But, as so often happened when she attempted a witticism, nobody laughed. They just looked at her strangely.

The first thing Tahiri noticed as she stepped over the threshold into *Sentinel* was the tension. It was like an overwhelming odor emanating from everything around her: the air, the walls, the floors, the light fittings—even from the people themselves. She winced; it was more a physical reaction to something she was sensing through the Force. What caused it, however, she couldn't tell. She just knew it was there.

The second thing she noticed was the briskness of the salute Princess Leia and Han received as they stepped through the air lock. The guards, dressed in dark green uniforms, fairly jumped to attention like wires snapping taut.

She didn't think the reaction came from any Palpatine-style discipline, though; Bakura was a peaceful world, with no history of dictators since the last Imperial governor, Nereus, had been overthrown during the Ssi-ruuvi crisis. More likely, she thought, the guards were reacting to the same tension in the air that she had detected. Something was making everyone jumpy.

A short, stiff-backed man with thinning red hair and a mustache stepped through the lines of Bakuran security guards.

"Grell Panib," he said by way of introduction, bowing sharply first to Leia, then Han. The rest of the party—herself, Jaina, C-3PO, Leia's Noghri bodyguards, and a small honor guard from *Pride of Selonia*—were acknowledged with a curt nod. "Welcome to Bakura."

"It's been a while," Han said dryly.

"You served under Pter Thanas, didn't you?" Princess Leia didn't miss anything.

A glimpse of sadness passed across General Panib's face. "You have a fine memory, Princess. We barely met."

"It was a memorable trip." She smiled as though at some private joke, then introduced the rest of the party.

"Thank you all for—" Panib began, but a commotion from behind the security guards interrupted him. There was the sound of scuffling as someone pushed forward. "I told you to wait for me to call you!"

Not some*one*, Tahiri thought, her heart suddenly pounding as, through the tangle of people, she glimpsed a reptilian creature bounding toward them. Some*thing*!

She instantly drew her lightsaber as the memory of her dreams lifted to emphasize her fears. *Tahiri . . .*

Tahiri . . . Tahiri . . . The godlike lizard creature from her dreams beckoned her.

She blinked once, twice, to clear her head as her lightsaber crackled in front of her.

"A trap!" Jaina shouted. She, too, withdrew her lightsaber. At the same time, the stormtroopers raised their blasters and the Noghri guards stepped forward to protect the Princess.

"No!" Panib quickly put himself between the reptilian creature and their weapons. "His intentions are not hostile!"

The creature emerged from the line of security guards, its claws skittering piercingly on the corridor floor as it came to a halt behind the general.

The alien was a beaked reptile with a long, muscular tail. Its scales were a dull brown, and beneath prominent ridges its golden eyes danced alarmingly. It wore a leathery harness to which were strapped numerous items that could have been either tools or badges of rank.

"This is Lwothin," General Panib said, clearly unsettled by the visitors' reaction. "I assure you that—"

A sudden burst of piercing tones from the creature interrupted him.

When it was over, Han pretended to clean out his ear. "Did anyone catch that?"

"I did, sir," C-3PO answered, oblivious to the fact that it had been a rhetorical question. "He says that he is the advance leader of the P'w'eck Emancipation Movement, and that he welcomes us. He refers to us as 'allies of the free.' "

Tahiri felt the uncertainty of those around her as more loud fluting sounded from the creature.

" 'I mean you no harm,' " 3PO translated.

"Well, that makes me feel a whole lot easier," Han said in a tone that suggested the exact opposite.

"I do apologize for this," Panib said. "The P'w'eck are

unaccustomed to advanced protocol—human or other-wise. They've only recently thrown off their shackles and started speaking for themselves, as it were."

Leia called for everyone to put their weapons away as she eased past the Noghri bodyguards, who parted for her without protest. She stepped up to Lwothin, wearing a thin, perhaps nervous, smile.

"Threepio, tell Lwothin that we are pleased to meet him," she instructed the protocol droid. "If indeed he *is* a 'him.' "

"He assures us that he is," Panib said. "And there is no need for your droid to act as mediator in your dialogue with him, either. He can understand what you're saying perfectly well. We don't like using droids much here, so if you prefer we can supply you with earpiece translators that will do the job equally as well."

C-3PO bristled at the suggestion that his talents might be unnecessary, or even distasteful. "With all due respect, sir, I was designed for precisely this kind of situation. I am fluent in over six million languages and—"

"What he's saying, General," Leia interrupted, "is that we'll get by."

Lwothin's nostril-tongues tasted the air as he followed the exchange. The P'w'eck was smaller than an average Ssi-ruu, although not by much—but he was still bigger than the average human. Muscles bunched under his leathery skin, and his thick tail swished back and forth in a regular, easy rhythm. It was an alarming presence, made all the more unsettling when Tahiri looked up into the creature's face to find his three-lidded amber eyes staring out at her—almost as if reading her reservations. She knew that Leia had instructed everyone to lower their weapons, but Tahiri found her thumb still hovering over the activation stud of her lightsaber.

"You bring Jedi Knights," Lwothin sang through C-3PO. "I had hoped to meet one. The lightsaber is a delightful weapon: an elegant blend of life energy and material design. Our divergent technologies become one in such devices."

Leia's cautious attitude became markedly frostier. "You still use entenchment?"

Panib stepped forward again. "I don't think this is either the time or the place for such involved discussions. Perhaps we should move to surroundings more comfortable for all species. Yes?"

"We're not going anywhere until Leia gets an answer," Han said, his hand back on his blaster. "I'm not about to have my life energy sucked out of me while my guard is down."

Lwothin danced agitatedly on the spot, fluting urgently to C-3PO.

"He assures us that the process is not the same as you remember it," the golden droid informed them. "It has been refined considerably. The P'w'eck come in peace, he says, not war."

Han looked around suspiciously. "Leia?"

"As uncomfortable as I am about all of this," Leia said, "I don't see the point in turning back now." She faced Panib. "But understand this: the Galactic Federation of Free Alliances will never sanction any form of alliance with a government that exploits the life energy of its subjects—no matter who they are, or were."

"You think the P'w'eck are getting back at their old masters?" Panib said. "I can assure you that's not the case."

"No one is entenched against their will anymore," C-3PO continued to interpret. "If you let us, we will explain."

Leia nodded solemnly. "I'd like to hear that. And then maybe you can also explain what's happened to Prime Minister Cundertol."

Panib bowed and Lwothin jigged on the spot.

"Please follow me," General Panib said.

Han came up alongside Leia and gently put an arm about her, and together they walked in the general's footsteps as he led them deeper into the *Sentinel*. Jaina and Tahiri followed, C-3PO between them and the Galactic Alliance guards behind. Jaina was a picture of controlled energy, eyes glancing all around—*except* at Tahiri. It was as if she was deliberately avoiding her eyes.

That hurt Tahiri. Jaina had exchanged barely a monosyllable with her since Galantos. And Jag Fel was no better. Every now and then, she felt as though they were watching her from afar. They hadn't had to say anything; she could feel their distrust in her, and that hurt her more than any words could ever hope to.

As they walked off together, Tahiri felt the scars on her forehead itching. She fought the urge to scratch. She felt self-conscious about them as it was, without drawing any more attention to the unsightly markings. The self-inflicted ones on her arm had all but healed, and remained hidden beneath the sleeve of her tunic. She had considered getting rid of them, but had decided to keep them, for now, out of an instinct she didn't entirely understand and didn't want to think about too closely. There were far more important things to dwell upon.

Sentinel boasted a large meeting hall on an outer level, with a transparent ceiling that afforded a magnificent viewport to the stars. During combat, steelcrete shields would slide shut over the top for protection, but during more tranquil times it offered a wonderful view of Bakura. The green-blue world hung like a fat moon above a ring-shaped conference table that floated on a bed of repulsors. There were enough seats for everyone who had entered the hall, but only those who'd be involved in the discussions were invited to sit around the table.

Jaina stood directly behind her parents, her hand on the hilt of her lightsaber. She didn't like being so far away from reinforcements in such an unknown situation, and having her weapon within constant reach went a long way toward easing her apprehensions. Everyone knew that the Ssi-ruuk were adept at mental coercion; who was to say that General Panib wasn't a brainwashed slave intending to deliver the delegates from the Galactic Alliance to his masters at the first opportunity?

The presence of the P'w'eck didn't particularly reassure her, either. In fact, when two more of the creatures had joined Lwothin, Jaina's misgivings had intensified immediately. She assumed them to be bodyguards by the way they took up position behind Lwothin, although she had to admit they didn't look any different in appearance from their superior. They wore odd-looking weapons fastened to their harnesses: flat disks with businesslike snouts protruding from one end. Paddle beamers, she assumed. The energy beams of such weapons couldn't be deflected by lightsabers, but they could certainly be bent a little.

Lwothin himself did not have a physique that allowed him to sit on chairs like the others present, so he was sprawled out on an assortment of cushions at his appointed place around the table. This didn't detract in any way from his intimidating mien.

"Blaine Harris, the Deputy Prime Minister, is on his way from Salis D'aar," Panib said by way of preamble. "But we shall begin without him."

"I wouldn't say we're a captive audience," Han said, sitting restlessly at Leia's side, "but we're prepared to hear you out."

"You've come at a very awkward time for us. I hardly know where to begin."

"You could start with entenchment," Leia said.

"We know that you think it an abomination," Lwothin said through C-3PO. "And I can sympathize with your feelings. My species has been exploited by it for thousands of years. We know its past evil."

"Be that as it may," Han said. "But I've seen plenty of slaves point the same weapons at their masters once they'd won their freedom."

"I'll admit the temptation was strong," Lwothin said, his beak clicking together at the end of the short phrase. "But perhaps I should tell you the story of how we came to be here. Maybe then you will understand us better."

Jaina saw her mother nod for him to continue, then settled back into the large, upright chair to listen.

"It has been almost thirty years since the Ssi-ruuvi Imperium waged war in this section of the galaxy," he began. Jaina knew the story. Initially courted by Emperor Palpatine, the Ssi-ruuvi Imperium had expanded aggressively into Imperial territories, starting with Bakura. Unfortunately for the Ssi-ruuk, that advance had been immediately repelled by the local Imperial government, with the unlikely help of the Rebel Alliance. Further incursions into the galaxy were discouraged by the New Republic, which forced the Imperium back to its homeworlds. Nothing had been heard from them since. Jaina gathered that everyone assumed they either had learned the error of their ways, or were gradually stockpiling for a more determined surge.

Just like the Yevetha, she thought.

"In fact," Lwothin said, "our former masters were assessing more than just their tactics in the wake of their defeat." Ssi-ruuvi society was strictly clan-based, he explained, with each clan designated by the color of their scales. The absolute ruler was the Shreeftut, assisted by the Elders' Council and the Conclave. The Conclave advised the Shreeftut on spiritual matters—another aspect of life considered very important by the Ssi-ruuk. Their belief system taught that the spirit of any Ssi-ruu who died away from a consecrated world would be lost forever. It was for that reason that the Ssi-ruuk preferred to use combat droids powered by the enteched souls of captives to fight their enemies rather than risk their own lives in battle.

"Entechment had served our masters well for many centuries. They had never seen any reason to change. The abhorrence with which you greeted the technology came as a complete surprise to them. They had assumed that all cultures would employ the same techniques. That you didn't only underscored the novelty of the technology you *did* use: that of fusion and ordinary matter.

"Clearly the Rebel Alliance beat our former masters for more reasons than different technology, but that was one aspect they could focus on. They had seen Imperial and Rebel Alliance vessels in action above and around Bakura. They knew enough material physics to back-engineer the technology and re-create it in their laboratories. Within ten standard years, they possessed prototype hybrid vessels that employed your technology for shields and engines but were directed by enteched minds. With a significantly reduced drain on their life forces, such pilots existed much longer and in less agony than before."

"But they were still enteched," Han interrupted.

"Yes. The mind of every prototype droid fighter consisted of a soul stolen from the body of a P'w'eck. The fact that their suffering had been lessened was balanced by the fact that they suffered longer. The situation was still undeniably wrong.

"Into this time, the Keeramak was born."

A new note entered the P'w'eck's voice. It might have been fear, Jaina thought. Or maybe awe.

"What is this Keeramak?" Leia asked.

"It is hard to explain in terms that you might understand. You know that those of the Ssi-ruuk with blue scales ruled the Ssi-ruuvi Imperium, and that the gold-scales were our priests. Yellow-scales studied the sciences of matter and energy. Those with russet scales were our warriors, while those with green scales were workers. Below them, barely above my own species, were those resulting from a mixed or unsuccessful breeding: the brown-scales. Some suspected them of being the progenitors of the P'w'eck in ages past. Regarded as dim-witted and brutish, they were fit only for the most menial of lives. Many, especially those born of a forbidden union, were destroyed at birth.

"That was the world into which the Keeramak was born. It is important you understand this, because the Keeramak should not exist. One of a brood of brown-scale Ssi-ruuk, the Keeramak alone possessed color. But it does not just have one color: the Keeramak has *all* colors. That is what makes it unique among the Ssi-ruuk."

Lwothin performed a complicated gesture involving the muscles of his tail and spine, as though shrugging his entire body. "That the Keeramak was a sport, a deviant birth, was clear. It had no clear gender, and its size was anomalous. But that was irrelevant. Its birth sent shock waves through the Ssi-ruuk. They place a great value on spiritual matters, as you know, and such a birth had been prophesied for millennia. The Keeramak, the birth of many colors, would be the one to take the oppressed and make them lords; the Keeramak would make the weak *strong*."

"What you're saying," Han said, "is that the Ssi-ruuk embraced the Keeramak because they thought it would lead them to victory over us, right?"

"That is correct," Lwothin said. "They raised it like a king, with every privilege and opportunity to learn and grow. The Keeramak soon proved to be exceptional in all respects: strong, intelligent, wise. It argued with the Shreef-tut over the limitations of power, it challenged the Conclave on matters of theology, and it rivaled the Elders' Council when it came to minor points of law. But ultimately it was the Keeramak's compassion that was its greatest point—as well as the Ssi-ruuk's undoing."

"It chose you over them?" Leia asked.

"The Keeramak was the one who led us to victory over our former masters. It conceived our revolt and consolidated the aftermath. Within a year, Lwhekk was ours and the Ssi-ruuvi Imperium a thing of the past. And now, five years on, the Keeramak still guides our destiny."

"Impressive," Leia said. "Throwing off an oppressor is only the beginning of a long and difficult journey."

Jaina nodded, knowing that her mother spoke from experience.

"In the wake of our liberation, we have continued research into entenchment," Lwothin said, through C-3PO. "We have found ways to nourish the stored minds reclaimed during our revolution. The life energy distilled from concentrated banks of algae and other primitive life-forms can prevent the decay common to previous soul-captures. It also goes a long way toward staving off the discomfort many feel when entenched. Now that we have diverted much of the life-draining work to your forms of technology and reduced the strain on the enteched soul, we have reversed many of the wrongs forced upon captives and slaves in the past.

"The droid fighters you saw today are piloted by those enteched in the last days of the Imperium." Lwothin's triple eyelids blinked in a complicated manner. "Although we do continue to offer entenchment as a form of military service, there are few who willingly sacrifice their physical lives. There's no way back, of course. Such a decision is not lightly made."

"I'm sure it wouldn't be," Leia said as she faced General Panib.

From the tone of her mother's voice, coupled with the set of her shoulders and the way she sat in the chair before her, Jaina could tell she wasn't entirely convinced by

Lwothin's lengthy explanation—even though it did con-
cur with the odd Force readings they'd had from the droid
fighters.

"General Panib, have you seen anything to contradict
Lwothin's statement that no one has been enteched
against his or her will?"

"None of us have been enteched, if that's what you're
getting at," the general said. "In fact, there have been no aggressive moves made against us whatsoever. Although . . ."

"What?" Han prompted, leaning forward slightly in
his chair.

"Well, that's something else we will need to talk about:
why you've come at such a bad time. The P'w'eck arrived
here two weeks ago, offering a treaty. Prime Minister
Cundertol and the Senate deliberated for days before arriving at the decision to accept the offer. The Prime Minister's announcement caused a few riots. It's hard to
explain to the general population that we haven't sold
them out."

"I can understand that," Han muttered.

"We thought the people were coming around," Panib
went on. "The defense advantages of joining with the
P'w'eck are obvious, given the Yuuzhan Vong's gradual
drift this way. And we had a lot be grateful to them for,
since they did get rid of the Ssi-ruuvi threat." Panib fidgeted
uneasily. "But there are complications—and conditions."

"Such as?" Leia asked.

"Lwothin has mentioned religion; the P'w'eck are like
the Ssi-ruuk in that they share some of the same traditions. In order to make them comfortable, there are details we have to attend to. Cundertol wanted this
Keeramak of theirs to come to Bakura to sign the treaty
in person, but he—it—wouldn't come unless Bakura was
consecrated. You see, it believes like the rest of the Ssi-
ruuk that if it dies away from one of the sacred worlds,
then its soul will be lost forever. And the fact is, assassi-

nation *isn't* out of the question—especially given the volatile temperament of some of the public right now." His glance to Lwothin was filled with apology. "We are neighbors; we must learn to trade and fight side by side. If Bakura and the P'w'eck are to work together, then we have to consider all our religious beliefs. We'd like them to feel safe enough to visit here. Toward this end, Cundertol managed to find a compromise: the Keeramak would come to Bakura to perform the consecration in person. The ceremony was planned for two days from now. That's where things stood when—"

"When Prime Minister Cundertol disappeared," interrupted a voice from the entrance to the chamber.

Jaina's grip on her lightsaber tightened instinctively as she turned to see a tall, aging man in a scarlet robe approach the table. His face was long and angular, the bones beneath clearly showing. Two Bakuran guards closely shadowed him, rifles held firmly across their chests.

"Deputy Prime Minister Harris," Panib said, standing. He sounded relieved. "Thank you for joining us."

Harris indicated for Panib to return to his seat, then nodded to everyone else around the table by way of greeting. "Princess Leia, Captain Solo: it's a pleasure to meet you again. And of course you, Lwothin."

An attendant brought up a chair, and he sat between the P'w'eck and Leia.

"I apologize for the delay," he said to Panib, "but there was a bomb threat at the main spaceport and I had to take a shuttle from Lesser Grace. As you can see," he explained to the rest of the table, "we are suffering from a pronounced civil unrest. Not on behalf of the majority, I imagine, but rather a violent and unprincipled minority who think they know what's best for Bakura. This minority has decided that the P'w'eck are no different from the Ssi-ruuk, and the Keeramak's visit here is nothing

more than an elaborate ruse that will result in the entechment of everyone. 'Once an enemy, always an enemy' is
their maxim. There is simply no room for negotiation."
He clenched his fists helplessly on the table. His gaze fell
upon Leia and Han. "I understand you have experienced
interference from them already."

"A secure transmission was interrupted by someone
warning us away," Leia said. "Whoever it was had access to comm channels that should have been restricted."

"They are everywhere," Harris said sourly. "As the
consecration looms, their desperation increases. They
have been behind at least five disruptions to subspace
communications in the last fortnight. Kidnapping Molierre Cundertol was an act of suicidal bravado. It is
strange but, while I have to condemn their methods, I
can't help admire their spirit." He shook his head sadly.
"Nevertheless, we will never negotiate with terrorists."

"What about Cundertol?" Han asked. "Any idea
where he's being kept?"

"We'll find out soon enough. Especially now that we
have the terrorist leader in our hands."

General Panib was clearly taken aback by this news.
"Since when?"

"She was taken into custody shortly before I left to
come here. We have her in a security holding cell, awaiting interrogation."

"Is she—" Panib hesitated. "—who we suspected she
was?"

"Malinza Thanas," Harris answered with a smug
smile. "Yes."

The surprise in the room was palpable. Jaina knew the
name. Malinza Thanas was the daughter of people her
parents and Uncle Luke had met on Bakura the first time
they'd visited. When Malinza's parents had died, Luke
and Mara had taken her on as a sponsor child, visiting

her a couple of times. She'd heard nothing about the girl being a terrorist leader, however.

"Malinza?" Leia asked. "Are you certain of this?"

"There's no doubt," Harris stated. "She admits it herself."

"She *admits* she kidnapped the Prime Minister?" Panib asked.

"Not yet, but it's only a matter of time."

"When you say 'interrogation'—"

"I don't mean to imply torture, Princess," Harris said. "We are a civilized people, and it would take more than a little civil unrest to reduce us to savages."

"This doesn't add up." Han was shaking his head. "Whoever we spoke to when we arrived warned us away because they thought we were after your ships. They implied that the P'w'eck were your *allies*. But that contradicts what you've just told us about the terrorists. If they're anti-P'w'eck they wouldn't want any association with them at all."

"What can I say? They are confused and directionless, their aims unclear even to themselves." Harris shrugged dismissively. "We have suffered at the hands of such isolationist groups ever since the overthrow of the Empire. There are indeed those who resent the intrusion of the New Republic into our affairs. Some of these may have allied themselves with the anti-P'w'eck movement to gain the illusion of numbers. Such people won't be happy until Bakura stands alone against the rest of the galaxy— and inevitably *falls* alone, too."

"So what now?" Panib asked.

"The first thing, General, is to put our house in order. While we look for the Prime Minister, I suggest we end martial law and begin preparations for the consecration. The treaty depends on it; the Prime Minister would not want it delayed for anything. With your permission, I shall convene the Senate and get things moving."

"Of course." The general's relief was obvious. "There's not much time, and a lot to be done."

Lwothin spoke up. " 'We understand that this is a difficult time for you,' " C-3PO translated, " 'and we are grateful for your continued efforts to bring our governments together.' " The P'w'eck's beak snapped emphatically. " 'I will convey my assurances to the Keeramak that all is in order and the ceremony will go ahead as planned.' "

"Thank you, my friend." Blaine Harris inclined his head in the direction of the P'w'eck ambassador. "And you, of course," he added to Han and Leia, "are very welcome to attend also. I'm sure it will be a fascinating glimpse into a culture we've theorized about for many years, but never had the opportunity to see with our own eyes."

"We'd be honored," Leia said. "The Galactic Federation of Free Alliances will be very interested to observe the ceremony."

General Panib stood, and the others around the table followed suit. "I hope you won't be offended if I call this meeting to an end, but I have urgent matters to discuss with the Deputy Prime Minister."

"Of course." Leia accepted the explanation with her usual diplomatic aplomb. "And thank you for taking the time to explain the situation here. There are still some aspects I'd like to discuss in more detail at a later date, if possible."

"It would be my pleasure to accommodate you," the general said. He spoke and moved with a confidence that had been lacking before the Deputy Prime Minister's news. "And I shall ensure that Salis D'aar spaceport is secured for your arrival. Hopefully with Thanas in custody, the situation will cool down a little now."

Leia bowed in acknowledgment.

The Deputy Prime Minister bowed also as Leia and

Han's party filed toward the exit. Lwothin and his two bodyguards followed close behind, and although he made no effort to come too close, Jaina still made sure to position herself carefully between her parents and the powerful saurian.

Once outside, the P'w'eck fluted in his loud, melodic way.

"Lwothin says that this is a pivotal time for all our species," C-3PO interpreted. More fluting and gesturing followed. "He also says that he is glad that you will be attending the ceremony. The Keeramak will be pleased when it hears the news."

Without waiting for a response, the P'w'eck headed off down the corridor, bodyguards in tow.

"Chirpy fellow, ain't he?" Han said.

"Something's not adding up here," Jaina said. She was glad the meeting was over and she was once again able to be involved in discussions. "How can the Bakuran resistance be everywhere and yet still be a minority?"

"Maximum disruption," Leia said, "for minimum effort. We could be seeing the Peace Brigade at work here."

"What's left of them," Han muttered. "It's like getting a dent out of a deflector grille, even after Ylesia."

"At least we're not too late this time," Jaina said, the destruction of N'zoth still fresh in her mind.

"That's assuming, of course," Leia said, "that we have the full story."

"The story, Yu'shaa. Tell us the story," whispered the acolytes crowding the darkened audience hall. "Tell us about the *Jeedai*."

The Prophet gazed down at them from his throne, his expression hidden behind a mask of truly horrific proportions. A maze of scars and tattoos, it was barely recognizable as a face.

"Who asks?" he demanded in accordance with the service.

"We do, Yu'shaa," the pilgrims responded with a unified bowing of their heads. "We are the Shamed Ones, and we come to you for wisdom."

The Prophet nodded, satisfied by the formal response. Warders outside the hall had carefully instructed the audience on how and when to speak. The being on the inside of the mask smiled to himself, knowing that these conventions were nothing more than a sham to encourage obedience to him and, ultimately, rebellion against his enemies.

Nom Anor rose from his seat on the throne and removed the mask. The hideous creation was meant to represent Shimrra and the gods, while its removal symbolized the casting off of the old ways. He had devised every detail of the ceremony with the help of Shoon-mi and Kunra, his chief acolytes, but no matter how many times he did it, it still felt clumsy. Only the reactions of the converts convinced him that it was working.

The acolytes looked wonderingly up at Nom Anor's "real" face—not aware that this was just another mask, an ooglith masquer designed to make him look like a member of the Shamed caste.

"The gods have granted me a vision," he announced. "It is a vision of a galaxy of beautiful worlds—worlds in which all Yuuzhan Vong can live in peace as well as in glory, free of shame, and with everything their hearts and souls desire."

In recent weeks, Nom Anor had learned to become more animated and expressive when addressing the groups that came to hear him speak. At first he had just sat there and spoken, but he soon found the attention of the Shamed Ones would drift beneath his dull monotones. So he'd adopted some of the techniques he had observed in Vuurok I'pan—a storyteller from the group of Shamed Ones

that had first taken him in during his initial exile to Yuuzhan'tar's underworld. Nom Anor clearly recalled how
I'pan had told the story of Vua Rapuung, and how those
gathered had listened intently, hanging from his every
word—even though they had heard the tale so many times
before.

"But as I gazed upon this vision," Nom Anor went on
with dramatic flair, "a dark shadow came between my
hungry eyes and the sight of the worlds that should be
ours. The huge, black shadow had rainbows that shined
from its eyes; its mighty hands were darkened from
bloodstains."

The congregation listened spellbound, just as I'pan's
audience had once listened to him. Nom Anor raised a
hand to demand silence—an unnecessary gesture since
the silence was already profound, but one that served to
reinforce his command over the gathering.

"The gods opposed the great shadow, the Rainbow-
Eyed One, and they brought forth their holy warriors to
strike it down!"

He stared down at the crowd. "You know the name of
these warriors."

The whisper surrounded him. "*Jeedai!*"

He nodded his approval, and leaned forward as
though to impart a great secret. And it *was* a great secret,
for uttering it could easily mean the death of everyone in
the room.

"Yes, the gods sent the *Jeedai* to drive away the
Rainbow-Eyed Enemy. For weeks and months they fought.
The Shadow killed many of the holy warriors, and kept
the rest at bay. Night fell across the galaxy, and it seemed
as though the war was hopelessly lost. Our home had
been taken from us! The Yuuzhan Vong were no longer
favored by the gods, for we had debased ourselves on the
altar of the Shadow!"

"No," moaned one in the congregation, shaking his

head. Even from his place at the front of the congregation, Nom Anor could smell the rank odor of the Shamed One's decaying arm.

He smiled inwardly. It was all too easy to work his will over the loose-knit congregations of heretics that infested the capital. Their members were weak and desperate, while he was strong and resourceful.

"No indeed," he said. "Even as despair overcame me at the defeat of the *Jeedai*, even as it seemed as though the Rainbow-Eyed One would never be stopped, the gods gave me hope. For just when all was dark, I saw the grasses of the field turn against the Shadow. I saw them rise and wrap around the feet of the Rainbow-Eyed One. The Enemy stumbled and fell—and then the grasses rose to bind the Shadow's mighty limbs! The grasses held this Foe of the gods to the ground, wrapping themselves around his throat and squeezing the very life from him, removing the influence of his black heart from the land!

"By themselves, each blade of grass was weak; but together they were *mighty*!"

The congregation sighed with relief and joy at the exclamation.

"Let us be as the grass and twine about the feet of our adversary to bring him crashing down. For individually we may be weak, but like the grass, together we can be strong."

The congregation hissed its appreciation, and Nom Anor basked in their approval. In all the years he'd served as an executor, he had never had such an audience. It had been impossible to speak honestly or openly for fear of offending the warmaster or the priests—or, through them, the gods. Now he had the attention of hundreds, and they would listen to anything he said.

He was wise enough to realize, though, that such attention would last only as long as they approved of his message. They devoured the nonsense about the Jedi along with his message of self-empowerment—and while he had no great belief in the former, he was very much in favor of the latter. The Shamed Ones were his ride back to the surface. He was happy to give them the means so he could achieve the end.

The allure of the means wasn't lost on him. As an executor, he hadn't properly appreciated the need and strength of the lower castes. The Shamed Ones were indeed weak individually, as he taught in his sermons, but this was easily made up for with their overwhelming numbers. The majority had belonged to the worker caste before their Shaming, but some had been of higher rank. Moreover, it wasn't just the Shamed Ones who answered his call. Converts to his Jedi cult were increasingly drawn from junior members of the un-Shamed—from the workers, the shapers, the warriors, the priests, and the intendants. The shapers knew the tools of their trade, the priests and intendants knew how to organize, and the warriors knew how to fight. Anyone who descended upon one of these meetings to make arrests was in for a nasty surprise.

Although it was hard to remember sometimes, those in his audience weren't particularly gullible. They weren't uneducated; they weren't stupid. They just wanted authority, and he would give it to them.

When the muttering died away, he returned to the throne and motioned the audience to gather around him. In reality, the chamber was just a large basement hundreds of meters below the spires of Yuuzhan'tar, and his "throne" was just a chair coated in moss of different shades to make it look better than it really was. It didn't matter. The congregation saw what it wanted to see, just as it heard what it wanted to hear.

Nom Anor leaned forward to talk to them with less ceremony. It was time to give them *the Message*.

"How many here have met the *Jeedai* face-to-face?"

he asked. "How many have heard the message from their own lips, in their own tongue?"

He waited for someone to answer in the affirmative but, as always, no one did. In all the sermons he'd given, not one of the Shamed Ones who came to him had ever met or even seen a single example of the ones they venerated and looked to for liberation.

"*I* have met the *Jeedai*," he said. "*I* have gazed upon the Twins and seen their power; *I* have wondered at the *Jeedai*-who-was-shaped; *I* witnessed the death of perhaps the greatest of them all, the one called Anakin Solo, who gave his life so that the ones he loved might live; and *I* have spoken to their elders and heard their message with my own ears. That I have done all these things and am here before you now attests to the truth of what I have told you. If what I say is not the truth, then may the gods strike me down here and now where I stand and erase this blasphemy from the heart of the galaxy!"

Nom Anor could feel the congregation holding its collective breath, and he hid another a smile as he dragged out the pause a little longer than was strictly necessary. He wanted the acolytes to realize that they were still afraid of the old gods, that old habits died hard.

He never grew tired of seeing the impact his words had upon the Shamed Ones. It never failed to amuse him how he could manipulate their emotions. Strictly speaking, Nom Anor's claims weren't lies. He *had* met a lot of Jedi in the course of his duty, just not in the capacity of an ally. Nor had he ever stopped to listen to their philosophy. They'd usually been on the receiving end of one of his schemes to betray and destroy them, or he'd been doing his level best to survive when those schemes went wrong.

When the silence was as taut as a stretched ligament, he began to tell them the story of Vua Rapuung, the Shamed One who had found redemption in the actions of the Jedi Knight called Anakin Solo. They had all heard it before, of course; none of them would have made it this far had they not been able to give at least a rough outline of the story, thereby demonstrating that *someone* thought them trustworthy. But this was the "official" version, as taught by the Prophet. It contained all the correct details in the right order, and was consistent with the known facts. It conveyed precisely the right message at exactly the right time.

So Nom Anor intended it, anyway. Again, lacking true belief, he could only judge by the reactions of those who came to hear him speak. They listened rapturously and left enlivened, empowered to spread the Message. All knew that being associated in any way with the Prophet would mean torture and death; the keepers of the old gods were jealous and did not tolerate challengers to their beliefs.

How far knowledge of the existence of the cult had spread was hard to say. Did Shimrra lose concentration during his nightly flagellations as he pondered the spreading rot? Nom Anor could only hope so.

". . . and there the *Jeedai* heresy might have ended, had it not been witnessed by the Shamed Ones watching from the edge of the battle—by the shapers' damutek. They spread the Message—and to this day the Message continues to spread, from mouth to ear among those like us. There is another way, a way that leads to acceptance, and a new word for hope: *Jeedai*."

Nom Anor paused at the end of the tale to sip from a drink bulb that Shoon-mi had ensured was at hand before the acolytes had filed into the room. The ending of the tale was identical to the ending he had first heard from I'pan. He told it this way to remind himself both of the story's origins and of I'pan's fate. I'pan's death at the hands of a band of warriors that had come searching for stolen provisions—thefts I'pan had conducted with Nom

Anor in order to keep their small band of outlaws alive—had galvanized Nom Anor into action. Without that to motivate him, he might have still been living in anonymity, waiting for his luck to run out instead of making his own.

"I shall answer your questions now," he said after a moment.

There were always questions.

"Did Yun-Yuuzhan create the *Jeedai*?" was the first, shouted by a female near the front.

"Yun-Yuuzhan created all things," he answered, "the *Jeedai* included. They are as much a part of his plan as we are. This will probably seem confusing to some, but you must remember that we should never assume to know Yun-Yuuzhan's plan in its entirety. We are as ghazakl worms before him. Would such a worm understand even the most menial task *you* perform?"

"Are they aspects of Yun-Shuno, then?" a male cried out from the back.

"As with all beings, different ones appeal to different gods. The twin *Jeedai*, Jaina and Jacen Solo, are often associated with the twin gods Yun-Txiin and Yun-Q'aah. Jaina is also associated with Yun-Harla, the Trickster. All the *Jeedai* are disciplined warriors, so they fight with the favor of Yun-Yammka, the Slayer. They revere life as does Yun-Ne'Shel, the Modeler. Self-sacrifice for the greater good is part of their teaching, as it is with Yun-Yuuzhan. And yes, they have acted as intercessors for the Shamed Ones in the fashion of Yun-Shuno.

"But in essence, they are beings like us. They are not themselves gods, any more than Shimrra is. They are mortal; they can be killed. I know this because I have seen them die with my own eyes. There are even stories of *Jeedai* who wreak destruction instead of good, so we know that they have flaws like us. It is their teaching we must follow so we can be strong like them, so we can be accepted as equals again."

"Yu'shaa, what is the Force?"

Nom Anor pretended to ponder this question before he answered. In reality, he had already given it a great deal of thought. He had seen firsthand the effects of the Force, but he had never understood it. Unlike those he had once served, however, he refused to dismiss that failure to understand as a failure on behalf of the Jedi. That was absurd. He simply could not hide from the fact that the Jedi Knights had access to *something* that the Yuuzhan Vong clearly did not.

It became worse the more he thought about it. If, as the Jedi claimed, the Yuuzhan Vong truly didn't possess the mystical life force or energy field that filled—or fueled— the galaxy they had invaded, did that mean, then, that the Yuuzhan Vong and all their works—and their gods— were as empty and lifeless as the machines they despised?

There were two obvious solutions to this problem, as far as Nom Anor could see. One was to embrace the teachings of the Jedi in order to learn more about what had gone wrong, and maybe save themselves from a pointless "non-life." The other was to find evidence, somehow, that the Yuuzhan Vong weren't entirely closed to this ubiquitous Force—that somewhere inside them existed the same spark of life that burned in the Jedi.

His answer to the question attempted to address both solutions in a way that left neither resolved.

"The Force is an aspect of creation, the same as matter and energy. It may even be an aspect of *the* creation, the primordial sacrifice that brought forth all things from Yun-Yuuzhan. We are taught that Yun-Yuuzhan is the source of all life, the Overlord who, through great pain to himself, created the lesser gods and thus, by connection, the Yuuzhan Vong. We assume that his sacrifice was of his body—as his followers might sacrifice an arm or a thousand captives in his honor. But why should that be so? Why do we limit Yun-Yuuzhan's generosity only to that which we can see and touch? Just as the wind is invisible to our eyes, there are many more things in the universe than we can sense with our corporeal bodies, and all these things spring ultimately from Yun-Yuuzhan. The Force is part of that, too.

"But what *is* it exactly?" Nom Anor shook his head. "I cannot address that question, my friends, because I simply do not have the answer. On this matter, I am as ignorant as all of you. The Force is a mystery—one that may haunt us forever. All we can do is grope in the darkness for that thing we know is missing, in the hope that we might somehow stumble across it by chance."

Nom Anor leaned forward again, dropping his voice to a whisper so they were forced to listen closely to his words. "So far in my groping, I have discovered two things that I want you to consider. The first is that our way and the way of the *Jeedai* are not necessarily at odds with each other. I'm not suggesting, as some have proposed, that we *replace* our pantheon with that of the *Jeedai* and the Force—but that we are both prophets of a new way."

He paused again, but not long enough for anyone to voice another question. "The other thing is no more than speculation, really, but I offer it to you anyway, for you to consider. I mentioned before that Yun-Yuuzhan's sacrifice might have been of more than just his body; that he might have offered up things in order to bring the universe into being—things that the likes of you and I can neither see nor sense. We see aspects of him reflected in everything around us. So is it not possible that the Force, in all its mystery and wonder, is what remains of Yun-Yuuzhan's soul?"

Nom Anor leaned back into the throne, leaving them to ponder that thought for a moment. He honestly didn't know if it meant anything or not, but the audience seemed to think it profound.

He let himself relax while they contemplated the notion. These were the toughest questions, and he was glad to get them out of the way early, but they were also the ones he had prepared for the most. From here on, if the acolytes followed the usual patterns, the questions would be relatively trivial.

"Who are you, Yu'shaa?" asked a disfigured warrior from off to one side of the gathering.

He dodged the answer with rhetoric, in much the same way he might have once deflected thud bugs with his amphistaff. "I am one of you: anonymous in servitude, remarkable only for my willingness to speak out against those who would have us defiled."

"Where did you come from?"

"Like you—like *all* of you—I was born and raised on one of the many worldships that crossed the gulfs between galaxies, following our ancestors' vision of a promised land."

It was the truth, of course, just not the *whole* truth. Nom Anor had acted as an advance scout, arriving many years before the main body of the migration. His mission had been to gather information about the governments and species occupying the worlds ahead. He had prepared the way for later agents, exploring pressure points and sowing seeds of dissent. Those seeds had flowered into rebellions and counter-rebellions, destabilizing the New Republic and widening the cracks that had ultimately led to its downfall. During the war, he had helped found the Peace Brigade that had so jeopardized the Jedi cause, and set many other schemes into motion. But there was no way he was going to let them know *that*.

"Is the war wrong?" asked one from the front, his eyes wide and hungry for answers.

That was a difficult question. Being pro-Jedi didn't

necessarily mean that the galaxy wasn't intended to be the Yuuzhan Vong's new home. It didn't mean that it was wrong to fight the Galactic Alliance, since it wasn't ruled by Jedi and didn't openly advocate Jedi values. It was perfectly reasonable to be soundly pro-Jedi and yet at the same time fanatically opposed to any suggestion that the war should be ended.

The trouble was, Nom Anor suspected that the Yuuzhan Vong were now losing the war. He had no confidence in Shimrra's ability to restore the situation. He understood the bankruptcy of the Supreme Overlord's regime—he knew of the lies, the betrayals, the desperate search for an antidote in the form of the eighth cortex. Without a radical change in direction or fortune, the Galactic Alliance was going to win.

For the worshipers of Yun-Yammka, the god of carnage, there was no such thing as losing. There was only winning or dying. A failure to defeat the Galactic Alliance would inevitably mean a fight to the end, and the destruction of all that Nom Anor held dear. His only hope, therefore, was to change the direction of the war from beneath, by muddying the waters for the enemy. Would the Jedi be so keen to attack when they had supporters in the Yuuzhan Vong ranks? He suspected not. They were warriors, but they were also guilty of compassion.

"The war is an aberration," he said, offering the reply he always used when fielding this kind of question. "It is a lie. We should never have been fighting the *Jeedai* in the first place, since they are the only ones who will speak up for those without voices—those like *us*. Nor should we be fighting those who call the *Jeedai* allies, either, since alone the *Jeedai* are insufficient to destroy the Supreme Overlord. We should be fighting the ones who pit like against like, who use fear and betrayal to keep the powerless in their place, who would strike down Yun-Yuuzhan himself in order to satisfy their greed! It is never wrong

to fight for what is ours, but you must make certain that
you do so for the right reasons. Be clear who your enemy
is. It is Shame. But together, like the grass, we can bring
an end to this Shame once and for all."

The audience responded enthusiastically to his words,
and this time Nom Anor did smile. They were his now,
would do anything for him. He had led them to the
noose, and they had happily put their heads through of
their own accord.

"What do we do now, Prophet?"

Nom Anor sought out the questioner, and recognized
him as the one with the severely decayed arm. The acolyte's
eyesacks were a deep, intense blue, almost visibly pulsing
with blood. His stare was the kind Nom Anor had seen
many times before—before and since he had formed the
cult. For some, belief was so much more than just a guide
to living: it became life itself. That was understandable,
he thought, when they had so little else to live for.

"You are among the first to receive the Message," he
said, addressing the whole room. "Your duty now is to
spread it to others so that they, too, will come to understand it. Some of these may choose to come here and
receive further instruction, themselves to become mes-
sengers. The Message will spread like a flood, washing
our Shame away."

A murmur of approval rolled around the gathering,
punctuated by the nodding of many heads.

"There will, of course, be those who will hear the
Message but do nothing with it," Nom Anor went on.
"They will keep it in their hearts—secreted away from
others as though it were some rare spore they have found.
For these individuals I feel nothing but pity. The Message
can only be of value if it is *heard*—for that, and that alone,
is its purpose. Remaining silent after you hear the Message
is akin to giving approval of the way you have been
treated, of being complicit with the enemy . . ."

He let the sentence trail off, then sighed. The time had come to end the audience. He had said everything he needed to say.

"My friends, I fear for all of you. Although we have right on our side, we are still fledglings who must confront hostility at every corner. Should word of our existence and identities ever reach the higher ranks, then every one of us involved will be hunted down and killed. Therefore, I ask you all to take every precaution as you spread the Message and recruit for our cause. A whisper will spread, but a shout would most surely be silenced. With patience and perseverance, we will prevail. I ask you to go now in the strength and knowledge that the spirit of freedom is with us!"

Nom Anor stood and opened his arms, as though to embrace them all. At the signal, the doors at the back of the cellar opened, allowing the newly recruited acolytes to file out. He smiled beneficently as they left, radiating goodwill and trust. It was very different from how he had once dealt with underlings. There was a time when he would have sent them off with curses and threats, trusting in fear to keep them loyal. But this wouldn't work on the Shamed Ones; threatening them with punishment would only demonstrate that he was no different from the rest of their masters. If he had learned one thing from his disguise, it was that when fear was a way of life and there was nothing left to lose, the only incentive remaining was reward.

When they were gone, he collapsed back into the throne. *Go now, in the knowledge that you are the instruments of my authority, and the means by which I shall attain the glory I deserve . . .*

"A good audience, Yu'shaa?"

He looked up. The Shamed warrior Kunra, who acted as his bodyguard and occasional conscience, had entered the room, closely followed by Nom Anor's truest believer, Shoon-mi Esh. Shoon-mi wore the robes of a priest, though without the insignia of any of the Yuuzhan Vong deities. Kunra wore no armor, belying the cowardice that had caused his fall from grace. Knowing their true selves, Nom Anor thought them a pathetic entourage for any would-be revolutionary; but he had to admit that the converts responded well to them.

"Nothing special," he said in his usual rough voice. There was no need to soliloquize with these two. "What we are gaining in quantity, we're losing in quality. A couple of them looked like they were about to die on their feet."

"I apologize, Master." Shoon-mi made fawning motions with his gnarled hands. "I did not feel it my place to turn anyone with need aside."

"Soon you will have to, Shoon-mi." Beneath his tiredness and irritation, Nom Anor felt an abiding satisfaction at the way the movement was growing. Every day brought more penitents to their door, seeking the truth of the Message spreading around Yuuzhan'tar. "Perhaps it is time to start training the Select. You have the list?"

Shoon-mi nodded vigorously, eager to please. "I have identified seventeen who qualify."

"Loyal without being blind," Nom Anor said, going over the prerequisites for those chosen. "Quick thinkers, but not *too* intelligent, yes?"

"Yes, Master."

"Then call them to me." He glanced around at his surroundings. "The sooner the better, for I grow weary of the stench down here."

Shoon-mi inclined his head. "They will stand before you tomorrow, Master," he said, making to leave.

Before he had gone five steps, Nom Anor stopped him. "Shoon-mi," he called. The Shamed One turned to face him. "I could not have done this without you. I want you to know that."

The highest of Nom Anor's acolytes beamed with pride as he scurried off to do his duty. The self-styled Prophet buried a flash of irritation. Although part of him wished he had killed the fool when he'd had the chance, he had to acknowledge Shoon-mi's usefulness. He was dedicated and resourceful, and Nom Anor felt he owed it to Shoon-mi's sister, Niiriit, one of the first true believers of the Message, not to kill him. Kunra would be sure to remind him if he tried, he was sure.

That wasn't the most irritating thing, though. Shoon-mi's willingness to work for nothing but praise stuck in Nom Anor's throat like a bone.

The ex-warrior stood in silence by the door, watching him. Nom Anor had come to know Kunra well enough to realize when he had something on his mind.

"What is it?"

"You'd better see for yourself." Kunra turned and walked through the hall's main entrance and into the antechamber. From there, he led Nom Anor along a short corridor to the small cell in which Kunra slept. There, immobilized by blorash jelly, lay a female dressed in rags. Her cheek was heavily bruised, but her eyes were open and filled with defiance.

"She was carrying this," Kunra said, offering Nom Anor the remains of a small, larva-like creature. Its leathery shell had been crushed and would have been barely recognizable had not Nom Anor seen such things many times before. It was a villip.

The female had obviously intended to bring it into the meeting so that the person on the other end could watch the Prophet in action. That in itself was not necessarily sinister; some of the acolytes had attempted to spread the Message via villips before—or so they had claimed. Nom Anor knew, however, that he couldn't afford to take the chance.

"Does Shoon-mi know?" he asked, keeping his stare fixed on the female.

"No. I make sure to check all acolytes before they reach him. This one came alone and was out of the way before he had a chance to suspect anything."

Nom Anor nodded his approval. It made things much simpler.

"I want the name of the person holding her master villip," he said coldly. "Find out how much she knows about us while you're at it—get the information any way you have to. Then kill her."

Kunra didn't argue. "I understand."

The female started to struggle, her protests muffled by the gag in her mouth. Nom Anor ignored her. "I shall explain to Shoon-mi that we have to relocate again."

"He won't like it."

He faced Kunra. "I'm sure he'd prefer it to dying."

Without a further glance at the prisoner, he turned and walked away.

PART TWO

DESTINATION

The freighter came out of nowhere from hyperspace far too close to Bakura and going into an instant spin. Its drive units stuttered at random, which wasn't helping the freighter's situation, while its subspace was transmitting nothing but static—which to Jag Fel sounded a lot like the buzzing of angry insects.

He had spent a lot of time and effort memorizing the manufacturers and model names of both Republic and Imperial vessels, but he was having difficulty identifying this one. Its distinctive asymmetric design suggested something from the Corellian Engineering Corporation— possibly somewhere between the YT 1300 and the YT 2400—although he couldn't be 100 percent certain. Either way, it was in poor shape, and that wasn't likely to improve in a hurry.

He would have happily ignored it had it not been for the fact that whoever was flying it was coming dangerously close to where *Pride of Selonia* was stationed.

"Flights B and C, stand by." Jag switched to a commercial channel. "Unidentified freighter, you are infringing upon our space. Change course immediately or we will be forced to take action."

More static was his only reply.

He swung his clawcraft away from *Selonia* in order to meet the incoming vessel. His wingmate followed, S-foils opening smoothly on her X-wing.

"Bakura Orbital Control," he commed on local channels, "has anybody given this freighter approval to occupy our orbit?"

"Negative, Twin One," came the instant reply. "This flight is unauthorized. But we've certainly seen her before."

"You have a registration listed?"

"Oh yeah. She goes by the name of *Jaunty Cavalier* and is owned by a Wookiee called Rufarr. In fact, I'm surprised to see him return here. He left owing me some credits."

Not your usual Wookiee, then, Jag thought as he watched the freighter tumble toward him. *And not your usual approach, either.*

"I think he's got more to worry about at the moment," Jag sent. "Requesting permission to nudge her out of harm's way."

"As long as you promise not to be too gentle," Orbital Control quipped.

"Do what you have to, Twin One," added Captain Mayn from *Selonia*. "Just make sure she gives us a wide berth."

"*Jaunty Cavalier,*" he tried again. "You have ten seconds to comply with my instructions or you *will* be intercepted. Please respond."

Still nothing but crackling over the comm.

"Okay, we're going in." He applied power to his thrusters and brought his clawcraft alongside the tumbling freighter. "Flight B, come closer and add your shields to mine. We're going to try to give her a little push."

Two X-wings and another clawcraft joined him and his wingmate. With half of Twin Suns all working simultaneously, the freighter's heading gradually began to change, but it required a redirection of all available power to both engines and shields from all ships. Jag kept a wary eye on the freighter, just in case she tried anything.

Five degrees would do it, he decided. That would take the freighter well past *Selonia* and clear of Bakura's atmosphere—

He caught a flash out of the corner of his eye. At that exact moment a dozen instruments on his console spiked, and he realized that a spray of neutrinos had just washed over him.

"Did anyone else catch that?"

"Affirmative, Twin One," the leader of Flight B replied. "Look at the drive units."

Jag craned to look out the rear of his cockpit's transparent canopy. The freighter's engines were stuttering furiously now, thrust ebbing and fading in wildly erratic energy swings.

"I don't like the look of this," he mumbled under his breath.

The words had barely left his lips when the drive units emitted a particularly bright flash, then died completely.

"Break off!" he called over the comm. "All fighters, disengage immediately!" He was already wrenching the controls of his clawcraft up and away from the stricken freighter. "Full power to aft shields! Put everything you've got between us and that thing! She's going to—"

There was a blinding white flash from behind him, then something picked up his clawcraft and spun it like a top around all axes. He clutched at the sides of his flight seat, hearing nothing but the scream of tortured matter over the comm.

Then the rough ride was over, and the stars reappeared.

Jag damped down his spin and checked on the four other starfighters. He was relieved to find them all present, if a little shaken by the experience. All that remained of *Jaunty Cavalier* was a jagged chunk of wreckage, possibly a section of the forward structural chassis. The rest had been blown to atoms by the drive failure.

"Bakura Orbital Control," he said solemnly into his comm. "I think you can kiss your credits good-bye."

"Don't write it off just yet, Twin One," came the voice of Captain Mayn. "We registered a launch from *Jaunty Cavalier* just before the detonation. It looked like a small pod of some kind."

This surprised Jag. "An escape pod? Are you sure? I didn't see anything."

"I'm positive," Mayn returned. "It was on the opposite side of the ship from you, which was probably why you didn't see it."

"Heading for Bakura, you mean?" Jag was still slightly disoriented from the shock wave, but he knew his up from his down. Every spacer did in a gravity well. "Does it have thrusters?"

"They're firing, but it's not enough. Reentry will be too steep. Want to go fetch it, or should we hand it over to Bakura OC?"

"Negative on that," Orbital Control said over the open line. "We wouldn't be able to get there in time. Sorry, Twin One, but it's going to have to be you or no one at all."

"Understood," Jag said, silently hoping there'd be no more surprises in store for him.

He sent his clawcraft swooping around the growing cloud of wreckage, his engines on maximum burn. The pod appeared on his scope a second later, streaking downward. Its velocity was increasing, but it was no match for a clawcraft at full throttle. He decelerated cautiously alongside as it loomed large in his scopes. There were no obvious booby traps or triggers, just the blinking of an emergency beacon, bright and repetitive on the subspace channels.

Jag didn't know exactly what sort of communications capacities the Corellian Engineering Corporation provided its escape capsules, but he didn't imagine they'd be much. Before locking on to the pod, he scanned the sub-space channels looking for any transmissions from the kind of local comlink the occupant—if there was one—would probably be using. He picked up various low-power transmissions, including just about every navigational beacon for a light-month, before finally lucking onto a faint voice calling stridently:

"—n emergency! *Someone* answer me, please! I'm in need of assistance. Can anyone hear this? I'm—"

"This is Colonel Jag Fel calling the occupant of life pod—" He checked the ident number visible on the stubby cylinder as it rotated into view. "—one-one-two-V. Can you hear this?"

"Yes!" The reply was immediate and drenched with relief. "Yes, I can! Thank the Balance you found me! I was beginning to think my escape had all been for nothing!"

Jag fine-tuned his trim preparatory to coming in closer. The voice clearly did not belong to the Wookiee captain of the destroyed freighter. "Want to tell me what happened back there?"

"The drive failed in midjump and I didn't know what to do to fix it. The navicomputer died in the energy surge following the engine failure. I was lucky that bucket of bolts made it as far as she did."

"Are there any other survivors there with you?"

"Just me. The crew is dead—and good riddance to them, as far as I'm concerned. Murderous fiends, every one of them!"

Jag hesitated. "You killed them?"

"Only in self-defense." The voice took on a more commanding tone. "Look, are you here to rescue me or ask questions?"

"I'm trying to ascertain *whom* I'm rescuing, that's all." *And what kind of monster you are,* he added to himself.

"You want to know who I am? I'm Prime Minister Cundertol, that's who—and I'm ordering you to pull me up this instant! After all I've been through, I'm not going to let some rookie pilot fumble my rescue. You put me through to Orbital Control this instant or so help me I'll have your license faster than you can—"

"I apologize, Prime Minister," Jag cut in, biting down on the reply he would have preferred to give. "Bringing you up now."

He pulled his clawcraft in closer to the pod. Magnetic clamps engaged, and he fired his thrusters only slightly more roughly than was necessary to bring the escape pod out of its headlong descent into the atmosphere. The roar of thrusters prevented further communication between Jag and his unlikely pillion rider, let alone Orbital Control. The Prime Minister was forced to ride out the long burn in silence, in whatever passed for acceleration straps among Corellian engineers. Although he probably had every reason to be impatient, if his use of words like *escape* and *murderers* was any indication of what he'd been through, Jag wasn't going to let him off easily.

Rookie, indeed . . .

". . . seven of them, four humans, two Rodians, and that wretched Wookiee captain of theirs. I resisted, of course, but they took me by surprise. Once they'd smuggled me out of the Bakuran Senate Complex, it was just a matter of getting me to the spaceport. No one stopped to question a group of traders carrying a crate of records—and not one person thought to scan the crate to make sure it contained what they said it did." The Prime Minister shook his head gravely. "Someone's head will roll for this, mark my words."

Prime Minister Cundertol was a big, solid man with thinning blond hair and a pink hue to his skin. He held his age well, overpowering any hint of frailty with bluster and exaggerated gestures. Safely recovered from the escape pod, he was sitting on a bench outside *Pride of Selonia*'s medical bay.

Jag and Captain Mayn sat with him. Mayn, as tall as Cundertol but half the weight, sat opposite him, her narrow features frozen in concentration. Only Jag, standing to one side, could see the tic pulsing in the skin beneath her shaved scalp.

"Go on, Prime Minister," he encouraged. "What happened next?"

"They took me aboard their ship and knocked me out, that's what happened next!" Despite his outrage, it was obvious that Cundertol was enjoying relating the tale. "When I woke up, we were in hyperspace. I had no idea where they were taking me. They'd stuck me away in an aft hold. Every now and then I would hear them talking, and it quickly became apparent that I wasn't in fact a hostage at all—as I had first suspected. From the little I could glean from the snatches of their conversations, I was to be taken somewhere and interrogated—then I was to be disposed of. Luckily, though, they hadn't fastened my bindings properly, so with a bit of effort I managed to work my hands free."

"Did your captors say whom they were working for?" Mayn asked.

"Not in so many words. Whenever they referred to him, it was only ever as 'the boss.' Or 'her,' of course," he added darkly.

"Well," Mayn said, "you should be pleased to know that your people made an arrest in your absence. Yesterday, Malinza Thanas was taken into custody and has been charged with conspiracy and disturbing the peace. It looks like your law enforcers could add attempted murder to those charges once we get you home and you can tell them your story."

"Malinza?" For a moment, Cundertol was nonplussed. "*Charged?* No, I don't believe it."

"It's true," Jag said. "Deputy Harris announced it himself."

The Prime Minister retreated into his thoughts, clearly stunned by the news.

"So you freed yourself," Jag prompted after a moment. "What then?"

"Huh?" Cundertol snapped out of his musings with a questioning look in his eyes. Then he said, "Oh, my escape. Well, eventually one of them came back to check on me. I overpowered him and took his blaster. I left him trussed up in the binders they'd failed to secure on me, then I crept forward to confront the others. There were three in the main cabin. They were surprised to see me up and about, as you can imagine. I confined them to a corner as two others arrived from the cockpit, leaving just the pilot in control of the vessel. It was five against one—not good odds, even for someone who trained with the Special Bakuran Troops." Cundertol's chest puffed up in pride at this. "I demanded to be returned, but was told that nothing could be done until the freighter had come out of its jump. I argued that they could cancel the jump and turn back immediately, but they continued to prevaricate with ridiculous excuses. It was obvious they were playing for time, though there was little I could do about it short of shooting one of them to let them know I was serious. But then that would have made me just as bad as them, right?"

He faced both Jag and Captain Mayn in turn, looking for approval. They nodded in response, but neither said anything.

"Anyway," Cundertol continued, "we argued for a few minutes until the Wookiee tried to jump me, and I was forced to fire upon them. I had no choice! If I let them take me, then I was as good as dead. It was either kill or be killed. So I killed them."

The Prime Minister looked down at his big hands as if disbelieving what they'd done.

"You did what you had to do, sir," Jag said after a moment. "No one can blame you for that."

Jag's reassuring words received a vague nod in reply, but it wasn't convincing. "I didn't kill all of them, of course," Cundertol said. "Just the five who attacked me. The one I'd trussed up, he was still in the hold, and the pilot had stayed in the cockpit until the fighting was over. I tied him up, too, when he refused to do as I told him. From there it was just a matter of turning the ship around and coming home. All would have gone well had the wreck not developed a raging case of system rot and fallen apart on me. When it came time to ditch it, the life support had failed in the aft holds, killing the two I'd tied up—otherwise I would've brought them with me to stand trial. They got off lightly, in the end. Death was too good for them—*far* too good."

Cundertol ground his teeth as if in frustration. He was clearly bitter, and rightfully so as far as Jag was concerned.

From the entrance to the bay, *Selonia*'s chief meditech was listening closely to the tale. When it became apparent that the Prime Minister had finished, she stepped forward and said, "Are you sure you're not hurt, sir? We really should examine you to see—"

"I'm fine," he interrupted, irritably waving her off. "It takes more than a scuffle to put me down."

The meditech backed away with a bony shrug.

"Have you found any evidence in the wreckage?" Cundertol asked Mayn.

"None, I'm afraid. There was very little left of the craft."

"That's a shame," he muttered. "Because I want whoever was behind this to pay dearly. If the Keeramak has been deterred by my kidnapping—or, worse, the consecration is canceled entirely—then I don't know where that will leave us. We can't afford tension with the P'w'eck. Not with the Yuuzhan Vong approaching us from the other side. Our defense fleet is stretched as it is without adding to our enemies."

"Do you know where your kidnappers were taking you?" Jag asked. "Because if we knew that then we might—"

"I'm sorry, young man," the Prime Minister said brusquely, "but you must appreciate that I had more important things to worry about at the time—such as staying alive. I didn't have the luxury of sitting them down and interrogating them, as you seem to be doing to me right now!"

Jag felt himself flush at the accusation. "Sir, I never meant in any way to—"

Cundertol cut off the apology with a grunt. "When's that shuttle coming?" he demanded, glancing at his chronometer.

"Soon, Prime Minister," Mayn said pleasantly. "General Panib is giving you a full military escort to avoid any further attempts on your life. In the meantime, you're safest here, with us."

"Better safe than sorry, eh?" The Prime Minister sniffed as he looked around at the cramped corridors of the frigate. "I'm just glad to be alive."

Something about the way Cundertol spoke those words told Jag that, perhaps for the first time since he'd been rescued, he was telling the whole truth.

The *Millennium Falcon*, with Jaina flying as escort, had left orbit barely an hour before the appearance of *Jaunty Cavalier*, heading planetside for a formal meeting with the Senate. The news of Cundertol's rescue and the destruction of the freighter came as they landed safely at

Salis D'aar spaceport. Tahiri watched over Han's and Leia's shoulders as Jaina climbed out of her starfighter to inspect security before anyone else disembarked.

Leia frowned. "You're saying he single-handedly over-powered a crew of seven? That's certainly not the Senator Cundertol *I* remember."

"I'm skeptical, too," Jag said from orbit. "But I suppose it's not completely impossible. He's fit, and he had the element of surprise. One thing that really bothers me is that he did it without taking any cuts or bruises."

"You're sure about that?" Leia asked.

"I'm telling you, I stood right beside him as he told his story, and there wasn't a scratch on the man. Ever known anyone to come out of a fistfight without so much as a fat lip or a grazed knuckle?"

"He's got a point," Han said. His posture indicated that he was devoting at least as much attention to Jaina's gesticulating at local security forces outside as he was to Jag. "But have you got anything else? Anything substantial?"

"Nothing. He refused a medical exam."

"Todra's chief medico is a Duros, though, right? And if I recall, Cundertol is pro-human through and through, right, Leia?"

"Definitely more than just a hint of Empire, Jag," Leia confirmed. "He could have simply wanted to avoid contact with an alien."

"Yet he signs an alliance with the P'w'eck?"

"He'd sign an alliance with an arachnor if he thought it politically expedient," Leia said.

Jag was silent for a second, then added, "This might not mean anything either, then, but Cundertol was as surprised about Malinza Thanas's arrest as you were."

"That it was her, or that they'd *caught* her?"

"I can't be positive, but I think the former."

"Well, Harris certainly seemed convinced of her guilt."

"It's possible my paranoia and suspicions are just getting the better of me," Jag conceded. "But one thing I am sure of: Cundertol certainly isn't someone I'd want to spend any more time with than I have to. I was quite happy to leave him with Captain Mayn until the Bakuran escort arrived. They've just left, so I'm happy to report he'll be all yours real soon."

Outside the ship, Jaina made a great show of exasperation, then turned and headed to the *Falcon*, signing a surreptitious *all clear* as she came. Keeping the locals on their toes, Tahiri imagined.

"Okay, then," Han said as he brought the ship's systems one by one off-line. "Apart from the fact that you're suspicious of the Prime Minister, do you have anything more substantial to add?"

"I guess not."

"And everything's under control up there now?"

"The wreckage has been cleared and our orbit corridor is clear."

"Good. Call us if anything else comes up. I think there's a meet-and-greet finally calling our name."

Han killed the comlink and turned to face his wife, who was shaking her head.

"What?" he asked, brow furrowed.

"I just find it amusing that someone who has navigated through his entire life on hunches could be so critical of someone else's."

Han pulled an indignant face. "Hey, I listened to what he had to say. It's just that I didn't think he gave us anything solid to go on, that's all."

"Is that the only reason?" Tahiri couldn't see Leia's expression, but she imagined the Princess to be smiling. "Or could it be that you're feeling a little put out at the idea of Jaina having a boyfriend whose instincts are as sharp as yours?"

Han performed a double take that would have been

amusing to watch had not Tahiri been acutely aware that she was listening in on a personal conversation.

"I'm going to leave the two of you to talk," Tahiri said, climbing from her seat. As she stepped from the cockpit, she heard the two start up again. As usual, there was no real malice in their argument. Beneath the words Tahiri could always detect the affection that the two obviously held for each other.

Outside the *Falcon*, the air was heavy with moisture and pollen. It was about midmorning, local time, and the temperature was rising. Within a minute, Tahiri could feel herself beginning to sweat, so she called on her Jedi training to regulate her temperature. The last thing she wanted to present to any officials she met was a sweaty palm—either metaphorically or literally.

A few minutes later, Han and Leia also emerged from the *Falcon*. Judging by the way the Princess was walking ahead of her husband and shaking her head, Tahiri guessed their friendly squabble was still taking place.

"At least he's got good taste," she heard Han say to Leia as they reached the base of the freighter's landing ramp. Any response Leia might have had to this went unheard, however, because at that moment Jaina stepped over to greet her mother and father.

They exchanged a few words together, but the combination of the distance and their hushed voices made it impossible for Tahiri to hear what was being said—although she presumed it to be about the current situation as Jaina saw it. Whatever, it was clearly something they didn't feel concerned her, so Tahiri decided not to intrude upon the discussion.

Instead, she checked out the docking bay they'd been assigned. Apart from the *Falcon* and Jaina's X-wing, it was completely empty—as requested by the Princess—and had only the one exit in the far corner. Through the transparisteel door of this exit, Tahiri could make out a small collection of dignitaries and guards. For some reason, the sight of their drab green uniforms all in a row made her feel uncomfortable, and one of the three scars on her temple began to itch. When she caught herself scratching at it, she quickly stopped, self-consciously lowering her hand and placing it behind her back. She still didn't know why this happened, but it bothered her that it did. It brought back memories; brought back dreams . . .

She turned away from the sight of the dignitaries beyond the transparisteel doors, and as she did so caught sight of a technician approaching the *Millennium Falcon*, a long black cable clutched in one hand. He was moving furtively, coming up behind where Jaina and her parents stood. At least Tahiri assumed it was a "he." The oversuit that the tech wore was designed to protect its wearer from hostile environments, and as such was too heavy and bulky to reveal the being's gender or even species.

She knew that Han hadn't authorized any maintenance on his ship while they were docked, though, so she stepped forward to intercept the tech before he could get any closer.

"Hey!" she called. "You're not supposed to be here!"

The suited figure hesitated, then changed direction to head toward Tahiri. She stopped in her tracks, the grip on her lightsaber instinctively tightening.

"Hold it right there," she warned.

"I bring a message," the figure said. The voice issuing from inside his helmet was distorted like a stormtrooper's.

Tahiri's brow creased with suspicion. "What kind of message? And who's it for?"

"Han Solo," the technician said. "I need to tell him to be careful. Things here are not as they seem."

"Things rarely are these days," she returned. Her grip on the lightsaber eased slightly. The precise form of the person inside the suit was hidden, but her instincts were clear.

"You're a Ryn, aren't you?"

The figure seemed slightly taken aback. "How did you—?"

"I met one of you on Galantos," she explained. More confident now, she took another two steps forward. "He was the one who suggested we come here, actually. He told us that—" She stopped in midsentence when the helmet shook.

"Now is not the time," the Ryn said, glancing around. "I shall contact you again later. For now, though, please pass on my message to Captain Solo."

Tahiri nodded. "Okay, but you're not really telling him anything new. He's always careful, and I think he's already guessed that something strange is going on here."

The Ryn didn't seem to be listening. He glanced around as though fearful he might be seen talking to her out in the open.

"I must go," he said. "You've been allocated quarters should you wish to stay longer than today. I urge you to take them. You'll find what you need there."

Without another word, the Ryn turned and made his way back the way he'd come. Tahiri stood watching him. She was finding herself becoming increasingly intrigued by the Ryn and their guarded hints.

"Trouble, Tahiri?"

She jumped at Han's voice so close to her shoulder. She shook her head, conscious of the security guards watching them closely from the edge of the landing field.

Han glowered at the Ryn's retreating back. "There'd better not be," he said. "What did he say, anyway?"

Tahiri lowered her voice. "That was our contact. The Ryn. He said to tell you that things here aren't what they seem."

Han rolled his eyes. "When are they ever?"

Tahiri smiled nervously. "That's just what I said."

"Anything else?"

She repeated what the Ryn had told her about accepting an offer of accommodation.

Han nodded, casting one final glance at the Ryn as if tempted to follow him. "Okay." He put an arm about her shoulder and guided her back to where the others stood waiting. "It's nothing," he called to them. "Let's get on with it."

Jaina gave Tahiri a penetrating once-over as she joined the group, but nothing further was said. Together they walked to where the security guards awaited them. As the uniformed guards surrounded them to escort them through the doors, Tahiri found herself filled with misgivings. It felt like they'd done all this before . . .

The harsh white of reflected sunlight belied the cold heart of Csilla. The briefest orbital scan of the icebound world revealed dozens of glaciers around the equator, as well as solid ice shelves that covered vast expanses of the planet. It made other frozen worlds like Hoth look positively temperate.

And yet, incredibly, it was inhabited. Huge cities skated the glacial fields like Mon Calamari water skimmers, riding the near-geologic flow of the ice; others buried themselves deep under the cold, tunneling into bedrock in search of geothermal warmth far below.

"Chilly," Jacen said, staring in muted awe out at the swarms of clawcraft that silently flanked *Jade Shadow* as she arrived in orbit. Images of the Chiss home planet had previously been nonexistent. Luke and Mara's last expedition to Chiss space, years earlier, had taken them nowhere near the heart of the alien empire.

"You talking about the planet or this reception?" Danni asked.

Jacen smiled at the quip. "You'd think with the pick of any of the worlds in the Unknown Regions that they'd have chosen one a bit more agreeable than this one. I mean, why stay here when there are so many warmer climates nearby?"

"Sheer obstinacy," Mara answered from her position in *Jade Shadow*'s pilot's seat. "You've seen how Jag and his pilots operate. Well, multiply that by ten and you might come up with something that approximates your average Chiss. Remember, Vanguard Squadron represents the imaginative, risk-taking extreme. The everyday stubbornness you'll find on Csilla would even make the Hutts look accommodating."

A brisk voice advised the incoming delegation from the Galactic Alliance of their allotted orbit. "You will not deviate from this vector," they were warned, "unless instructed to do so."

"We understand," Mara replied, unable to hold the irritation from her voice. "But is there someone who can—"

"Commander Irolia is the intermediary you have been allocated. She will attend you on this frequency and address any queries or concerns you may have at this time."

With that, the line went dead.

"Looks like our friend Commander Irolia beat us here," Mara said.

"Well, at least it'll be a familiar voice," Jacen said.

"Ask for her," Luke said from the navigator's chair. "Tell her we want permission to send a landing party."

"Are you sure that's a good idea?"

"Which: landing or asking?" Luke smiled fleetingly. Then, soberly, he added, "Listen, Mara, if it's not safe to deal with the Chiss now, with Imperials on our side, I fear it never will be."

Mara acquiesced without further comment, and Jacen leaned back in his seat to listen to the conversation. It was brief, as expected. Irolia replied to Mara's request with a briskness suggesting that she had anticipated it days ago. She gave them a window and uploaded a reentry corridor to R2-D2's navigation banks. The stubby droid whistled to indicate that he'd received it, and that was that.

"Do you require the shuttle?" Captain Yage asked over the command frequency.

"I think we'll take *Shadow* down this time," Luke said. "Instruct Hegerty to gear up and—"

"Actually, Soron Hegerty won't be going along on this trip," Yage cut in. "The incident on Munlali Mafir proved a little too much for the doctor. She's opted to stay aboard and sit this one out, if that's all right."

Jacen could see his uncle's disappointment. Since leaving on this mission, the doctor and Lieutenant Stalgis had assisted Luke and his party on a number of occasions. His uncle was thankful for this, as it reflected cooperation between the Empire and the Galactic Federation of Free Alliances—and the more this could be seen happening, the easier it would be to sway the cynics in the Alliance. Her decision to sit this mission out would no doubt start rumors among those cynics.

"Okay," he said, nodding. "Can you organize us a ground party? That window's in an hour, so we'll need to move quickly."

"Testing our mettle," Yage said, almost audibly grinding her teeth. "We're more than a match for that trumped-up power princess."

Luke smiled at his wife as Yage closed the line. "I think Irolia might have won herself an enemy."

"Not hard," Mara agreed. "After all, the commander isn't particularly trying to make any friends."

A thought struck Jacen then. "Do you think she's been sent to us deliberately?"

Luke turned in his seat. "To see how we'll react?" He

thought for a moment. "Could be that someone much higher up than Irolia is testing us."

"Don't worry," Mara said. "Arien is right. We're more than ready for the Chiss."

"I've no doubt about that," Luke said. He faced the front again. "But it's not Chiss I'm worried about."

Jade Shadow came in low over the western arm of what would have been a crescent-shaped continent on a more temperate planet. Deep-surface radar revealed scoured rock two kilometers down, buckled and split by the weight of the ice above. Melt channels and refreezing fissures had created a fiendishly complicated network of caves and tunnels throughout the ice, and it was in these tunnels that the Chiss had built the city of Ac'siel.

Above the ice shelf, all that was visible was an equilateral triangle consisting of three craterous spaceports linked by lines of towers that could have been massive observation antenna and weapons installations.

Or perhaps, Jacen thought, *just there to intimidate.*

The wind howled like a lovelorn wampa, tearing at the hull of *Jade Shadow* as Mara brought her down to the spaceport they'd been allocated. Her hands moved deftly over the controls, guiding the ship with natural ease.

Back in the passenger bay, Jacen waited with the rest of the landing party. Outside, heat differentials whipped the storms into a fury, creating an illusion of dynamic processes that might eventually lead to life, but the ice always won out in the end. Where water froze, only the meanest organisms could evolve, and only the toughest survive. The Chiss clearly fit into the latter category, clinging to their world tooth and claw, no matter how much it tried to freeze them out.

Danni followed Jacen to the air lock when they had touched down.

"Ready when you are," she said as the air lock hissed open.

Together, they stepped outside.

He had expected to find himself in the middle of an icy storm, but instead the air was warm and still. They had landed inside a large docking bay that was sealed against the elements by a flickering force field high above. The ferrocrete platform beneath his feet was clean and dry, and sloped down to where a small welcoming party waited for them. Seven officers dressed in purple-and-black uniforms stood to attention, their blue skins looking like marble under the arc lights. Jacen couldn't tell if Commander Irolia was one of them, but he offered a small wave of acknowledgment anyway. There was no response.

"Nothing untoward," he sent to Mara and Luke via comlink.

Moments later they joined him and Danni outside *Jade Shadow*. Luke came first, followed by Lieutenant Stalgis and Mara. A second stormtrooper would stay with *Jade Shadow*, along with Tekli and Saba. The air lock sealed behind them.

There was a brief pause during which nothing happened. They simply stood awkwardly by the air lock, waiting.

"You know, I expected the Chiss to be more punctual," Luke said.

Jacen caught the wink that his uncle sent Mara. "Perhaps we caught them with their pants down," he put in.

At that moment the formation of guards dissolved. Two people walked through the entrance behind them and up the ramp to where *Jade Shadow* had settled. One of them was Commander Irolia, her expression as steely as her hair was black. The other was a human—a solid, muscular man of about Luke's height. Completely bald, he had a thin mouth, deep-set eyes, and a nose large enough to rival a Toydarian's. When he spoke, he made no pretense of welcome.

"I am Chief Navigator Peita Aabe," he said, his voice as sharp as the creases in his uniform. He came to a halt before them, his cold gaze touching each of them in turn. "We have made arrangements for you to meet with the necessary authorities."

"Wouldn't you like to know who we are?" Luke asked.

Aabe's attention settled on the Jedi Master with an expression that suggested he was making the best of a bad situation. "That isn't necessary. Commander Irolia has ensured that we have the relevant information. If you will come this way."

Aabe turned to lead them across the docking bay.

"Wait a second," Mara said. "I'd like to know more about you, first. You're human."

He didn't attempt to hide his annoyance as he swung around. "And that troubles you?"

"No, of course not. It's just that apart from Admiral Parck and Soontir Fel, I wasn't aware that any others had joined the Chiss."

"Many would have, but few were accepted." Aabe's frosty facade melted for a moment, allowing a glimpse of burning pride beneath. "I serve Assistant Syndic Fel in his absence. My origins are not important."

He turned and continued down the ramp. Irolia waited to ensure that they followed, then did the same.

Assistant Syndic Fel? Jacen thought as they followed the Chiss officer. The Baron must have been promoted. Whether that was a good thing, though, he couldn't decide.

"A cheery lot, aren't they?" Danni mumbled as they walked.

"Be that as it may," Jacen replied, "I'd sooner deal with them than the Krizlaws, any day."

As they passed through the exit from the docking area, the seven guards standing there fell in line behind them.

"Where are we going?" Mara asked.

"I have already told you," Aabe said gruffly.

"You told us that we were going to meet the 'necessary authorities,' but you haven't told us who they are or where we're being taken to meet with them."

Aabe strode a few more paces before speaking again. "Is that really important at this time?"

Mara rolled her eyes at Luke, clearly annoyed with the evasive responses. "You tell me: *is* it?"

Surprisingly, it was Irolia who answered Mara's initial question.

"You are being taken to meet representatives of the Four Families and Chiss Expansionary Defense Fleet." Mara half turned to face the woman as they walked. "There we will discuss the role the Chiss will play in your mission."

"You work for the Nuruodo family," Mara said. "That's military and foreign affairs, right?"

Irolia didn't answer. She didn't need to. The Chiss didn't give anything away, but the broad structure of their government was common knowledge. Jacen knew that four families dominated public affairs: Nuruodo, Csapla, Inrokini, and Sabosen. The Csapla oversaw resource distribution, agriculture, and other colonial affairs; industry, science, and communications were the concern of the Inrokini; the Sabosen ensured that justice, health, and education services were maintained equitably across the colonies.

"Which of the families do you work for, Chief Navigator Aabe?" Jacen asked.

"I work for none of them," their stiff-backed guide said without so much as a glance in Jacen's direction. "I am employed by the CEDF. The fleet is always in need of those with experience outside the inhabited territories."

"Incursions from the Ssi-ruuvi Imperium and the Yuu-zhan Vong," Irolia explained, "plus our experience with Grand Admiral Thrawn, taught us that insularity could be a weakness as well as a strength. It's not enough to be strong; a truly successful culture needs to be flexible as well. And in order to be flexible, we must look beyond what we consider familiar; we must come to know our neighbors as well as we know ourselves."

"Most governments would open diplomatic ties," Mara said. "Either that or just send in spies."

"Those are methods we have certainly tried, and indeed to an extent still employ. After all, we are talking to you now, are we not?" Her smile flickered briefly. "However, sometimes we find that integration is the optimal way to achieve our goals. Your former Emperor accepted Thrawn as an ally because he was a brilliant strategist, despite his nonhuman origins; so, too, are we prepared to accept non-Chiss into our fold."

"Would you accept a Ssi-ruu into the fold? Or perhaps a Yuuzhan Vong?"

Irolia didn't miss a step. She regarded Luke, who had offered the challenge, with not the slightest change in expression.

"If they were exceptionally talented and trustworthy," she said, "then yes, of course."

Jacen was unsettled by the response, and he sensed the others were, too. It wasn't hard to understand. The pain of loss was still fresh in the hearts and minds of everyone around him. Lieutenant Stalgis had lost many troopers and friends on Bastion; Danni had seen her colleagues die on Belkadan, right at the start of the war, and had probably seen more death and mayhem as a result of the Yuuzhan Vong than anyone Jacen knew; Mara had almost lost her infant son Ben on Coruscant; and Jacen himself still felt the terrible absence of his brother Anakin in his heart . . .

His uncle's feelings were kept carefully hidden, and Jacen wondered what he was thinking. Intellectually he knew that at some point loss had to be put aside to make room for hope. Clinging to the past only made the future that much harder to achieve; and it was only in the future, ultimately, that peace lay.

With Irolia's comment having effectively killed any further discussion, the party continued along in gloomy silence. In the absence of any conversation, Jacen studied their surroundings, his curiosity piqued by the strange translucent substance that made up the walls. It appeared to be ice, but when he reached out to touch it he found it warm and dry. Visible in the substance every meter or so was a frame of silver metal that seemed to define the boxlike corridors, each possessing a green light that flickered on as they approached and then switched off after they had passed. At first glance he could see no discernible reason for the frames' existence, although he had no doubt that they performed some function. The Chiss didn't seem the types to enjoy decoration for its own sake.

Danni noticed his interest. "Field generators," she whispered.

He frowned, momentarily puzzled. Field generators? Why should they need field generators to hold their corridors together? Surely the power drain would outweigh any possible security benefit.

Then it hit him: the walls really *were* made of ice. The field generators provided a boundary between the bubble of warm air in which they walked and the slippery surface beneath their feet. They also kept the cold at bay, and stopped the ice from melting. The generators switched on as they approached then switched off as they passed, meaning that the power drain on each unit was minimized. Overall, the cost would be much less than sealing and heating every single cubic meter of the tunnels—especially when the cost of manufacturing and laying insulated materials around the tunnels was factored in. It was an elegant solution to a tricky problem—particularly in areas that weren't frequently traveled. Jacen was impressed.

Eventually they came to an area that was insulated and sealed with more conventional materials. His ears popped as they passed the last of the field generators and the heated bubble dissolved around him. A smell of flowers struck him, and he found himself in a wide, tiered space that was thick with vegetation. The ceiling hung at least twenty meters above, with a bright tube that ran its length, lighting the area. The atmosphere was peaceful and serene, and Jacen's first impression was that it was a residential space—perhaps an underground park for the public. However, he soon dismissed the idea when he realized that, apart from themselves, there was no one else present. For that matter, he hadn't seen *anyone* other than their escort since they'd arrived at Ac'siel. All the corridors they'd walked down had been empty.

Whatever the reason for this was, he didn't have time to ponder it. Chief Navigator Aabe had led them to one of three doors on the far side of the gardenlike area and was now impatiently trying to hurry them through. Jacen and the others complied, filing into a relatively small and circular room containing a dozen black chairs set around an equally circular table. The walls, floor, and ceiling were black also, while tiny globes floating high above stabbed beams of light through the room's shadows to give prominence to the chairs around the table below. On the far side of the chamber, opposite where they'd entered, was another door.

Taking the seat nearest to him, Aabe indicated for the others to sit also. They did so, occupying a semicircle of chairs opposite him—all except Stalgis, that is, who opted to remain at the door with Irolia. Guarding the guard, perhaps, Jacen thought.

The door behind Aabe slid open without a sound, and four figures entered the room. Their faces were hidden by hoods, and each of their head-to-foot robes was a different color—bronze, rust-red, silver-gray, and copper-green. Without a word, they took seats at seemingly random positions around the circle, spreading themselves out on either side of Aabe.

An awkward silence followed, only broken when Mara asked, "So, do we find out now who we're talking to?"

"No," said the hooded figure in bronze—a woman with a rich contralto voice. "Just as our families are defined by their function in society, so are we defined by our roles as representatives of those families. We are here before you not as people, but as the beginning and end points of a decision-making process."

"No names?" Mara asked, not attempting to hide her annoyance.

"No names," agreed the green-robed figure. This one was a male—and young by the sound of his voice.

"But you know who *we* are."

"As is our right," Bronze said. "After all, it is you who come to us for help. You do not need to know who acts on behalf of the Chiss. We represent everyone."

"You must tell us what it is you want," said the figure in rust-red.

Gray nodded in agreement. "Then we can give you our decision."

"We do not decide lightly," Copper-green added.

"But our decision will be final," Bronze concluded. "Do you agree to these conditions?"

"What if we don't?" Mara asked, resting back in her seat and folding her arms defiantly across her chest.

"Then you will be asked to leave," Aabe said. His tone left no doubt that *asked to leave* was a euphemism.

"Our request is simple," Luke said, heading off a protest from Mara. "We are looking for the living planet, Zonama Sekot. We have reason to believe that it might be hiding in what we refer to as the Unknown Regions. As the major power in these regions, you have every right to question our presence here. It is my hope that you will assist us—either passively, by permitting us to cross your borders unhindered, or actively, by allowing us access to any information you have on the subject."

"That is all?" Gray asked, possibly surprised by the simplicity of the request.

Luke nodded. "That is all."

"And what have you achieved in your quest so far?" Bronze asked.

Luke explained where their mission had taken them, outlining the numerous systems they'd surveyed on the inner edge of the Unknown Regions, the various civilizations they had briefly touched upon, the hints of Zonama Sekot they had received. Invariably the clues came to them in the form of a story told by grandparents, or a dimly recalled memory. Their efforts had been frustrated by the absence of solid evidence. Since the planet had a tendency to avoid systems containing any sort of advanced civilization, there were no actual physical records to prove that it had ever really been anywhere. It was as if they were chasing a ghost that had vanished decades ago.

"And yet despite this, you seem confident of success," Copper-green said.

"We would not have taken on the mission in the first place had we not believed it achievable," Luke said. "And we will do what we must to ensure its success."

"And *why* must you do this, exactly?" Rust, the second woman of the four, sounded genuinely puzzled. "Commander Irolia is uncertain on this point. Although she believes that you are trustworthy, your goal seems incredible and your motives are obscure. You cannot blame us for being cautious."

Luke sighed. "No, I cannot. And if I were you, I would be wary, too. I can only say that we are willing to take any steps you require in order to demonstrate our veracity in this matter."

"Except discontinue your quest," Gray said.

"Except that, yes. We will continue to search for Zonama Sekot, with or without your help."

There was a moment's silence in which Jacen sensed that the Chiss representatives were conferring behind their hoods, but he couldn't read exactly what it was they were saying. Strong-willed people were notoriously hard to read, and the Chiss were about as strong-willed as a race could be.

"What of this new Alliance of yours?" Bronze asked. "Are we required to join it?"

"No," Luke said. "Although the fact that we have common enemies suggest that there might be advantages in doing so, someday."

"Indeed, there might be," Rust said, nodding slowly.

"On the matter of your presence within our borders," Copper-green said, "it is an issue upon which we find ourselves somewhat divided."

"Two of our number are willing to allow you free access to Chiss territories," Gray said, "on the grounds that there is little you will find here that either we do not already know or will do us harm."

"If Zonama Sekot truly existed within our borders," Bronze added, "we would surely know about it already."

"On the other hand," Copper-green said, "the vagueness of your motives calls into question the true purpose of your mission. It can be argued that the issue of Zonama Sekot is a cover for something more sinister."

"While it is true," Rust said, "that we have as yet seen no evidence of hostile intent, your presumption to come here without first asking questions is arrogance of the first order and should not be encouraged."

"So we find ourselves at an impasse," Bronze said.

"A tie," Copper-green said.

Gray inclined his head. "This is not an uncommon situation, given the diversity of our needs."

"As in all such situations, we turn to the Expansionary Defense Fleet to cast the deciding vote." Rust turned to her left. "Chief Navigator Aabe?"

Jacen inwardly groaned. There was no way Aabe was going to vote in their favor.

The ex-Imperial looked superciliously down his nose at Luke and the others seated before him. "The case seems quite clear to me," he said. "We cannot allow intruders to travel unchecked through our territory, for that would betray the trust of the Chiss people. There have been numerous incursions of late by the Yuuzhan Vong, and any relaxation of security now will only encourage such problems to go unnoticed. From the position of internal as well as external security, I advise that we do not give permission for this expedition to freely wander Chiss space."

Both Luke and Mara moved simultaneously, as though each was about to protest the decision.

"However," Aabe went on, raising a hand to cut off whatever it was they'd been about to say, "I am reasonably certain that the Skywalkers' intentions are honorable, and it is not in the Chiss nature to turn away those genuinely in need. Therefore, in the interest of good relations, and the hope that something may actually come of this quest, I would like to suggest a compromise. The thing the Skywalkers need more than freedom of access is information. No single mission could cover the entire Unknown Regions in a practical amount of time, even with the records of the Imperial Remnant as a guide. I propose that the Skywalkers and their allies be given full access to the Expeditionary Library here on Csilla, in order that they might conduct their search in safety."

Mara sank uncertainly into her seat, while Luke beside her could only lift his eyebrows in surprise. Jacen had to admit that Aabe's suggestion did make a kind of sense—although exactly for whom it was "safer" remained unclear. Was the chief navigator referring to the crews of *Jade Shadow* and *Widowmaker*, or was he implying that Chiss space would be better off without these ships roaming through it? Either way, Jacen was as surprised as his uncle that the ex-Imperial officer had actually suggested it at all.

"There is one condition," Aabe said.

Ah, Jacen thought. *Here comes the catch.*

"I would not want the Galactic Federation of Free Alliances to mistake our intentions," Aabe continued. "This offer should be open for a strictly limited period. If the Skywalkers and their companions have failed to find what they require within that time, then the offer will be rescinded and they will be required to immediately leave Chiss space."

"How long do you think will be necessary?" Coppergreen asked.

"Two standard days should be sufficient," Aabe replied. "After all, how hard can it be to search for a living planet that appears and disappears across the galaxy? There are only so many legends one can trace, and our library is second to none."

The four robed figures nodded in unified agreement. "We regard this as an acceptable compromise," Bronze said. "Master Skywalker?"

Luke straightened his shoulders and rose to his feet. "I accept the terms of your offer."

Jacen sensed Mara begging to differ, but outwardly she agreed.

"Then you are free to begin whenever you wish," Bronze said.

All four representatives rose from their seats in unison, but it was Gray who spoke. "A guide from the Inrokini family will be assigned to instruct you on the use of the library. If you are ready, Chief Navigator Aabe and Commander Irolia will take you there now."

"Thank you," Luke said, bowing.

"That concludes our business," Rust said. Without another word, she and the others turned and walked from the room.

"That's it?" Mara said, watching their backs disappear through the far door.

"What more do you want?" Aabe asked. "We have been generous with our time and we will continue to be generous with our resources. There is no obligation to help you hanging over our head. You should be—" He stopped and shook his head. "I was about to say *grateful*, but that would be incorrect. Gratitude is an emotional response not necessarily contingent on what has been offered. *Appropriately honored* might be closer to what I meant to say."

"We are," Luke said. "And we are also keen to start work as soon as possible." He indicated the door. "May we?"

Aabe nodded as he made for the door, saying, "I'm glad to see at least one of you appreciates the way of the Chiss."

The doors opened into the gardenlike hall, and Irolia and Aabe led the party through. They had barely traveled half the hall's length when a tall figure stepped out of a small niche to intercept the group. Broad-shouldered and as solid as a wall, he stood in front of them as though daring them to try to get past him. A black patch covered one eye, matching his uniform; iron streaked his black hair and goatee.

"Mara Jade," he said. "We meet again."

She moved forward a step while Jacen and the others stopped.

"That's Mara Jade *Skywalker*, Soontir Fel," she replied.

Fel nodded in acknowledgment but made no effort to correct himself.

"Chief Navigator Aabe had led us to believe that you were 'absent,' " Mara commented.

"That is patently not the case."

"So were you just avoiding us earlier?"

"Avoiding the decision-making process, yes." Fel's voice was gravelly but strong. Jacen could see where Jagged Fel inherited his father's presence, if not his width. "My thoughts are not unclouded by emotions over this issue. I recall offering you an alliance some time ago."

Mara nodded. "The irony wasn't lost on me, either."

"You didn't take it then, yet you expect us to take yours now." The enormous frame of the man who had once been the Empire's greatest TIE fighter pilot shifted minutely. It might have been a shrug, Jacen thought. "It is the way of the Chiss," he went on, "to stand down and let another decide when one is unable to be impartial. I trusted Peita to view with clarity what I could not."

Fel's gaze was as cold and sharp as an ice dagger. Jacen didn't understand where the man's hostility came from. It was one thing to be old enemies, but that didn't explain the passion that so obviously burned behind the man's gaze.

Luke moved to stand beside his wife. "I believe we reached a satisfactory conclusion." He held out his hand. "Under other circumstances, perhaps it'd be a pleasure, Soontir."

Fel hesitated, then returned the gesture, gripping Luke's hand in his enormous fist. "We're not allies yet, Skywalker."

"But we're not enemies, either. Surely that counts for something."

Mara made a show of glancing at her chronometer. "We should really be going," she said. "Those two days aren't going to stick around forever."

"Indeed," Fel said. His dark gaze swept the group gathered behind the Skywalkers. "The Expeditionary Library is some distance from here, in another enclave. Rather than move your ship, I suggest you allow me to provide you transport. The resources at my disposal are more secure than even those the Chiss normally offer."

Luke hesitated, and Jacen could sense his uncle conferring with Mara. He was sure that Luke's concerns reflected his own reservations. Aabe's decision to allow them access to the library had surprised him, but Jacen could see how it might be a ploy to separate them from the ship. And he knew Mara wouldn't want to be any farther from *Jade Shadow* than was absolutely necessary.

But did they dare risk offending Fel by refusing his offer? Or could they afford the time it would take to move their own ship when a convenient alternative was available? After all, as Mara had said, two days wasn't a lot of time to play with.

"Thank you," Luke said in the end. "Your offer would certainly save us some time."

"But if you *try* anything, Soontir . . ." Mara let the threat go unstated, but there was no mistaking it in her tone or body language.

Fel almost smiled. "Believe me: if I had wanted to try something, I would have done so long before now." He turned away. "Time is wasting. We cannot afford to be standing here chatting like fools. If you're going to come with me, then I suggest you do so now. Because the deadline is not going to change."

"You'll make sure of that, will you?" Mara asked.

He fixed her with another steely gaze. "You can count on it, Mara Jade Skywalker."

Jaina was exhausted by the time they returned to their quarters after the first day on Bakura. The meeting with the Senate had been postponed so Prime Minister Cundertol could attend, leaving them stuck with junior officials and restless flunkies. When the time finally came, the presence of the Galactic Alliance delegation was completely swamped by Cundertol's triumphant appearance and the banquet that followed. His long, somewhat rambling and self-congratulatory speech was greeted with cheers from the Senate and the press galleries, but left her agreeing with Jag's impression: The Prime Minister of Bakura was a good-looking figurehead, but a little too obsessed with his own interests to be a good statesperson.

Nevertheless, the banquet hadn't been too bad. Men and women in formal attire had provided attentive service, rather than droids, making Jaina feel very out of place in her expedition uniform. The food had been excellent, and she'd had the chance to sample some of the Namana nectar she'd heard so much about, a liqueur the Bakurans were particularly proud of. And rightfully so, she had to admit. Orange in color, it caressed her taste buds like a slow-burning ray of sunlight. She'd only taken a sip, however; she didn't want her reflexes dulled. Judging by its effects on the people around her, her decision had been a wise one.

Two people who had also stayed resolutely sober were Cundertol and his deputy, Blaine Harris. She wondered if that explained her impression that, despite the seemingly friendly and polite exchanges between them, underneath the surface simmered a powerful tension. It might have been a mutual dislike of each other, but why that should be, exactly, Jaina wasn't sure. They were political running mates, after all. It could have been nothing more than the fact that both were powerful personalities and dominating men. Working together in such close but clearly defined roles would undoubtedly chafe.

Still, it made her curious. She wondered how Harris had felt upon receiving the news of Cundertol's kidnapping. She imagined that part of him would have been secretly relieved to be rid of him. If the Prime Minister died or disappeared, his deputy would be the natural successor. The question of whether Harris had been involved in the kidnapping itself therefore had to be asked. And if he had, then Malinza Thanas's arrest would have been little more than a deliberate attempt by Harris to find a scapegoat.

Really, though, there was nothing she could pin down to justify either Jag's nebulous suspicions, or her own. Cundertol's Force presence was strong and clear: He was who he said he was, and his thoughts were his own.

Even Lwothin, the P'w'eck advance leader, seemed nothing but pleased at Cundertol's return. A little relieved, perhaps—but that was understandable, given that the consecration of Bakura was due to take place the very next day. With Cundertol back and the popular leader of the resistance behind bars, there was no reason for the Keeramak to further delay its arrival. The dull-scaled saurian hadn't partaken of the local delicacies, preferring instead to stick to a dish of fft—a multilegged lizard that had been imported from Lwhekk especially for the occasion. Throughout the banquet he seemed to be carefully observing the people and the goings-on around him, and although Jaina's eyes met his on several occasions, she found his golden gaze completely unreadable.

"Anyone else feel like we're the odd ones out?" Han asked, collapsing onto a floating couch. Their rooms weren't as finely appointed as the ones they'd had on Galantos, but that suited Jaina just fine. Too much hospitality only made her edgy.

"They're just caught up in their own affairs." As was often the case, Leia's input on the matter was in opposition to her husband's, but to show she wasn't being argumentative, she sat on the couch beside Han and took his hand in hers. She didn't mean to be contrary; she simply wanted to make sure that every situation was properly viewed from all angles. It had taken Jaina a long time to understand the way her mother's mind worked, something her twin brother seemed to have picked up instinctively a long time ago. "They'll get around to us when they have reason to."

"Perhaps they should be reminded of those reasons," Jaina said, talking over her shoulder as she set up the same anti-bugging equipment they'd used on Galantos. "They've got problems a simple treaty isn't going fix, because if that illegal transmission we received is anything to go by, then the resistance infiltrators are high up the command chain. Locking Malinza Thanas away isn't going to magically erase that fact. If anything, it could make it worse."

In the corner of her eye, she noticed Tahiri moving restlessly through the rooms, as though searching for something, and wondered what the younger Jedi was doing.

"It depends on what they want," Leia was saying. "One group seems in favor of an alliance with the P'w'eck as opposed to an alliance with us. Another wants nothing to do with the P'w'eck." She shrugged. "If our being here exposes the cracks in the underground, then that might be a good thing. Instead of one concentrated assault on the local government, their objectives may fragment, resulting in a number of small and relatively ineffectual attacks."

"Scattershot might be inaccurate," Han said, absently playing with Leia's fingers in his hand, "but it usually hits something. Personally, I'd rather be on the receiving end of a single sniper than a dozen people spraying wildly. At least with a sniper you know when the threat is—"

He stopped midsentence, his attention also caught by Tahiri's unusual behavior. Now she was inspecting the underside of an antique drink cabinet.

"Tahiri?" Leia said. "What are you—?"

"A-ha!" Tahiri stood bolt upright, brandishing a small object in her outstretched hand. "This is it!"

Jaina and her parents exchanged confused looks.

"This is what?" Jaina asked.

Tahiri brought the thing closer for the others to see. Jaina leaned in to examine the object and found it to be a metallic capsule no larger than a baby's tooth.

"The Ryn said we'd find what we needed here," Tahiri said. "This has to be it."

"The Ryn?" Leia repeated.

Han quickly outlined what he had learned about Tahiri's encounter with the Ryn on the landing field.

"Did he say anything else?" Leia asked Tahiri.

"Only that he thought you should be careful," Tahiri told her. "But he couldn't talk properly there, so he said he'd contact us later. Perhaps that's what this is: a note of some kind."

She fiddled with the capsule, turning it over in her hands and picking at a seam around its middle. Nothing happened until she squeezed it between two fingers; then one end clicked and there was a brief but intense flash of light.

Jaina blinked in surprise, waiting for something else to happen. But nothing did. The capsule was inert again, and no matter how much Tahiri poked at the thing, she couldn't get it to repeat the flash of light.

"That can't be right," the young Jedi muttered. "You'd think he'd make sure it worked before leaving it for us."

"Excuse me, Mistress Leia," C-3PO said, "but—"

Han raised a hand to motion him to be quiet. "Hang on, Goldenrod. We're busy right now trying to figure out how this thing works."

"But, sir," the droid said. "I already know how it works."

All four stopped what they were doing and turned to C-3PO.

"Well?" Han asked after almost fifteen seconds. "Come on!"

"It would seem, sir," C-3PO said, "that the flash of light contained a compressed message—a holographic page of writing, to be precise. My photoreceptors were able to collect the data and store it in my memory banks."

"A note?" Tahiri asked excitedly. "What does it say?"

"It appears to be written in an obscure Givin code."

"But can you translate it?"

The droid bristled at the very idea he might not be able to. "Of course. The message reads: 'Malinza Thanas has information you will need. She is being held in Cell Twelve-Seventeen of the Salis D'aar Penitentiary. You can gain access through Rear Entrance Twenty-three at midnight tonight. The code word is *fringe dweller*. I will try to contact you properly tomorrow.' "

Jaina committed the details to memory. "Is that all?"

"I'm afraid so, Mistress Jaina."

"It's not much, is it?" Tahiri put in, disappointed.

"It's enough for now," Leia said. "I'll go and find out what Malinza has to say as soon as the time is right."

Jaina shook her head. "Let me go," she said. "You'll be missed. They'll expect you to stay to investigate the situation with the P'w'eck. If you send me or Dad in your place, they'll wonder why."

"Will Malinza listen to you, though?" Leia asked. "Right now she has no more reason to trust you than we have to trust her."

"I'll just have to use my winning ways, I guess. Besides, it's not as if she's going to find many willing ears in prison. This could be the last chance she gets."

"Okay." Leia stood and put a hand on her daughter's shoulder. "But be careful, won't you?"

Jaina smiled, then brushed off her mother's concern—sweet though it was—and went to her room to prepare.

"Halt!" The image of a guard appeared in the stolen villip. Nom Anor watched as the Shamed One carrying the villip—cunningly concealed in a dead and hollowed k'snell vase—unhesitatingly obeyed the warrior's command—as would be expected of a member of the lowest social class who had just wandered into Lord Shimrra's antechambers.

The guard advanced slowly upon the Shamed One, his face set in a sneer. "In your haste to rejoin Yun-Shuno, you have forgotten that no one enters these chambers without permission from the Supreme Overlord himself." He stopped a couple of paces from the Shamed One, his grotesque visage thrust into close focus. "Explain why it is that your vile presence now dirties these floors."

"I-I was sent by High Priest Jakan," stammered Nom Anor's spy. She had practiced the excuse many times before leaving on her mission, but it had never before sounded so unconvincing. "He or-ordered me to present this offering—"

"Lies!" The warrior's amphistaff uncurled from around his uniformed waist, snapping into an attack position. "You will tell me what it is you are doing here, and then, for your transgressions, you will feel the wrath of Lord Shimrra's palace guard."

As the warrior took another step closer, the Shamed One dropped to her knees, clutching the k'snell vase and the villip within to her chest. "Please—" Nom Anor couldn't see her face, but he could imagine her fear.

"Your begging is an affront to all Yuuzhan Vong!" the warrior growled as he raised his amphistaff. "Prepare to die!"

"Jeedai!" the Shamed One screeched suddenly, her tone no longer obsequious and sniveling. As was planned, she triggered the patch at the base of the k'snell with the palm of her hand. *"Ganner!"*

The image died with the villip and the Shamed One a split second before the amphistaff came crashing down. The last thing Nom Anor saw of the antechamber was the twisted and hateful snarl of the warrior.

"She wasn't supposed to say anything about the Jedi," he said, using the infidel pronunciation he had become accustomed to during years of undercover work. A rising tide of anger was hard to contain. They had been so close!

"At'raoth was devoted to the cause," Shoon-mi said. He stood to one side of Nom Anor's new throne, situated in a hiding place that was far removed from the last one. The former Shamed One was clearly uneasy in the aftermath of their failed attempt to infiltrate Shimrra's chambers. "She went willingly, knowing that she might die."

"But whether she died the *right* way remains to be seen," Kunra said. "Will she be captured and tortured? Will they learn about us?"

"No!" Shoon-mi seemed shocked by the suggestion. "She will have taken the appropriate precautions."

Nom Anor was certain his highest acolyte was correct. "The appropriate precautions" meant, in this case, breaking the false tooth at the back of her mouth and swallowing the irksh poison they had provided her with. It would have killed her instantly. Her fanatical loyalty to the cause guaranteed that she would have obeyed that last command.

But even suicide might not be sufficient to avoid disaster, Nom Anor thought. The spy had openly declared her allegiance to the Jedi heresy, so Shimrra would certainly be alerted now to attempts to infiltrate his walls. It would be even harder to get in next time—and riskier.

That didn't mean he'd give up trying, though. He didn't care how many acolytes died in the attempt. Information on his enemy's activities was vital. Any campaign, covert or overt, depended on intelligence, which meant he needed to get someone on the inside of those walls—and *soon*. If he couldn't, then he wouldn't know what measures were being taken against him, and that left him unacceptably vulnerable.

"We did well just to get this far," Kunra said. It was a desperate attempt to make good out of a bad situation, but there was no hiding his weariness. "At'raoth made it farther than any of the others."

"I believe I even heard voices," Shoon-mi said.

Nom Anor nodded. He had heard voices, too, from within the chamber on the far side of the threshold the spy had attempted to cross. He was sure that those voices had belonged to High Prefect Drathul, High Priest Jakan, and Lord Shimrra's abominable puppet Onimi. Someone had been arguing with them—one of the warriors, perhaps. The argument had been too faint to discern any actual words, but it had been close. Had At'raoth made it just a few steps closer . . .

He growled an ancient oath under his breath. Mistakes risked the ruin of everything he was trying to achieve. The heretical movement was still too weak to survive a concerted purge.

"We have to try again," he said shortly. "We need access to those chambers." Frustration boiled inside him like a magnetic storm. He missed his old networks, his chain of informers, the many spies who had fed him information. Bloated on data, he had not known how fortunate he'd been before his fall. Starved, weakened by ignorance, he longed for a return to those glory days. "If we can't get a villip inside, then we will need an informer."

"But who?" Shoon-mi asked. "And *how?*"

"Our numbers are increasing," Kunra said by way of reply. "Word is rising up the ranks. It's only a matter of time before we infiltrate the upper echelons."

"I cannot wait that long!" Nom Anor snapped. "The closer we get to the top, the riskier it becomes for us. Without knowing what Shimrra knows, we are like one of his sacrifices: on our knees with a coufee at our throats, waiting for the killing blow to finish us off." He shrugged under his robes. Lately in his dreams he found himself fleeing a band of warriors bent on his destruction. He never saw them, but he could always sense them close behind, and could always hear them. In his dreams, he was nothing more than an animal being hunted.

He shook his head; the waking hours were no time to waste on nightmares.

"I will not die down here," he said. "I will not become like the corridor ghouls: blind and vulnerable to anyone with light."

"It will not happen, Master," Shoon-mi said lamely. "We would let no such thing happen to you."

Shoon-mi's attempts to reassure him were like those he would use on a child, and Nom Anor brushed them aside with the contempt they deserved.

"Enough!" He stalked back to the throne and collapsed into it. "Find me another volunteer. We will try again; we will *keep* trying until we have achieved our goal! We must crack Shimrra's security before he cracks ours. It's either that, or perish."

Shoon-mi swallowed and backed away, bowing. He didn't know anything about the spy they'd captured at their last headquarters, but he understood the reality of their situation. They were heretics, anathema to Shimrra and the priests, a contamination to be purged. A *rust*, Nom Anor thought, remembering his musing on the rotting of iron he had observed in the belly of Yuuzhan'tar before adopting the mantle of Prophet.

"It will be done, Master."

"Make certain of it," Nom Anor said. His glare fell upon Kunra, also. "*Both* of you."

Kunra nodded grimly, not needing to say that there were only so many volunteers left to be wasted on such hopeless missions. The more that failed, the fewer there were to choose from next time. Sacrifice needed a *point* to be noble.

But he, too, understood the harsh reality of the situation. It was either kill or be killed. If the most the Shamed Ones could gain was to choose the manner of their passing, then that, at least, was something. It was certainly more than Shimrra had ever offered them.

Jaina crouched behind a stone balustrade on the roof of a warehouse across the road from the penitentiary. She kept herself low to avoid being spotted by the powerful floodlights sweeping the area. Regular patrols around the perimeter of the prison she had expected, but the Ryn hadn't warned them about the swarm of G-2RD sentry droids that accompanied them, and she hadn't anticipated them. The Bakurans' usual dislike of droids had obviously been overcome by pragmatism in this case. Surveillance of the area was frequent and random, making it difficult to predict when sweeps would next take place. Worst of all, she had tripped some sort of concealed alarm when she'd dared make her first dash for the rear entrance. The entire compound was now on full alert, ready and waiting for someone to break in.

Half an hour's careful observation convinced her that it was unlikely she could sneak in unobserved. And if the security on the inside was as stringent as that on the outside, then she wasn't going to last a minute in there—let alone reach the cell she needed. No, she was going to have to try another way . . .

Slipping out from her hiding space, she crossed the roof of the warehouse and descended a narrow ladder fixed to the far wall. The laneway at its base was cluttered with rubbish, suggesting it was rarely used. Following it to its end, she allowed a trio of deep and calming breaths to fill her with a sense of control and authority.

I am not a covert agent, she told herself. *I am the representative of visiting dignitaries, and the people here are our allies.*

With a brisk, measured pace, she walked around the corner and into full view of the security droids. A spotlight instantly hit her full in the face, but she didn't break step—the slightest hesitation could destroy the illusion she was trying to create.

Two G-2RD droids swooped from emplacements in the high ferrocrete wall that was the rear of the prison. Floating spheres equipped with several means to inflict discomfort, they converged on her, buzzing furiously like agitated insects.

"Halt!" exclaimed one. She couldn't tell which.

She stopped within three meters of the rear entrance, radiating patient obedience.

"State your name and purpose here," ordered the other, its voice a nasal whine probably designed to irritate.

"My name is Jaina Solo," she replied easily. "I'm here to speak with Malinza Thanas."

Both droids buzzed as they performed a quick check on her clearance. After a couple of seconds, one of the droids advanced with its stun prod crackling. "No such visitation has been authorized."

"Please don't threaten me," she said, sending the small droid into a spin with a push from the Force. "I really don't take too kindly to things like that."

The second droid emitted a piercing wail that Jaina was quick to cut short. She reached deep into the droid's circuitry with the Force and fused its vocabulator.

More droids and spotlights converged on her. She couldn't have drawn more attention to herself if she'd wanted to. Nevertheless, she maintained her calm exterior and kept her hands well away from her lightsaber.

"I am here to speak with Malinza Thanas," she repeated, patiently and firmly. "Please let me through."

The first droid recovered from its spin and faced her again, this time speaking with a different voice, that of a guard from within the compound, obviously watching through the droid's sensors.

"I'm sorry, but we cannot allow visitors without authorization."

She folded her arms in front of her. "Then I suggest you get it, because I'm not going anywhere until I've seen Malinza. And I have no intention of leaving quietly. I'll give you one minute to comply."

The droid buzzed, bobbing up and down as though itching to be given the okay to attack her. She watched it warily while counting from one to sixty in her head.

At the end of the minute, she heard hurried footsteps coming toward her from around the nearest corner.

"I can't wait all night, you know," she said, brushing the droids easily aside and taking three more paces toward the rear door that the Ryn had specified in his message. There she spoke the code word she'd been given.

"Fringe dweller."

The door instantly hissed open, lifting sharply up into the ceiling. She strode through into a glowing white corridor that led as straight as a beam of light into the heart of the building.

A chorus of buzzing from the droids followed her. A new voice issued from the nearest droid's casing.

"This is a flagrant disregard for regulations!" There was no disguising the guard's annoyance. "Whoever you are, I must insist that—"

"As I have already explained," she said, "my name is Jaina Solo, and I'd appreciate it if you could make up your minds as to whether you intend to assist me or arrest me. I really have no desire to fight you, but if you force my hand then I—"

"You can't expect to just walk in here and see any prisoner you like! Ever heard of protocol?"

"You ever heard of a diplomatic incident?" she shot back. "Because that's what you're going to get if I don't get to see Malinza Thanas."

The pause was longer this time, and she sensed the droids backing off slightly. A squad of guards had appeared behind them, and waited uncertainly to see what she would do next.

"Well?" she prompted after a while. "What's it to be?"

"Please wait where you are." The voice seemed more cowed than it had been a moment before, and Jaina suspected the guards had been instructed by their superiors to let her through. "An escort will arrive shortly."

No sooner had this been said than four Bakuran security guards came hurrying around the corner—their weapons, she noted, carefully holstered.

"Come with us," ordered the one nearest to her. He spoke firmly, gruffly, but there was no escaping the fact that he was a little uneasy. Jaina allowed herself a slight smile at this; they weren't as good at hiding their nervousness as she was.

She didn't move. "Not until I know where you're taking me."

"You're to be taken to see the prisoner," he replied. "As requested."

There was derision in his tone, but it was all bluster

and show. He knew that Jaina had the upper hand in this situation.

Her smile widened. It never hurt to boost respect for Jedi on outlying worlds, and respect wasn't always earned at the end of a lightsaber.

She offered a polite bow of her head in the direction of the droids, knowing that whoever had authorized her would no doubt be watching. There would be no further need for any aggressive posturing this evening—not unless she was provoked, of course. "I apologize for this inconvenience. The sooner I can see Malinza Thanas, the sooner I can be out of your hair."

Her senses finely attuned for any sign of deception, she let herself be shepherded by the four guards deep into the heart of the penitentiary. The high-security wing was identical to the regular wings except for G-2RD droids stationed at every junction. They hummed menacingly when she passed, as though warning her not to try the same tricks she had employed on their fellow sentries. She tried to memorize every turn and corridor as she went, but it wasn't easy. They all looked the same to her, and the cell numbers didn't seem to follow any particular pattern.

Finally they arrived at Cell 12-17. The door looked like all the others they'd passed along the way: sterile white with no window or openings. One of the lead guards keyed a short code into a keypad, then stepped back as the cell door slid open with a dull grinding sound.

Inside, on a narrow cot, sat a thin, dark-haired girl of about fifteen years. Despite the gray prison uniform and the bruises to her face and arms, she still had a defiant look about her—but there was also exhaustion behind that defiance.

"What now?" the girl asked.

"A visitor," the first guard said, motioning Jaina to

enter. He indicated a green touchpad by the door. "When you're done, just hit the CALL button."

"Kinda late for visitors, isn't it?" Malinza said, looking Jaina over suspiciously.

Jaina stepped into the brightly lit cell. "My name is Jaina Solo," she said as the door closed behind her. She examined the girl quickly, wondering what sort of treatment she'd been subjected to.

Malinza's sharply defined face tilted upward. She studied Jaina for a moment before nodding. "Uncle Luke has spoken about you. He once showed me a holo of you and Jacen when you were little."

Jaina felt an unaccountable stab of jealousy at the girl's words. *Uncle* Luke? Who was this girl she'd never met, claiming Jaina's uncle as her own?

Indignation quickly gave way to understanding, however, when she remembered that Malinza was Luke's sponsor daughter. With both her parents dead—Gaeriel Captison, former Prime Minister of Bakura, had sacrificed her life to destroy a large chunk of the troublesome Sacorrian Triad, while Pter Thanas died of Knowt's disease some years earlier—Luke Skywalker was probably the closest thing she had to family. What right did Jaina have to deny the girl that?

"I wish we could have met under better circumstances," she said, moving deeper into the small room, close to the girl. She gestured to the bunk. "May I?"

"You sure picked a bad time to visit," Malinza said as she moved to make room for Jaina to sit down.

"Want to tell me about it?"

Malinza studied Jaina with a maturity that was at odds with her age. Her gaze was piercing, made even more disconcerting by the fact that her eyes were different colors. Her left iris was green, her right gray.

Just as her mother's had been, Jaina thought.

For a long moment it seemed as though Malinza wasn't ever going to reply to Jaina's question.

"You know why I'm in here," she said after a while.

"You've been charged with kidnapping the Prime Minister."

"Actually, the official charge is disturbing the peace and conspiracy."

"Doesn't it amount to the same thing?"

Malinza shook her head. "The difference is an important one, actually."

"Why? Now that Cundertol has returned—"

"I had nothing to do with him," Malinza interrupted. "But the rest is true enough."

"Sorry, but I find it hard to picture you as a disturber of the peace."

Malinza smiled faintly at Jaina's comment as she held out her arms to display the bruises. "Look at me," she said. "If they wanted to beat me, there are ways they could have done it without leaving any marks. I earned these while resisting arrest. It took three of them, as well as two droids, to bring me down."

Her expression held a burning pride, but it failed to hide the terrible weariness that Jaina recognized all too clearly. She remembered that feeling from when Anakin had died: of there being nothing left to lose; of desperation; of despair. It was so easy to mistake the signs of self-destruction for battle scars.

"What are you fighting for?" Jaina asked.

"That's the strange thing. A week ago, I wasn't fighting at all." Malinza's defiance dissolved altogether then, and became a look of genuine bemusement. "You've no idea what you've just stepped into. I tell you, it's crazy around here."

"In what way, Malinza?" Jaina leaned in closer to encourage a feeling of trust.

The girl chuckled. "That I'd even *think* about telling

you is probably the craziest thing of all," she said, slumping back against the wall. "If anyone here is the enemy, it's you."

Jaina frowned but said nothing, sensing that there was no point pushing. It would come or it wouldn't.

After more than a dozen heartbeats, Malinza sighed. "Whatever. It's not as if I haven't tried to tell everyone here already."

"They don't believe you?"

"Why else do you think I'm in here?" The girl pointed at where a security cam watched them. "I guess it couldn't hurt for them to hear it one more time. And who knows: they might even listen this time."

"And even if they don't," Jaina said, "you can be assured that I will."

Malinza smiled and nodded. "Okay," she said, leaning forward again to begin her story. "About a month ago I was in charge of a cell of activists, capitalizing on my parents' reputations to get our message heard. There were sixteen of us in all. At first we just organized protests, spread the word—but it's grown much more over time. We called ourselves *Freedom*." She rolled her eyes. "It's lame, I know, but it gets the point across."

"And what point is that?"

"That we're tired of kowtowing to Imperial doctrines, of course. It's time for us to throw off our shackles and govern ourselves."

"*Imperial?*" Jaina echoed, confused. It had been almost thirty years since the Imperial presence had been repelled from Bakura.

"Not *the* Empire," Malinza explained. "The thing that took its place: the New Republic. Don't you know that nature abhors a vacuum? Especially a *power* vacuum. No sooner had we won our freedom than we held out our wrists to be shackled again. We offered ourselves up to the New Republic like pets begging for a scrap of affection. And that's all we got, too: scraps."

Jaina winced at the description of the government her parents had helped create.

"Of course, you don't call it the New Republic anymore, do you? It's been given a new name ever since it lost its war against the Yuuzhan Vong." Malinza snorted derisively. "No one wants to be associated with losers, do they? Therefore, your only hope of fighting back was to pretend to be something else. But cratsch droppings by any other name still stink, don't you think?" She shook her head and looked away. "If you do beat the Yuuzhan Vong, you'll just chain everyone up like before. And if you lose, you'll drag everyone else down with you."

"It's not like that."

"No? You'll probably tell me that we'll all die unless we band together to defeat the common enemy. But there's *always* a common enemy, Jaina. Oppressive regimes don't function without them. The Empire had its Rebel Alliance; once, we had the Ssi-ruuk; and right now, you have the Yuuzhan Vong. Who will it be next time you feel the cracks spreading?"

"I'll be happy just to reach the next time," Jaina said. "But tell me, Malinza, what would happen if we did lose this war? What would you do if the Yuuzhan Vong turned up on your doorstep and we weren't there to help you, like we did with the Ssi-ruuk?"

"We'd fight them, of course," the girl said simply. "And yes, we would probably all die in the process. But it would be *our* decision, not one made by some faceless bureaucrat on the other side of the galaxy."

"Is that really the issue, Malinza? Does it really boil down to who controls you? Or who makes the decisions for you?"

"Of course it does!"

"I don't recall the New Republic ever demanding anything of Bakura. You were always asked."

"And we always said yes. I know that. That galls me more than you could possibly understand. While we abased ourselves before the New Republic, it was happy in return to steal our defense fleet, our families—"

Malinza stopped there, leaning back heavily against the wall with a troubled, weary sigh. Jaina was relieved to see tears in the girl's eyes. She had already guessed what lay at the heart of Malinza's dislike of the New Republic, no matter how she dressed it up in rhetoric. Behind her stoic defiance, she was still just a fifteen-year-old girl. One pushed into defying a government she regarded as being oppressive, forced to learn skills no teenager should have had to know—but still only fifteen. That she had risen above that disadvantage spoke volumes about her ability and her determination. She had taken the example of her adopted uncle to heart, it seemed.

Jaina herself hadn't been much older when the war with the Yuuzhan Vong had broken out. People were capable of extraordinary things when circumstances demanded it, she reflected.

"I'm sorry about your mother, Malinza," Jaina said, putting a hand on the girl's shoulder. It wasn't pushed away. "I met her briefly at Centerpoint before she died, but I was just a kid then. I know Uncle Luke held her in very high regard."

"I barely remember her," Malinza said, trying to be casual as she knuckled away the tears she was fighting. "I recall her leaving, and my aunt trying to explain what had happened when she didn't come back, but I was only four years old, and I never really understood. I just knew who had taken her from us. The New Republic dragged her into a war she wasn't part of, and she gave her life to save others. She did a very good thing, and I suffered because of it." She shrugged helplessly. "I guess the universe found its balance, as it always does. It's just that in this instance I was on the receiving end, that's all."

"Balance?" asked Jaina. "What do you mean?"

"Cosmic Balance. The wheel of fate, you know?" She shifted her position on the bunk so she was facing Jaina fully. "Every action causes a reaction. A great force for good can't exist without there also being a counterbalancing force for evil, somewhere. In the same way, good works lead to evil results for someone else, quite unintentionally. It's just how the universe works, and the Force, too. Save someone on Bakura today and you might kill another later. That's why I don't want this Alliance of yours here. It's too dangerous. I have no desire to see my home get caught in friendly fire."

"So you want no part in the Galactic Alliance and the war against the Yuuzhan Vong. Is that what you're saying?"

"Don't get me wrong, Jaina. I have nothing against Uncle Luke. Apart from Aunt Laera, who raised me after Mom died, he's the only family I have left. Dad died not long after I was born, so I never got to know him. If I should side with anyone, it would be you. It's only my fear of the backlash from the Balance that stops me."

"So how does kidnapping Cundertol help you, then? He's all for an alliance with the P'w'eck. They'd make viable alternatives to the Galactic Alliance and give you a fighting chance of defending Bakura against a Yuuzhan Vong attack."

"Exactly!" she said. "That's why it makes no sense for me to have kidnapped Cundertol in the first place."

"But you could have ordered it—"

"No," Malinza cut in firmly. "I didn't. Just because I'm young doesn't make me automatically stupid!"

"I'm not saying—"

"Maybe not, but you're still listening to what they're telling you—and they're telling you that I'm stupid." A humorless laugh broke her somber mood. "Then again, to have attempted a stunt like that, perhaps they're right."

"You're not stupid, Malinza," Jaina tried to reassure her, but the girl didn't seem to hear.

"I keep trying to explain that the goal of Freedom is simply to kick the New Republic off Bakura. We don't use violence, and we certainly don't kidnap people. Call us idealistic if you want, but we do have principles. The last thing we want to see is the old regime replaced with one equally as bad."

Jaina's mind boggled at the thought of sixteen people attempting to take on a galactic civilization. It smacked of either madness or incredible bravery.

"How did you ever hope to succeed?"

"Ah, well, there's the thing," Malinza answered with a half smile. "You see, we had some funding from private sources, and with that money we were able to dig deep into the infrastructure, looking for things that might assist us: evidence of corruption, brutality, nepotism, and so on. You'd be surprised what we turned up."

Jaina seriously doubted that; she'd heard plenty about dodgy politicians over the years from her mother. "Who funded you?"

"They would consider that private, I'm sure," Malinza said firmly. "Especially where you are concerned."

Jaina respected Malinza's reticence on the matter, but quietly suspected that the Peace Brigade might have been involved at some point in the past. Such an underground organization would be just the thing for stirring up dissent. "You say you're not into violence, Malinza, but what about the others?"

"*None* of the sixteen core members of Freedom was into violence. It wasn't our style. But . . ."

"But?"

"Well, there were others who joined us," she said.

"And it's possible that they might have had violent intentions. In fact, with some of them I'd have to say that violence was high on their agenda. But we didn't encourage them to stay."

"So who else would join?"

"All sorts, really. Not all of Freedom's actions were covert; we had a recruiting front and our policies were well known. This is a democracy, right? Or it's supposed to be. Some of our members were bored with their everyday lives and were looking for excitement. Sometimes we'd get people coming over from similar underground movements." She shrugged. "Ever since the P'w'eck arrived, we've attracted all sorts of malcontents."

"Why is that?"

"Well, for one thing, my involvement in Freedom was never a secret, and I have some sort of profile with the media because my mother was once prime minister. We've had cranks trying to come along for the ride since we started, but they've always been easy to weed out. Until recently, anyway." She looked down at her lap. "It was getting hard to control, to be honest. The anti-P'w'eck movement made it clear that if we weren't with them, then we were against them. As I said, I'm not a xenophobe; I think the P'w'eck could be a good thing for Bakura. I don't want to be against anyone, really, because that makes them against me. The Balance kicks back just as hard as we lash out. And trust me, I have no desire to get kicked again."

"I think I'm starting to understand that," Jaina said. And she was. She didn't necessarily believe everything Malinza had said, but she also didn't believe that the girl was the sort to order kidnappings and murders to further her cause. "So why do you really think you're in here, then?" she added.

"We were too good at what we did," Malinza said. "We were making too many inroads. We'd uncovered some dirt on a few Senators and threatened to go public with the information."

"Blackmail?"

"Is it blackmail if you're acting in the public's best interests?" Malinza shrugged. "Whatever. They were getting nervous, but they couldn't put us away without whipping up an even bigger storm. We hadn't done anything really wrong, you see. It would have been difficult for them to incarcerate us for very long, because once we made their secrets known then public sympathy would have been on our side. So we reached a kind of impasse, I guess. It was only a matter of waiting to see who snapped first."

"During which time you kept digging for more dirt, I presume," Jaina said. "Which means that if they don't genuinely think you kidnapped Cundertol, then you must have uncovered something new that they very much wanted kept quiet."

"If we did, then I honestly have no idea what it could've been." Malinza shook her head again. "We were tracing some financial deal that went through just after the P'w'eck arrived. An awful lot of money went offworld, but we couldn't work out who was behind it or where it was going. It looked like some sort of commercial transaction, and may well have been just that. The fact that the endpoints had been obscured made us wonder." She looked at Jaina, eyes narrowed slightly. "Your Galactic Alliance isn't looking for money now, is it?"

"No. Not from Bakura, anyway." Taking money from Bakura would have been like taking small change from a child in order to finance a starship purchase. "It could have been legit, as you say."

Malinza nodded, taking in the confines of the cell with one sweeping gesture. "Nevertheless, here I am." She paused, fixing Jaina with a sober stare. "I'm not responsible for Cundertol's kidnapping, I swear. But that's not going to stop the people behind this. They never let the truth get in the way of what they want."

"If you didn't do it, they won't be able to make the charges stick."

Malinza laughed. "You're assuming I'm going to get a fair trial." She shook her head. "There's bound to be circumstantial evidence."

Perhaps the young woman was right, Jaina thought, recalling Blaine Harris's certainty over Malinza's guilt on announcing the news of her capture. On the other hand, though, there was also Cundertol's reaction on hearing the news to consider. Clearly, he hadn't been as convinced as Harris had.

"The Prime Minister's testimony will count for something," she said by way of reassuring Malinza. "He was there, after all. If *he* doesn't think it was you, then I doubt they'd ever be able to convict."

"Maybe," Malinza said faintly. Some of the fire had gone out of her; she looked more than ever like a lonely, frightened teenager caught out of her depth. "I just have to have faith in the Balance. If a wrong is done to me now, then some good will come of it another day. That's some comfort, at least."

A very lonely one, Jaina thought. But then, perhaps Malinza's belief in the Balance was no less lonely than Jaina's own faith in the Force.

She stood, glancing at her chronometer. It was well past midnight, and her parents would be starting to get worried. "I should go now."

"But you haven't told me why *you're* here yet," Malinza protested.

"I'm just doing my job," Jaina said with a smile. "You know what Jedi are like: we're always getting in the way."

"As well as always getting their way." The smile was

halfheartedly returned. Then it was lost altogether. "I have to admit I would be glad to be out of here."

Jaina nodded sympathetically. "I'll see what I can do about that." She palmed the green CALL button and faced Malinza one last time. "Maybe we can apply some pressure to get your hearing processed more quickly and—"

She broke off. The door had opened onto an empty corridor.

"That's strange," she muttered.

Malinza peered past her. "What is?"

"The guards said they'd escort me out of here." Jaina stepped cautiously out of the cell, every nerve screaming *trap*. "But there's no one. Not even so much as a droid."

Malinza joined her outside the cell. Jaina could tell from the girl's expression that she was as surprised as Jaina that no sirens sounded when she did this. Surprise soon became excitement, though.

"It's Vyram!" she said. "It has to be!"

"Who?"

"He's one of Freedom's core members," Malinza said. "In fact, he's what you'd call the brains behind the group. If anyone could slice into the system and get me out of here, it would be him."

"I don't know, Malinza," Jaina said, glancing around uneasily. "This doesn't feel right to me."

"That's easy for you to say. You get to walk out of here no matter what happens." Malinza straightened until they were almost eye to eye. "I'm going for it."

Jaina grabbed her sleeve as she went up the corridor. "Wait! That's the wrong direction." She was unable to shake her suspicions; something told her that what she was about to do was what someone *wanted* her to do. Nevertheless, her options were limited. "At least let me show you the way."

Malinza's grin was both appreciative and mischievous. "I thought you'd never offer," she said.

* * *

Tahiri moved through the canyon, tired and weary, every muscle in her body aching terribly. It felt as though she'd been running for years. Fifty meters away on either side of her were mighty, craggy walls curving up and around her, making her feel as though she were walking in the palm of some impossibly immense fist. She paused for a moment to look up, and saw the stars twinkling overhead. No, not stars! These glistening specks were too close for that. They were no more stars than the blackness that held them was the night sky.

A sudden howl and a cry reminded her that her pursuers weren't far behind. Across the vast and empty plain she could make out nothing but varying degrees of darkness; there was no sign of the thing with her face or the lizard creature. But they were out there somewhere; she knew that without a doubt. And if she ever stopped moving, stopped running, then they would catch up with her and—

She pushed the thought down, turning back to the task of continuing through the darkness in search of the light. However, where moments before there'd been nothing but barren ground, now trees crowded around her from every side. For a moment she felt strangely comforted by this, believing that nothing could possibly find her amid such a tangle of branches, limbs, and trunks. But this comfort was short-lived. Her pursuers didn't need to see it, she realized; they could *smell* her. That's how they'd been able to follow her all this time—and how they would continue to follow her until she finally relented and surrendered to their hunger.

The howl of the lizard beast rang out through the spindly foliage, its cry carried on a wind that rustled the daggerlike leaves hanging down from the trees around her. She moved faster, wincing as each leaf she brushed aside cut into her arms and hands.

The bitter forest gave way to a rock face that rose sharply into the dark. For a moment, she panicked that she had nowhere left to run, but then off to her right she noticed a small crevice in the rock.

"Tahiri . . ."

The voice came as a whisper on the breeze. It seemed far away, but not so far off that she could afford to relax.

Sucking in her stomach and bringing her arms in close to her side, she managed to make herself small enough to be able to squeeze through the narrow opening, the mildew covering the rocks expediting her movement. She closed her eyes, forcing out the disquieting thought of *being swallowed* as she wriggled between stone. Better that, she thought, than face what was following her.

The narrow crack widened around her. It had brought her safely out on the far side. She opened her eyes and her heart sank at what she saw: the path ahead was narrow and straight and lined with trees filled with ysalamiri. She climbed out of the crack and stood trembling for the longest time, too scared to move or even breathe. But her fear came not from the idea of passing between the trees, but rather from what she thought she could make out in the distance beyond them: a dark, reptilian figure, silhouetted against the sky.

"Tahiri . . ."

Crying out in fright, she spun around to see the thing with her face glaring through the crevice in the mossy rock. Its arm was reaching out to her; its bloodied fingers clawed for a touch of her sweat-soaked skin.

"You can't leave me here, Tahiri . . ."

Tahiri woke with a half-formed cry on her lips. Her hand was halfway to her lightsaber before she realized where she was: Bakura. She sighed in relief. It wasn't the worldship orbiting Myrkr. She was safe.

Safe? Was she *really* safe?

She groped in the darkness for the light panel, relaxing as a yellow ambience filled the room. The bed rocked beneath her as she sat up and swung her legs over the edge. Almost everything on Bakura floated; wherever repulsors could possibly be included, they were—lifting chairs, counters of food, almost everything, it seemed.

As unsettling as it was to have things floating around her, it wasn't this that troubled her most right now. Neither was it the tension suffocating her like a thick fog. No, the discomfort she felt now was like a tingling at the back of her mind—a suspicion that those around her, the "family" that Jacen had assured her she was a part of back on Mon Calamari, were conspiring against her.

Jaina had talked to her mother before going off to find Malinza. Leia had gone into Jaina's room to stir her daughter from a Jedi trance and hadn't emerged for some time. When she had, she had carried in her eyes a stare that was both wary and distant. Leia was seeing something that troubled her—something in *Tahiri.*

Tahiri felt it keenly, like ice water trickling down her spine. No matter how she tried to ignore it, the feeling simply wouldn't go away.

Feeling like she was still dreaming, she stood up and crossed the room to the doorway. Opening it, she crept into the hallway linking their rooms. Unlike on Galantos where they had five rooms all opening onto a central common area, on Bakura they occupied rooms designed as though in a hotel. Han and Leia's was the largest, with an adjoining area that could be used as a common room. Tahiri and Jaina were up the hall, adjacent but not connecting.

Tahiri stopped outside Jaina's room, pressing her ear against the door to listen. There was no sound whatsoever; Jaina must still be out on her mission, even though it was well past midnight. A distant concern for Jaina's well-being penetrated the fog. But not for long. Jaina was one of the ones who suspected her, who constantly watched her for any sign of—

What? What was it Jaina searched for when she looked at Tahiri? The truth, perhaps, of who she really was?

The thought hit her like a blow from behind. *No!* She performed a mental forward somersault, rolling with the punch and coming up fighting. *That's* not *who I am!* In her mind, she slashed at the thought with her lightsaber, cutting the notion to ribbons. *You can't make me be someone I'm not!*

Then the terrible moment of clarity faded and the fog fell around her once again. She embraced the vague dream state, letting it dissolve her concerns and reduce her anxieties to just one. She could still feel it tugging at her, as though a hook had pierced her soul and some dreadful angler was reeling her in.

It *had* to stop. She didn't know how much more of this she could take before she snapped—or something altogether worse happened.

She moved from Jaina's door, silently walking the short distance to Han and Leia's room. There she repeated the same process, pressing her ear against the door to listen for any movements. She couldn't hear anything.

Keying the access code into the lock, Tahiri eased open the door. It surprised her that Leia's Noghri bodyguards were nowhere to be seen. But she didn't have time to dwell on it. The fact was, they wouldn't be too far away, and if they returned now they'd be sure to question her late-night activities in the Princess's room . . .

From the darkness inside, C-3PO's glowing photoreceptor eyes turned toward her.

She raised a finger to her lips. "Not a word, Threepio," she whispered. "I just need to get something from the other room, okay?"

"As you wish, Mistress Tahiri," the droid replied, making no effort to speak in a voice lower than he normally would. "But shouldn't you—"

"*Shhh,*" she insisted with a hiss. "I promise not to be long."

C-3PO nodded uncertainly in the gloom as Tahiri continued through to Han and Leia's bedroom. They were asleep when she entered, their restful breathing the only sound. She stood there motionless, extending herself into the shadows, feeling for the thing that called to her. And there it was; she could *feel* it, pulling her ever closer . . .

I must destroy the evidence, she breathed to herself. *Destroy it, and the problem will go away.*

Using the Force to guide her through the darkened bedroom, she made her way to a small table containing a bowl of flowers and a glass of water. There was something else there, too—something that the Force couldn't reveal to her. Now that she was closer she could see it, the small object caught in a fine sliver of moonlight from the open window. And just as on Galantos when she'd first found it, every one of her physical senses was tingling from the echoes emanating from the small pendant.

She reached out with her hand to pick up the silver totem molded into the likeness of Yun-Yammka, the slayer. At the very moment her fingers touched it, a hand reached out of the blackness to grab her wrist, and a voice called out her name in a language that disgusted her.

If the voice said anything else, she never heard it, as darkness suddenly swirled around her and swallowed her senses.

"Here we are," said the librarian, a thin, shorthaired woman whose name was Tris. She had brought them to two broad, solid doors deep in a secure installation buried deep under the ice in an isolated sector of the Chiss homeworld. Soontir Fel had ferried them there on the back of a large, black ice barge, an armored craft that used powerful repulsors to sweep across the icy planetary crust. It was big enough to hold fifty people, but the passengers had consisted solely of Luke and his entourage, Commander Irolia, Chief Navigator Peita Aabe, and Fel himself. There appeared to be neither pilots nor any security staff, so either they were keeping carefully out of sight or Fel had supreme faith in automatics.

Upon arrival, they had been introduced to their guide from the Inrokini family, who had whisked them deep underground via a turbolift that seemed to take forever, while Fel and the others went off on official business.

"We're here at last?" Jacen asked. Like the others, he was restless from the long journey and keen to get started on the search for Zonama Sekot.

Their guide nodded and pushed open the doors with a dramatic sweep. "Welcome to the Expeditionary Library. You are among the very few non-Chiss to step through these doors."

She waved them through. Jacen and the others, mindful of the honor, moved respectfully forward into the giant chamber. It took him a second to grasp the scale. Vast and rectangular, with lines sharply defined, the library space was as large as a docking bay. There were four levels of walkways surrounding the walls, with steep stairwells leading to each, and endless rows of rectangular dividers subdividing the floor. Yellow lights hung suspended from the ceiling on long cables, casting a warm glow across the space. The air was still, warm, and fresh. A deep silence filled the space, as though the enormous volume of air was soaking up every sound.

"Nice," Mara said, her long red hair waving as she turned to look around her. "We'll have lots of elbow room, at least. If you show us to the holoscreens, we'll get started."

Tris frowned. "Holoscreens? There are no holoscreens here."

"Then how do we get at the data?"

"I'll show you."

The librarian led them across the floor of the giant chamber, along a path between two long shelves. Jacen idly studied the contents of the shelves as he walked, wondering what they were. They looked like bricks of some kind, and he wondered if they were some sort of data storage device. A high-security installation such as this one would, he assumed, have a highly sophisticated means of keeping its data safe. Perhaps the bricks had to be fed by hand into some kind of reader, which would then display its contents. Each of the memory bricks could hold vast amounts of data, safely sealed away.

Tris turned right at the end of the shelves and took them down to another aisle. "Here are the exploration notes for the world you visited last, Munlali Mafir, translated into Basic for permanent record." She reached up to the top shelf and selected one of the bricks. "Everything here is meticulously cataloged. It may take you a while to get the hang of our system, but I am here to assist you in that task."

She handed the brick to Mara, who hefted it uncertainly, then gave it to Jacen. It was heavier than he had expected, and there were no obvious jack-in ports. The front and back were made of the same material as one side of the thing—a deep red material, with gold writing in Basic. The other three sides were curiously rough and soft.

Seeing his puzzlement, Tris took it back from him and opened it. The top folded back like the lid of a box, only the interior wasn't empty. It was full all the way through. Full of text.

Only then did Jacen understand. He felt like an idiot for not getting it sooner. But judging by the gasp of surprise from Danni, he knew he wasn't the only one.

Not a brick. The object in Tris's hand was a *book*.

"You're kidding," Mara said, her eyebrows rising.

It was Tris's turn to look puzzled. "The Chiss have always stored sensitive information in this fashion. It is safe, secure, and permanent. We have lost too much data in ice storms to trust other, more complicated forms of storage."

"But how are we going to find anything?" Danni asked. "We can't do keyword searches through . . . *this*!"

"There are ways to search, and I am here to assist you." Tris seemed serenely confident, but Jacen's mind balked at the thought of poring through the millions—maybe billions—of pages contained on the shelves around them. The library was full of mission reports, xenobiology tracts, anthropological assays, and contact histories from the Chiss Expeditionary Defense Fleet's exploration of the Unknown Regions—and that exploration had been ongoing for *centuries*.

How hard can this be? he told himself. *If I can fly an X-wing with my eyes shut, then surely I can leaf through a few books!*

Something similar must have been going through Saba's mind. "We wish to search for referencez to Zonama Sekot," the saurian Jedi Knight said. "Pleaze assist us in that."

"Of course." The librarian put the book back in its proper place and walked briskly through the aisles, humming softly to herself. "Follow me."

Luke exchanged glances with Jacen and Mara, then followed.

It was a huge pit: easily thirty meters deep and almost a kilometer across. Mighty columns stretched up into the sky, reaching for the planet that hung in the blackness like an overripe fruit about to fall. Around her on the ground were a number of ships, some secured in their birthing bays by restraining carapaces, others just lying on the ground in various stages of disrepair and decay.

She knew the place to be an old spaceport—one that was both comfortingly familiar and disconcertingly alien. She wanted to climb into one of the derelict spaceships and fly off to the planet up above—for she knew that here, at least, she might be safe—but the dilapidated condition of the ships told her that this simply wasn't an option. The spaceport and all its craft had lain unused for many years. It was abandoned, just like the world beneath her feet—as abandoned as she felt herself to be.

Someone was standing behind her. She turned, startled, and found herself staring at a distant reflection of herself. Only it wasn't her at all. This person had scars across her forehead. Reaching up, she realized she didn't carry any such scars. The only scars she carried were the ones on her arms, and they felt completely different. Her reflection's scars stood out boldly, proudly, and had been carved into the flesh with *purpose*. Hers, on the other hand, were a product of anger and an intense desire to remove something she'd thought she had seen lurking beneath her skin . . .

"There's nowhere left to run," the ghostly reflection said.

In the distance came the howl of the lizard beast.

"Not for you, either," she pointed out.

Despite obvious effort to hide it, there was fear behind the reflection's gaze.

"Why do you want to hurt me?" she asked it.

"Because you want to hurt me."

"I want to be left alone! I want only to be free!"

"As do I."

"But I *belong* here!"

The reflection surveyed their surroundings, then faced her again. "As do I."

The howl of the creature sounded again, louder this time, and closer.

"It can smell us," the reflection said. "It can smell my fear, and it can smell your guilt."

"I have nothing to feel guilty for."

"No, you don't. And yet there it is, nonetheless."

She looked into herself, then, and saw the guilt of which the reflection spoke. It had always been there, she knew; she just hadn't wanted to *see* it. But now the amorphous and neglected emotion took shape, forming into words that rose in her thoughts, in her throat, finally demanding release:

Why am I alive when the one I love is dead?

And with this came a deafening roar from the lizard creature. It was a roar of anger, of remorse, and of regret; it was a bellow whose echo called back to her out of the dark over and over again, fading each time until it became little more than a far-off whisper, a distant speck in the dark . . .

Tahiri . . . Tahiri . . .

"Tahiri?"

The hand shaking her shoulder did more to dispel the dream than the sound of her own name being spoken. She blinked, then looked around vaguely at her surroundings. The walls so close around her seemed small in comparison to the dreamscape she'd just left—so much more restricting.

"Come on, kid—snap out of it."

Han's voice was rough and hard, like the hands shaking her. She looked at him through tear-stained eyes and saw his worried and fatigued expression. Leia stepped between them, her gentle features smiling reassuringly at Tahiri.

"Are you okay?" she asked.

"I'm awake," the girl mumbled hazily. Then, realizing

she hadn't answered the question, she nodded and added: "I think I'm all right."

Her head was pounding, and the harsh light felt like a naked sun burning into her eyes. She winced, blinking back more tears as she tried to sit up. She felt strange, confused—and this confusion was only magnified when she saw where she was: lying on the bed in Han and Leia's suite.

"What happened?" she asked. Even as she spoke the words, she knew the answer: the same thing that happened before, on Galantos and elsewhere. The illusion of ignorance was her only defense. "What am I doing here?"

"You don't remember?" Leia asked.

Both of Anakin's parents were standing over her, dressed in their night robes.

"I—" she started. How could she tell them the truth when she herself wasn't even sure what it was? "I was looking for something."

Leia held out the silver pendant. Its many-tentacled, snarling visage seemed to mock her from its cradle of soft, human flesh. "You were looking for this, weren't you?"

Tahiri nodded, embarrassed. "It—it calls to me. It reminds me of . . ." She trailed off, unable to put what she was feeling into words.

"Of who you are?" Leia suggested.

The words seemed to stab a sharp pain in her mind, to which she responded with anger. "I know who I am! I'm Tahiri Veila!"

Leia crouched down beside the bed to look up into the girl's face. Tahiri didn't want to meet her eyes, but the Princess was hard to resist. "Are you?" she asked in a low, searching tone. "You don't seem like the Tahiri I once knew."

"What are you talking about, Leia?" Han said, looking

equal parts exasperated and tired. "What exactly is going on here?"

"Sometimes I think we forget what happened to her on Yavin Four, Han." Leia kept her warm, reassuring eyes on Tahiri as she spoke. Then she stood and addressed her husband fully. "The Yuuzhan Vong did something terrible to her while she was in their hands—something we can't even begin to understand. They tried to turn her into something other than human. You don't just get over that easily. It takes time."

"But I thought she was given the okay. Wasn't that why she was invited to join us on this mission?"

The two kept talking, but Tahiri had stopped listening. Although he probably didn't mean it, there was a suggestion of mistrust in Han's words that was hurtful to her, and for a brief moment she felt overwhelmed by grief—a grief that was exacerbated by the way Anakin's parents kept talking about her in the third person, as if she weren't even there. It made her feel strangely removed from what was taking place around her . . .

"*I* wasn't asleep," Leia was saying to Han in response to something he'd said. "Jaina told me what Jag found on Galantos; I was *expecting* Tahiri to come for it. That's why I instructed Cakhmain and Meewalh to stay out of sight—to *let* Tahiri come for the pendant."

As she said this, Leia gestured off to one side, and for the first time, Tahiri noticed the Princess's Noghri guards standing there.

Han sighed. "I still would have preferred it if you'd told me what was going on."

"There was no need, Han. I wanted to see what would happen."

"So what's causing this?" he asked. "You think it might be Anakin?"

Leia shook her head. "It's more than that; much more.

She's hiding something—from herself as well as everyone else."

The accusation stabbed at Tahiri's heart, making her jump to her feet. "How can you say that?" she cried, taking a step forward. But a single step was all she managed before Cakhmain moved to stop her, taking Tahiri by the shoulders to hold her back from Leia. She wriggled in his slender hands but couldn't break free. "I would never hurt either of you! You're—" She stopped, remembering Jacen's note back on Mon Calamari. "You're my *family.*"

Han stepped over to her, then, taking her hands. "Hey, take it easy, kid." He wiped at the fresh tears on her cheek with the back of his hand. "No one's accusing you of anything, Tahiri. Just relax, okay?"

She did so, feeling oddly calmed by the large man's rough but friendly voice. She saw Leia motion to her Noghri guard, who immediately released Tahiri and retreated to the shadows.

Leia came forward. "I'm sorry, Tahiri. I didn't mean to upset you."

Tahiri didn't know what to say—she felt foolish and ashamed at her outburst—so in the end just nodded her acceptance of the Princess's apology and said nothing.

"Tell me, though, Tahiri," Leia said. "Do you have *any* idea what's been going on in your head these last couple of years?"

"I-I—sometimes I black out," Tahiri stammered awkwardly. "I have these . . . *dreams* that—"

"That tell you you're somebody else?" Leia offered.

This brought her up defensive again. "My name is Tahiri Veila! That's who *I am!*"

Leia took Tahiri's shoulders in her hands and looked the girl in the face with her penetrating brown eyes. "I know this isn't easy, Tahiri. But you must try to understand. I want you to think back to just before you blacked out. Do you remember what I said to you?"

Tahiri thought about this. "You called my name."

Leia looked over to Han.

"What?" Tahiri said, angered by the almost conspiratorial looks being exchanged between them. "You *did* call my name! I heard you!"

Sympathy shimmered in Leia's eyes. "I didn't call you by *your* name, Tahiri. I called you Riina."

A feeling as cold as ice spread across Tahiri's shoulders and ran down her back in a horrible, clammy rush. At the same time, a terrible blackness rose up in her mind, threatening to engulf her. "No," she mumbled, shaking her head slowly and fighting the feeling. "That's not true."

"It is true, Tahiri. Before, when you blacked out, you were shouting at me in Yuuzhan Vong. You were calling me something that not even Threepio could understand. You weren't Tahiri, then." She paused uncomfortably before pronouncing the terrible truth. "You were Riina of Domain Kwaad, the personality that Mezhan Kwaad tried to turn you into. Somehow, the Riina personality is still inside you."

Tahiri shook her head again, more vigorously this time, wanting to deny the spreading darkness as much as the words themselves. "It—it *can't* be true. It just can't be!"

"It is, Tahiri," Leia said. "Believe me. And the sooner you accept that, the sooner we can start doing—"

"*No!*" Tahiri screamed in a pitch that surprised herself as much as it obviously did Leia, who took a step back at the outburst.

As though a dam had burst, she was suddenly in motion. With the full strength of the Force flowing through her, fueled by her desperation and her need to escape, she snatched the pendant as she pushed past Leia and Han and headed for the door—too quick for even Cakhmain to grab her. C-3PO was standing on the other side of the door when she went through, but she didn't even give him time to utter a single word of objection; she just shoved him aside as hard as she could, throwing the golden droid clean off his feet and into the wall. Then she was through the door and out of the suite, running as if her very life depended on it.

She saw nothing but corridors flashing by, and could feel nothing but the cool pendant of Yun-Yammka against her palm, grinning in vile satisfaction.

And somewhere beyond the sound of her own sobbing, she could hear a name being called. That she couldn't be sure the name even belonged to her made her cry that much harder, and run that much faster.

Jag listened intently as Han and Leia detailed the incident with Tahiri over the secure subspace channel. The two sounded exhausted, which was hardly surprising given what they'd just been through—and the fact that it was still the middle of the night where they were probably wasn't helping, either.

"She didn't hurt anyone, did she?" Jag asked.

"No," Leia said. "And I don't believe she would have, either."

"What about the Riina personality?"

There was some hesitation from the other end. "We're more concerned about what she'll do to herself than what she might do to others," Leia said firmly.

"So where is she now?"

"She ran off," Leia said.

"And we haven't heard from her since," Han put in wearily. "Poor kid was in quite a state when she left."

Jag acknowledged his frustration at being too far away to be of any direct help with a sigh. "Have you notified security on the ground?"

"And tell them what?" Han asked. "That there's a

lone Jedi on the loose who's possibly under the control of a Yuuzhan Vong mind? That'll really go down well with the authorities."

"They'd probably lock the lot of us up," Leia said. "Anyway, it's not an option. But she does need to be found—and soon. I don't like the idea of her being alone while she's trying to deal with this. She needs our help right now."

Jag shook his head. "I just don't understand how this could have happened. From what I understood, she was over her experiences on Yavin Four."

"So we all thought," Leia said. "But her conditioning went deep. She could speak the Yuuzhan Vong language and fly their ships; and there were moments when Anakin himself said that she acted strangely. But outwardly she *seemed* okay; she appeared to be holding herself together."

"But then Anakin died," Han said, "and that must have changed everything." Jag could hear the echoes of the still-painful grief in Han's words. He seemed to steel himself against the emotion as he carried on with: "And if this Riina personality is still with the kid, then we have to do something about it."

Jag agreed, but he knew it wasn't going to be easy. Tahiri could have been anywhere by now, and if she was as panicked as Han and Leia said she was, then she probably wasn't going to *want* to be found in a hurry. While Leia was probably right in that Tahiri wouldn't hurt anyone, Tahiri might see things differently. *Without any control over when the Riina personality emerges, she may see herself as being a threat to her friends and want to keep away for fear of causing them any harm . . .*

"What bothers me, though, Jag," Leia went on, "is that you and Jaina suspected something was wrong and yet you kept it to yourselves."

Jag swallowed, wishing it were Jaina, not him, fielding the question.

Leia had every right to be upset, of course. After he had shown Jaina the pendant that Tahiri had found back on Galantos, the two of them had discussed what they should do about the young girl. Clearly she was finely attuned to anything Yuuzhan Vong; and just as clearly there were moments when the alien personality rose up and tried to take over. However, the girl was a trained Jedi, and they felt she should be given the chance to solve the problem on her own. It had never been their intention to keep Han and Leia out of the loop indefinitely, and neither had imagined that anything could go wrong as long as one of them was close at hand to keep an eye on her.

"I'm sorry," he said shortly. "But we really didn't expect anything like this to happen."

"Well, it did," Han said. "And if Leia hadn't suspected that something was up, things could have gotten quite ugly down here."

"Well, again, I'm sorry," Jag said. "Where is Jaina? She was supposed to be looking out for Tahiri while you were all down on Bakura."

"Jaina hasn't returned yet from interviewing Malinza Thanas," Leia replied. If there was any concern for her daughter, the Princess was hiding it well.

"She still hasn't reported in?" Jag had been apprised of Jaina's mission when he'd first come on duty. "But it's hours past midnight down there. She should have been back by now."

"We know," Han said.

Jag felt his fists clench at this news. He wished again that he were down on the surface where he could do more good. "Maybe I should ask Captain Mayn to send a shuttle with backup and—"

"No," Leia interrupted. "I have faith in Jaina; if she

needs assistance, then she'll be in touch. Wherever she is, I'm sure—"

An alarm sounded from the console, cutting off the last part of her sentence.

"Hang on a second," Jag said. "I have another call coming through on a separate channel." He flipped a switch to hear the incoming message. "Go ahead."

"Colonel Fel, we have contacts emerging from hyperspace in Sector Eleven." The voice belonged to Selwin Markota, *Pride of Selonia*'s second in command.

Jag forced the problems on Bakura to the back of his mind. His duty as squadron leader took precedence for the moment over his concerns for Jaina and Tahiri. "How many?"

"Thirty, with more on the way; at least two capital vessels so far. It looks like a fleet."

"Have they contacted Bakura?"

"They're being hailed now. I'll patch you into the defense fleet net."

"Copy that." Jag flicked back to the secure channel. "I'm sorry, Leia, Han, but I have to go."

"We just got the call, too," Leia responded crisply. "We'll let you know if anything changes."

"Flights A and B," Jag said on the Twin Sun frequencies, "stay here and mind the big bird. C, you're with me." He peeled out of formation and was followed by two X-wings and a clawcraft. On the scanner before him, the ships emerging from hyperspace stood out like a nebula in the deep void. The number of contacts now stood at forty, with still more coming.

"This is Bakuran Defense Fleet," called the local traffic control. "Please identify yourself and state your intentions."

The response came in the form of a warbling, dissonant fluting.

Jag had been briefed; he knew enough to recognize the language. The fleet had originated from Lwhekk—but who was commanding it? The Ssi-ruuk or the P'w'eck?

The voice of C-3PO came over the comm. "The message says: 'I come in peace, people of Bakura, to consecrate this world and bond our two cultures in alliance.'"

Another voice spoke from Bakura in response to this. Jag recognized it as belonging to Prime Minister Cundertol.

"We welcome the Keeramak to Bakura in the hope that this new friendship will bring prosperity and enlightenment to all."

The sickly sentiment made Jag roll his eyes. Luckily the speeches didn't last any longer than that.

"Keeramak Entourage, please assume the following orbits," the first voice from Bakura said. There followed a long list of requests designed to minimize the disruption caused by the many new arrivals, at the end of which there came a brief burst of alien song, which C-3PO interpreted to mean, simply, "'Understood.'"

Jag turned his interception flight into a sweeping, exploratory cruise, examining the alien vessels with a critical eye. The Chiss had fought the Ssi-ruuk on several occasions, contributing behind the scenes to the Imperium's retreat at the advance of the New Republic. He himself, though, had never seen one outside of a simulation. While their battle droids consisted of simple, angular pyramids with weapon and sensor arrays at each corner, the larger ships possessed a smoothly organic appearance. Great sweeping hulls with relatively few breaks formed bulbous, shell-like structures that bulged in odd but beautiful ways. He spotted two ovoid *Sh'ner*-class planetary assault carriers, accompanied by numerous *Fw'Sen*-class picket ships. The assault carriers were crewed by more than five hundred P'w'eck—plus over three hundred enteched droids, if they were still used—and were nearly

750 meters long. Overall, given their structure, they displaced a greater volume than a *Victory*-class Star Destroyer.

It seemed an awful lot of hardware to accompany a diplomatic mission. But then, he supposed, the P'w'eck were probably just as nervous of the Bakurans as the Bakurans were of them. With their freedom only recently attained, they wouldn't be keen to send their leader into the middle of a potentially difficult situation without sufficient backup.

At least they weren't shy about sharing their battle data, though. On the screen before him, names rapidly appeared next to all the major P'w'eck vessels. The cruiser in the middle of the formation was called the *Firrinree*, while the one lagging slightly behind was designated the *Errinung'ka*. He didn't even bother to attempt to remember the names of the picket ships.

As he watched, the last of the stragglers arrived and the formation broke in three to assume the orbits given them by the Bakuran Defense Fleet. The maneuver was accomplished smoothly and without fuss—and that spoke loudly of the discipline and flexibility of the P'w'eck fleet. One thing was for certain: they might be new to the idea of being in charge of their own destiny, but the P'w'eck had been exhaustively trained by their Ssi-ruuvi masters to fly battleships. It showed.

He hung around the main chunk of the fleet long enough to follow security negotiations with the reception team on the ground, and to witness the launch of seven heavily armed *D'kee*-class landing ships. The Keeramak was on its way.

Jag only hoped that Bakura was ready for it.

PART THREE

AGGRESSION

The warm, dry air of the library was making Saba's scales itchy, and she scratched absently at them while skimming through one of the many books suggested by Tris. She barely noticed the discomfort, however; her thoughts were too focused on the information she was reading. It surprised her how effortlessly she had taken to this form of research. When they'd first started, she had thought she'd never get used to the turning of pages—it seemed so time-consuming! And yet now she was skimming through the books with an ease and confidence similar to that with which skotcarp lizards back home would skate down the shaley slopes of Mount Ste'vshuulsz.

"Found anything yet?"

Saba looked up to see Mara peering at her from the end of an aisle of towering bookcases. She shook her head with some apology as she closed the book she'd been browsing through. She'd been reading up on a world on the outer edge of the Unknown Regions where a species of stilt-legged insects lived in a densely oxygenated atmosphere. Their legends spoke of a fire god who burst out of the planet's core every three years to burn large swaths of their world to the ground, initiating a new cycle of death and rebirth. But as interesting as it was, it didn't help their search. There was nothing about mysterious planets appearing in the sky anywhere in the text.

"This one has found nothing," she replied.

Mara nodded. "None of us has, unfortunately. I guess we're all still trying to come to grips with these books. It's frustratingly slow."

"It would be slower still if not in Basic. Our persistence will pay off," Saba told her. "It alwayz does."

Mara smiled, then moved off in the direction of Danni; probably, Saba thought, to check on the young scientist's progress also.

Saba pushed the book she'd been reading to one side and took another from the stack that Tris had supplied. Another species, another dead end. She didn't mind, though. She was reveling in the diversity of life in the Unknown Regions. The search was a far cry from any of her previous duties as a Jedi, and in many ways she knew it could turn out to be one of the most difficult, given the amount of material they had to work through. But she also knew that finding the data itself would probably turn out to be the easiest part; examining it and determining if it was relevant or not would undoubtedly take a lot longer.

Two books later, it was time to get up and stretch. Her eyes were starting to ache from reading, and her back was stiff and sore. Seeking a new list, she loped through the narrow aisles to the center of the vast room, from where the voices of Jacen and the others came. Luke and Mara looked up from three massive piles of books as she approached. They had conscripted a massive snow-wood table for their use; broad and square, it was easily large enough to seat twenty people. Datapads lay scattered before them, into which fragmentary notes had been entered. Lieutenant Stalgis emerged from one of the aisles, staggering under yet another stack of books. No one could be spared from the effort. The only person missing was, ironically, the one who would have been the most fascinated by it all: Soron Hegerty. Worn out from the episode on Munlali Mafir, the doctor had elected to wait out this mission to the Chiss from orbit. But she was still there in spirit, and her voice could often be heard issuing from comlinks, requesting more data in annoyed tones.

"Look at this," Luke announced, holding up a book before him for the others to see. Saba leaned over Jacen's and Mara's shoulders. While the bulk of the text had been translated into Basic, there were still portions in the native Cheunh that demanded assistance from the librarian. Saba concentrated to make sense of the words before her.

The pages Luke had opened to showed the location and history of a world called Yashuvhu. It had been settled by humans some three thousand standard years earlier, but had only recently encountered the Chiss. A quick scan of the pages revealed no reference to any wandering planets, although there was a description of an ancient woman called the Prophetess who oversaw the spiritual development of the colony. This woman taught that there was a living energy field pervading and connecting all things, which, when tapped into in the correct way . . .

"She's talking about the Force," Mara said.

"I think so," Luke said. "Look." He opened to a page containing pictures of the Prophetess, whose real name, it turned out, was Valara Saar. It showed a woman of advanced years in a state of excellent preservation. The Chiss contact team had attempted to visit her home in the Yashaka Mountains, but they'd been repelled. No one, it seemed, came to the Prophetess's retreat uninvited.

The images were sketchily drawn and portrayed the chaos of a hasty retreat, but one thing was plain to see.

"She's wielding a lightsaber!" Jacen exclaimed.

"It looks very much like it," Luke agreed, displaying a bit more calm than his excited nephew.

"How long haz she been there?" Saba asked.

"The records don't say," Mara said. "But if she was trained as a child, it could be decades."

"Either that or she found a Holocron," Jacen suggested.

"Let's not jump to any hasty conclusions," Luke said. "Strictly speaking, this isn't what we're here to look for."

Nevertheless, he had dived deep into the information on Yashuvhu and the Prophetess. Saba noted other books open around him, all tracing the same topic. The woman herself had not deigned to speak to the Chiss landing party, but many of her acolytes had. The records contained a list of her primary teachings: patience, humility, compassion, clarity of thought, balance between physical and mental prowess, strict observance of diet, and, lastly, a solitary lifestyle. In all the years that Valara Saar had been teaching the people of Yashuvhu, they had never known her to take a mate, so she never had any children. In fact, her only constant companion was a creature called a duuvhal, which she had raised from a pup.

"Hey, I think I've found something!"

All attention shifted to Danni, who emerged from an aisle clutching a very large book. Beneath the overhang of her unkempt hair, there was excitement in her eyes as she placed the book heavily on the table and flicked through some pages.

"See: here, and here . . ."

Saba and the others looked to where she was pointing. The young scientist had found a reference to an asteroid belt that had been perturbed by recent tidal forces. Millions of chunks of rock ranging in size from grains of dust to giant boulders had been knocked out of orbit by something very large within the last three decades. That in itself wasn't so unusual; solar systems were frequently unstable, with planets drifting in from interstellar space, wandering across orbits, or leaving at the whim of chaotic perturbations. What made this one unique was a record made by the civilization on an inner world before their atmosphere clouded. More than a dozen large rocks had impacted on the planet, rendering it uninhabitable.

The ruins contained murals depicting a new star in the sky—a blue-green star that had appeared one summer as though out of nowhere, then disappeared half a year later. Its appearance had triggered a terrible religious war that had seen one entire nation subjugated and another reduced to rubble. The victors had celebrated the star's visit. But their celebrations had quickly turned to mourning as first fire rained from the sky, and then the new sun vanished. Within two generations, they'd been reduced to savagery.

"Another fleeting visit, another violent culture," Mara said, cutting through the silence. "The correlation gets stronger."

"I see no evidence that Zonama Sekot is deliberately trying to harm the people it comes across," Luke said thoughtfully.

"Nevertheless," Mara said, "this is what it's doing."

"Inadvertently, perhaps," Luke said. "Not deliberately."

"Maybe it just isn't thinking straight," Stalgis suggested.

"Or *wasn't* thinking straight," Jacen added. "This is an old reference, after all."

"True," Luke said. "And until we see something more recent, I don't think we can judge it."

Saba realized only then that Luke was warring within himself over Zonama Sekot. Something as powerful as an intelligent planet might just as easily be influenced to do evil as it could to do good. So even if they did find it, the Galactic Alliance would still have to decide whether or not to trust it. Any evidence to suggest that it had been responsible for destroying a civilization—inadvertently or not—would be viewed unfavorably.

"Good work, Danni," Luke said. "And that goes for everyone. It may be slow, but we are making progress."

Obtaining another list from Tris, Saba followed Danni back into the maze of books.

"You know, Saba," the young human scientist said, "I think we've got the easiest job here. Have you ever tried to extrapolate star maps from the sort of old sketches we're finding here? It's almost impossible!"

"This one suspectz that'z the idea," Saba responded, sissing deep in her throat.

Danni pulled out a book on a new system near the one Saba was exploring. It was a long way from any of the other known contact regions. If they found something there, that would suggest that Zonama Sekot's search for a hiding place had ranged extensively across the Unknown Regions. If it had followed a random search pattern, then a clear trail might not even exist, which meant that no amount of searching here would help them find it. She had to assume that this wasn't the case—otherwise there was no real point in even trying.

Worlds upon worlds upon worlds . . . Saba ranged among the records of civilizations dead, thriving, or newly born. There were a thousand new species to examine, but time didn't allow her to linger too long on any of them; she could only touch fleetingly upon each, skimming over their aspirations and philosophies like a pebble across a pond.

"Be sure to take a break if you need to," Luke said the next time she returned for another list of books. "You've certainly all earned it."

"That might not be a bad idea, actually," Jacen put in, eyeing the towers of books building on the table. "You and Danni have been searching for six hours. We have plenty of data to pore over while you rest."

Saba was speechless for a moment. *Six* hours? It didn't feel anywhere near that long. It had been so pleasant to be apart from the world, to forget her own troubles for a while. Now that she thought about it, though, she could feel her body's fatigue. Her tail was as limp and lifeless as the trail of Zonama Sekot itself.

She shook her head.

"Time iz passing," she said, picking up the next list. "And hunting iz this one'z specialty."

Then, with the scent of old books and cold trails rich in her nostrils, she resumed her patient, determined prowl of the data.

Jaina kept her head low as she followed Malinza across the flat, tiled rooftop.

"Are you sure you know where you're going?" she asked after a while.

"Positive." The escapee didn't look over her shoulder to reply, nor slacken her pace. "This way."

Malinza sidetracked to the edge of the roof, jumping off without hesitation into space. Jaina hurried to the same spot in time to see Malinza land heavily on another rooftop two floors below. Despite her growing reservations, she followed easily with a similar leap.

Salis D'aar from the air had seemed a lot more sophisticated than the side of it she was seeing now. Its weblike radial layout and high towers had reminded her of many other affluent colony worlds she'd visited. On Bakura, the beginnings of rot had seeped in at basement level, with the high water table and humidity attacking steel-crete and other preventives directly, or encouraging plant life to grow around and into it. The cultural unwillingness to use droids meant that menial repair work often went undone. Since fleeing the penitentiary, she had become quite familiar with the sort of decay the city was capable of. The farther she went out from the center of the city, the more unattractive it became. The paint jobs were rougher, the streets themselves were considerably grubbier, and fewer repulsors meant that things like street-lamps, vehicles, or buildings didn't float. It was almost like an entirely different world than the one she'd initially been introduced to.

Jaina maintained Malinza's pace perfectly, staying half a dozen steps behind at all times. She wasn't trying to catch up; watching the girl's back was her priority right now. This whole escape had been way too easy, and her tingling senses were screaming for her to keep her eyes peeled. Her only consolation was that their route through the city had been far too convoluted for anyone to follow.

They descended a stairwell to the third floor of the building. There they climbed through a window and went hand-over-hand along a dead power line to yet another building. This one appeared as if it had been empty since the Ssi-ruuvi invasion. Its outer shell held empty offices and reception areas; the interior was a giant atrium filled with tropical plants gone wild. The faceted roof far above consisted of dirty transparisteel that seemed as though it had been designed to let the sun in during the day and open at night, although it obviously hadn't done so for a long time. The opening mechanism had long since turned to rust, and now, apart from a narrow slit through which the rain crept in, it remained permanently closed.

Malinza stopped briefly at a balcony on the second floor, quickly checking on Jaina. She was about to continue when Jaina grabbed her by the shoulder and held her back. Malinza faced her, confused, and Jaina put a finger to her lips to indicate that she should remain still. The sense of walking into a trap was stronger here than ever.

The only noises she could hear were dripping sounds from within the dense vegetation at the heart of the building. If Bakuran security forces had managed to follow them, then they were being exceptionally stealthy about it. Still, she had more than just a sneaking suspicion that Bakuran security weren't the only threat awaiting them.

From above her in the trees, Jaina heard a soft *click*. In an instant her lightsaber was out. With her free hand she pushed Malinza behind her, protecting her from any attack.

"She's fast."

Jaina squinted into the trees, but she couldn't make out the owner of the voice.

"Who is she?"

"Look at the lightsaber," replied another. "She's a Jedi."

"One lightsaber against three blaster rifles," returned the first. "She couldn't be *that* fast."

"Just try me and find out," Jaina challenged the voices, tightening her grip on her lightsaber while pinpointing the exact location of the voices in the trees. There were three of them at different heights, two male and one female. A subtle movement of the leaves suggested that perhaps there was a fourth slightly higher, silent for now. The leader, perhaps?

Whatever, she thought. A quick tug of the branches with the Force would soon bring them down.

"It's okay," Malinza said, taking a step forward so she stood between Jaina and those in the trees. "At least I *think* she's okay, anyway."

"What's she doing here, Malinza?"

"I brought her." Malinza faced Jaina. "It's all right. You can put your weapon down. This is Freedom."

Jaina reluctantly relaxed her posture, deactivating the lightsaber and dropping her hands to her sides. She wasn't completely convinced everything was all right, but the last thing she wanted to do was give the rest of Malinza's rebel cell the wrong impression.

The mini forest rustled as leaves parted and three people emerged. The woman was striking, with the sides of her skull shaved and the remainder of her blond hair tied back in a whiplike ponytail. The man nearest to her was dressed in a tatty security uniform about two sizes too big; his brown hair was wild and he looked as though he hadn't shaved in a week. The third was a Rodian, his green skin blending almost perfectly with the foliage.

"This is Jaina Solo," Malinza told them.

Jaina acknowledged them with a curt nod, glancing uneasily toward the tree for a glimpse of the fourth person she suspected to be still hiding there.

"And what is it, exactly, that Jaina Solo wants?" the blond-haired woman asked.

"There's something going on here, on Bakura," Jaina replied for Malinza. "I'd like to find out what it is."

"You mean something other than the usual?" the human male asked. "The exploitation of the weak by the powerful, the rape of natural resources, the corruption of innocents—"

"Easy, Zel," the blond said. "Let's not scare her away before we've heard everything she's got to say."

"Be mindful, Jjorg," the Rodian said in a rasping voice. "A Jedi is likely to put things into a mind as open as yours."

"That only works on the weak-minded," Jaina said. "Besides which, I'm not here to brainwash anyone."

"And we're just supposed to take your word on that?"

"Hey, that's enough," Malinza said firmly. "Where's Vyram, Jjorg? I need to talk to him."

"He's lurking about somewhere," Zel said. "As usual."

"I suspect that's him up in the trees over there," Jaina said, pointing to where she suspected the fourth person to be hiding.

A short laugh escaped from the greenery. "You have good eyes, Jedi," said a voice. "If that is indeed what you're using."

The leaves parted again and the fourth person emerged. He was a rakishly thin, black-haired male who was perhaps a little older than Jaina. His cheekbones were prominent even beneath a patchy beard, and his movements were sure in the treetop.

"I've learned not to rely on my eyes alone," she responded.

The man Malinza had described as the brains of Freedom smiled faintly. "Well, you come here with Malinza," he said. "That's enough for me, at the moment."

Jaina practically felt the spark that passed between the young woman at her side and the black-haired man in the tree, but neither of them openly acknowledged any connection other than professional.

"Take it down, Zel, so we can come aboard," Malinza said. "I'm getting tired of calling out to you from down here." The scruffy-haired human disappeared into the foliage. Jaina was shepherded toward a nearby stairwell, and as she descended, she experienced a momentary giddiness. The strange sensation caused her to stop and grab hold of something to steady herself—and it was then that she realized that the forest she was standing in wasn't what it appeared to be. The entire area was an artificial construct draped with vines and other plants, suspended in midair on a bed of Bakura's ubiquitous repulsors so a casual glance would miss it completely. She wondered if it was an existing structure that Freedom had found and occupied, or one they had slowly built up so as not to attract attention. From this distance, there was no real way of telling.

By the time she and Malinza reached the ground floor, the base of the structure was at arm's length above their heads. It wasn't a particularly elegant arrangement, resembling nothing more than several large, rectangular freight containers joined and surrounded by numerous layers of scaffold tubing and heavy cables, with pots and lattices for the plants covering it, but it did make for an effective disguise. Jaina glimpsed dark spaces within, and ladders leading higher up still.

Malinza reached up to grab one of the horizontal bars hanging over them and hauled herself into the dense canopy. Clipping her lightsaber onto her belt, Jaina did the same. With a groan, the structure ascended back to its original position, leaving the floor some distance below.

Jjorg and Salkeli, the Rodian, were at the entrance to the lowest container and helped Malinza inside. No such assistance was offered to Jaina; she had to manage by herself—which she did without difficulty. Vyram was waiting inside the container, seated in a corner on a packing crate.

"Welcome to the Stack," he said to Jaina with a sweep of his arm to take in his surroundings. "It's not much, but it's all we have, I'm afraid."

"Where are the others?" Malinza asked him.

"Scattered about," he replied. "Or out on patrol." His dark eyes glistened in a faint electrical light. "Things have been . . . difficult."

"Your arrest really had us worried," Salkeli said.

"Not me, though," Zel said, dropping into the container through a hole in the roof. "I'm cool."

"Yeah," Jjorg scoffed. "About as cool as a red dwarf."

Malinza ignored both of them. "I'm sure the others will come back when word spreads that I'm out."

"And I presume this one had something to do with your escape," Salkeli said.

"Jaina? Actually, I'd assumed it was you, Vyram."

The black-haired man shook his head. "I tried, but the defenses were way too tight. I was going to have another go at it tomorrow, when everyone's attention was on the consecration."

Malinza frowned. "If it wasn't you, then who was it?"

"One of the other groups, perhaps," Vyram said. He shrugged. "Or someone on the inside. A sympathetic guard, maybe."

"Or someone sympathetic higher up, perhaps," Jaina mused.

"How do you mean?" Malinza asked.

"Cundertol didn't believe you were guilty," Jaina answered. "So if you were framed and there was nothing official he could do about it, maybe he decided to at least try to make escape easier for you."

"The *Prime Minister*?" Zel looked more unnerved than he was before. He used a short laugh to hide it. "No way! That would just be *too* bizarre."

"It's not important right now," Vyram said. "I'm just glad that we have you back."

Again Jaina sensed a surge of something more than just respect between Vyram and the young leader of Freedom. "She's not out of the woods yet," she said. "Remember, Malinza is still a fugitive—regardless of who helped her. She'll have to stay hidden until we can find out who really kidnapped Cundertol."

"I've been digging around," Vyram said, "but none of the data I've come across has revealed any clues."

"Would it be possible for me to see that data?" Jaina asked.

The young man glanced uncertainly at Malinza, who nodded. "Come on, then," he said, standing. "I hope you're not afraid of heights, though. My workshop's at the very top of the Stack."

"I'm sure I can handle myself."

With a crooked smile, Vyram hauled himself up through the hole in the container, and Jaina and the others followed. From there it was up ladders and through other boxy room-spaces for another fifteen meters to the very apex of the interior jungle, where Vyram's workspace balanced on top of the rebel heap. Jaina had no doubts that the Stack was structurally sound, otherwise Freedom wouldn't have used it as a base in the first place, but her instincts were telling her otherwise. Any sudden movements made the upper reaches sway unnervingly.

"Pull up a seat," he said, indicating a pile of empty crates in one corner. His own seat looked a lot more comfortable, consisting of a floating orthopedically designed chair positioned in front of a complex array of computer screens and keyboards, many of them also levitated by repulsors. Jaina pulled up a crate, closely followed by Malinza, Zel, and Jjorg. The green-skinned Salkeli remained standing.

Vyram brought the system to life. "I know it's not much, but . . ."

"Given your circumstances," Jaina said, "I'm quite impressed." She noted insect fibers in the corner of the crate, and what appeared to be a bird's nest under a desk. "You're actually patched into the planetary network from here?"

"Not permanently. We've a holocomm up on the roof, but we only use it when we need direct access. It's less risky to get a link-up, take what we want, then trawl through it afterward to see if we can find something interesting. That's what the system's doing at the moment. Comm scanners flag anything that looks vaguely suspicious for me to check out later. If I need to, I go back in to find more."

That made sense, Jaina thought. Illegal nodes on any network were difficult to trace, even if suspicions were aroused, but it wasn't impossible. Accessing the planetary network irregularly would certainly make it more difficult for anyone to pin down Freedom.

"What have you found so far?" she asked. "Malinza told me that you've uncovered evidence of corruption at a Senatorial level. You'd be naive to think that this is anything remarkable. Every government I've ever seen suffers from that to some degree or another—including my own."

Vyram nodded. "That's why we oppose the government we have. There has to be a strong opposition to keep the Senate and Prime Minister honest. They might try to shut us down, but we need to be here for the Bakuran people. We're the planet's conscience."

"You keep things in Balance," Jaina said.

Malinza smiled. "Exactly."

"But how do you finance yourselves?" she asked again. "I can't imagine any of this setup would have been cheap."

"You'd be surprised." Vyram's smile was full of pride. "The equipment is actually secondhand or on loan, and the Stack was here already. We just adapted what we found to our needs. It's a better strategy than becoming indebted to people, don't you think?"

"Our allies today could be our enemies tomorrow," Malinza agreed. "You see, we're not naive, Jaina. The only way to be truly objective is to stay independent."

"I admire your efforts," Jaina said, speaking with absolute honesty. She might not have agreed with Freedom's goals or methods, but the fact that its members had managed to stay out of serious trouble for so long was in itself a remarkable feat. "But something has changed. The obvious question is: what?"

"The only thing we can think of is this." Vyram's hands flickered across the keyboards as he accessed encrypted memory. "We uncovered a secret leak of government funds through several intermediaries. The amounts were all different and the payments weren't regular, but our software was sophisticated enough to spot and flag them."

"Where did the money leak to?"

Vyram shook his head. "There's no information about that at this end; whoever set up the leak was careful in that respect. Barely had we begun to dig when the communications blackout came down on us."

Jaina had heard about the infamous cluster over the

years, but her own knowledge was scant. Aunt Mara had entertained a younger Jaina with stories of adventures in the cluster with Talon Karrde—tales of pirates and outlaws and renegades. If only a small percentage of the stories she'd heard were true, then she had no doubt that there were probably many places within the cluster that would be more than happy to take credits from Bakura— whether it was stolen government money or not.

"So you think this led to Malinza being arrested?" she asked.

"What else could it be?" Vyram replied. "Nothing else we've found is as big as this. I mean, we're talking millions of credits here. It has to be someone in government behind it, because no one else would have the codes needed to access those funds and set up the system of automatic payments from within. If word got out, the scandal would be huge."

"We're guessing we tripped something when we sliced the data," Malinza said. "There would be safeguards against detection. The person behind this must have realized that we noticed the leaky funds. They acted immediately, before we put together a strong enough case to go public. At the moment, we have no idea who's behind it, or why."

Vyram nodded glumly. "It comes down to our word against the government—and following Malinza's arrest, our word isn't looking so good anymore."

"So you need a suspect," Jaina said, thinking quickly. "Someone high up in the government. High enough to set the payments in place and to order the fake arrest."

"Such as?"

"What about Blaine Harris?" she suggested. "He's the one who told us about Malinza's arrest. And he's certainly in the right spot to do everything else."

Malinza and Vyram exchanged a look that Jaina couldn't interpret. Then Malinza shrugged. "It's possible."

"I can have a closer look at his records," Vyram said, hands moving again across his equipment. "Let me patch into the network and I'll see if we can find something on him."

This took Jaina back a little. "You've sliced into the Deputy Prime Minister's private files?"

Vyram smiled fleetingly up at her. "Give me a minute and I will have."

Jaina looked on as Vyram closed the documents he had opened for her and set new programs running. His fingers were quick and confident as he prepared the Stack's system for connection to the Bakura's planetary network. Jaina wasn't the only one admiring his skill, either. Malinza's face was practically glowing with admiration as he worked. This quickly turned to concern, however, when a series of warning bleeps issued from the board before them.

Vyram frowned.

"Problem?" Jaina asked.

"I can't establish a link." He tried something else, but received the same warning bleeps in response. "There seems to be some sort of interference."

"Jamming?"

"I don't think so. More likely it's a nearby signal swamping the microwave feed from the satellite. Let me see if I can tap into it." Data flashed across the screens as he switched rapidly from one program to another. "Here, listen."

A regular bleeping began to pulse from the network's speakers.

"I know that sound," Zel said from behind them. "That's a homing beacon!"

The dynamic inside the Stack instantly changed, with everyone suddenly rising to their feet and facing Jaina.

"So that's why my escape was so easy," Malinza said, advancing a pace.

"Wait a minute!" Jaina protested, but was quickly shouted down by Salkeli.

"You led them right to us!"

"She's a spy!" Jjorg said, advancing on Jaina. "I say we kill her!"

"Hold on," Vyram said, fiddling with the array of computers and adjusting a directional antenna. "She isn't the source of the transmission."

"What?" Jjorg stopped in her tracks and turned to look at Vyram. "Then where's it coming from?"

Vyram pointed at Malinza.

"Me?" The rebel leader's face went pale.

Vyram checked the computers. "I'm afraid so, Malinza. The signal is strongest where you're standing."

The others were staring at their leader with stunned expressions, unsure how to react. Even Vyram seemed frozen by indecision.

"Can we narrow down the location of the beacon?" Jaina asked. "Maybe we can remove it before they home in."

Vyram adjusted the antenna and passed it over Malinza's body. The program's bleeping went up in pitch as it passed her midriff. She lifted her prison tunic to expose the waistline of her pants. There, embedded between two lines of stitching, was a tiny bump in the fabric.

"They've had a bead on you the whole time." Zel's eyes darted around him, staring wildly at the walls of the container—almost as if through them he could see security guards converging on the Stack. "They could be here right now!"

"Get a grip," Jjorg said in a manner that suggested his panic offended her. "We have perimeter alarms, don't we? They couldn't get anywhere near the place without us knowing."

"Why now?" Salkeli asked.

Jjorg turned to him. "What do you mean?"

"They could've planted something on Mali like this months ago," he said. "So why now?"

"Because she's an escapee now," Vyram said. "And we're aiding and abetting her. They're clear-cut criminal charges, not something as gray as slicing."

Malinza stood. "They're only clear-cut if my original charge isn't a fake," she said. "Which it is."

"Either way," Jaina said, "we're going to have to get out of here."

"Running will only make us look guilty," the Rodian said.

"I agree with the Jedi," Zel said. "Staying here will get us caught."

A fierce buzzing from the computer system suddenly filled the room. All eyes turned to Vyram at the computer console for an explanation.

His expression was grim. "That's the perimeter alarm."

"I knew it!" Zel shouted, nervously pacing the confined space. "I just knew it!"

"Shut it, Zel!" Malinza snapped. Then, more calmly, she turned to Vyram and asked, "Which one is it?"

"North-Fourteen and South-Seven. They're coming in from both sides."

"Air?"

"Not as yet."

"Good." Malinza turned to the others. She no longer looked the frightened teenager; now she appeared every bit the leader of a covert group under threat. "I'm open to any suggestions at this time."

"Why not let the Jedi fight for us?" Zel said, his expression just a little too eager and manic for Jaina's liking. "She could easily take on—"

"No!" Malinza said sharply. Zel fell instantly silent. "There'll be no fighting. You know that I will never approve of violence."

"We might not have a choice, Malinza," Jjorg said.

"No, there is an alternative," Jaina said. "You could remove the bug and give it to me. I could take it elsewhere, to throw them off your scent."

"Isn't it a bit late for that?" Jjorg said. "They're right outside!"

Jaina resisted the urge to snap back. Although Vyram had proved that she was not responsible for having led the enemy to the Stack, she still felt as though everyone was blaming her for the situation they were in.

"They're not here yet, though," Vyram said, looking thoughtful.

"Yeah, but they're not stupid, either," Jjorg said. "They'll know when they're being duped."

"Not if we present them with many variables at once. We've had a distraction in place for some time, just in case a day should come when they'd find us." He took a deep breath and looked at Malinza. "I'd say that day has arrived, wouldn't you?"

Malinza nodded, then hastily tore the bug from her waistband and handed it to Jaina.

"They're getting closer," the young leader said, glancing at the screens as another siren went off. "I'd hurry, if I were you."

"I'll go with you," Salkeli said. "I know the streets better than you do."

Jaina hesitated briefly, then relented with a nod. She couldn't deny that what the Rodian said made sense. "Okay," she said. Then, to Malinza, she asked, "Will you at least tell me where you're going?"

"I think it would be best if you didn't know." The girl extended a hand; Jaina took it and shook. "We'll meet again, though, I'm sure."

Jaina just nodded. There wasn't time for long farewells.

"After you," she said to Salkeli, and the Rodian dropped feet first out of the container.

* * *

The work in the library was a painstaking process, and after so many hours poring over books, Saba was beginning to feel fatigue pressing at the stiff muscles beneath her itchy scales. Thankfully, though, there were enough allusions to a wandering planet in the innumerable cultures to keep everyone optimistic. After Danni had found the first reference, Saba had quickly discovered two more, and shortly after that Jacen had found yet another. Since then, as the trail grew warm, appearances came at a regular rate. When what they thought was Zonama Sekot had passed near a relatively civilized world, they were able to pin down its appearance with precise dates; otherwise they were able to guess, based on more or less inaccurate records and physical evidence. Luckily, Saba thought, they weren't chasing an event that had happened centuries ago. In many cases, witnesses were still alive to relate to the Chiss contact teams their firsthand experience of the "Coming of the New Star," or the "Dawning of the Death Sun," or whatever else it happened to be called. From these recollections, along with more recent surveys of every system in the Chiss's domain, they gradually began to reconstruct the planet's movements.

Zonama Sekot had first appeared on the Imperial fringes of the Unknown Regions, visiting three systems within a couple of years. Then it had jumped clear across to the outer edge of the galaxy, where habitable systems were fewer and far between. There it had encountered a species that, before its enslavement by the Yuuzhan Vong early in their invasion, would relate to the Chiss visitors the coming of a world that hung in their sky for a month, burning and smoking. This certainly didn't match the description of the lush and peaceful world given by Vergere, but it did match predictions of the sort of stresses the crust of a planet might experience by jumping in and out of gravity wells through hyperspace. No one had ever heard of such a feat before, so there was no experimental data on record, but the most basic planetary science suggested that Zonama Sekot would not have been unscathed by its precipitous jumps across the galaxy.

Following this, it had retreated inward, toward the Core of the galaxy. There it encountered several species in quick succession before finally settling down in one particular system for almost a year. The new light in the sky had inspired a competitive surge from the normally content denizens of that system's habitable world, with the two main countries entering into a kind of "space race" to see who could be the first to land a probe on the mysterious visitor. However, well before the vying probes made orbit around the planet, it vanished once more.

Again, images taken before it disappeared showed a world completely covered by smoke and ash, simmering in its own heat. Saba felt a pang of pity for the fleeing world as she once again contrasted these images with that of Vergere's own testimony, reported by Jacen, of a world rich with life, in constant harmony with the Force.

Oddly, though, later reports from farther around the galactic rim spoke of a world that was green again— so either Zonama Sekot had managed to heal itself, or it was getting the hang of making hyperspace jumps without causing itself any further grievous damage. It came and went without warning, flitting shyly from star to star in search of . . . *what?* Saba wondered, but she couldn't begin to imagine. Perhaps, she thought, somewhere along the way it had lost the only company it had ever known—the Ferroan colonists who had for generations lived on its surface—and was now seeking replacements . . .

Then again, she was also aware that as one of the few

remaining members of her own species, still mourning the loss of her home planet, she might be externalizing her own problems and transposing them onto Zonama Sekot. She couldn't presume to know what went on in the mind of such an incomprehensible being that—

A sudden high-pitched squeal startled Saba, causing her to jump and almost drop the book she was returning to the shelf. She turned to see a tall woman in her middle years dressed in a green jumpsuit beneath black robes standing at the end of the aisle, both hands covering her mouth. She was clearly surprised to have stumbled upon the huge Barabel.

Behind her stood a blond human girl who looked to be in her early teens; she was dressed in a black uniform that looked like a miniature version of the CEDF dress code. The girl looked disdainfully at the older woman, as though thoroughly mortified by her exclamation.

"I-I—" the woman stammered, lowering her hands. A nervous smile failed to hide her obvious embarrassment. "I'm sorry; you startled me."

"There iz no need to apologize," Saba said. "This one was startled also. We thought we were alone in the library."

"You are. I mean, you were." The woman still seemed a little unsure of Saba.

"What my mother means is that we just arrived," the girl said. "We were looking for my father, Soontir Fel."

There was something in the way the girl glanced to the ground as she said this that suggested she wasn't telling the truth. Nevertheless, understanding dawned for Saba at the mention of the Baron's name. "Then you must be Syal Antillez?"

The woman smiled more easily this time, dissolving some of her awkwardness—although not all. "Yes. And this is my daughter, Wyn."

Saba executed a short, respectful bow. The wife of Soontir Fel, mother of Jagged Fel, and sister of Wedge Antilles was an acquaintance she was pleased to make. "This one iz Saba Sebatyne."

"What're you looking for?" Wyn asked, craning to look at the spine of the book Saba had just replaced.

Saba hesitated, unsure how much she should reveal. "This one waz tracing the history of a speciez called the Hemes Arbora."

The girl shrugged. "I've never heard of them."

Saba stretched up to pull the book back down and flipped it open to one of the strange, two-dimensional maps the archive preferred. She tapped it with a claw.

"They originally came from here, Carrivar, and migrated to Osseriton here, via Umaren'k. This one detected their influence on the Umaren'k'sa culture."

"What does that mean?"

"Wyn," her mother cautioned.

Syal Antilles was waiting some distance away—a "safe" distance, Saba observed. Despite her years living with Baron Fel among the Chiss, she was probably still wary of nonhuman aliens—as so many Imperials seemed to be. To Saba, she said: "I must apologize for my daughter's prying. I'm sure you have enough to do without her bothering you with questions."

"This one iz not bothered by your daughter," Saba assured. Then, blinking at the girl, she turned to answer her previous question. "Our search iz for a particular planet. Apart from itz one habitable world, Osseriton iz an empty system. The Hemes Arbora would have noticed a new world."

Wyn laughed lightly. "You have a strange way of saying things."

"Wyn!"

The girl, easily half a meter shorter than Saba, looked up at the Barabel and rolled her eyes, all the while keeping her back to her mother.

Saba smiled, saying to Syal Antilles: "It iz all right. This one iz not offended by her words."

Wyn returned the smile at this, then turned her attention to the maps, her eyes almost shining in wonder. "You must lead such an amazing life. Traveling to all those place, having all kinds of adventures!"

Saba nodded, supposing that from a child's point of view that must seem true. Jedi Knights carried with them an aura of mystique wherever they went. However, it was unlikely that Saba's current work in the library was even remotely connected to the adventures that Wyn was obviously imagining . . .

"So it's true," Syal muttered as she took a step forward. There was a look of suspicion on her face. "You're really expecting us to believe that you're looking for Zonama Sekot."

Saba didn't bother denying it. "This iz our quarry, yes."

"But Zonama Sekot is nothing more than a legend, a *myth*." Syal shook her head, eyes narrowing as her suspicion came to the fore. "What is it you're really after?"

"This one does not know what you mean by—"

"I mean that I find it hard to believe that you came all this way to chase shadows!"

Saba frowned, her eyebrow ridges contracting thickly on her brow. She didn't understand why the woman's temperament had suddenly changed, or indeed what she was trying to get at. "Why else would Master Skywalker bring uz here?"

"The CEDF Library, of course. It gives you access to everything we have on all the people and places known to the Chiss!"

"But why should we want to know thiz?"

"Because you're looking for allies," she said. "We've resisted the Yuuzhan Vong better than you have. You need us far more than we need you."

"You think we're looking for a way to convince you to join the Galactic Federation of Free Alliances?"

"Or maybe coerce us," Syal returned bluntly.

"Mom," Wyn said. There was a hint of embarrassment and reproach in her tone. Then she faced Saba with a look of apology. "She doesn't mean what she says. She's just worried you're going to try to take Dad away from her, like you took Jag."

The woman's eyes flashed anger at her daughter, and her voice carried denial. "Wyn!"

"Oh, come on, Mom," the girl said, wheeling around to face her mother. "You've been worried about Dad ever since Jag left!"

"That's not true," Syal said firmly, but there was something in her eyes that suggested that what her daughter said *was* true. After a moment, she sighed and shook her head slowly. "It hasn't been since Jag left, Wyn; it's been since Coruscant fell."

Saba was beginning to feel out of her depth. She wished that Master Skywalker was here to face these accusations instead of her; he was far more adept at handling such matters.

"Before Coruscant, I was actually trying to talk Soontir into joining the fight against the Yuuzhan Vong." All acrimony had gone from her tone, for which Saba was grateful. She seemed to speak now as a means of explaining her prior hostility toward Saba's presence. "I wanted him to join the New Republic like Jag did, either with the rest of the Chiss or without them. But he didn't want to fight; he said that the New Republic could handle the Yuuzhan Vong, just as we were handling it on our side of the galaxy. Then you lost the capital and—" She hesitated briefly, as if collecting her thoughts. "I knew two things, then: that he would change his mind; and that you were going to lose." Her eyes flitted between Wyn and Saba as she said, "I won't let you take him down with you. I won't."

"Do you think he will be safe here if the Chiss don't join uz in the war?"

The expression on Syal's face told Saba everything she needed to know. The woman knew that the Chiss had no hope if the rest of the galaxy fell to the Yuuzhan Vong; within years, the alien invaders would be replenished and able to overwhelm even the strongest Chiss defense.

"Don't make the mistake of underestimating the Yuuzhan Vong," Danni suddenly put in from the other end of the aisle. All eyes turned to her. Saba hadn't heard the scientist arrive, and wasn't sure how long she'd been listening in. Her expression was heavy with tiredness, but her words were uttered with the clarity of personal experience. "Too many of us have already paid a terrible price for doing just that. The New Republic, the Empire, the Hutts, the Ithorians, the Rodians—the list keeps getting longer with every year this war continues. You obviously know what's been going on; you must realize how serious a threat these invaders are. Do you really think that hiding out here will save you forever? They may decide to wipe you out on a whim, just like they tried to do with the Imperial Remnant."

"Your position iz untenable," Saba added. "Denying it will not make it otherwise."

"I don't want to lose him," Antilles whispered, her expression one of someone caught between two conflicting emotions. "I can't take it anymore. I can't . . ."

"Mom . . ." The daughter looked frightened.

"Do not be afraid," Saba said, putting as much compassion as she could into her rough, reptilian voice. "We are not your enemies; we understand your fearz." Wyn looked up at her with wide, staring eyes. "But there iz no easy solution to this war. Turning your back on it won't make it go away. We need long-term solutions; we need to work together. Of that, this one iz absolutely certain, Syal Antilles."

Syal nodded, then, although her uncertainty clearly remained.

"You're Syal Antilles?" Danni asked, coming closer.

"Yes," the woman replied. "Why?"

"Baron Fel just arrived," she said. "But he didn't mention that he was expecting you."

"He wasn't," she said, confirming Saba's earlier suspicion of Wyn's lie. "We just heard that someone had come from home, and we wanted to see them." Gone was the frightened mother and wife; in her place stood a composed and confident woman beaming a pleasant smile to a stranger who might not have heard every doubt she'd just expressed. "And now that we have seen you, perhaps we should be moving along." Her eyes met Saba's briefly, exchanging all manner of emotion—the most prominent of which was gratitude. "Thank you for your words, Saba. And please accept my apology for mine."

"There iz no need," Saba said, effecting a slight bow.

Syal Antilles returned the gesture. "Come along, Wyn."

"I think I might stay and help them, if that's all right?" The girl directed this to Saba and Danni, both of whom nodded.

"I don't think that's a good idea, Wyn," her mother said. "They don't need you getting in their way while they're trying to work."

"No, it's fine," Danni said. "Actually, we could use the help."

"Are you sure?" Syal asked. There still seemed to be a residue of embarrassment for her earlier outburst.

But Saba knew that an injection of youthful enthusiasm from Wyn would be just what they needed. "This one iz certain that Wyn would not be a burden."

Wyn's face immediately lit up. "You won't regret it. I

know these records better than most people—including Tris!"

"That I seriously doubt," her mother said.

Wyn didn't respond; instead she faced Danni and asked: "Is it true that one of the Solo twins is here with the Skywalkers?"

Danni nodded and smiled. "Jacen Solo, yes."

"And will I get to meet him, too?"

"I'm sure you will," Danni said.

"Don't get too far ahead of yourself, Wyn," her mother said. She still seemed hesitant about her daughter staying. "We still have to clear this with your father."

"He'll be fine with it, Mom," Wyn said, fairly bouncing on her toes. Her enthusiasm suggested that not much in the way of excitement had happened in her life for a long, long time.

"This one will mind her while you check, if you wish."

Syal nodded, still with some uncertainty, as Danni led her away.

"Thank you so much for this!" she exclaimed once her mother and Danni had disappeared down another aisle. "This will be fantastic!"

"It will also be hard work," Saba cautioned. "And it iz very important work, too."

"Oh, I understand that," Wyn said, forcing herself to settle down. Then, looking around, she spread her arms as if to encompass the entire library and said: "So where did you want to start?"

Jaina followed as quickly as she could as Salkeli slithered down the pipes and vines to the bottom of the Stack. The entire structure shuddered as it lowered slightly to make their drop to the ground less severe. She looked around to make sure the area was clear. It was. However close the Bakuran guards were, thankfully they hadn't yet breached the ground floor.

Salkeli waved for her to follow. With the bug tucked deep in one of her jumpsuit pockets and her deactivated lightsaber in hand, she did so. Her feet fell silently among the plant debris and rubble that made the abandoned building look more like ruins in a jungle than an abandoned office block. The Rodian led her out of the atrium space and through a series of short corridors. They entered what had once been a public refresher and, after a brief pause to listen for sounds outside, pushed out the window.

"After you, this time," Salkeli said. Jaina slipped through the narrow space and into the darkness outside.

She found herself standing in a long and very narrow alley. She was grateful that there were no guards waiting for them, because there wouldn't have been much room to fight if there had been.

It was still night by the look of the sky. She hadn't yet adjusted to local time, but she suspected that dawn wasn't far off. If Malinza and the other members of Freedom were going to make a clean getaway, they'd have to do it soon.

"What sort of distraction does Vyram have in mind, anyway?" she whispered to the Rodian as he emerged from the window beside her.

"Wait and see," he answered with a wink.

He hurried up the alley, moving carefully but quickly. Jaina followed, alert to the slightest change in the environment around her. A fitful wind blew from ahead of her, throwing up dust and rustling discarded paper and rubbish. She was acutely aware of the fact that the guards didn't have to be supersleuths to find her. All they had to do was follow the signal from the bug in her pocket. Ideally, what she needed was a feral cratsch or a lost droid to which she could attach the bug, after which she could make her own escape. Until then, though, she would just have to keep moving and stay attentive.

Salkeli was within ten meters of the end of the alley when an aircar suddenly swept over them, landing lights and powerful arcs flashing down the narrow gap between the buildings. In a second it was gone. Jaina could hear the whine of its turbines as it circled to come back around and pinpoint them again.

Through the Force, Jaina sensed the blaster come up from behind her before the woman holding it had even had chance to fire. In one smooth motion she wheeled around in midstep and activated her lightsaber, bringing it up between her and the guard at the distant end of the alley at the exact instant the laser bolt fired. There was a bright flash as the bolt discharged into the wall beside her, spraying chips of stone into the air. More bolts followed, but the smoke in the air spoiled the guard's aim, and Jaina was easily able to back away after Salkeli, providing cover.

The Rodian hissed for her to hurry. Sensing no one lying in wait for them, she turned and ran full tilt for the exit from the alley. Salkeli had his blaster out, ready to fire at anyone who got in his way. Jaina, on the other hand, wasn't so committed to attacking people who, despite her current situation, were supposed to be her allies.

Out of the alley, she found herself on a wider, more exposed street. Salkeli was already halfway across it, heading for a smashed window in a building on the far side. Jaina followed without hesitation, deactivating her lightsaber as she went. She dashed across the road and dived headlong through the window just seconds after Salkeli. She rolled as she landed, coming up into a crouch to examine her surroundings. A quick look around told her they were in the remains of an open-plan office, long abandoned, with broken furniture strewn about the floor.

Salkeli was clambering to his feet just as the guards emerged from the alley across the street.

"Keep moving!" he urged, dashing from the room with his head low.

He took her deep into the building, then down into one of its sub-basements. Kicking open a stuck door, he revealed a long tunnel that, judging by its length, stretched to several other buildings along the street. They hurried along it, passing entrances to other basement levels.

"I trust you have a plan?" Jaina said.

"More or less," he called back to her. "We'll go back up in a second, to throw them off track. Once we're sure Malinza and the rest are safely away, I'll take any suggestions you have."

Footfalls came from the corridor behind them. Jaina spun around, igniting her lightsaber and deflecting a handful of blaster bolts that had been aimed at their fleeing backs. Salkeli took the next stairwell on their right; Jaina followed.

He didn't stop at the ground floor, but instead continued on to the top of the building. When they emerged, the aircar was waiting for them, hovering above the roof like the remotes she'd once trained with—only much larger, and much deadlier. Two guards hung over its sides, blaster rifles pointing down at Salkeli and Jaina. Dodging and deflecting laser bolts, the two of them took cover behind a ventilation shaft. Jaina used the Force to rock the aircar while the Rodian returned fire. That evened the score, but they were still in a no-win situation because they had nowhere to run.

She was about to point this out when a loud explosion from nearby brought a halt to the firing from the aircar. The attention of the guards in the vehicle suddenly turned to a huge ball of burning gas rising up from a nearby building—the same building, Jaina noted, that had contained the Stack. She was so surprised by the turn of events that she barely noticed the arrival of other guards from the stairwell. Thankfully, though, they were also attracted to the spectacle, staring in amazement at what was emerging from the newly formed hole where the building's skylight had once been.

The Stack itself—its ragtag jumble of containers loosely tied together with scaffolding and hidden by vines—rose gracefully into the predawn sky, glinting shards of shattered transparisteel falling like silver rain onto the building below. Propelled by repulsors, the entire structure was as buoyant as a hot-air balloon, and moved in much the same way. As soon as it had cleared the top of the building, it began to drift with the prevailing wind, trailing a spreading cloud of smoke and debris beneath it.

The aircar sped away to intercept the floating structure, leaving the guards on the rooftop staring at the spectacle.

"Now's the time for suggestions," he hissed. "Before those guards over there remember what they're here for. Right now they stand between us and our only means of escape."

"There is one other," Jaina said, staring at the edge of the roof a dozen or so meters away.

Salkeli laughed, following her gaze. "Don't tell me that Jedi can fly, too?"

She shook her head and smiled at him. "No, but we can jump. Come on!"

With that, she bolted for the edge of the rooftop, not stopping to check that the Rodian was following. Then, trusting in her instincts and the Force, she threw herself into the air.

Instead of landing on another rooftop, however, she found herself plunging into a deep and wide aqueduct half filled with fast-moving water. The current instantly grabbed and held her down. Her limbs flailed as she struggled to orient herself and come up for air. Lungs burning, she finally broke the surface, desperately trying to suck in some oxygen while at the same time coughing up some of the water she'd inhaled. Then, from somewhere nearby, above the sound of rushing current, she heard the wheezing laughter of the Rodian.

"Over here!" he called as the current swept them along into a high-ceilinged tunnel. He was paddling strongly a meter or so away from her.

She spat out some more water and swam to his side. "I presume the Stack was the distraction you mentioned. It was empty, right?"

"Right." His voice echoed in the tunnel. "While the guards chasing us split up to check, the others would have slipped out through the basement."

"But all that equipment," she said. A loss like that for a small group such as Freedom had to hurt. "All that data!"

"Data and equipment are replaceable; lives are not." An open shaft passed by overhead, briefly affording them some light. It reflected off Salkeli's multifaceted eyes. "Okay, we're there," he said. "Swim for the edge."

"You actually *know* where we are?" She was genuinely surprised.

"A Rodian always has an escape plan," he said, kicking vigorously for the edge of the tunnel. "I thought everyone knew that."

"But it was my idea to jump!"

The Rodian snorted, a nasal bleat that sounded unusually loud in the tunnel. "I had already thought of it; I just wanted to check out your mettle."

He reached the wall and found purchase on its slimy surface. Jaina wasn't far behind. Her fingers dug into the gaps between bricks where ancient mortar had eroded away.

"Up there," Salkeli said. "See?"

Jaina looked up and to her right, and saw an open access cover. Descending from it was a rusting metal ladder. She followed Salkeli's lead and began to edge her way toward it. The current was stronger here than it had been before, and she had to fight not to be swept away. From farther down the tunnel she could hear a faint rumbling sound, like that of a distant roaring. She guessed that either the tunnel continued to narrow the farther it went, or it ended in an underground waterfall of some kind. Either way, she didn't particularly want to find out.

"I'll help you up," Salkeli said, coming up beside her when she reached the base of the ladder.

"That's all right." She nudged him upward with the Force and enjoyed the look of surprise on his green face. "I have something I have to do first."

He ascended the ladder while she reached into her pocket and removed the bug, releasing it into the current. She was happy to let the security guards search through the drainage system to find it. Then she lifted herself out of the water, pulling herself up and out into the relatively fresh air.

The sun was rising over the horizon when she scrambled through the access hatch. Looking around, she could tell they had come out in a completely different section of the city than they'd just been in. The streets were wider, the buildings lower and better maintained. It looked more like a warehousing suburb than the abandoned business complex they'd left behind.

"We made it," she said, laughing in relief.

"You ditched the bug?"

Jaina nodded, already thinking about what to do next.

"I think you've helped Freedom enough for one day," Salkeli said. "Would you like a lift back into town?"

"As long as it doesn't involve swimming again."

He grinned, motioning for her to accompany him to the nearest building—a low, long container hold. There was a metal roller door securing the premises. Salkeli tapped a code into the lock and it obligingly slid up, revealing a dusty but serviceable two-seater speeder.

"You're not going to tell me that's yours, are you?" she said.

The Rodian's multifaceted eyes twinkled. "Would you believe me if I did?"

"Well, you know what they say," Jaina said lightly. "A Rodian always has an escape plan."

He smiled at this, gesturing with his long, green fingers for her to climb aboard while he moved around the back to adjust the airfoil. In the second it took for him to do this, her senses told her that something had gone terribly awry—something she hadn't anticipated. But it was too late. She was climbing into the speeder when a searing pain caught her in the back.

She turned as she fell, catching a fleeting glimpse of Salkeli as he lowered his blaster.

"Always," she heard him say as darkness claimed her.

She ran as fast as she could along the mostly empty corridors, not knowing where she was or where she was going. For all she knew—or cared—she might have been running in circles. It didn't matter. The only thing that mattered was that she keep running in the hope that it might distract her from the pain in her mind.

Try as she might, though, she couldn't outrun the memories. Her life seemed to be made up of one long tragedy, from her parents' deaths on Tatooine to her latest breakdown on Bakura. And, of course, Anakin . . .

Remember—together, you are stronger than the sum of your parts. Master Ikrit's last words to her, communicated via the Force, had helped her accept her feelings for Anakin. But it wasn't about *strength*; it was about being *together*. She loved Anakin, and always had. As a child, she had loved him as a friend; then, as they grew older, she had been learning to love him as a woman. But now, because of the Yuuzhan Vong, because of the voxyn and Myrkr, that love would never be realized.

Her body shook with sobs as she doubled up, clutching her stomach. Anakin's absence was like a yawning gulf in her life, a hole that *nothing* could fill. The future they should have had together would never happen, and nothing could ever take its place. Not even becoming a full Jedi Knight was any comfort. The Force without him in it was an empty thing.

It's not supposed to be like this! she wanted to shout at the universe. *Change it back! Make it right. Make it better. Make the pain go away!*

She fell to the floor, rolling tightly into a fetal position, desperately wanting to push back the pain. Anakin had sacrificed himself for the greater good, and the thought of that only enhanced the love she felt for him. She wanted to go back and kiss him that last time, instead of holding off as she'd done. She wanted to go back and fight at his side, to help him overcome the Yuuzhan Vong warriors who had ultimately brought him down. She wanted to die with him, because life without him was so incomprehensible.

Memories . . .

"You aren't immortal," Corran Horn had told them on an asteroid near Yag'Dhul, *"and you aren't invincible."*

"Everybody gets a nasty surprise someday," Anakin had replied. *"I'd rather get it standing up than lying down."*

Memories . . .

"I've thought about the dark side for most of my life. My mother named me after the man who became Darth Vader. The Emperor touched me through her womb. Every night I had nightmares that ended with me in my grandfather's armor. With all due respect, I think I've probably thought a lot more about the dark side than anyone I know . . ."

Memories . . .

"You were scarred up and tattooed like Tsavong Lah,"

Anakin said. "You were Jedi, but dark. I could feel the darkness radiating from you."

"You don't still think that could happen to me?" she responded, horrified by the vision. "How could I? You saved me from them, stopped me before they finished." His doubt, his fear that she might join the other side and destroy the Jedi, had cut her more deeply than any physical wound she had ever sustained. "Anakin, I'll never join the Yuuzhan Vong . . ."

Memories . . .

"Might be simpler if we don't make it."

After their first kiss, when there was no going back to the way they'd been before.

"Yeah. Are you sorry?"

"No. No, not even a little bit."

"So let's survive so we get a chance to figure this out, okay?"

Sobs tore through her like knives. She was so lonely; she was so *alone*. Anakin's family could have been hers, but now instead they were frightened of her. They were suspicious of her and tried to push her away. *Everyone* was pushing her away. Everyone except—

"Tahiri?"

The voice came from outside her head, beyond her memories. The use of her name was so unexpected that she was on her feet in an instant, her lightsaber crackling, rising defensively before she'd even seen who had said it. Then, when she did look, she couldn't see him properly because of the film of tears over her eyes.

"No, wait!" Whoever it was, he backed nervously away, arms outstretched in a desperate request for her to lower her weapon.

"You come anywhere near me," she hissed, "and so help me I'll—"

"I won't, I promise." She didn't recognize the voice. "I

just heard that you were lost. That's all. I came to help you."

"Help me?" she repeated suspiciously, the lightsaber unsteady in her hands. "Why should you help me? You don't even know me!"

"Sure I do," he said. "You're the Jedi-who-was-shaped. You're—"

She felt the blood drain from her face. "Don't ever call me that!"

He backed away another step as the tip of her light-saber stabbed toward him. "I'm sorry!" he said. "I didn't realize you found it offensive."

"Well, I do," she said, pouring all of her anger into the words. "It reminds me of things I'd sooner forget."

"I can understand that. You are like us in many respects."

Anger flared again. He was trying to manipulate her. "Who *are* you?"

"I'm a friend. We met back at the spaceport, remember?"

"The Ryn?" She blinked back the moisture covering her eyes and looked more closely at the being before her. He was gray-skinned and had a beak for a nose. A pre-hensile tail lashed the air behind him. There was a smell about him, too: a smell that was inherent to his species.

"It *is* you," she said with some surprise, sensing his familiarity even though she'd never seen his face before.

He nodded. "The name is Goure," he said, trying to force a smile but clearly finding it difficult with her lightsaber still raised toward him. "Look, could we put that away for now? I think we might attract unwanted attention."

With some embarrassment, Tahiri realized that they were standing in a public access way. At the other end of the corridor, people were starting to gather, staring curiously at the Jedi and the Ryn. She quickly deactivated her lightsaber and reattached it to her belt.

"I'm sorry," she said, appalled by her foolishness. "I'm not thinking straight at the moment."

Goure shrugged good-naturedly. "It's nothing to be ashamed of," he said sotto voce. "Come, follow me and I'll take us to a place where we won't have an audience. But try not to make it seem as though you are following me, okay? I'm a servant; you must order me to lead."

She nodded slowly. "I was lost, and you are taking me home."

"Exactly." He rearranged his body under the simple gray robes he wore so he was hunched forward, as though with age. "This way."

She followed him with head held high and her expression devoid of any of the emotions she'd felt just moments earlier. She pushed through the crowd at the end of the corridor, her cold stare daring anyone to obstruct her. It took all her control of the Force to placate the more curious, and the irony wasn't lost on her that she couldn't apply the same trick to herself. Behind the facade, her mind was still very much in turmoil.

Goure led her through the corridors and malls of Salis D'aar, past floating statues and elegant fountains. Plant life encroached heavily on the city, thriving in the thick air and fertile soils. Tree trunks snaked through carefully arranged holes in the pavement and walls, their vine-covered coils diverting the eye from security checkpoints, public comm stations, and information outlets. In some places, Salis D'aar seemed so heavily overgrown that it looked like the jungle was taking over, but ferrocrete was strong and resisted the tide of root and tendril with stubborn defiance. The city would last awhile yet; it was civilization's strongest bastion in its battle against nature.

"Here," Goure said, waving her ahead into a narrow corridor between two ornamental statues. She did as he told her without hesitation or question; he projected no sense of threat or danger. After looking up and down the corridor behind them, he followed. When inside, he flicked a switch; a small holoprojector flickered to life, covering the entrance with the illusion of solid wall.

"It won't actually keep anyone out," Goure said, walking ahead of her along the corridor, "but it'll at least stop them from stumbling in on us."

"Is security looking for me?" she asked.

"Oh, no. This is nothing to do with you." His tail coiled and uncoiled restlessly. "We just prefer not to leave too many odd connections in our wake, that's all."

The room at the end of the corridor was empty apart from two simple chairs and a low box. Bare stone walls and a single, naked light source leant it a forbidding air, but Tahiri didn't feel threatened by the Ryn at her back. He radiated nothing but surety and reliability.

"Take a seat." He fished around in the box and produced two scuffed metal cups and a bottle of water. Tahiri eased herself into the chair closest to the entrance, thankful to be resting her feet. She felt drained right to the very core of her being, as though she had been running for days.

He offered her a cup of the water, which she gratefully accepted. It felt good and refreshing in her mouth, and she closed her eyes in appreciation as she sipped it.

"What happened to your arms?" Goure indicated the scars showing beneath her thin tunic.

"Nothing," she answered uneasily, folding her arms in a way that hid the self-inflicted wounds from back on Mon Cal. There was nothing she could do to hide the marks on her forehead. "What time is it?" she asked to change the subject.

"A couple of hours before dawn."

That surprised her—although it did explain her exhaustion. She didn't want to ask the next question, but she had to in order to ease her mind. "What have I been doing?"

Goure looked sympathetic. "You haven't hurt anyone, if that's what you're worried about."

"You said you'd heard that I was lost." A useful euphemism, she thought. "How?"

"I have many means of learning what's going on," he said. "I'm a Ryn. We're ignored at best. We work on the lowest rungs of society, doing the jobs no one else wants to do. That allows me to get into places and gives me access to information most people wouldn't even know existed. I listen to gossip, scan the security frequencies, go through the trash—" She inadvertently pulled a face, which made him smile. "Yeah, I know. It's not the most glamorous of jobs at times, but I get results. Anyway, your name came up in a security report. They were watching you carefully, unsure what you were up to. I thought it might be best to get to you before they decided to bring you in." He shrugged. "It wasn't difficult to work out where you were and where you might be headed."

She hated to think what she might have done had the security guards closed in on her at any point during her strange fugue state. The feelings of anger and hurt had been so overwhelming; she may well have used those guards as a means to vent her emotions.

Still, Goure had said that she hadn't hurt anyone. That was something to be grateful for, at least.

"What about Han and Leia?" she asked. "Do they know?"

"They have other things to worry about, I'm afraid." The Ryn's expression turned serious. "A warrant for Jaina's arrest was released shortly after midnight."

"What? *Why?*"

"Security droids caught images of her helping Malinza Thanas escape from where she was being held. She's been charged with aiding and abetting, along with sedition—or she will be, when they find her. She's listed as being armed and dangerous. Guards are to use force if necessary."

The news shocked Tahiri out of concern for herself. Jaina on the run? Her first thought was to help. The tug of the family she'd nearly had was strong, but not as strong as the sudden sense of warning that rushed through her.

I called you Riina.

It came back to her in a rush: Leia's face in the gloom of the bedroom, the silver pendant—

Jaina told me what Jag found.

She reached into the pocket of her robe and felt the pendant, its bumps and edges worn by Yuuzhan Vong claws. The Peace Brigade had left it on Galantos, probably by accident. It had fallen under a bed in the diplomatic wing, where the Brigaders had been staying. Something about the pendant had called to her, triggering her instincts. They told her that something was up; there was more to Galantos than met the eye. Searching, she'd been drawn to the pendant's dusty hiding place and—

She's hiding something—from herself as well as everyone else . . .

Then she had blacked out. When she had woken, the pendant had gone. Jag must have found it and passed it on to Jaina, who had aired her suspicions to her mother. All the while, the pendant had nagged at Tahiri like an unscratchable itch, preoccupying her mind, calling out to her . . .

No. Not *her*. It was calling out to Riina of Domain Kwaad—the monster the Yuuzhan Vong had tried to turn her into!

Somehow, the Riina personality is still inside you.

A deep darkness rose up in her mind, threatening to consume her—just as it had so many times before. She fought it now as she had then, fighting down the persona that kept trying to take her over.

I am not Riina! I am Tahiri Veila! Despite her determination, her mental voice sounded feeble. *I am a* Jedi!

The darkness receded and she sagged back into the chair with a sob. What was she going to do? If the slightest hint of Yuuzhan Vong was going to destabilize her so deeply, how could she possibly hope to be of use in the war against the enemy? And what if Riina took over completely? What then would become of her and the people around her?

"Tahiri?"

Despite the softness of the voice, it cut sharply into her thoughts, startling her. So relieved was she to hear her own name that she suddenly burst into tears.

"Hey, I'm sorry, Tahiri. Are you okay?"

Lost in her thoughts, she had forgotten all about Goure, the Ryn. He was crouched down before her now, his powerful scent filling her nostrils, thrusting deep into the old places of her mind, forcing itself into the spaces buried beneath her thoughts. It seemed to sweep out the cobwebs as it went, working its way through the tangled corridors of her mind like a powerful cleansing wind.

Jaina couldn't be blamed for the position Tahiri was in. Nor could Jag, or Anakin's parents. There was only one person responsible, and that was herself. She had to be the one to prove to everyone that she could be trusted, that she was the one in control and *not* Riina.

"Don't be sorry," she said to the anxious Ryn. She wiped the tears from her face and quashed down the darkness still threatening to rise to the surface. The pendant was in her hand, and she pushed it back into the inner pocket of her robes where she didn't have to look at it. "Just help me rescue my friend."

"That I will," the Ryn said, his tail snapping like a whip. "The first thing we have to do, though, is find out if they've caught her. The warrant only mentioned Jaina, so Han and Leia might be in the clear for now. But I can't be certain. We'll need to be closer to things in order to keep an eye on them."

"I'll do whatever it takes," she said determinedly. "I just want to put things right."

"And the best way to do that is with my help, if you're willing to stick with me awhile longer."

She met his gaze with all the strength she could muster. Part of her wanted to go straight back to Han and Leia, to try to repair the damage, but another part of her was nervous of doing that just yet. Not until she was certain of where she stood. And besides, she told herself, if she could find more about what the Ryn were up to, that would stand her in good stead when she did go back. It was important who was helping them, and why.

Goure nodded as though in approval.

"Very well, Tahiri Veila." He rose to his feet. "The first thing I need you to do is to wait here. You can't go wandering around looking like that."

She looked down at her robe and frowned. "Like what?"

"Like *you*. Even if they weren't already watching you, they certainly wouldn't let you walk freely into where we need to go. The trick to being like us, you see, is to make sure you're not noticed."

"I need a disguise, right?"

He nodded, smiling. "I won't be long, I promise."

"*How* long?" she asked quickly, standing. The emptiness of the room was already crowding in around her. There would be nothing to do while he was gone, no distractions from her thoughts. The idea of being on her own in an unfamiliar city put her even more on edge. What if the security guards came for her? What if Goure didn't come back?

"Try not to be scared, Tahiri. You'll be all right."

She could tell from the hesitant movements of his

hands that he would like to reach out and reassure her physically, but was reluctant to do so. Probably, she figured, because he was worried she might have another panic episode and threaten him with her lightsaber again.

"I-I'm just worried about being alone, that's all." She looked down, embarrassed by the admission. It was a weakness, and did not become the Jedi Knight she was supposed to be. "I feel very lost right now."

"We have a saying," Goure said. " 'In the darkest hole you can always find some light. You just have to open your eyes to see it.' "

"We also have a saying," she responded. " 'The darker the shadow, the brighter the light that casts it.' "

"Very wise," he said, nodding. "But tell me, Tahiri Veila: when you say 'we,' do you mean the Jedi or the Sand People?"

She smiled at the memory of the first time Sliven said those words to her. "The Sand People," she said. "And what about you: Ryn or Bakuran?"

"Ryn." His beak twitched for a moment, then broke into an unusual smile, as though he'd been amused by some profound joke. His hand reached out carefully to touch her shoulder. "I won't be long, Tahiri."

She nodded briefly and then he was gone, hurrying up the short corridor and disappearing through the holographic illusion hanging across the entrance. The city murmured through the stone walls, distantly, impersonally. It didn't care about her—who she was, what she wanted, or whether her friends lived or died. Its coldness was, oddly, a remedy for her dour mood, reminding her that in the larger scheme of things, perhaps, it simply didn't matter who she was.

But it *did* matter. If she gave in to Riina and Anakin's vision became fact, who would stand up against the Yuuzhan Vong then? Life in the galaxy would vanish under a creeping tide of darkness that no dawn could ever hope to dispel.

She shook her head to clear her mind of the thought and sat cross-legged on the stone floor to wait for Goure's return. With a grim determination, she fell into a Jedi rejuvenation trance. It had been a long time since she'd last slept, and she was going to need her resilience. Her body must be strong, she told herself, her senses sharp; her concentration was a crystal spear, cutting through the layers of deception to the truth beneath . . .

A worm of doubt burrowed into the trance, however, as something unsettling occurred to her. No matter where she went, she could never again be the same. There would always be Riina at the back of her mind, trying to come forward. There would always be that question niggling at her thoughts: *Who am I, really?* How could she live a life like that, let alone get through one more day?

I am Tahiri Veila, she told herself again, *Jedi Knight and child of the Sand People. I will prevail!*

Or I'll die trying . . .

The audience was not going well.

"Yu'shaa, your word spreads farther with every day, yet still we are reviled. We are beaten and killed as we have always been. How long until we will be free to be as we were?"

Nom Anor replied: "We will only be free when the un-Shamed accept us as their equals, as we are in the eyes of the gods. Our Message—the philosophy of the *Jeedai*—will persuade them if we spread it far enough. If it doesn't convince them we then will *make* them accept it, and us with it. Only then will we achieve our goal." He paused significantly. "It is a hard road, I know—but it is one that must be walked."

"But if we do Yun-Yuuzhan's work, then his will must

become clear to the enemy, too. Surely they would come to see the truths the *Jeedai* bring?"

"You can show a blind person something a thousand times and he will never see it; you can speak a message to a deaf person until the universe turns cold and she will never hear it. So, too, it is with our enemies. Only those who are open to the truth will accept the truth that the *Jeedai* bring. Moreover, those who do not, those who continue to espouse a perverted philosophy of pain and pointless sacrifice, these are the ones who must in turn be sacrificed. Redemption can only be achieved by those with the capacity to be redeemed."

The questioning acolyte nodded slowly, unsurely, as though Nom Anor's answer only partially satisfied her. Nom Anor studied the Shamed One closely, seeking anything that made her stand out from the rest of the congregation. The usual procession of the disabled and the sick was increasingly diluted by numbers of the hale and the higher-ranked, all dissatisfied with the status quo on the surface. But despite the mass of scars and failed bio-implants that marked this particular member of the congregation as a Shamed One, Nom Anor couldn't help but feel there was something that set her apart from the others. Dressed in unadorned robes, she was slender without being skinny. Her eyes were filled with the furious intelligence of one consumed with doubt. She lacked the bent, cowed frame possessed by so many of the usual penitents.

"But, Master," the acolyte went on, "what if one of the enemy *was* to question the ways he'd been taught? A lifetime of lies is difficult to fight—especially if the truth is hidden from him. The enemy you revile hears only that which he is told, filtered through many ears and mouths along the way. The message is distorted, clouded by those who are indeed your enemy, who will ascribe to you all manner of heresy simply in order to damn you. What of the one who wishes to hear the truth, but cannot obtain it? Is ignorance an excuse in Yun-Yuuzhan's eyes?"

Nom Anor's eyes narrowed behind his ooglith masquer. "Our mission should be to reach *all* Yuuzhan Vong, regardless of caste or rank, in order that they may have the chance to see the truth. We start at lower echelons not only because they are easiest to access, but also because they are the most numerous. We see the greatest need among them."

"The need for freedom is not the same as the need for redemption, though, Master."

"One does not come without the other."

"No, but should you amass every one of the Shamed Ones and all the disaffected, you would still be fighting those at the top who wield overwhelming power over the instruments of state. It would take years to overthrow them—years I don't believe we have. Even as we speak, plans are put into motion to eradicate your movement and trample your dreams into the dust."

The congregation was transfixed, now. Nom Anor, too, was filled with a morbid fascination. This was no ordinary penitent. She spoke too well, had thought the issue through too thoroughly, and she didn't just regurgitate the same vacuous questions that so often spilled from the mouths of those who came to see the Prophet, all looking for the answers that simply didn't exist in the real world. No, this one had seen the problems Nom Anor grappled with, and considered them carefully. And, like Nom Anor, she'd only been able to come up with incomplete solutions—if any at all.

There had been others with minds as keen as this. Kunra and Shoon-mi had taken them aside for training as disciples, taught them the lessons that Nom Anor wanted preached, and then sent them back out into the world to spread the Message further among the masses. There were six such disciples now, and Nom Anor knew he would need many more if he were to reach all of those who hungered for redemption. More like the Shamed One before him today.

But the doubt in those eyes . . .

No, thought Nom Anor again: this was no ordinary penitent.

"We hear rumors of countermeasures," he said, choosing his words with caution. He would have liked to clear the room to end this one's challenging questions, but that would be seen as a sign of doubt. "We have made efforts to ascertain the truth behind them."

"But those efforts have failed."

"Yes."

"They have also been noticed."

Nom Anor fixed his stare upon the acolyte for a few lingering seconds before responding. "Of course. But there is nothing else we can do."

"There are always alternatives, Master. Attacking a stronghold is pointless when it is unassailable. It must be weakened from within."

"Easier said than done," Nom Anor returned. "How are we to achieve this when we cannot enter it?"

How have you turned this around, he wanted to ask, *so that you now have* me *asking the questions?*

"You must wait for the opportunity to come to you," the penitent said. "And when it does, you must take that opportunity and use it to your best advantage."

There was complete silence in the room. At last, Nom Anor understood.

"Who *are* you?" he asked.

"Does it matter?" she responded. "I am here, and I wish to join you. I think—and I am coming to believe— that you hold the answers the Yuuzhan Vong have come to the galaxy in search of. Or if not you, then certainly the *Jeedai*. The gods no longer speak through those who claim to speak for them, and I no longer wish to be the enemy of the truth."

Nom Anor saw the sincerity in the words, even as he understood their fragility. Here was one who thought like him. This was not the mind of a simple follower, consumed by passions little nobler than those of animals. No, this was a higher mind, like Nom Anor's. Those who looked to Yun-Yuuzhan for answers would invariably be disappointed because, even if the gods did exist, why wouldn't the truths they served be infinitely more complex than those any mere mortal could ever hope to understand?

The penitent's face showed none of this, but that was because the face was as false as Nom Anor's own. She, too, was wearing an ooglith masquer designed to give the appearance of a Shamed One. All was illusion, deception . . .

Could this be the one? Nom Anor wondered. *Could this be the link to Shimrra I've been waiting for?* He wasn't so naive as to hope for a high-ranking warrior or intendant. They were all thoroughly brainwashed. A simple servant would be enough—someone who had access to the private places he could no longer see; someone who could overhear the meetings at which policies were decided. With a spy right in the heart of the Supreme Overlord's inner circle, he could indeed eat away at his enemy from within, just as the penitent had said, using the knowledge gained from such a source to direct his campaign—and all the while recruiting others to reduce his reliance on that one person.

But how could he trust someone without knowing her name? What if the penitent had been deliberately planted by Shimrra to spread false information about his intentions? Did the Supreme Overlord have the capacity for such subtlety?

Doubt flowered in his gut.

"Come closer," he said, motioning the penitent forward. He could feel the weight of the entire audience's stare upon him. They were present during a significant moment, and they knew it. How he handled the next few minutes was vital.

The penitent approached within arm's reach—close enough to kill honorably, Nom Anor thought. He waved her closer still, until their mouths were at each other's ears.

"How do I know I can believe you?" Nom Anor whispered.

"You can believe me." The penitent's voice was little more than an expelled breath. "The gods have brought me this far, have they not?"

Nom Anor pulled back slightly to stab his steely gaze into the penitent's eyes. "We screen for infiltrators, not for piety."

Those eyes smiled back at Nom Anor. "I pass on both counts, then."

"Perhaps," Nom Anor said. "But we are not so foolish as to believe that we will catch every spy that comes our way. They come in all shapes and sizes, and they present many different faces."

"You would know more about that than I, Nom Anor," the penitent whispered. "That was your specialty, after all."

Nom Anor went cold, pushing the penitent away from him. "How—?"

"I recognized you as soon as I saw you—even behind your ooglith masquer." The eyes of the penitent didn't leave his; they were filled with something approximating triumph, as though Nom Anor's reaction had confirmed what had until that moment been only a guess. "It didn't seem possible, at first; we'd been told you were dead. But the more I listened to you speak, the more sure I became that it was you. Audacity and surprise were always your hallmarks, Nom Anor. When Shimrra cast you out—"

"Enough!" Nom Anor pushed her farther away, as he would repel something unclean. "I have heard enough!" He looked around desperately for Kunra and Shoon-mi. They had planned for such an eventuality; there were contingencies. They should have been sealing off the room and preparing for slaughter; there was no way he could allow anyone to leave this room now that his true name had been spoken.

But they weren't moving. They stood at the back by the door, looking puzzled. They hadn't heard the penitent's whisper! They didn't know what was going on!

The penitent was determined. "Wait," she said, pushing forward, one gnarled hand reaching under her robes. "I have something for you."

Nom Anor reacted instinctively. There wasn't time to think. Someone who recognized him was threat enough; the slightest suggestion that a weapon might be drawn on him was enough to make him act.

Blood rushed to the muscles around his left eye socket. Pressure peaked where the eyeball had once been. He felt a short, sharp pain as his plaeryin bol exploded, spitting poisoned darts into the face of the penitent.

With a harsh cry, his attacker fell backward onto the ground.

The audience erupted. Nom Anor fell back against his throne, his muscles turned to jelly. He heard screaming, confusion, cries for order. Inside he felt only emptiness. He had come *so close* to death. The plaeryin bol where his left eye had once been had saved him, as he had always known it would, one day. But he also knew that the respite was only temporary. An assassin had been sent to destroy him, and he had come *so close*. Others would follow; he would never be safe again!

He forced himself up, to think, to act. Kunra and Shoon-mi were getting the crowd in order, looking to him for instructions. At his feet, the penitent writhed as the paralyzing poison seared through her system. Nom Anor knelt beside her and pressed his claws on either side of the penitent's nose, looking for the pressure point that would cause the ooglith masquer to release itself. He didn't care if the creature took off half the spy's face. He had to know who it was that Shimrra had sent; he had to look at the face of his would-be assassin.

The ooglith masquer came away with a grotesque noise, like that of fabric tearing. Underneath was a face more familiar than Nom Anor had expected. It didn't belong to a guard or a nameless servitor. Far from it.

The penitent was Ngaaluh, a priestess of the deception sect. He knew of her from the sect's attempts to infiltrate the infidels in the past. He had seen her in the company of Harrar, another priest rising in Shimrra's court.

"You?" Nom Anor frowned deeply. "Why *you*?"

"I—" Ngaaluh's eyes were wide and frightened, the bluish sacks beneath them almost invisible. The poison was sending fire through her nervous system, making breathing difficult. Soon her heart would stop, and it would all be over. Through the pain, she was trying to say something. She reached up, but Nom Anor flinched away.

Then he looked again as something spilled out of the priestess's failing three-fingered grasp. It wasn't a weapon, as Nom Anor had suspected. It was a living unrik—a chunk of tissue excised from Ngaaluh's body as a votive offering to her gods. Kept alive by biotechnology, the unrik served as a symbol of Ngaaluh's servitude—and she had been offering it to Nom Anor!

"You fool!" He knelt over Ngaaluh as the priestess's body began to shake. There was an antidote to the plaeryin bol poison, but he had never expected to use it. The neural pathways were rusty, and he had to concentrate to stir the buried bioconstruct to life. The knuckle of his right thumb snapped straight with a click. He bit down on a gasp as a searing pain burned in the joint. A hair-thin needle extruded from under the claw. He slid it into Ngaaluh's neck where the vein still throbbed. There was more pain as the antivenin shot into the priestess's blood-stream, but it was nothing compared to that suffered by the female before him. Nom Anor held Ngaaluh down as every muscle went into spasm, burning energy in one final paroxysm of agony. A keening, hissing sound escaped the priestess's clenched jaw, growing louder with each spasm.

Then, suddenly, the priestess went limp. Fearing the worst, Nom Anor bent over her.

"Yu'shaa . . ."

The word was little more than a sigh, and with that, Ngaaluh's eyes closed. Nom Anor pressed his hand to the spot on the priestess's throat where he'd injected the antidote. Despite appearances to the contrary, the faint, lingering pulse was testimony to the priestess's continuing existence in the world.

He looked up. The members of the audience were staring at him in alarm and amazement. How much they understood of what had just taken place he didn't know, but he doubted that any of them would come close to grasping its true import. The gods had provided the answer to Nom Anor's prayers, in the form of the priestess—and he'd almost killed her!

The unrik rested beside Ngaaluh's unconscious form. Nom Anor picked it up. It was warm and pulsed gently in his grasp. Ngaaluh must have stolen it from the high priest's sanctum sanctorum before coming to offer it to the new gods. How and why she had come to believe in them, Nom Anor couldn't imagine. Nevertheless, he knew an opportunity when he saw one, and he did not intend to pass this one up.

He indicated for Shoon-mi to come to him. His servant did so immediately, pushing his way through the agitated crowd. "Master, is everything well?"

"This acolyte is to be given the best care we can offer." Which wasn't much, given their meager resources, but it was better than nothing at all. "She is important, Shoon-mi. Do you understand? *Nothing* is to happen to her."

Shoon-mi bowed. "It shall be so, Master." The Shamed One scurried away to organize a stretcher.

Nom Anor gestured for Kunra next. The ex-warrior came and knelt down beside him so he could whisper.

"What has happened?" he asked. "Who is this female?"

"She is a priestess, and close to Shimrra. I knew her before my fall. She named me, Kunra." The ex-warrior's eyes widened, and Nom Anor knew that he understood the significance of that fact. "But I think we can trust her. She has given me . . . assurances." The slow throbbing of the unrik matched the pulse visible in the great vein in Ngaaluh's neck.

"She could be just what we need," Kunra said.

"Exactly. But first we have to make sure that no one overheard." The members of the audience were growing more restless by the second, shuffling aimlessly and muttering among themselves.

"I should take precautions, perhaps?"

"No." Nom Anor knew that Kunra would happily kill all the penitents to ensure their safety, but that wasn't an optimal solution. Ngaaluh would wonder what had happened to them, and so would Shoon-mi. "We can't afford to waste resources, or to provide fuel for rumors. If they all disappear, some will be missed. Better to find out if my secret is safe and let them go. Who knows? Maybe it will work in our favor."

"Feeding the legend," Kunra mused, then nodded once. "It shall be done."

Nom Anor stood to address the crowd. "This is an auspicious day!" he said dramatically, knowing that the truth was too dangerous to reveal. "I have survived an attack and am stronger for it. Go, now, and tell everyone! It will take more than this to keep us from the respect we deserve!"

The crowd accepted this pronouncement with some uncertainty, but accept it they did. He had delivered the bulk of his message before Ngaaluh's interrogation had thrown him off. They had heard everything they needed to hear. Once Kunra had satisfied himself that they hadn't heard anything else, they would be allowed to leave to begin their missionary work.

"Our time draws ever nearer," he said to them as they began to file out. "And with the events of this day, it might come sooner than even I expected . . ."

"I'm going to melt if it gets any hotter in here," Tahiri said, wiping her brow with the back of her hand.

"Adjust the ventilation controls," Goure said, his muffled voice coming from within his own hostile environment suit. A super-strong exoskeleton a meter taller than he was, the HE-suit hid his face behind a collection of droid sensors and allowed him to use its superior strength for any manner of distasteful chores. Tahiri's own suit was identical to his—painted a dull, metallic brown with scuffed ident markings on back and chest—and she watched the world through a bewildering array of views and senses. She felt as though she were wearing an ancient suit of armor. "Turn the thermostat down and you should start to feel better."

"It's already down as far as it'll go," she said. They could have communicated by comlink, but Goure had said he didn't want to take the risk of being overheard. The suits had external speakers and microphones and they did the job well enough—unlike her air-conditioning unit.

She jabbed at the controls with her chin, trying to blink away the salty sweat stinging her eyes. Having grown up among the Sand People, she was used to being enclosed in hot environments—but this was ridiculous.

Something thumped her from behind, followed by a distinct *click*. A flow of icy air instantly rushed through the suit, offering a relief that was so intense that Tahiri could only sigh her thanks.

"Your coolant line was clogged," said Arrizza, the Kurtzen sanitation worker who accompanied them on their long turbolift ride. Goure had described him as a part-time conspirator, but not part of the Ryn network. He had explored the inner workings of the Bakuran Senate Complex with no interest in taking it further. Having no political agenda, he was quite happy to help Goure get Tahiri in and out of the complex without being noticed.

"I think you just saved my life," Tahiri said only half jokingly, wriggling in her suit to help the cool air reach every centimeter of her sweat-soaked body. Her HE-suit—designed to take minuscule movements of her limbs and magnify them, giving her increased strength and flexibility—made odd half-stepping motions as she did so.

"I once knew someone who died from overheating on the job," was the Kurtzen's reply. "You got to look out for each other down here."

She didn't quite know what to say in the face of his gruff pragmatism. "Thanks," she said after a moment. "I'll try to remember that."

The turbolift clanked to a halt and the wide steel cage opened before them. Arrizza went first, his suit scruffier than Goure's, if that was possible. The only real difference between them was a belt of leather pouches tied around its waist. Tools, Tahiri presumed—although she doubted the suit's stubby fingers could handle anything so small with any precision.

They walked in single file along the sub-basement access corridor. It was easily high and wide enough for the HE-suits, designed to accommodate all sorts of maintenance machines. None of them droids, of course, she reminded herself—not with Bakura's distaste for automated machinery. If droids couldn't do the dirty work, people had to. Hence the suits they were wearing.

Arrizza was taking them to another turbolift that led directly under the main Senate chambers. There they could enter the complex itself, avoiding the tight security employed by the normal entrances. As part of a waste cleanup crew performing the usual morning rounds, they would be able to move unobserved—or at least unhindered—through the lower levels of the complex. They might not get into the Senate chamber itself, but they should be able to access the internal data networks with relative ease.

"Do you have any idea what's going on?" she asked.

"No. Security has been on edge since Cundertol's kidnapping. I haven't worked out who was behind it, but I know it wasn't Malinza Thanas. That's not her style."

"Then who?"

"I'm not sure."

After walking awhile in silence, Tahiri switched to a private channel and ventured another question.

"You always get around in these things?" she asked as they trundled along, steel boots clomping heavily on the reinforced floor. "There must be easier ways to travel."

"Unfortunately the security scare has shut down my usual sources," he said. "Especially with the arrival of the Keeramak and today's ceremony. It's crude, I know, but it's all I have left for now. I just hope it doesn't result in me getting caught and my activities being discovered."

"What would happen if you were discovered? Would you be replaced?"

"Once word got out, then yes, another of my kind would be sent to replace me."

"But how would word get out? If communications are down like they are now, I can't see how that could be possible."

"Well, the first thing we do when we arrive at our posts is set up plans to cover such emergencies. Those of my family don't use the Force; nor do we rely on conventional communications. That, you see, is our strength. We get into places we're not supposed to simply because we are ignored, not by virtue of arcane technology or powers, which people are always looking for. In the same way, who notices a note or two slipped into a cargo manifest? A whisper from a dock handler to a droid? Or a story innocently exchanged in a tavern? Even during communications embargoes, Bakura receives its fair share of freighters and traders. Everyone needs repulsors. I use the simplest and most universal techniques of spreading my word via those travelers. It may be slow at times, but it is effective."

Tahiri fumbled with the concept. "Are you telling me you're sort of a pan-galactic gossipmonger?"

"You make it sound like a bad thing. It's actually very effective. If one of my regular messages fails to arrive at a certain place at a certain time every day, then a message will be sent to the next Ryn along the chain, who will request a replacement."

"Who from?" Tahiri was unable to suppress her curiosity about the Ryn network. Their existence had been completely unsuspected until Galantos, but their influence seemed to be as insidious as the Peace Brigaders had been.

Goure chuckled softly. "I can't tell you too much, Tahiri. A secret organization can only operate efficiently if its workings *remain* secret. Since you already know we exist, I can tell you that we Ryn don't have a strictly hierarchal system like the Jedi. We do have, however, a leader who ultimately receives the information each of us supplies. It is he who makes all the major decisions."

"Does your leader have a name?"

"Of course. But to reveal it would compromise his safety. Toward this end not even *we* know his real identity. We know that someone perceived the need for such a network of information seekers; it was that same someone who trained me—and many others like me—in the art of infiltration and sent us to our posts. Mark my words: a time will come when there will be songs sung about him, if they aren't already."

Goure stopped as they reached the second turbolift. It was as battered and well used as everything else on this level. With a deep groan it slid open; when they were inside it lurched upward. Tahiri found her hands reaching for the sides to steady herself; every muscle tensed uneasily. She distracted herself with another question.

"How can songs be sung about someone who has no name?"

A noise like wheezing issued from Goure's HE-suit speakers that, while it might not have particularly sounded like it, Tahiri knew nonetheless to be a laugh. "You're so practical, aren't you?" Before he could answer her question, however, Arrizza had raised a hand and waved the two of them to silence.

"We're almost there," he said. "Remember the arrangement."

Tahiri nodded inside her all-encompassing helmet. From now on, they were to address each other only as Yon, Gaitzi, and Scod, members of an underground cleaning gang nicknamed the Tripod.

The lift platform grated to a halt a second later, and the massive doors slid open again, revealing another service corridor that seemed little different from the one they'd left below—except this one terminated in a set of thick blast doors after only a few meters. Tahiri followed

Arrizza as he approached it, imitating the heavy lope of his HE-suit in the hope of radiating the impression that she was as comfortable in the bulky outfit as she would have been in normal clothing.

"Identify," a voice blared from the other side of the door. Laser beams tracked the suits, reading ident codes painted in various reflective paints.

"Tripod duty," Arrizza said in a bored tone. After only a few seconds' waiting, he added gruffly, "Come on, Schifil! Let us in, will you? I haven't got all day."

"And so much important work to do, eh?" The double door slid open with a hydraulic hiss. "There's a block in Compactor J earmarked for your attention, Yon. You must've been a bad boy last night."

Arrizza just grunted as he led them past the security checkpoint. Two guards in an open booth watched them pass, weapons slung across their laps and smirks on their faces. The HE-suits could have crushed them like bugs, but physical strength was no match for superior social status.

Tahiri filed subserviently past, putting a hunched sway to her heavy lurch that she thought suitable for a low-grade worker. So focused was she on her performance that it took her a moment to realize that one of the guards was talking to her.

She stopped, turning slowly, using the seconds to reach into the guard's mind to discover that he thought he was talking to the cleaner called Gaitzi.

"Got a kiss for me today, Gaitzi?" the guard asked, puckering grotesquely while his partner laughed.

Tahiri improvised a suitably moist smacking sound with her lips before turning away and moving on.

"Delightful," Goure muttered once they had cleared the checkpoint and were safely following Arrizza into the underbelly of the Bakuran Senate Complex. "It never ceases to amaze me what happens to the males of most species when you give them a gun and put them in a uniform."

"I suppose the male Ryn are above all that, are they?" Tahiri said dryly.

"Actually, we are!" he defended indignantly. "That's why we work in secrecy, with no fancy titles or privileges. We exist to oppose such self-aggrandizing methods used by groups like the Peace Brigade. In fact, rumor has it that our founder was inspired by the Great River—the network of safe houses and escape routes founded by Master Skywalker in order to save the Jedi from betrayal."

"Is that why the Ryn helped us back on Galantos?"

"News of what happened there has yet to filter down to me," he said. "But yes, if the Peace Brigade were there then we would have done what we could to resist them. Look on it as our contribution to the war effort. We can't take on the Yuuzhan Vong directly—not even we could infiltrate *their* society—so we aim lower, at those who rot the Galactic Alliance from within."

"A second line of defense," Tahiri suggested.

"We like to think of it as the first line," he countered. "There's no point defeating the Yuuzhan Vong if we defeat ourselves in the process."

As cryptic as that sounded, it echoed Jacen's philosophical uncertainties regarding the consequences of winning the war by violence alone. It also hit a little close to where her own problems lived.

"We're not really going to have to unclog that garbage compactor, are we?" she asked by way of changing the subject, thinking not just of the mounds of steaming refuse but the closing walls as well.

"No," Arrizza said. "You just go about your business. I'll make sure the chores get done."

"We have signals we can send each other if we're needed at either end," Goure explained.

"If you're bothered by anyone," the Kurtzen added,

"or you split up, just tell security that your localizers have been scrambled and you're looking for Sector C. I'll find you there."

Tahiri nodded.

They reached a T-junction and split up without another word: Arrizza heading off to the right to perform the functions of the cleanup crew, Tahiri and Goure stomping down the left corridor to begin their reconnaissance. From that moment on, Tahiri knew, the risk multiplied. She didn't know how closely the cleaning crews were monitored, or how deeply they could move through the complex before someone noticed that they weren't following the usual routine; all she could do was work quickly, and hope that they were given enough time to do what they'd come to do.

Goure led her on a long and winding route through the sub-basement levels, occasionally taking turbolifts up or down floors, or detouring through warehouses full of sealed containers.

"There's more to the complex than meets the eye," she commented after passing through an enormous underground bunker packed to the ceiling with food rations.

"After the war with the Ssi-ruuk, it was redesigned as a shelter," Goure explained. "The Senate and a large proportion of the population of Salis D'aar could survive down here a considerable length of time—as long as the barriers to the surface weren't breached, of course."

"And if they were?"

"There's a weapons cache, too," the Ryn replied. "Enough for a small army. Believe me: they wouldn't go down without a fight."

Given the horrors of entrenchment, Tahiri could understand the lengths the Senate had gone to avoid them. With the specter of enslavement and death hanging over them for decades, fear of a return invasion must have been deeply entrenched. No wonder, then, that some people were reluctant to have anything to do with the P'w'eck, whether they were former slaves themselves or not.

So why the sudden turnaround? she wondered. Princess Leia had commented that Prime Minister Cundertol had been anti-alien when serving on the New Republic Senate, so why had that changed now?

She forced herself to put the matter aside and concentrate on the issue at hand. "If they put food and weapons down here," she said, "there must be some sort of command hub as well."

"Exactly," Goure replied. "And that's where we're headed."

They took a small detour to gather a floating floor-polishing machine, then continued on their way. They passed through an empty security checkpoint and went down one more turbolift. Tahiri constantly checked the spaces around them for any sign of habitation, but the sub-basement was uniformly empty. They could have been wandering the well-preserved ruins of an ancient, abandoned city, for all she could tell.

But there were still security cams at every corner. All it would take was for one person to become suspicious . . .

Two large, molded doors slid aside to reveal the unused command hub. Tahiri and Goure strode confidently inside, as though they visited there every day. Rather than crane her hydraulic neck, she sent her HE-suit sensors sweeping across the empty workstations and dormant holoprojectors. There was room for fifty or more people to work around a raised circular dais where, she presumed, the Prime Minister and his chief officers would conduct business in times of war. Although it had clearly been empty for many years, there was an air of preparedness to the place—a hint of anticipation in the dusty durasteel—as though it was waiting for its moment to come.

It might yet, she thought cynically, *if the Keeramak's intentions are not what they seem.*

Goure came to a halt in the middle of the vast room and activated the cleaning machine. Swinging it back and forth, he spoke over its patient whine:

"Look like you're cleaning. I'll slice into the systems and see if I can find Jaina. Switch your monitors to channel seventeen so that you can monitor my progress."

"Won't someone notice what we're doing?"

"Not if I'm good enough." He smiled at her through his faceplate. "And I *am* good enough." More seriously he added, "Although we need to be in the hub to access its networks, we don't want to do anything obvious like switch on the displays. The HE-suits can do the job for us." Again the heavy shoulders of his suit flexed. "I suspect we're only going to get one shot at this, so we have to make it count."

Tahiri acknowledged the instruction and did as he told her, making a big show of using her suit's strength and flexibility for the sake of anyone that might be watching. All the time she was working, she kept one eye on Goure's progress, using the upper half of her helmet's interior as a crude VR hood. At first, she saw nothing but line after line of complex machine code as he used a number of simple techniques to infiltrate the complex's low-security networks. From there the job became much tougher, and it took him a while to break into the next layer. There he gained access to administrative data, such as arrests and releases, but there was no mention of Jaina.

Another twenty minutes' code work took Goure right into the heart of the Bakuran bureaucracy, where he said the true secrets were stored. At first Tahiri was amazed at his ability, until she remembered that the Ryn had a reputation for being capable slicers. Not only that, but Bakura, a system on the isolated edge of the Rim worlds, probably didn't possess the sophisticated software required to guarantee silence—the kind she took for granted back on Mon Cal. Nevertheless, peeling back the system's strongest defenses in under an hour and a half was still impressive.

"Interesting," he muttered at one point.

"You found something?" Tahiri was immediately interested. She was growing tired of polishing and dusting.

"Not about Jaina, I'm afraid. I've managed to access hidden holocams in rooms that aren't supposed to have them." The view through the top half of her hood changed to a video feed, and she saw a wide, circular bed surrounded by lush drapes.

"Looks like someone has been doing a little spying," Tahiri said.

"I doubt it. Probably just an overzealous security chief. You see this kind of thing wherever you go. It's a case of the left hand not trusting the right."

He scanned through more hidden cams, glancing at more supposedly secure rooms. The picture quality varied from full 3-D to grainy black-and-white 2-D. Mostly the footage was of empty offices or of Senators going about early-morning preparations for the consecration ceremony. Nothing terribly exciting.

After flitting through numerous cam points of view, Tahiri was starting to wonder whether they were ever going to find anything useful. Then—

"Wait!" she called out. "Go back!"

But Goure was already onto it, recalling the image of Han and Leia and manipulating it to bring it into focus. They were standing in a plushly appointed office opposite Prime Minister Cundertol's broad, polished desk. Leia's expression was carefully composed, as always, but there was no mistaking Han's frustration.

Tahiri was about to ask if there was any sound when Goure provided it.

"—understand your concern," Cundertol was saying, "but at this stage there really is nothing I can do— especially when it appears that she might have been complicit in the escape of a dangerous criminal."

Han bristled. "If she helped Malinza escape, then it had to be for a good reason."

"Be that as it may, Captain Solo, the fact remains that she broke the law. If your daughter believed in Malinza's innocence, then there are legal avenues she could have pursued. However, as things stand, you have to see that my hands are tied. From a legal point of view, it is hard to deny that she is guilty."

"Of helping an innocent woman escape!" Han said.

"Malinza Thanas is hardly an innocent," the Prime Minister said gravely. "She and her band of insurrectionists have done more than enough damage to the peace of Bakura to warrant her outlaw status. It was time she was put away."

"But you yourself thought she was innocent!" Han blustered, incredulous.

Cundertol's expression was one of mystified puzzlement. "Whatever gave you that idea?"

Leia broke in calmly, averting an explosion of Corellian proportions. "Prime Minister, it's my suspicion that Jaina has been set up. We were contacted by someone claiming to have information for us. Acting on that information, Jaina went to visit Malinza Thanas—but only to speak with the girl. She certainly never went there to help Malinza escape. If she did participate, it would only have been under coercion."

"So why hasn't she come forward to explain herself?" Cundertol asked. "The footage clearly shows her leading Thanas out of the penitentiary of her own free will. There was no coercion."

"Then she was tricked into it," Leia said.

"Why?"

"If we knew that," Han snarled, "then we wouldn't be wasting our time with you, would we? We'd fix the problem ourselves."

Leia put a hand on her husband's shoulder. "We don't mean to criticize," she said. "We are simply concerned about the well-being of our daughter."

"And what about your other companion? The other Jedi? Has she returned yet?"

Han's scowl deepened, but Leia's expression remained calm and sober. "Unfortunately, no. And I'm becoming concerned about her safety, too."

"So that makes two Jedi Knights roaming Salis D'aar unchecked. I'm sure you'll forgive me for suggesting that anything underhanded is going on, but the timing is uncanny. One day before Bakura is due to cement a lasting peace with its old enemy, the Galactic Alliance turns up and throws everything into disorder. I can't help but wonder whether you want us to sever ties with the rest of the galaxy. Or perhaps there is something you still need from us that you fear we will no longer give you . . ."

"I don't think you believe that, Prime Minister," Leia said, unruffled by the accusations. "You know us, and you know that we only act in the interest of peace."

"I'm afraid I have yet to see any evidence whatsoever to support this, Princess."

At that moment, a high-pitched buzzing sound issued from the Prime Minister's desk. In one smooth movement, Cundertol stood and smoothed back his hair. The change in his behavior was striking. As unperturbed as he had been by Han's threatening manner, a tinny alarm seemed to leave him quite flustered.

"I'm sorry, but you really must excuse me; that will be my next appointment. You can rest assured, though, that we will be doing everything in our power to find the missing Jedi Knights—along with Malinza Thanas." Almost as an afterthought, he added, "I trust we will see you both at the consecration ceremony. It's only a short time away now, and I do not wish you to feel that because of the recent developments, we would be so churlish as to rescind our invitation to you. Princess Leia, Captain Solo: you remain our honored guests until such time as we have cause to think otherwise."

Leia practically had to drag her husband from the office. They were both clearly unsatisfied by the audience with the Prime Minister, but even Tahiri, watching from afar, could see that they could do little about it just then.

As the door shut behind them, Cundertol sat back down. For a long moment he was completely still—as though gathering his thoughts in meditation.

"Leia mentioned you," Tahiri said to Goure. "You're the who contacted us, who sent Jaina into the penitentiary. She probably thinks you're involved in whatever trouble Jaina's in."

"Which is all the more reason to find out what happened to her. Let's see if we can pick up something in—"

"Wait; look!" The door to Cundertol's office had opened again. Four dull-scaled P'w'eck guards walked in, dressed in elaborate leather harnesses and wearing paddle beamers at their sides. They spread out on either side of the desk and gazed suspiciously around the room. Lwothin then lumbered in, and behind him, walking serenely and with consummate grace, came a figure that, broadly speaking, resembled a P'w'eck, but was in almost every detail something quite different.

The Keeramak, Tahiri thought. She couldn't help but admire the creature's beautifully swirled, multicolored scales. The pattern they made shimmered with rainbow hues under the bright lights of the office. Every movement sent new sparkles dancing. The Ssi-ruuvi physique was that of a refined hunter, honed by thousands of years of dominance over the stunted, nervous-looking P'w'ecks. The Keeramak's posture was straighter and its poise more balanced; its limbs were longer, its muscles sleeker, and its eyes glinted with an intelligence and cunning that made Advance Leader Lwothin look about as threatening as an Ewok.

Two more P'w'eck guards followed. The doors shut firmly behind them. The Keeramak strode right up to Cundertol's desk and stood there, its thick tail swishing.

Cundertol rose and bowed formally.

The Keeramak said something in the powerful, deep fluting of the Ssi-ruuvi tongue. Tahiri listened for a translation, but none came. Cundertol had an earplug, she assumed, feeding the Keeramak's words in Basic directly to him. That was unfortunate, but not a disaster.

At least we can still hear his *reply,* Tahiri thought.

But what happened next took her completely by surprise. When the Keeramak had finished speaking, Prime Minister Cundertol opened his mouth and replied to the alien in fluent Ssi-ruuvi—a language that no human could possibly dream of pronouncing.

Tahiri stared at the screen, watching Cundertol's larynx bob up and down in a highly unusual fashion as a rapid series of flutes issued from his mouth.

"This isn't possible," she said, stunned.

Cundertol's speech was interrupted by a loud interjection from the Keeramak. A clawed hand grasped air between the two of them. Cundertol protested at something, but the Keeramak cut him off again. Finally, with a sour expression, he nodded and sat back in his seat, folding his arms across his chest.

He spoke again in the alien language, to which the Keeramak responded with a snort that might have been Ssi-ruuvi laughter. Lwothin tried to lean into the conversation, but the Keeramak batted him roughly aside. Cundertol smiled at this.

"I don't like the look of this," Tahiri said.

"Me neither," Goure replied. "If only there was some

way I could record this—or at least patch it into a trans-
lator. But I can't do either without alerting security."

"Then maybe that's what we need to do," Tahiri said.
"I mean, *someone* needs to know about this!"

The words had barely left her lips when the exchange
between Cundertol and the Keeramak ended. The Prime
Minister stood and offered another slight bow. Lwothin
and his Ssi-ruuvi leader left the room, flanked by their
armed bodyguard.

When he was alone again, Cundertol fell heavily into
his seat once more, this time with a relieved expression
on his face.

"I've no idea what just happened," Goure said, "but
you're right: we have to tell someone about it."

"Tell them what, though?" Tahiri asked. The incident
was only seconds in the past, and already she was finding
it difficult to credit—so how were others going to believe
them without proof? "Do we just come out and say that
the Prime Minister might be some sort of human/Ssi-ruu
hybrid? They're never going to believe us!"

"There is someone who might," Goure said
thoughtfully.

"Who?"

"This kind of thing would undoubtedly end Cundertol's career—regardless of what his intentions might be.
Who do you think would stand to gain the most from
that?"

Tahiri nodded. "The Deputy Prime Minister."

"Exactly. He has a motive for doing something, as well
as the power to make it happen quickly. If we can just get
to him—"

"—before the ceremony!" she finished for him. "If the
Keeramak is planning to double-cross Bakura, then we'll
need to act before then. The only thing stopping them
from attacking openly is fear for their souls. Once Bakura
is consecrated, there'll be no stopping them."

"Agreed. And that doesn't leave us much time." The image of Prime Minister Cundertol winked out and was replaced by a flowchart of the complex's communications network. "Now, where exactly is Harris at the moment?"

Before he could pinpoint the Deputy Prime Minister, a blaring voice rang out through the empty command hub.

"Attention, cleaning crew. On whose instructions are you acting?"

Goure activated an external comlink, his voice erupting uncomfortably close to Tahiri's right ear. "Supervisor Jakaitis, sir."

"Supervisor Jakaitis denies requesting a crew in that location," came the instant reply. "Your presence is not authorized."

"I'm sure if you were to ask him again—"

"You are in violation of Sections Four through Sixteen of the Secrecy Act. Remain where you are until a squad arrives. You will be escorted to a holding area where you will be formally processed."

The feed from the command hub ceased.

Tahiri cursed under her breath and, despite the air-conditioning unit of her suit, started to sweat again. They'd been paying too much attention to Cundertol, and not enough on maintaining the pretence of manual labor.

Now that they'd been sprung, security would almost certainly be listening in on them. Goure butted the helmet of his HE-suit against Tahiri's to ensure they could speak without being overheard. At least their identities hadn't been revealed.

"There goes that plan," he said.

"We have to get out of here." An uneasy feeling was growing inside her. She couldn't sense anyone nearby, but the security squad might just as easily consist of droids.

"Don't worry," he said. "We will. Follow me and do exactly as I do."

"What about Harris?"

"I found him before they cut us off," Goure said. "All we have to do is get to him."

"And Arrizza?"

"He can look after himself. Come on!"

Before she could ask anything else, he'd pulled away and was powering his suit toward the exit. Although bulky and not designed exclusively for speed, the massive constructs could move quickly when they had to. She followed, the pounding of her heavy feet vibrating up through her metal legs and jarring into her body. The sound of hydros straining was loud in her ears.

Goure led her back to the first turbolift they'd taken. Knowing that security would be watching them, he didn't even consider taking it. Instead, he took Tahiri along another series of corridors to a spiraling stairwell. The stairs shook precariously under their combined weight, but it was better than being trapped in a lift, waiting to be arrested.

They climbed ten floors without interruption. Concern about the stability of the stairs became a worry of a very different kind when two black spheres dropped from above, wailing and flashing warning lights.

"Security droids!" Goure yelled, his voice echoing from his speakers through the stairwell.

Tahiri looked up. Restricted to the stairs, the droids had dropped down the center of the stairwell shaft. Thankfully there were only two, but she had no doubt that others would soon follow. Their stun prods would be harmless against the HE-suits' armor, but they had more powerful weapons at their disposal.

"You are under arrest!" they announced. "You are under arrest! Drop your weapons and cease all movement!"

Not likely, Tahiri thought, opening a metal hatch on the outside of the suit and reaching inside. Before climbing into the suit, she had hidden her lightsaber among the cleaning tools in case of an emergency such as this. It felt tiny in her giant metal fist, and she would have to concentrate twice as hard to fight the natural clumsiness of the suit, but she instantly felt better for having it in her hand.

"No!" Goure shouted, seeing what she was doing. "If you activate it then they'll know who you are!"

What difference will that make? she wanted to shout back. If they didn't already know, they would as soon as she was arrested and forced to step out of the suit.

But an instinct told her to trust Goure. He didn't seem to be running without purpose. Wherever he was taking her, he obviously thought they could get away. And there were ways to fight that didn't involve using a lightsaber.

She sent a psychokinetic pulse to knock out the nearest droid. It spun out of control, showering sparks as it rolled crazily around the stone wall before plummeting to the bottom of the stairwell. The second backed away a meter or so, its weapon arms rising threateningly. She sent a power surge through its repulsorlift circuits, sending it upward to a fate similar to the first. Its screams of protest faded rapidly as it disappeared into the shadows above.

"Good work," Goure said, reaching up to smash a nearby security cam. "Now, through here."

They left the stairwell thirteen floors above the level of the secret command hub. The area they entered wasn't designed for heavy maintenance, and Tahiri had to stoop to fit into the corridor. Goure didn't bother. The top of his metal head scraped against the ceiling, lifting tiles and smashing light fittings, leaving a trail of wreckage behind him. Whenever he passed a security cam, he didn't pause. He just reached out and crushed it without so much as breaking step.

"I take it you know where you're going?" Tahiri asked. Her previous confidence in him was starting to wane. She couldn't help wonder whether he really did have a plan or whether he was just intent on causing as much damage as possible.

"If my memory serves me correctly, there should be a maintenance shaft somewhere . . ."

Ahead of them was a two-meter-wide, cylindrical column running from floor to ceiling. Goure stepped up to it and used his suit's strength to tear through the column's side. Within, Tahiri saw numerous coiled cables and pipes. Clearly, the column stretched many floors above and below them, delivering essential services to the areas around it.

Goure spent a moment searching for the cable he needed. Frustration soon took hold and he started pulling out handfuls at random.

"Come *on*," Tahiri muttered, glancing around nervously, checking for signs of the other security droids. They couldn't be far behind.

Sparks and steam hissed and spat from the column as the powerful hands of Goure's HE-suit tore through wires and conduits. When he was up to his elbows in bubbling fluid and smoking insulator, he clutched both hands around something he'd found deep inside and gave a mighty wrench.

Instantly the lights went out around them and the entire floor was plunged into darkness.

"Okay," she heard him say somewhat breathlessly. Tahiri switched to infrared to see him step back from the column, then move over to a ventilation shaft and pull it open. "We haven't got much time. This isn't going to hold them for long."

There was a hiss as his HE-suit cracked down the back. His head emerged from the seam, followed by his arms. Tahiri reached around to give him a hand. Her HE-suit lifted him as though he were a doll, his tail lashing in obvious relief at being freed from its confinement.

"Slave your control circuits to mine before you come out," he instructed her. She did so, and then clicked the FAST-RELEASE button. She inhaled deeply, appreciating the fresh, cool air that immediately swept across her body.

"Now what?" she asked, retrieving her lightsaber from the suit's unresisting fist.

Goure pointed at the open shaft. "We climb. But first . . ." He reached under his suit's armpit and flicked a switch. Both suits whirred shut and turned to stride quickly away, each leaving a trail of destruction as they walked through the low-ceilinged corridors.

"Now that's a trail no one could miss," he said, his face briefly lit by sparks as the suits marched away into the darkness. "I've programmed them to run free, heading up whenever they can. If they reach the stairwell, things could get interesting. If not—well, they'll gain us a minute or two, at least."

He helped her into the shaft, then followed, replacing the cover behind him.

"There should be a central air shaft not far from here," he explained. "When we find it, we go up. Once we reach the surface, we can look for somewhere to come out of the shaft. From there we're free."

"Hopefully," Tahiri added.

Goure nodded grimly. "Hopefully."

"And what about the Deputy Prime Minister?"

"As long as Harris doesn't go too far, we should be able to find him in time. But we've only got an hour before the ceremony starts, and we have seventeen floors to climb."

"Then we'd better get moving, wouldn't you say?"

Outside the shaft, emergency lighting flickered into life. In the distance, they could hear the pounding of the suits' feet and the crackle of blasterfire.

In the shadowy and reddish darkness, Goure nodded

again, and without another word the two of them began to crawl.

"What do you mean, you prefer to leave the fighting to your sister?" Wyn Antilles stared at Jacen as though he'd gone mad. With her severe black uniform and blond hair pulled back, she looked like a schoolgirl trying to impersonate a Grand Moff; she might have known the rules, but she didn't have the maturity to pull it off.

"Where I come from," Jacen responded good-naturedly, "we don't have customs prohibiting women from fighting in battle. In fact, I didn't think you had here, either."

"We don't," she said. "That would just be stupid—wouldn't it, Commander Irolia?" The Chiss officer nodded stiffly from the far side of the table, where she was watching Jacen input data from the library search into datapads for further analysis. Wyn had joined Jacen and Danni as they reviewed their data electronically, while the other members of the group had continued to talk with the girl's parents. Initially, Wyn had been very excited at meeting Jacen, and was keen to talk to him about the search for Zonama Sekot. But when this conversation ebbed, the girl had obviously decided it might be fun to lock horns with Jacen, determinedly teasing out his place in the mission and the universe in general. He couldn't figure out if she was genuinely interested in what he had to say or if she was deliberately antagonizing him, trying to see how far she could actually push a Jedi before his patience cracked . . .

"All I meant was that you should fight when you have to. Your preferences don't come into it. Your enemy won't stand down just because you don't want to fight. You either rise to the occasion or you die."

Harsh words, Jacen thought, coming from one so young. But with her pedigree, he reminded himself, and the culture and times in which she'd been educated, perhaps it wasn't so surprising.

"I guess what I should have said was that I prefer to put myself in situations where skills other than those involving combat will save the day." He tried to put his feelings into words with consummate precision, not wanting to give her the chance to leap on another ambiguity. Fatigue wasn't making it easy, though. "Not every conflict can be solved with violence, Wyn. Some become exponentially more difficult to solve once violence has entered the equation. The Force may need both sides of life—birth and death—in order to be balanced, but that doesn't meant we can't look for peaceful solutions. It's the same if violence seems to be the only—or indeed the easiest—option."

To his relief, Wyn acknowledged his point with a thoughtful nod. "Okay, I can understand that. But what about your sister? How does she feel about you letting her risk her life exercising the 'easy' option?"

"I don't think it's a case of me *letting* her do anything," he said. "She's simply better at following that path when the need for it arises. While I spend half my life philosophically pondering the way of things, she focuses her energies on the exterior, on what she can change. But as far as I'm concerned, deep down we're still addressing the same problem—just from different angles."

"You carry a lightsaber," Wyn pointed out.

He shrugged. "It's a symbol of a Jedi—just like the insignia on Commander Irolia's uniform."

"Nevertheless, the weapon at your side seems out of place on a man who says he dislikes violence."

How do I answer that? he wondered. *If I say that I don't hate violence, I undermine everything I've told her. If I confirm that I do, I make a mockery of my own convictions. Is this the corner I've backed myself into?*

"Haven't we drifted off the topic a little here?" Danni

said, stretching tiredly. "We were looking for Zonama Sekot, remember?"

Jacen nodded. It had been an exhausting session, and one that had only been partially successful. The number of "hits"—systems where stories of a wandering planet had been recorded—was reaching a plateau; they quickly ran out of the ones that were easiest to find. So far they had sixty confirmed or suspected appearances in a forty-year period spanning from shortly before the formation of the Empire to some years after. Wherever it was that Zonama Sekot had settled down, it seemed to have done so about twenty years before the arrival of the Yuuzhan Vong.

"But you said before that you were probably looking in the wrong place," Wyn said.

Danni sighed, and when she spoke there was no mistaking the frustration in her tone. "We're looking primarily through sociological records," she said. "Astronomical data would be our best bet. We need to look specifically for systems that have adopted a new planet in their habitable zones, whether those zones are inhabited or not."

"But there are hundreds of thousands of stars in and around Chiss space," Wyn said. "Plus about the same number again of orphan worlds drifting in interstellar space. There must be planets captured and lost all the time."

"Actually, no." After Danni's success at cracking the biological secrets of the Yuuzhan Vong, it was easy to forget that her original specialization was astronomy. "Although the capture of extra-solar planets does happen quite naturally, it's a very rare event—and even rarer right in the middle of the habitable zone. A large percentage of those systems have been visited more than once by droid probes on deep-survey missions, and the basic configurations of the others would have been at least recorded by large-scale interferometric detectors in nearby systems. The Chiss checked every target system at least twice in the last sixty years. Any discrepancies would show up in even the most basic scan."

Wyn nodded. "We could set up a sweep to look for stuff that was added to any of the systems on record. I can talk to Tris and—"

She stopped as Luke appeared from one of the aisles, followed closely by Saba. "Sorry to interrupt," he said. "We've decided to bring *Shadow* to a closer spaceport. If you'd like to clean up and have a rest, then this might be your best chance."

"I think I'd settle for either, right now," Danni said.

"What about you, Saba?" Luke said, facing the Barabel. She was bringing another heavy-looking tome to read.

"A shower soundz good," she said. The exhaustion was clearly evident in her voice. "Even the best hunterz need to wash."

"Okay, then we'll see you all shortly at the barge," Luke said. "When we come back, we'll bring Artoo with us. He might be able to help us search through the less obvious data."

"That's a good idea," Danni said, rising to her feet. She faced Jacen. "You coming?"

He shook his head. "I think I'll stay here. Someone has to keep looking through the data we've collected. There's a lot to get through, and we've only one day left."

Danni's disappointment was obvious, but Luke agreed with a cautious nod. "Don't overdo it, Jacen. I'm sure Commander Irolia can provide you with a bunk and a 'fresher if you decide you need one."

"Of course," the commander said.

"Syal and Soontir will be coming with us on the ice barge," Luke went on. "Obviously you're welcome to come as well, Wyn, if you're interested."

"Actually, I think I'll stay and help Jacen, if that's all right?"

Jacen nodded. "No problem. We can begin that search you thought of, Danni. And if anything comes up, I promise to call, okay?"

Danni glanced at Jacen and Wyn, offering a curt and unenthusiastic nod. "Sure," she said, then faced Luke. "How soon do we leave?"

"Right now if you like."

"Sounds good to me," Danni said. Then, with the faintest glance at Wyn, added: "The sooner the better."

Jacen's uncle, aunt, and Lieutenant Stalgis left for the barge with a brief farewell to everyone, followed shortly by Danni and Saba.

"So, what do you want to do?" Wyn asked when everyone had gone. "I could show you around, if you want. Or there's always—"

"I don't think that's such a good idea." Jacen cut her off firmly but gently. Commander Irolia silently took up position against the far wall—a position that allowed her to keep an eye on both Jacen and Wyn. "There really isn't much time before the deadline runs out, and if we don't learn anything, then we're back where we started."

The girl rolled her eyes, sighing with only a half-serious look of rejection on her face. "Then we'd better get going," she said.

No, thought Jacen. That's exactly what they wouldn't be able to do. If they ever did find what they were looking for, then everything would be blown wide open. It would be the beginning of the end of everything they had come to take for granted these last few years.

He kept this to himself. When he thought of the future, the image he received from the Force was invariably clouded. His vision of a galaxy slipping into darkness still burned inside him, and he didn't like to think that any failure on his part might contribute to such an outcome. He was determined to bring his uncle's peaceful solution into being. And despite a twinge of guilt, he couldn't allow Wyn's feelings to get in the way of that.

I should have known better . . .

Jaina struggled to get a grip on the world around her as suffocating folds of unconsciousness tried to drag her back down. The only signal she received from her body was that of a burning sensation between her shoulder blades, where she'd been shot. She suspected that she hadn't been seriously hurt, but the blaster's stun setting had been on the high side, and her nervous system was still a bit scrambled.

When the darkness finally began to recede and she managed to haul herself out into daylight, she couldn't tell if weeks or minutes had passed. Moaning, she tried to move, but found that Salkeli had bound her arms and legs tightly together. There was a translucent hood over her head, too.

"I see you're awake," she heard him say from close by, his voice raised over the steady whining of his landspeeder's motor. From the way the world bumped and slewed beneath her, she guessed that she was slumped on the reclined seat of the vehicle. Despite her situation, she actually found this thought reassuring; it suggested that she hadn't been out too long, after all.

"Where are you taking me?" she asked.

"To meet someone."

"Who?"

"It's not important. He has money, and that's all that concerns me right now."

She reached into herself to find her still center, hoping to pluck his intentions directly from his mind, but her focus was scattered by the pain and disorientation.

"You betrayed them," she said disgustedly.

"Do you mean Freedom?"

"You sold them out."

"They did it to themselves. I mean, what do they expect? You go up against the big cannons, you have to expect to get shot."

"But you were the one pulling the trigger."

"Better that than be on the receiving end. Besides, if they hadn't caused so much trouble, this might never have happened."

"So they *were* getting close to someone?"

"You really think you're going to get any information out of me?" He laughed. "I don't think so, Jedi."

She tried again to use the Force and this time felt a flicker of response. She clutched at it as though it were a life raft. "You could just release me," she said, putting as much persuasion as possible behind the words. "I'm of no importance—"

"You're right," he said. "So I might as well shoot you now and be done with it."

She heard him pull the blaster from its holster.

"No, wait!"

The bolt took her in the shoulder, hurling her again into darkness.

Hundreds of thousands of stars.

It was easy to say the words, but much more difficult to comprehend what they actually meant. On a map, the Unknown Regions comprised only 15 percent of the total volume of the galaxy; but when that 15 percent became the search area for something as small as a planet— which, on a cosmic scale, was much, *much* smaller than a needle in a haystack—the true immensity of the task became all too apparent.

And they had to do it in just two days!

Jacen concentrated on scouring through data Saba and Danni had discovered, while Wyn worked on the search algorithm. There were thousands of mission reports to scan through. Wandering asteroids and close encounters with comets were common, and it wasn't always easy to distinguish these from a mysterious planetary appearance. He soon lost track of all the unfamiliar names among the thousands of people and places he came across.

"Who's this Jer'Jo Cam'Co who keeps cropping up in the records?" he asked Wyn.

The girl looked up and shrugged. "Beats me."

"Jer'Jo Cam'Co was one of our founding syndics," Irolia said from where she'd kept patiently out of the way while Wyn and Jacen worked. "He proposed the Expansionary Defense Fleet after a series of exploratory expeditions turned up numerous vital resources."

Jacen nodded. That would explain why the man's name was on so many of the older reports. There were at least seven vessels named after him, and two systems. There had been no mention of him in any of the old or recent Republic records—which only went to show just how much there was still to learn about the Chiss.

It amused him, therefore, when Wyn demonstrated that the ignorance worked both ways.

"Tell me," she said, "what's it like on Coruscant?"

Jacen did his best to describe the capital world as he remembered it. His recollections were tainted by his recent experiences with the Yuuzhan Vong, however, and the knowledge that so much that had been beautiful was now lost or sullied in his memories. It made him sad to think of the former Imperial Palace in ruin, or the Monument Plaza turned into yorik coral fields, but they were very real possibilities. And the saddest thing of all was that even if the Galactic Alliance defeated the Yuuzhan Vong tomorrow, the actual damage inflicted upon Coruscant might never be undone. Memories could be all that remained to future generations.

Wyn listened soberly, only occasionally interrupting

with a question. The idea of a world devoid of natural life, on which most people lived underground, didn't seem to surprise her as he thought it might. But then, perhaps her world wasn't all that different. On Coruscant, the bedrock was covered with city; on Csilla it was ice, but the effect was essentially the same.

"I think I'd like to go there someday," she said when he'd finished talking. "When the war is over, of course. I'll see if I can get Father to let me take *Starflare*, our family yacht. I'm licensed to fly her, you know—not that I get much of a chance because Cem's always taking her out!"

She was probably fishing for a personal invite from him to show her around the place sometime, but he refused the bait. He smiled, saying nothing.

"Oh well. If Saba and Danni are right then I guess it doesn't matter anyway." She went on when he frowned at her. "Sometimes they talk about stuff when they forget I'm there." She paused, looking uncomfortable. "You really think there's a chance that we won't be able to beat the Yuuzhan Vong?"

Jacen nodded slowly. "It's a very real possibility, Wyn, yes."

She nodded also, equally as slowly, but infinitely more sadly—as only a teenager who'd been told she might not have long to live could. "Sometimes I think—" She stopped in midsentence, dropping her gaze. The notion obviously scared her.

"Sometimes you think what, Wyn?"

"It doesn't matter," she said. "No one cares what I think, anyway."

"I wouldn't have asked if I didn't," Jacen said soberly.

She looked up again, flashing an appreciative smile. "Sometimes I think that the sooner we can be rid of the Yuuzhan Vong, the better. I don't want what happened to Coruscant to happen here, Jacen. I think we should do whatever we have to to make sure of that."

"Even if it means joining up with us?"

"Yes," she said, nodding. "Unfortunately, though, Dad and I are in the minority there. Most people believe that the Yuuzhan Vong would strike twice as hard if they found out we'd sided with you. Others just worry that you will corrupt us with your ways, making it easier for the Yuuzhan Vong to walk all over us when the time comes. And Jag's behavior has only helped support this argument, I'm afraid."

"What do you mean? What about Jag's behavior?"

"Jag and his squadron were supposed to return months ago," she explained. "To some, the fact that he hasn't only proves that you've been a bad influence on him. He would never have gone off for so long before."

"I wasn't aware that this was a problem," Jacen said, wondering if Jaina had any idea, either. "But I can say that he's been a great help to us in the fight against the enemy. I hope your people realize that."

"That's just it, though. Because he hasn't reported back as he was supposed to, no one really knows exactly *what* he's been doing."

"Maybe he's just been too busy fighting the Yuuzhan Vong to communicate."

"Maybe," Wyn said. "Or maybe he's just been spending a little too much time with his new girlfriend."

Jacen studied her curiously for a few seconds. "How could you possibly know about that?"

"I didn't say he hadn't reported in at all, just that he hadn't reported in *as he was supposed to*." She grinned impishly. "That's an important difference for the Chiss, you know."

Her expression was one of exaggerated innocence mixed with mischievousness. And her smile left no doubt in Jacen's mind that the girl knew that Jag's girlfriend was in fact Jacen's own sister. "Well, perhaps he might prefer his private life to remain private," he returned in a tone that said this was a path he was not prepared to take.

Her eyes twinkled; she knew how to press people's buttons. "Hey, if he's sweet on her, then that's just fine by me. It keeps him out of my hair for a while, at least. He can be such a pain."

Despite her obvious intelligence, comments such as this only served to remind Jacen of just how young she really was—hovering as she was on the cusp of adolescence and adulthood. He didn't doubt that she loved Jag, but she was clearly unimpressed by her older brother's achievements at the same time.

"What about your father?" Jacen asked, moving the subject along. "What does he think?"

"Well, he's been something of a disruptive influence himself," she said. "The Chiss don't like to use droids in combat, arguing that they're too slow and vulnerable. Dad agrees mostly, but not *all* the time. He says, um, that 'expendability can be a deciding factor in a war.' He has a team of engineers working on a prototype droid fighter that should—"

She stopped abruptly when Irolia pointedly cleared her throat. The commander stared warningly at Jacen, her expression telling him quite clearly that she didn't for a moment believe that he was asking such questions out of idle interest.

"I'm sorry," he put in quickly, directing his apology to both of them. "I shouldn't have asked. My mission here is to find Zonama Sekot, not to pry into your affairs." Then to Wyn specifically, he added, "You've been a lot of help, Wyn, and I'm grateful for that. I'd hate for you to get into any trouble because of me."

"I won't," she said, offering a fleeting, somewhat chastened glance to Irolia. "Perhaps we should change the subject, though."

The two of them returned to the holodisplay before them.

"How's that algorithm coming along, anyway?" Jacen asked after a moment of studying the data. "You almost there?"

"It's ready to roll. All you need to do is give me the constraints."

"As we discussed earlier: any system that has gained an extra, habitable world in the last sixty years should be flagged for our attention. If Danni's right, that should narrow our search dramatically. Can you do that?"

"Of course." The girl bent her head to the task, not looking up as footsteps approached across the library floor.

Jacen didn't need to turn, either, to know who it was; he could tell both from the way that Commander Irolia instantly snapped to attention, and from the hostility the man radiated as he entered the room.

"At ease, Commander," Chief Navigator Aabe said.

Jacen and Wyn swiveled around to face him.

The bald man glided smoothly to the table, flanked by two Chiss guards. He walked to where Wyn was sitting and placed a hand on her shoulder. "Your father has asked me to fetch you."

The girl looked worried. "It was an honest mistake, mentioning the droids," she said. "I swear. If you'll just let me stay to—"

"This has nothing to do with that, child." Aabe's voice was firm. "But disobeying his instructions won't make him any more pleased with you, will it?"

She sagged into herself, and then stood. "Sorry, Jacen," she said, nervously glancing down to him. "Good luck with the search, though."

"Thanks." He watched, unable to protest, as Aabe led

her from the room. "Hopefully you'll get the chance to come visit me at my home someday."

She briefly smiled back at him as the door closed between them. Then she was gone, leaving him alone with Commander Irolia. The commander sat down wearily, her red eyes avoiding his. He sensed that she, too, didn't like the way in which Wyn had been whisked out of the room.

Nothing was said, but he couldn't help feeling a twinge of misgivings about what had just taken place. Something didn't feel right, somehow.

Wyn's search was indeed ready to roll, as promised. He called up a list of references on his datapad and considered where to start. He sat as though he was deep in thought for several minutes, but for once he wasn't thinking about Zonama Sekot.

He unclipped his comlink from his belt and turned away from Irolia.

"Uncle Luke? Can you hear me?" He kept his voice and the volume of the comlink down to a minimum.

"I hear you, Jacen. Have you found something?"

"Not yet. I just wanted to make sure you're okay."

"Everything's fine. We're still on the ice barge, not far from the spaceport. We should be back within two hours." There was a slight pause. "Is everything all right at your end?"

"Well, something odd just happened. Do you know if Soontir Fel has been in touch with Chief Navigator Aabe in the last half hour or so?"

"Not that I'm aware of. He's been with us the whole time."

Aabe had lied about being sent by Fel to collect Wyn. But *why?* Jacen thought hard. What was Aabe up to? he wondered. To isolate Jacen, perhaps? He looked over to Commander Irolia. She was sat perfectly still, silently watching him. He sensed nothing untoward in the tone of her thoughts—no anticipation, no nervousness—and there was nothing in the Force to suggest she was about to attack him. The threat had to be directed elsewhere. But where?

"Jacen?" His uncle sounded concerned. "What's wrong?"

"It's probably nothing," he answered. "It's just that—"

Before he could finish the sentence, however, a sense of extreme alarm surged through the Force. It hadn't come from Luke, either, but rather from someone *close* to his uncle. And tangled up in the thought was an impression of a cold, white wasteland and howling winds.

"We're under attack!" came the urgent cry over the comlink.

"Aunt Mara!" Although she was thousands of kilometers away, he found himself instinctively jumping to his feet and going for his lightsaber.

Irolia stood also, startled by Jacen's inexplicable outburst, automatically reaching for her own weapon.

"What's going on?" she asked anxiously, clearly confused.

Jacen ignored her.

"Uncle Luke! Aunt Mara!" he called into the comlink. "Answer me!"

It could have only been a few seconds before his uncle replied, but it felt like eons of tortured silence to Jacen.

"Jacen, I can't talk now," Luke said, voice crackling.

Then he was alone, desperately wanting to know exactly what had happened, but understanding that it could be a while before he found out. There was betrayal in the air, so thick and cloying that he felt for a moment as though he couldn't breathe.

"May the Force be with you," he muttered quietly to his uncle, reluctantly releasing the handgrip of his lightsaber. His thoughts turned to Wyn, wherever she was. "And you."

*   *   *

Jaina's eyes opened to bright light. She winced and re-coiled from the sudden rush of information.

"Where am I?" she croaked, squinting around as she tried to sit up. Just these simple tasks caused every muscle in her body to cry out in pain, and she fleetingly wished she'd remained unconscious.

She appeared to be in a study of some kind, although the details were still hazy. The smell of leather was strong in her nostrils, and her questing fingers quickly discovered the plush couch beneath her.

"Welcome back, Jaina."

She turned slightly in the direction of the voice and made out a vague, green-faced blur standing by what appeared to be a door. She hadn't really needed to look, though; she knew who the voice belonged to.

"Salkeli, you treacherous little—"

"It's not there," someone else said when her hand crept down to her side in search of her lightsaber. The voice was familiar, but a name didn't immediately spring to mind. "It's all right. No harm will come to you—*if* you behave yourself, that is."

She felt naked without her lightsaber, especially in such a weakened state. Two stun bolts so close together had left her nervous system profoundly scrambled. Her eyes were only slowly remembering how to focus. Her light-saber wasn't all that was missing, either; her comlink was gone, along with everything else that might have enabled her to call for help.

She forced herself to sit up straighter, turning to face the second person. He, too, was just a blur, but he wasn't to know that.

"Salkeli said someone wanted to talk to me," she said. "I presume that someone is you."

Whoever he was, he was seated behind a wide desk and dressed in richly red garments. "You presume correctly."

"So where exactly am I?" she asked again, glancing

around the confines of the room, hoping for something familiar to fall into place.

"You are in my private chambers," the man answered. "These rooms are soundproofed and protected against all forms of electronic infiltration. The door is blast-proof, and its lock can only be opened by my thumb-print." The leather of his chair squeaked beneath him as he leaned back into it, obviously trying to exude a calm and confident air. "Trust me when I say that you will not be leaving here without my consent."

"Yeah, I'm getting that impression," she said, looking around again. Her depth of field was gradually return-ing, allowing her to make things out more clearly. The study was lavishly appointed; polished wood cupboards containing delicate crystal ornaments—small glasses and bowls, mostly, some of them veined with bright colors—lined the walls. The beauty of the objects, however, was somewhat diminished by Salkeli standing in front of them, his green face staring back at her with an expres-sion of extreme smugness.

When she returned her gaze to the person sitting be-hind the desk, her vision had snapped back into focus. Long-boned and sharp-eyed, Deputy Prime Minister Blaine Harris looked at her with a questioning look on his face.

"Well?" he asked, arms outstretched imploringly. "*Will* you cooperate?"

She kept her surprise carefully in check. "That all depends."

"On?"

"On what you plan to do with me, of course," she an-swered. "And also what you did with the credits."

He frowned deeply. "Credits? What credits?"

"The credits you've been siphoning from the Bakura treasury, of course," she said, taking a gamble on a plau-sible theory. "Freedom discovered the leaks; that's why you had Malinza put away. What I don't get, though, is what you wanted that much for in the first place. I mean, what could you buy with all those millions of credits?"

"Ah, yes." Harris nodded his understanding. "Salkeli told me something about your little theory. Correct me if I'm wrong, but didn't Freedom fail to pin anything on me?"

"Yes, but I'm sure Vyram would have, if he'd been given the chance."

"I very much doubt that." Harris steepled his fingers in front of him, smiling thinly behind them. "You see, it really wasn't me who stole those credits."

Jaina forced a disbelieving laugh. "You expect me to—"

"Quite honestly," he interjected, "I don't care if you believe me or not. Because the truth is, it *wasn't* me. If I had access to that many credits, do you really think I'd be employing spies like *this*?"

He gestured at Salkeli. The Rodian seemed completely unfazed by the obvious insult.

"Sorry to disappoint you, Jaina," Harris went on, "but I'm not your thief. I was interested to learn about it, though, and I'm as curious as you are to find out who is responsible. When this ridiculous farce is over, I'll certainly make a point of looking into it more closely. I'll not allow the Bakuran public to be bled dry."

Jaina's eyes narrowed, scrutinizing the Deputy Prime Minister for any hint of duplicity. No matter how hard she looked, she couldn't find anything. Nevertheless, she didn't believe him. "You're up to *something*," she said finally. "I know it."

"Oh, I'm not denying that for a second," he said with a laugh. "It's just not what you think."

Harris pressed a control on his desk, and a section of the office wall slid to one side. The space behind it contained a holoprojector three meters across. The Deputy Prime Minister stood up to gain a better vantage point as an image came to life within it.

Jaina recognized it from her approach path to Salis D'aar: a massive amphitheater whose walls were bedecked with multicolored streamers and pennants bearing the P'w'eck and Bakuran emblems. Banners scrawled with greetings for the visiting aliens stretched between huge stone pillars around the outside, while overhead floated an enormous canopy that offered cover for the central arena, its underside painted with Bakura's flag. The sun was rising into the sky behind the point of view of the holocam, casting a golden glow across the stone steps and pillars. People were already filing into the seats, with guards in dark green uniforms making sure nobody strayed into a circular area in the center of the stadium—easily the most decorated section in view.

"The ceremony," Jaina said.

Blaine Harris nodded. "It'll be under way within the hour. From what I understand, it's supposed to be quite impressive, too."

"You're going to try to stop it?"

Harris glanced momentarily away from the holo to cast her a scornful look. "Don't be a fool, girl," he said with obvious contempt, and then turned back to the image. "My intentions are far more complex than that."

Jaina tried to force herself to think. Something was going on, but *what*? "You said 'farce,' " she prompted.

"I wasn't referring to the ceremony, if that's what you're thinking."

In the holo, a squad of P'w'eck guards appeared. With powerful muscles gliding smoothly beneath dull scales, they spread out to inspect the circle at the center of the stadium where, Jaina presumed, the ceremony itself would take place.

"They're keeping tight-lipped about the ceremony," Harris went on thoughtfully, still staring at the events unfolding. "I guess that's their prerogative. It's a privilege for us to be part of it."

"I thought the people on Bakura were only meant to be spectators."

"Oh, we are. But our planet is becoming sacred, and that's not something that happens every day."

"You really believe in this stuff?" Jaina asked.

He found this amusing. "Of course I don't believe in it. But the P'w'eck do, and that's enough for me." He turned back to Jaina. "Have you ever noticed the similarities between the Ssi-ruuk and the Yuuzhan Vong? Both cultures are xenophobic, stratified, religious, and expansionist. Both express these tendencies in violent methodologies. Both are, or have been, potent enemies of the New Republic."

"Just like the Yevetha," Jaina said.

Harris frowned. "What do they have to do with this?"

She shook her head. "Perhaps nothing." *Or everything,* she added to herself. "Go on."

"Both the Ssi-ruuk and the Yuuzhan Vong use defeated foes as slaves—an ugly practice that I'm pleased to see the P'w'eck abandon. That's one of two ways they've learned from their old masters."

"The second being? . . ."

"No more xenophobia, of course," he said, as though stating the obvious. "I'm hoping we can make it three ways. By allowing them their ritual, they might also learn to turn their religion into a nonviolent activity. Then we'll work on their caste system and see if we can't make the slave mentality a little more flexible. Acceptance, you see, can be as effective a tool for change as domination and force."

She frowned, understanding what he was saying but not getting the context. "I'm sorry but I think I'm missing the point you're trying to make."

He moved away from the holo with a sigh and began to pace. "My point, Jaina, is that we don't need the New Republic telling us what to do here on Bakura. We can make our own decisions, and you breathing down our neck only makes things more complicated."

"But we're not here to do that," she protested. "We're just trying to make sure that everything is okay with—"

"Really?" he cut in. "I find that very hard to believe." He stopped a few steps away from her, staring fiercely down into her eyes. "On the eve of our greatest moment— alliance with the heirs of our old enemy—you turn up to sow the seeds of dissent. Coincidence? I don't think so."

"Wait a minute. We were called to Bakura by someone who was concerned that something bad was going on."

"And who was that exactly?"

She glanced away. "An informant," she said, unable to be more precise.

He snorted. "If there's one thing I learned in the military, it's that an ill-informed informant can do more damage than a convincing double agent. The only way to be certain of anything, my dear girl, is to see it with your own eyes. And even then . . ."

He turned back to the projection, sentence unfinished. When he spoke again, his tone was softer, the subject changed. "I never thought I'd see this day. After all the years of fear and doubt, Bakura has finally found a means to become what we have always wanted it to be: independent and safe. From this day forward, Bakura will be a world in its own right—not one shackled to the Empire or the Republic or the Ssi-ruuk. With the P'w'eck, we can forge a new alliance—an alliance of our own choosing, not one forced upon us by circumstance. Peace will never again be ripped out from under us by powers from afar. It is time for us to be strong, at last."

Remembering the stories she'd been told of riots and disturbances, Jaina said, "I take it not everyone feels the same way about this as you do."

"That is only to be expected. It can take people time to

realize what is good for them." An apologetic smile flickered across his angular features. "I am self-aware enough to understand that I am betraying some of my own principles here. But as those who believe in the Cosmic Balance might say, sometimes it takes a great evil to bring about the greatest good."

"Exactly what sort of evil are we talking about?"

He ignored her question. "It's odd, you know, that we here on Bakura should defy the will of the Jedi so blatantly. I mean, not just that it was your uncle, Luke Skywalker, who played such an important part in saving us from the Ssi-ruuk so long ago, but that our beliefs so closely mirror yours. You, too, believe in a cosmic system of checks and balances that, ultimately, ensures life will thrive. I don't know if you're familiar with the beliefs of the native population of the planet, the Kurtzen, but they cling to a faith in a universal life force not dissimilar to your all-pervasive Force. Combine the two, and we might have become you—but there has never been a Jedi from Bakura that I am aware of. I find that strange."

"You think we're neglecting you, Deputy Prime Minister? Is that it? There are thousands of worlds out there. It takes time to search them all—time we don't have at the moment with the Yuuzhan Vong—"

His laughter cut her off. "My motive is not one of jealousy! You see—"

A buzzing sound came from the door.

Harris glanced at Salkeli, who straightened and raised his blaster. "This could be it." The Deputy Prime Minister came back around the desk to check something, and nodded. "And not a second too soon." He looked up at Jaina with a smile. "It would seem that the reinforcements have arrived. Quite unintentionally, I might add, but still . . ." He gestured to Salkeli, and the Rodian crossed the room to take Jaina by the arm, pressing the blaster into her side. She decided to play along for the moment. The Rodian's will was weak, and it probably wouldn't take much to make him turn the blaster on Harris. However, she thought it would be more prudent to wait for a while to see if she could find out just what Harris's plan was—and whether there was a way to stop it.

Salkeli walked her to a position in the corner of the room, out of sight of the door. He raised the blaster to her neck, pushing it firmly under her chin as he clamped one leathery hand over her mouth. Then he signaled to Harris, and the Deputy Prime Minister crossed the room and pressed his thumb against the lock.

The double door slid open with a hiss and three people entered in a rush. Jaina didn't recognize them at first—they were hooded and cloaked—but she could tell that it wasn't her parents and Tahiri. Clearly, they weren't who Harris had meant by the "reinforcements" arriving. It wasn't until the door shut behind them and the one in front turned to face Harris that Jaina saw who it was.

"We're in trouble," Malinza Thanas said. The others pulled back their hoods, revealing Jjorg and Vyram.

Harris looked concerned. "What happened to Zel?"

"He was shot when we fled the Stack," Malinza said, her voice caught somewhere between anger and tears. "They *shot* him, Blaine!"

"The main thing is that you're safe," he returned coolly. "Everything will be all right now."

"How can you say that? It was all we could do just to get here without being seen! And that's only because security is distracted by the ceremony. We're never going to be able to show our faces again unless you find out who's behind this!"

"Behind what, my dear?"

"Framing me for kidnapping, for one—then letting me escape to make it look like I'm guilty. I'll probably get blamed for Zel's death, as well!" Malinza sounded like she was on the edge of breaking down, but with obvious effort she brought her emotions under control. "We've lost Salkeli, too. He created a diversion while we got away, but he didn't meet us at the rendezvous. I'm worried that—"

"You should know I'd never let myself be caught or killed, Malinza," the Rodian said, stepping out from where he'd kept himself hidden and dragging Jaina with him. "But I guess you didn't know me that well, did you?"

Malinza turned, her look of surprise deepening when she saw Jaina. "I-I don't understand."

"That is becoming increasingly obvious," Harris said, producing a blaster of his own from beneath his scarlet robe. "Your weapons on the floor, if you would be so kind."

Malinza's face was pale as she dropped her small blaster onto the rug in front of her. Jjorg obeyed with a snarl, while Vyram calmly complied, keeping his thoughts to himself.

"What do you intend to do?" Malinza asked, fighting even harder now to keep her emotions in check.

"Do?" Harris waved Salkeli forward, and the Rodian pushed Jaina over to the others. "The job you set out to do, of course. Why else would I have funded you, Malinza, if our goals weren't the same in the first place? I'm going to unite the people against the Galactic Alliance. With the P'w'eck's help, I will make Bakura as safe as it can possibly be from outside invasion. We will govern our own destiny, forever." He smiled coldly. "The only real difference between your plans and my own is that, when mine come to fruition, the people of Bakura will be united behind me, not you. Which is a shame, really, because it will be your tragic death that finally mobilizes

them. That and the terrible betrayal of the Jedi who came
to enslave us once again."

"*What?*" asked Malinza and Jaina at the same time.

"All will be made clear in due course, I assure you.
Now, Salkeli, if you could bind their hands, please."

The Rodian dragged Jaina to join the others, holstered
his blaster, and produced electronic binders for the four
of them from a drawer in Harris's desk. With only the
one blaster on them now, Jaina felt a heightened edginess
in the Freedom members. She tried to catch Malinza's
eye, but the girl was steadfastly ignoring her—although
whether from embarrassment or anger, she couldn't tell.

"You're crazy if you think you're going to get away
with this," Jaina said, trying to divert the burden of rebellion onto her shoulders.

"Get away with what, exactly?" Harris laughed.
"You don't even know what it is I intend to do!"

The Deputy Prime Minister was finding the whole
thing entirely too amusing for Jaina's liking. That troubled Jaina deeply. That and the cool readiness with which
he held the blaster trained on his captives.

Malinza glared at Salkeli as he started to put the
binders around her wrists.

"We trusted you," she hissed.

"If it makes you feel any better, Malinza, it'll probably
be the last mistake you're ever going to make."

"Malinza, no!" Jaina called out when she saw the girl
noticeably stiffen.

But it was too late. Not waiting for the binders to snap
shut and tighten about her wrists, Malinza pushed Salkeli's
hands aside and brought her knee up into his groin. As
he jackknifed forward, she clubbed him to the ground.
Barely had the look of surprise begun to form on his face
when Jjorg was moving forward also. The long-limbed
blond lunged across the room, her strong thighs propel-
ling her forward, reaching for Harris's gun.

He didn't even move, except to pull the trigger. A single shot rang out and Jjorg hit the floor with a sickening thud.

Then the blaster was on Jaina.

"Whatever you're thinking," he said softly, "I advise against it."

Malinza backed away, mouth open in horror as she stared at Jjorg's limp body. Vyram made a move as though to help his fallen comrade, but Jaina quickly pulled him back.

"He means it," she said. "That blaster's not set to stun."

"Why didn't you do something?" Malinza asked, her words steeped in accusation and her cheeks soaked with tears.

Jaina shook her head. There was no way to say it nicely.

Harris saved her the trouble. "If Jjorg hadn't resisted, she'd still be alive."

Jaina would have perhaps phrased it less bluntly—and added something to the effect that there would come an opportunity to escape later, when they found out what exactly Harris was up to—but that was the essence of it.

Salkeli had climbed back to his feet, looking a little gray. Stepping up close to Malinza, he snarled, "Don't ever try that again."

He fastened the binders then, and Jaina saw Malinza wince as he set them to tighten around the girl's wrists—obviously tighter than they needed to be. Malinza didn't complain; she just let him do it with her jaw firmly clenched, her eyes unable to hide the anger and betrayal she was feeling.

"This actually works out well for me," Harris said as Salkeli bound Vyram next. "You saved me the trouble of trying to decide which one of you to shoot. There's nothing quite like a body to prove that there was a struggle, don't you think? Unfortunately, security was so distracted by the Keeramak and the ceremony that they didn't notice a slight glitch in the cams monitoring my office antechamber and the corridors outside. When they do, I'll be sure to point out your prowess, Vyram, at slicing into official systems. Such a disruption would be well within your capabilities, wouldn't you say?"

Jaina held out her hands when it was her turn for the binders. As Salkeli reached around her wrists to seal the durasteel binders she slid a simple thought into his mind: the *click* of the binders locking. She reinforced it with a wince similar to Malinza's, as though they were pinching her skin.

He leered at her as he stepped back, confident that all of the captives were now effectively bound. Jaina smiled back at him defiantly. The binders were tight around her wrists but not locked. A good tug would have them open, when the time was right. *Then* she would help Malinza and her friends escape.

Salkeli produced his blaster and took his place beside Harris. Malinza glowered at him, eyes filled with hate, while Harris stopped to check the growing crowd in the holoprojector before switching it off and closing the panel.

"Within the hour, this planet will be a consecrated part of the P'w'eck Emancipation Movement. And you, my dear Malinza, will be a martyr to your cause. Doesn't that fill you with pride?"

Malinza spat on the carpet at his feet.

Harris simply smiled back at her, his eyes triumphant and gloating. "Spoken like a true rebel." He faced his accomplice, then. "Salkeli, in position, please."

The Rodian ushered his three prisoners closer to the door, and Harris opened it with his thumbprint. Jaina, Malinza, and Vyram filed outside with the blaster pointed at their backs.

"Where are you taking us?" Malinza asked.

"Wait and see," Harris said. "I guarantee you won't be disappointed."

PART FOUR

CONSECRATION

"Disappointed?" The note of incredulity in Jag's voice could barely hide his irritation. "Jaina is still missing and you think I might be disappointed that I'm not going to see the ceremony?"

The voice of Twin Sun Three fell silent, her attempt at lightening the mood having fallen painfully flat.

Jag clicked twice to remind his pilots not to clutter the airwaves, even as he chided himself for being snappy. He was concerned by Jaina's continued absence, but at the same time he had to trust in Jaina's ability to look after herself. Besides which, if anything terrible had happened to her, he was sure Leia would sense it. That Jaina hadn't called for help yet through the Force suggested that she was at least still in control of her situation—whatever that might be. And until such a time as she did get in touch with anyone, he would just have to continue on as though everything were normal—and that meant concentrating on flying.

He had taken a mixed flight out to patrol the edges of *Selonia*'s orbit, wary of any "unauthorized" activity while attention was focused below. Both P'w'eck and Bakuran contingents were quiet, the two big alien assault carriers, *Errinung'ka* and *Firrinree*, orbiting in quadrants diametrically opposed to the two local defenders, *Defender* and *Sentinel*. The latter had two full squadrons of P'w'eck fighter craft stationed at close quarters, plus two squat picket ships. If things were to turn nasty, for whatever reason, they could do a lot of damage while the Bakurans tried to get their balance. While Jag obviously hoped nothing untoward *would* happen, he had to think tactically.

"Don't just outguess your enemy," his father had once said, "but out*see* him, too. Always assume that he's two steps ahead of the current play, and be *three* steps ahead yourself."

Jag took his clawcraft and his two wingmates in a wide arc around *Selonia*. The frigate basked in the light of Bakura's sun, unmolested and apparently completely ignored by the forces surrounding it.

He could sense games all around him, moving slowly toward their endplays. It irked him once again to be so far away from the action taking place below on Bakura's surface. But if nothing came of it, and all his second-guessing proved unfounded, he wouldn't be disappointed. A large part of him agreed with Leia that maybe, just maybe, this deal with the P'w'eck would turn out to be the best thing that had ever happened to Bakura . . .

The voice of the comm operator on *Selonia* suddenly cut across his thoughts.

"Launches detected!"

"I'm on it," he said, quickly swinging his clawcraft in the direction of the numerous vessels his sensors detected emerging from *Sentinel*'s launching bays. His wingmates were close behind him, following him in for a closer look.

"Has Bakuran Defense Fleet advised us of the launches?" he asked. The number of ships leaving the cruiser was already up to twenty and still rising.

"As far as they're concerned, I don't think they feel they have to," came the reply. "But I'll check with them anyway."

Jag was already close enough to pick out the types of craft emerging from the launching bays, but this only confused him. It was a mixed bag, consisting of Y- and X-wings from the Bakuran Defense Forces, along with an equal number of Ssi-ruuvi—*P'w'eck,* he reminded himself—*Swarm*-class droid fighters. They flew in elegant formation out of the bays and into orbit, peeling off in threes and fives, still divided more or less equally between both forces.

"Apparently it's an honor guard," came back *Selonia*'s operator. "I've notified Captain Mayn."

Honor guard? It was plausible enough, he supposed. The ships were flying tightly together, and had obviously rehearsed their maneuvers well beforehand. That showed a degree of cooperation between the two forces—as well as trust.

But it still troubled him. The number of ships was approaching fifty, far too many for the depleted Twin Suns to tackle on its own—especially if it was caught off guard.

Be three steps ahead . . .

"Do you think they'd mind if the Galactic Alliance joined them to show our respects, too?" he asked *Selonia*.

"I'll ask."

While he waited on a reply, on another channel he alerted the Twin Suns pilots on standby, telling them to kit up and launch as soon as possible.

"We're on our way," Jocell said, adding dryly: "I don't think any of us really expected this to be a slow day, did we?"

Jag picked a flight of three ships, two of them droid fighters, and tailed them around the planet. The trio didn't react to his presence, but a transmission from *Selonia* not long after confirmed that they'd been noticed.

"They're requesting we stay well clear," came Captain Mayn over the open channel. "I informed them that we would happily comply, but that we would have to take the necessary steps to ensure our security."

Jag smiled tightly to himself. What Mayn was saying was that, short of Jag provoking an altercation, he had a free hand to do whatever he felt necessary.

With this in mind, he continued to shadow the trio of fighters. The total number of ships in the "honor guard" had just reached an even hundred—and it was still climbing.

We're under attack!

In an instant, Saba was awake and clambering to her feet. Disconcerted, she tried to get her bearings. Then she remembered: she'd been resting in a large chair on the ice barge's opulent observation deck. She'd nodded off and fallen into a peaceful dream of being up on the slopes of the Listian Hills. The sky had been red and cloudy, the scent on the breeze relaxing, and she'd lain there among the warm rocks, listening to the restive growlings of her hatchmates nearby . . .

Then Mara's cry through the Force had snapped her back to reality, and she realized with some disappointment that the growling she'd heard in the dream was in fact the rasping of the barge's many repulsors over the surface of the ice beneath them. With a grunt, she shook herself free of the dream and made her way over to where the others were standing.

The barge was a shallow, oval-shaped vessel that skidded across the surface of glaciers and ice fields with more speed than grace. The three passenger decks bulged out of the top like an afterthought, ringed by the powerful generators and repulsors that kept it in the air. It possessed heavy shields that kept the icy wind at bay, but the howling was still audible as a thin, far-off Ixll-like wail. There were four weapons emplacements around the curved edge of the barge, and they currently pointed at something flickering in and out of sight through dense snow spray off to the starboard side.

"There are two more behind us," Soontir Fel said. One thick finger stabbed at a display. Ten swift targets surrounded the barge. Software identified the objects as smaller than a snowspeeder, but just as heavily armed and shielded. They looked like fat coins tipped on their sides, ripping edge-first through the air. "Single-person fliers, I imagine, given the speed they're moving."

A warning shot on the port side bounced off the barge's shields and into a snowbank. Steam exploded from the point of impact, sending a white cloud high into the air.

"Pirates?" Master Skywalker asked.

"Possibly." Fel rocked the barge in the direction of the snow-flier, forcing it to swerve away.

"Shouldn't we try to contact the spaceport to let them know what's happening?" Mara asked.

"Already tried," Fel said, shifting the barge suddenly to starboard. A loud *thump* sounded as the barge's shields connected with one of the fliers. "But we're being jammed."

"If they're not pirates, could they be enemies of yours?" Stalgis asked.

"Sure, but which ones?" Fel grunted. "Whoever they are, we can't outrun or outshoot them. Our one advantage is the shield, which I'm fairly certain they can't take out. Unless they bring in something bigger, we should be safe in here."

Syal Antilles put a hand on his shoulder. "When we reach the spaceport, security will drive them away."

A nearby explosion rocked the ice barge from nose to stern. Fragments of ice ricocheted off the barge's shield and swept into its wake. Another explosion cracked the ice ahead of them, sending spreading fingers across the endless white plain. Fel banked to avoid the instability.

When he tried to return to his original course, more fire from the snow-fliers forced him back.

"That's *if* we can make it there," he belatedly responded to Syal's comment.

"They're trying to force us off course," Mara said.

"I think you're right," Fel growled. "If it was just me, I'd take my chances over those crevasses. But—" He glanced at Syal, standing behind him with her hand still on his shoulder. He shook his head. "I'm not prepared to take that risk right now."

"I'm sorry," Luke said. "It's us they want."

"Don't be too sure. I'm not popular with some of the syndics because I want to change their ways. All it would take is for one of them to decide to make a move while I'm distracted—"

Another explosion rocked the barge, forcing it to turn farther starboard.

"Either way," Mara said, "we're all in this together right now."

"Maybe if I give myself up to them, they'll leave the rest of you alone," Fel said.

"No!" Syal responded instantly. "I won't let you do that!"

Luke agreed. "It would be a pointless sacrifice. They won't leave any witnesses. You know that. In fact, if anything they'll use us as scapegoats. What could be more believable than a spat between old enemies—especially if the accused are killed resisting capture?"

Fel acquiesced with a nod. "So what do you suggest?"

"There's clearly no point running, and we can't beat them with brute force." Luke's gaze wandered around him as he thought for a moment. "I suggest we stop trying altogether."

"I thought you just said we shouldn't give them what they want," Syal said.

"I did."

"So what are you saying?" pressed the woman.

Master Skywalker smiled. "I'm saying we should maybe give them a little more than they're expecting."

Leia followed an usher to their seats, accompanied by Han, C-3PO, and her two Noghri bodyguards. The stadium was enormous, practically a giant crater lined with stalls, with the more comfortable booths higher up, affording the more privileged guests a better view of the proceedings that would soon be taking place in the stadium's center. The delegation from the Galactic Alliance was, of course, among those privileged guests. They had reserved seating to the right of Prime Minister Cundertol's stand, where he would be surrounded by senior Senators atop a large podium that jutted out from the ring of seats. The day was warm; floating sunshades circulated lazily above the crowd, propelled by the ever-present repulsors. Among the crowd, she made out signs and banners, although she couldn't quite make out exactly what they were saying. She guessed that they'd belong to both protestors and supporters of the Keeramak and its P'w'eck revolutionaries. This was a big day for Bakura, and a lot hung in the balance.

Nothing much was happening just yet, though. The Prime Minister had still to appear and, after the early-morning meeting, he would no doubt be avoiding the Galactic Alliance when he did. Fifty P'w'eck soldiers maintained a perfect ring around the area on which the ceremony was to take place, well away from the nearest seats in the center of the stadium.

Han's hand found hers and gave it a tight squeeze. Warmth flooded through her, reminding her of why she loved him. Even in difficult times, when events threatened to overtake everything, he was always there for her. Flashes of irritation hid a depth of emotion that surprised even him, sometimes, and of which she was always grateful to be the recipient.

"Do you think the rain's going to hold off?" he asked.

She followed his gaze. Dense clouds were building on the western horizon, promising a tropical storm.

"If it doesn't," she said, "then I guess we're going to get wet."

"Great. That's really going to add insult to injury."

A fanfare sounded as they took their seats, announcing the formal arrival of the Bakuran and P'w'eck leaders. Prime Minister Cundertol, dressed in a magnificent purple robe, and the Keeramak led a large group of human, Kurtzen, and P'w'eck officials in a cleared path from the base of the stadium to the central ring. There, to the stirring sound of the Bakuran anthem, they turned to address the crowd and, symbolically, Bakura itself.

"My people," Cundertol began, his voice magnified a thousandfold by speakers floating high above the stadium, "welcome to you all on this magnificent occasion. With our new allies, the P'w'eck, we join together to usher in a new era of prosperity and peace. As neighbors and friends, we will embrace the universal truths that bind together all cultures. Today, Bakura achieves its destiny, free from fear of old enemies and working with new allies to build a common future."

The crowd responded with equal parts cheers and boos as he stepped back to allow the Keeramak to speak. The mutant Ssi-ruu looked radiant in a shining silver harness trailing multicolored ribbons and tiny bells that jangled delicately with each movement. Its scales glinted in the weakened morning light, making it hard to tell where its outfit stopped and its skin began. Not even the growing cloud cover could dim its unique beauty.

The powerful tones that issued from its throat boomed deafeningly across the stadium.

"People of Bakura," came the translation when it had

finished its address, "I am proud to be here as the leader of a liberated people. The P'w'eck species, no longer bound to an oppressive regime rooted in cruelty and bloodshed, joins with you in spiritual communion as our two great nations create a bond that will run much deeper than mere friendship. With the signing of the treaty, we will be one, our fates forever linked!"

The response from the crowd was as mixed as it had been for Cundertol, but it didn't seem to faze either leader. They bowed to one another, then the Prime Minister and his contingent made their way back through the crowd to their seats. As Leia had guessed, he acknowledged her and Han with only a formal nod.

Han muttered something to the effect that he wouldn't trade a bootful of mynock droppings for Cundertol on a good day. Leia shushed him. There was no sign of the Deputy Prime Minister—an absence no one had mentioned, but which she found interesting.

There was no time to ponder it, however, as the ceremony was immediately under way. P'w'eck priests bedecked with streamers began warbling some monotonous chant as the Keeramak prowled the edges of the cleared space, scattering glinting shards in a perfect circle around the alien contingent. Every few seconds, in counterpoint to the chanting, the Keeramak would raise its head and intone a phrase in its own tongue. This time there was no public interpreter to explain what was being said.

"Can you translate this?" Leia whispered to C-3PO.

"Only in part, Mistress. The dialect is not the same in which the P'w'eck converse. It appears to be an ancient, ritual tongue, perhaps preserved for—"

"Spare us the details, Goldenrod," Han said in an irritable undertone, "and just get to the point, will you?"

"As you wish, sir. The Keeramak is addressing the life spirit of the galaxy, beseeching it to hear him and grant his wishes. 'The golden light of this morning is yours,' it is saying. 'The blue-tinted skies and white clouds are yours. Where leaves are green and flowers bloom in many colors, you are there. Where children grow strong in limb and heart, you are there.' "

"Very poetic," Han muttered. "How much more of this is there?"

"The ceremony is scheduled to last one hour, sir."

"That's just great." Han stretched his legs in front of him and locked his hands behind his head. "Wake me when it's over, will you, Leia?"

The floating van pulled up outside an unguarded entrance to the stadium. Goure, at the controls of the aircar following the van, drove past, rounded a corner, and came to a halt. Tahiri was the first to climb out, running back to the corner. Goure was close behind. Once there, the two of them cautiously peered around just in time to see Blaine Harris lead Jaina, Malinza Thanas, and two others into the stadium.

"So much for security," Tahiri muttered over the sound of chanting coming from speakers within the stadium. "There's no one at the gates. They just walked right in!"

"I suspect it was arranged that way." The Ryn's tail brushed rhythmically against her legs. "And if we're quick enough, we might be able to take advantage of the situation, too."

Together they approached the entrance, their pace hurried but wary, aware that at any moment alarms might start to ring out. In the end, they managed to reach the gateway without incident and slip inside undetected. The rumble of the crowd within wrapped around them like a warm and comforting embrace. Whatever was taking place inside the stadium, Tahiri thought, it certainly sounded impressive.

"Can you sense your friend?" Goure asked.

Jaina's mind had been shining like a beacon since well before she'd left Blaine Harris's office, just minutes after Tahiri and Goure had arrived. While she and the Ryn had been trying to convince a security guard to let them in to see the Deputy Prime Minister, Tahiri had detected that Jaina was on the move. Retreating from the ministerial offices, Tahiri and Goure had found a droid interface, via which the Ryn had been able to determine from security cam images that Harris was moving with Jaina. Although they had no idea of where exactly the Deputy Prime Minister was taking Jaina, they'd set out in pursuit, with Tahiri beginning to despair of being able to reach Harris in time to stop the ceremony. That they had ended up at the stadium where the ceremony itself was taking place was indeed a stroke of luck. Perhaps, she thought, the Deputy Prime Minister had the same idea they had, and was wanting to stop the ceremony before Cundertol's plan—whatever it was—came into effect.

But there was an edge to Jaina's thoughts that undermined Tahiri's confidence. Something wasn't quite right. If Jaina was Harris's prisoner, then what did that mean? Tahiri was finding it increasingly difficult to tell who was on what side—which made knowing what to do almost impossible.

"Well?" Goure asked.

Tahiri nodded. "Yeah, I can sense her all right."

Then together they padded silently down the corridors, following Jaina's presence deep into the bowels of the stadium.

"Where are you taking us?" Jaina demanded.

Harris, a few paces ahead, ignored her. Salkeli gave her a shove in the shoulder from behind with the butt of his weapon. It was a simple message: *Shut up and keep moving.* She did so, following the Deputy Prime Minister down a wide ramp and through a series of archways barely high enough to accommodate his large frame. A short time later, they stopped before a sealed door that looked big enough to drive a landspeeder through.

It opened when Blaine Harris keyed a long alphanumeric sequence into the lock.

"Move," he ordered curtly, waving her and the surviving members of Freedom ahead of him.

Jaina found herself in an equipment locker, empty except for a single metal container in the center of the room.

"A little bare for my tastes," she said dryly. "But I guess it will do for now."

"As good a place as any to die, you think?" Harris countered. He closed the door and strode over to stand beside Jaina. "Take a look at the box; tell me what you see."

Jaina squatted to take a closer look, carefully maintaining the pretense that her wrists were still securely bound. After a moment's consideration, she shrugged. "A remote detonator?"

"Very good," said Harris. "Now press the red button."

She laughed humorlessly. "You can't be—"

"*Do* it," Harris insisted, raising his weapon and pressing it to Malinza's forehead. "Do it or I shoot the girl."

Jaina glanced at Malinza. Her expression was determined, but her eyes couldn't hide her fear. They both knew that Harris's threats weren't idle.

"Okay," she said, reaching out with her seemingly bound hands and depressing the button. A numeric timer came to life, counting down from ten standard minutes.

Harris nodded in satisfaction, lowering the blaster to his side. "And now that your fingerprints are on the button, your fate is effectively sealed. Once you're dead and the bomb goes off, there'll be no one to plead in your defense."

Jaina focused her energy, forcing herself to remain calm. *Soon,* she told herself. *Just a little bit longer . . .*

"You know," she said, standing, "blowing up the stadium isn't going to help relations with the P'w'eck." It was as much to stall Harris as it was to fish for information from the man.

"If that was my intention," he said, "then yes, I have no doubt that such an action would seriously compromise relations with the P'w'eck. But it's not. Well, not the *entire* stadium, anyway. Just the part where my enemies are seated."

My enemies . . .

"Prime Minister Cundertol?" Then, with a terrible realization spreading through her, she said, "My *parents*?"

His smile was wide and cruel. "Yes, my dear. What will become evident when the pieces are put together is that you planted the bomb to derail the treaty with the P'w'eck. The Jedi didn't want Bakura to leave the Galactic Alliance, and they were prepared to stop at nothing to prevent this from happening. Your parents, unfortunately, were simply necessary sacrifices to the cause. Thinking that you were helping her, Malinza Thanas was convinced by you to kidnap me and force your way into the stadium, where a bomb awaited. But just in time, your evil plans were discovered by the misguided but loyal young Malinza who, at the cost of her own life and the lives of her friends, helped release me. Alas, not in time to prevent the detonation of the bomb. The Prime Minister will be killed, along with much of the Senate."

"And you step in to make sure the ceremony goes ahead as planned, right?" Jaina finished for him.

"In memory of the brave Malinza Thanas, of course," he added, still smiling widely. "It's all rather poetic, don't you think?"

"It's abominable," Malinza muttered, unable to hide the tremor from her voice.

"I think *efficient* sounds better."

Jaina glanced at the timer while Harris gloated. She had only seven and a half minutes left to deal with both Harris and Salkeli, as well as deactivate the bomb. Even for a Jedi, that seemed a tall order.

Leia watched with interest as the P'w'eck priests added a swaying, fluid dance to their weird chant. The Keeramak had completed the circle and was addressing the sky above, opening its arms as if to encompass the entire world.

" 'The oceans of space have parted to create this island of bounty,' " C-3PO continued to translate. " 'Even in the desert of the void, oases must exist. We invite you to share this one with us in the spirit of galactic unity: one mind, one body, one spirit, one . . .' I'm afraid I am unable to translate this particular phrase."

"Remind me again why we had to be here," Han whispered. Leia shushed him again.

"The stars shine kindly upon this world," the Keeramak said, "for it is a blessed place."

Leia wasn't so sure about that. Bakura had seen its fair share of trouble, and she doubted some alien blessing was going to change that. If the Yuuzhan Vong kept coming, it was going to take more than hand-waving and the jingling of a few bells to keep them at bay.

Mind you, she thought, if the P'w'eck turned out to be as good at fighting as the Ssi-ruuk had been, the chances were they'd give the Yuuzhan Vong a run for their money. The Ssi-ruuk fought well when forced into it. Their fear of dying away from a consecrated world lent any engagements outside the Imperium a hurried, almost frantic air—which was probably why, Leia thought, they were so good at the quick strike. They had honed this tactic over the years until they had become the masters of it. And the more such raids they won, the stronger they became, since the object was as often to take captives for entechment as it was to destroy.

Still, she couldn't help feeling a growing edginess as the ceremony built in intensity. The chanting had reached an almost fever pitch—so much so that C-3PO was barely able to keep up with the Keeramak's intonations.

The crowd was utterly silent now. Even Han abandoned all pretence of disinterest, leaning forward as though hypnotized by the swaying, singing aliens.

". . . tighten the bonds . . . conjoined in glorious synergy . . . although space may separate . . . as one in the crèche of stars . . ."

Then suddenly a stab of urgency cut though her. She didn't know where it was coming from, at first—until she identified its source as the Force, and from *outside* her.

"Han," she whispered. Then, louder, to be heard over the P'w'eck: "Han, it's Jaina!"

He instantly snapped upright in his seat. "Where?" he asked, looking vaguely into the crowd in search of his daughter. "*Where?* Is she okay? I don't see her!"

"She's not here!" Leia struggled to interpret what she was feeling. "She's calling to me through the Force. She's in trouble—but her thoughts aren't focused on herself. She's trying to warn us. She's—" She shook her head, unable to get a proper reading on the message. "Something's about to happen."

Han turned to his wife. "What is it?"

Leia closed her eyes to sort out a mad jumble of wordless impressions. Images she couldn't interpret flooded into her on a tide of growing urgency.

"Han, I think we need to get out of here. Quickly!"

Han rose to his feet immediately. He knew better than to question the instincts of both his wife and his daughter. With Cakhmain and Meewalh gathered close around Leia, he got to his feet and started to lead the way out of the stadium. No one paid them any attention; they were all too busy concentrating on the spectacle taking place down below in the stadium's center.

They reached the edge of the prestige stand unmolested. No assassins had lunged at them out of the crowd, nor any threats been issued. But there was no denying Leia's nervousness. Whatever Jaina was sending her via the Force, it was getting more urgent with each passing moment.

"What's going on, Leia?" Han asked at one point. "Where is she?"

"She's near here. I don't want to distract her, Han. She's—"

A near-perfect image formed in her mind: explosives, a timer, seconds decreasing rapidly in number.

"Oh—it's coming!" she gasped. "We have to get down! Run, everyone, run!" She shouted this last comment to the people around her, but no one seemed to pay her any mind. They were still taken by what was going on below. Her Noghri bodyguards bustled their two human charges and C-3PO toward an exit from the stadium. "No!" she shouted. "There's not enough time! Get down! Get down!"

Her bodyguards pressed her to the ground, saurian eyes scanning the crowd for any sign of what was to come. The alien chanting was at its peak, screeching over the channel, making it almost impossible to hear anything else.

Then another desperate image from Jaina, so clear it formed words in her mind:

Tahiri, no!

The world turned white and her connection to Jaina instantly went dead.

The ice barge slowed to a halt in the lee of a giant snow dune. The grating whine of its repulsors ebbed as it settled onto its wide belly. Fel's hands worked the controls with practiced ease, guiding the craft to a near-perfect landing.

When everything was still, the burly human glanced at Luke as though to ask, *Are you sure you know what you're doing?*

When Luke nodded his reassurance, Fel killed the shields. The barge instantly shuddered as the howling, icy wind swept over it.

"We'll need survival suits," Syal said.

Fel shook his head. "We won't be out there long enough to need them. This should be over in a minute or two."

Danni glowered at the ten circular shapes swooping around the landed barge. Her eyes were dark with fatigue. "Here comes one now," she said, pointing at a snow-flier arcing in to land near the barge.

"And another," Stalgis said, also pointing.

Saba watched as the strange-looking craft came down on one edge. Its engines burned brightly in infrared, outshining the cold sun. Four spindly supports emerged to support the vertical disk in the snow. When it was stable, a circular panel on its side irised open and a black-clad female pilot stepped out, her uniform unadorned by rank or other identifying markers. The figure was tall and slender, just like every other Chiss Saba had ever encountered. Saba watched as the woman strode confidently to the curving flank of the barge, then jumped lightly up onto it.

A second pilot joined her, holding one of the two-handed rifles Saba had seen in the immersion room. The Chiss called them charrics, she had learned. The first pilot removed her helmet, revealing craggy, weathered features under close-cropped hair. The blue skin of her face looked colder than the ice around her.

"Ganet," Fel said darkly. "I should have known."

"Who is she?" Luke asked.

"She commands a phalanx for a rival syndic, one who doesn't approve of the changes I'm encouraging. And I know she wouldn't approve of you, either."

Master Luke dismissed the implied warning with a smile. "Then maybe it's time we meet her," he said. "See if we can't change her mind about us."

Fel didn't smile back in response. He just slipped his hand into a pair of thin black gloves as he turned to his wife. "Everything ready?"

Syal nodded and pressed a button on the ice barge's controls. A display to one side of the main instrumental panel began to count down.

Two minutes . . . one minute fifty-nine seconds . . . one minute fifty-eight seconds . . .

The main door lifted up and out, and warm air in the cabin was instantly sucked outside. An icy chill wrapped itself around Saba, who clenched her teeth, bracing herself for the freezing temperatures. As with most saurian species, the cold would slow her down, so she would have to draw upon the Force to counter this—which she did, igniting a ball of warmth in her chest that spread outward through her limbs. Only her extremities retained any sensation of the cold, and she kept them tucked in close, curling her fingers into fists and tucking her tail near her legs.

Soontir Fel exited the barge first, exuding a calm self-assurance. He surveyed the scene before him, then stepped over the threshold to make way for the others. Master Luke went next, followed by Saba, Mara, and Stalgis. Danni and Syal stayed inside.

One minute forty-five seconds . . .

Fel stopped in front of the female pilot, looking her up and down with quiet disapproval. Finally he shook his head. "You don't seem the type for open rebellion, Ganet."

"I prefer the term *excision*, myself," she answered calmly.

"Whatever it takes to justify your actions, is that it?"

Another pilot stepped up behind the craggy woman and waited there with charric at the ready. Two more snow-fliers landed nearby.

"I'm not here to banter with you, Fel," Ganet said. "I want your cooperation. And I will get it, too, because we have your daughter."

Saba detected a slight stiffening to Fel's posture, but his expression and tone remained firm and steady. "Who exactly are 'we,' Ganet?"

"It's not important," she said as she raised her weapon and pointed it at his chest. "All that matters is that we have her, yes?"

"At least tell me *why*." Fel stepped forward, his barrel chest defying the nozzle of her weapon. "I have given the Chiss my all since I joined you; surely I have the—"

"You joined *Thrawn*, Fel! That's not the same as joining the Chiss. We have ways and traditions he turned his back on, and by joining him you proved that you don't respect them, either."

"Isn't one of those traditions not to fire upon an enemy until he has fired upon you first?"

Ganet smiled calmly. "But you aren't my enemy, Fel. Don't mistake me on that. You are merely an inconvenience that I will soon be rid of."

One minute . . .

"And what about us?" Master Luke asked.

Ganet took a step to her right, out of Fel's reach, turning her attention to the others. "You were invited here on a pretext the CEDF does not credit," she said. "You may have fooled the Houses, but your fables don't impress us. Zonama Sekot is a smokescreen for something more sinister. We just don't know what it is yet."

"Then you intend to dispose of us, too."

Ganet laughed. "It was always our intention to dispose of you, Jedi! We never intended to let you leave here."

"Then the deadline—" Stalgis started.

"Was a ruse to give us an opportunity to move against you, of course."

"So we're all just pawns in Chief Navigator Aabe's little power game?" Luke shook his head. "What did you promise him? Soontir's position once it was available?"

Thirty seconds . . .

"He delivered us the means to fix a difficult situation," she said, nodding. "He will be suitably rewarded when the time comes, yes."

"The same way you're 'rewarding' Soontir right now?" Mara said. "Don't you people have a conscience?"

"We are aware of the concept," Ganet said, raising the charric, "but it has no place in war. And this *is* war, Mara Jade. Have no doubts about that whatsoever. In the fight against the Yuuzhan Vong, there can be no gray areas: there are only allies and enemies. The Chiss do not need allies, so I'm afraid that leaves only the other option." She motioned the other snow-flier pilot to come forward as two more stepped up onto the ice barge. "Please move away from the door and turn around—*all* of you."

Ten seconds . . .

"That includes your wife, Fel."

Fel motioned for Syal and Danni to join them, which they quickly did.

"I promise you a clean death, Fel," Ganet said. "There is no dishonor in accepting your fate."

Three seconds . . .

"For the Chiss!"

"Indeed," Ganet said, mistaking Fel's battle cry for a qualifying statement. "For the—"

Now! Luke commanded.

Saba, Danni, and Mara sprang immediately into action—along with Soontir Fel—a split second before all the ice barge's cannons simultaneously fired.

The intended distraction worked. Ganet and her accomplices were momentarily thrown by the explosions—and a moment was all the Jedi needed.

Fel stepped nimbly to his left. Ganet instinctively followed, the charric in her hand ready to fire. With a hiss, Luke's lightsaber flared to life, slicing smoothly up to sever the barrel of Ganet's weapon. Fel snap-kicked her legs from beneath her as Luke turned upon the second pilot, effortlessly knocking him to the ground with a Force push.

"You *heard* me?" Luke called to Fel. "I didn't know you were Force-sensitive."

"I'm not," Fel responded. "But I can count!"

Mara spun around as a bolt of energy flashed by Luke's head, and saw the other two pilots adopt sharpshooter stances on the edge of the barge. She deflected the first shot with her lightsaber, exploding a snow dune a hundred meters away into a puff of white. The second shot missed altogether. Saba reached out with a mental hand and wrenched the pilot's rifle away from him. The remaining pilot turned his charric on her and fired. The shot was a good one and would have connected with Saba's head had she not deflected it back at him with her lightsaber. He fell backward off the barge and into the snow.

A screaming sound heralded an attack from above. Blaster bolts scored thick black lines across the top of the barge, barely missing Saba as the snow-flier swept by and swung around for another pass. Two of the other five were already lining up to do the same.

"Get those shields back on!" Stalgis yelled, picking up a charric and taking a potshot at the retreating flier. The shot pinged from the craft's side but didn't slow it even slightly.

"Come on, Saba," Mara said, pointing at two of the landed fliers. "While we have the chance!"

Saba understood instantly what she meant. Even with

its shield up, the ice barge would be vulnerable to the remaining six snow-fliers. If they were going to reach the spaceport, then they were going to have to take a more offensive role in this fight.

Flexing the muscles in her powerful legs, Saba ran for the edge of the barge and threw herself forward into the snow.

Not a moment too soon. Her tail caught the edge of the shield as it snapped into life. Flexing it to get rid of the tingling, stinging sensation, she ran up the snow dune for the nearest of the fliers. Mara took the one to their right, using the Force to assist her movement through the thick snow. The fliers were larger than they looked in the air—at least twice as tall as Saba and as thick across as three of her body lengths. Like a glossy, black wheel stuck in the snow, it towered over her as she reached its base and hauled herself up the egress ladder.

The controls were different from any she'd seen before but, like the charrics, operated on principles she understood. The craft didn't possess a sophisticated security system, and responded to the touch of her cold fingers. Wrapping her tail around her hips, she fired up the engines.

The flier's legs retracted with a faint whir as it lifted smoothly from the ground; then, with the cockpit vibrating to the tune of the craft's powerful repulsors, it swung up into the sky, forcing Saba back into the seat, grunting in discomfort as her tail was momentarily squashed.

The flier's weapon system was uncluttered and simple to operate. She armed the blaster cannon and targeted one of the six enemy snow-fliers coming around to respond to the new threat. Her first shot went wide. She adjusted her trim, rapidly familiarizing herself with the snow-flier's responses. Her second shot was closer to the mark, but she still had to make some adjustments. She fought to ignore the giddying rolls of the horizon as the flier she was following banked sharply in an attempt to throw her off its tail. It had been a long time since her last dogfight around Barab I, but she was pleased to find that her skills hadn't atrophied.

A low growl emerged from her throat as the flier edged up into her crosshairs. She fired.

Sparks flew in a comet tail: her shot had blown her target's port stabilizer. It wobbled in an ungainly fashion across the sky as the pilot fought to bring it down in a controlled ditch. Saba didn't stick around to see if it made it or not; she was too busy bringing her own flier around in search of another target.

Mara had downed one flier, too, but that did nothing to deter the remaining four. Regrouping in a tight square formation, they abandoned their attack of the ice barge—now firing its own cannon through its shields at the enemy fliers. Saba and Mara were disadvantaged by their inability to communicate with each other, but the Force more than compensated for that. Subtle instructions from Mara nudged Saba in new directions, toward new targets. She followed them without question, even when they appeared to conflict with what her own instincts were telling her.

When the Force told her to take her flier in a barrel roll right through the heart of the Chiss's diamond-shaped formation, she did just that, breaking them up and scattering them in four different directions. Mara picked one off as she swept by in Saba's wake, reducing the odds to a more comfortable three-to-two.

On your tail, Saba!

Saba twisted in her seat to see what was behind her, but immediately regretted her impulsive reaction. The sudden movement in the restricted seat made her tail cramp. A shot from behind sizzled horribly close to her starboard cockpit shell. Forcing herself to ignore the discomfort, she jerked the flight stick down hard, then up again, rolling the flier up and over in a loop that brought her behind the flier that had been chasing her. It pitched forward in an attempt to lose her, but wasn't quick enough to avoid a volley of blasterfire that sheared off its cannon and scored a hole in its canopy. Wind snatched at the damage, twisting it off course and plunging it into a snowbank in a bright explosion that scattered debris far out from the impact site.

Mara performed a spectacular maneuver that knocked another flier out of the sky and left her on a head-to-head trajectory with the sole remaining flier. The Chiss pilot didn't deviate from his course in the slightest, however, as the two fliers sped toward one another. Saba felt distinctly uneasy as she watched, knowing that Mara would never back down from such a challenge. Opening herself completely to the Force, she closed her eyes and fired three rapid cannon bursts. When she opened her eyes again, the Chiss flier was spiraling toward the ground with damage to its maneuvering flaps.

They performed a quick circuit of the grounded ice barge before landing. Master Skywalker and the others had rounded up Ina'ganet'nuruodo and the other three pilots and placed them in binders. The four were on their knees on the flank of the barge, watching bitterly as Syal killed the barge's shield and Saba and Mara landed nearby.

Saba's tail whipped gratefully behind her as she climbed aboard the barge and rejoined her friends. After the heat of battle, the air felt even colder than before.

"Nice flying," Luke said, addressing the compliment to both Mara and Saba.

Coming from such an accomplished pilot as the Jedi Master himself, Saba couldn't help but feel pleased. "Thank you," she said, feeling herself flush dark green beneath her scales.

"The jammer is in Ganet's flier." Luke nodded at one of the fliers still parked nearby. "We didn't deactivate it, so they haven't been able to call for help."

"But we could now, right?" Mara asked.

All eyes turned to Fel, who knew best of all how the local security forces would react to the development. "I think we should make our way to the spaceport, as originally planned," he said after a moment's consideration. "While we're out here, there's still an opportunity to dispose of us and erase the evidence. I think it best we present them with a fait accompli by coming back alive." He shot a dark glance to Ganet, glowering on her knees before him. "Showing the Chiss the worst they can do usually brings out the best in them. This is probably just what we need to demonstrate the futility of our inaction while the rest of the galaxy is at war. There's no point pretending we're strong while our own command structure falls apart around our ears."

Syal came to stand next to her husband. "I don't want you to go to war," she said, "but I'd rather that than seeing you betrayed by our own people."

Fel put a hand on her shoulder and squeezed gently. He said nothing, but his eyes betrayed the affection he obviously held for her.

"We should gather the other pilots from the downed fliers," Luke said. "We can't leave them out here to die in the cold."

"Why not?" Stalgis said, glaring at Ganet. "They seemed to have no qualms about killing *us*."

Ganet glared back at him without apology.

"But we're not them," the Jedi Master pointed out soberly. "Saba, can you sense any of them out there?"

A quick Force reading of the wasteland around them located the remaining pilots with ease. "Four of them are alive; three of those are injured. This one will guide you to them."

Fel urged the four captives to their feet. "Inside," he said. "And don't try anything, Ganet, because believe me when I say that I won't display the same compassion that the Jedi have."

The woman turned her red eyes upon him malevolently, but she did as she was told without argument.

"And what about Wyn?" Syal asked. "What do we do about her?"

"Don't worry," Luke said. "If I know Jacen, that's already being dealt with."

Despair was a feeling Jaina had never succumbed to—not entirely—but frustration was a completely different story. She had tried twice to distract Salkeli, but the Rodian was watching her far too closely. With the blaster trained on Malinza and the others, there was no way she could risk an open attack.

Then she felt a touch through the Force that was at the same time familiar and strikingly unfamiliar.

Tahiri was nearby and coming closer.

Unnerved though she was by the thought of touching minds with the young Jedi, Jaina made her presence as strong in the Force as she could. If Tahiri was homing in on her and arrived in time . . .

Unaware of the subtle life energies flowing around him, Harris had produced Jaina's lightsaber from the folds of his robe and triumphantly activated the shining blade.

"There remains only one thing to do to make the story watertight," he said. "If the Jedi really are to be the enemy, our hero needs some realistic wounds. Don't you think?"

Salkeli grinned as Harris approached Malinza. The girl backed away in horror. Vyram pushed himself between the Deputy Prime Minister and the girl. Harris, however, wasn't fazed in the slightest.

"Either one of you will do," he said, raising the violet

blade over his head, ready to strike. "I really don't mind which one gets it first."

Jaina couldn't wait any longer. If she was going to act, then she needed to do it now.

A swift outward movement of her arms got rid of the binders, and one solid Force push knocked the lightsaber out of Harris's hands. She duck-rolled as Salkeli brought his blaster to bear on her, his eyes widening in surprise at the abrupt turn of events. She kicked the Rodian's legs from beneath him. Harris wasted no time getting his own blaster out, but Jaina was on her feet in time to deflect his first two shots, directing them harmlessly into the wall. Another two bolts hissed by, exploding loudly somewhere behind her. Then with three quick steps, she lunged at the Deputy Prime Minister, clubbing him with the handgrip of her lightsaber. He collapsed back against the wall, a look of startled annoyance frozen on his face as he slumped to the floor.

Confident that there was no longer any threat from Harris, she turned her attention back to Salkeli. Malinza, however, had already taken care of him. The girl had him pinned to the ground with one arm twisted up behind his back.

Jaina nodded, impressed. "Well done," she said. Then, holding out her lightsaber, she added, "Here, give me your hands."

She cut the binders from both Malinza and Vyram with two deft flicks of her blade.

"You'll pay for this!" Salkeli snarled from the floor. "Your time will come soon enough, Jedi filth!"

"Want me to shut him up?" Vyram asked, collecting Harris's blaster.

"Not yet," Jaina said, deactivating her lightsaber. "We might yet need his help."

Then, with dismay, she saw the ruin of the remote detonator. One of the stray blaster bolts had struck it square in the top casing. The Rodian followed her stare to the smoking, half-melted box, and burst into a fit of mocking laughter.

Malinza looked, too. "What do we do now?"

Jaina thought frantically. "How much longer did we have on the timer?"

Vyram shook his head. "I have no idea."

"You've lost, Jedi!" Salkeli cackled.

"Not yet, we haven't," she said, grabbing him under the chin. "Tell me where the bomb is, and tell me now."

The Rodian stared at the crackling lightsaber close to his face. "Not that you can do anything to stop it now, anyway, but it's under the premium stalls, tucked safely away behind a ferrocrete support."

"But it still doesn't help us," Malinza said, "because we're trapped in here!"

The sound of pounding erupted from the far side of the locked door.

Jaina reached out through the Force and felt Tahiri trying to attract her attention, but the door was too thick to shout through, and two Jedi weren't enough to form a Force-meld.

Frustration returned, but only for an instant. Looking over to Salkeli, she suddenly remembered . . . She hurried across the room to where the Rodian lay pinned by Malinza. A quick search of his pockets and she soon found what she was looking for: her comlink.

"Tahiri, can you hear me?"

A second's pause before: "Jaina? We're right here outside the door!"

"I know. Can you get it open, though?"

There was some hesitation. "The code sequence might take a minute or two to get through, but yes, we should be able to get you out."

"We don't have a minute or two, Tahiri. Listen: there's a bomb. You have to get to it and defuse it."

"Where is it?"

Jaina repeated the information that Salkeli had given her. "How long do we have?"

"I'm not sure, but I'm guessing not much. There was a ten-minute timer, and it's already been ticking away for some time. You'd better get going while I find out how to disarm it."

"Okay. Goure's going to stay here and try to get the door open."

"Who's—?"

"He's the Ryn who's been helping us. You can trust him."

Jaina nodded. "Don't worry about us. We're probably safer in here than you are. Just get going!"

She sensed Tahiri hurrying away up the corridor, calling on the Force to maximize her speed. She could feel the girl's exhaustion, too, and wished she could send some of her strength to help. But there was little she could do in that regard. She had to direct her efforts elsewhere.

Jaina turned away from the door and squatted down next to the squirming Salkeli, still futilely trying to break free.

"I thought Rodians always had an escape plan," she said. The Rodian spat at her and glared. She didn't let it bother her. "How do I disarm the bomb, Salkeli?"

"How should I know?" he growled. "And what makes you think I'd tell you even if I did? I've already told you too much."

Jaina sighed. "I'll try again," she said, this time with some Force persuasion behind it. "How do I disarm the bomb?"

His eyes glazed over slightly as he said, "It can't be de-activated now."

That threw her for a moment. "There *has* to be a way!" She pushed even harder with the Force. She didn't believe for a moment that the Rodian wouldn't have had at least *some* knowledge of Harris's bomb. "Now tell me what it is, Salkeli. How is the bomb disarmed?"

"The remote detonator," he answered without resistance. Then, glancing over to the ruined box, he smiled nastily. "But like I said, there's no way to disarm it now."

Jaina cursed under her breath. It was unlikely the Rodian had the will to resist the Force persuasion, so he was probably telling the truth—or the truth as he saw it, anyway. And even if the Deputy Prime Minister did know of another way to deactivate the bomb, it was unlikely they'd be able to rouse him in time to get that information.

"I'm almost there," Tahiri said over the comlink, her voice crackling through dozens of meters of durasteel and ferrocrete. "Do you have the information?"

Jaina shook her head, beginning to feel nauseous. "Tahiri, I don't think it can be disarmed."

"What?"

"Harris rigged it so that it can't be switched off without the remote detonator—and that's been destroyed!"

"There has to be a way, Jaina."

"There isn't. I've seen devices like these before. We're lucky it didn't automatically go off early."

"Then what are going to do?"

"We try to warn Mom and Dad, and get them to alert Cundertol. If we're quick enough, they might be able to clear the stand and get everyone away before—"

"How much time do we have?"

"I still don't know, Tahiri. But not much, so get out of there as quickly as possible, okay?"

She tried to raise her mother on the comlink, but its signal was too weak. Instead, she reached out through the Force. Leia Organa Solo was one mind among thousands, but her mental signature was instantly recognizable. Jaina felt secondhand the hypnotic power of the consecration ceremony gathering force throughout the stadium, and fought to punch through it.

Mom! You have to get out of there. There's a bomb!

It was difficult to convey more than sense impressions through the Force, but she tried her best, and did receive a faint hint of a response for her efforts. She couldn't tell, though, if her mother understood.

"I've found it," Tahiri said. "I have the bomb right here in front of me."

Jaina's anxiety doubled. "What are you still doing in there, Tahiri? I told you to get out!"

"I'm going to try to disarm it."

"Tahiri, do as I tell you! Just get out of there and try to warn the others!"

"Jaina, we don't know how much time we have. What if they can't clear everyone out in time?"

Jaina bit back an angry response. "You don't know what you're doing, though!"

"Then I'll just have to improvise, won't I?" came the reply.

Jaina reached out with all her strength and tried to Force-meld with Tahiri. The link was faint, but she did receive a brief clear view through Tahiri's eyes. The bomb in front of her was not equipped for manual disarming, but it did have a timer. In bold blue digits, Jaina could see they had seventy seconds left.

Sixty-nine . . .

Then something cold and dark pushed her away and the link ebbed.

Mom! Can you hear me? Jaina called, fighting a mounting desperation. *Get everyone out of there—fast!*

The locker door hissed open and the Ryn called Goure rushed in, his tail straight out behind him. "What's going on?"

Jaina checked her chronometer. They had only thirty seconds left.

"Get that door shut!" she told him sharply. "That bomb's about to go off!"

The meld with Tahiri returned, faintly.

"I'm making progress," the girl said over the comlink. "I've got the cover off and I think I can—"

Sparks flashed and Jaina received the sharp tang of burning wires through the Force. At the same time she felt the equally sharp stab of hopelessness as Tahiri realized she didn't have a clue what to do next.

"Tahiri, you've got to get out of there!"

"No, there has to be a way!"

"There isn't! Now, move!"

"I can do it, Jaina. I have to!"

"Why? So you can die like Anakin?" The backlash of pain surprised Jaina and made her instantly regret her words. "Tahiri, I'm—"

"You don't trust me, do you, Jaina?"

"You don't have to prove anything to me, Tahiri. Please, just—"

"I *can* do it! I know I can."

"Can we argue about this later, Tahiri?"

But again something dark and powerful broke the meld between them, its presence casting a black shape in Jaina's mind.

"Mon-mawl rrish hu camasami!"

The words cut into Jaina like a jagged blade. "Tahiri!"

"No!" Tahiri cried, her desperation shattering the fragile darkness. "Leave me alone!"

Her will was not as strong as the darkness, though, and the broken pieces of the shadow reassembled, twice as powerful as it had been before.

"Do-ro'ik vong pratte!"

The voice over the comlink didn't sound like Tahiri's, but Jaina recognized the words. She'd heard it on the lips of her enemies many times in the past. It was a Yuuzhan Vong battle cry.

"Riina?" Jaina asked.

The voice changed to Basic with uncanny ease. "Anakin killed me—and now you want me dead, too! I won't let that happen! *Krel nag sh'n rrush fek!*"

"Wait, Riina!"

It was too late: time had run out. The bomb went off with a muffled concussion that Jaina felt rather than heard. The floor bucked beneath her, throwing everyone to the ground. The lights went out; someone screamed.

Jaina collected herself when the shaking died down. She frantically reached out into the darkness for Tahiri's mind. No matter how much she tried, though, she couldn't find it anywhere.

Tahiri was gone.

Wyn's fear was strong in Jacen's mind as he tracked her and her Chiss escort along the ice tunnels far below Csilla's frozen surface. He sensed that she was frightened, but had nothing concrete on which to pin her concerns. Although she clearly didn't like Chief Navigator Aabe, as yet he'd done nothing overt to threaten her.

Let's just hope it stays that way, he thought.

"I don't understand," Irolia hissed from behind him. "Why would Aabe kidnap Assistant Syndic Fel's daughter?"

"I have no idea, Commander. All I do know is that he has taken her, and that we have to stop him before any harm comes to her."

"But *how* can you know this?" she asked. "This Force of yours is something we don't have. How do I know you're telling me the truth? For all I—"

He motioned her to silence. They had reached an intersection, and his breath puffed into thick, frosty clouds as he peered around the corner. He didn't have time to justify his actions to Irolia, or try to convince her of the existence of the Force. Wyn was close; he could feel her.

The way ahead held a faint glimmer of light: the bubble of warmth and heat containing Aabe, the two guards, and Soontir Fel's youngest daughter was moving rapidly away from them.

"They're heading for the iceway terminus," Irolia said, looking past him.

"Which is?"

"An underground transport station. There are excavated tunnels through the bedrock, far below the ice. Carriages travel through them."

Jacen quickly considered their options. "Then we'll just have to stop them before they reach it."

"Agreed—because if they manage to get onto a carriage, then they could be on the other side of the planet within an hour."

He turned to look at her. The Chiss commander was staring ahead with a determined expression, her blue skin and red eyes contrasting powerfully in the icy gloom. All suggestion of the skepticism she'd voiced just moments earlier appeared to have left her. Even if she wasn't convinced about his motives, at least she was determined to help him get Wyn back in one piece.

He felt vaguely sorry for her. She'd been put in charge of baby-sitting the visitors from the Galactic Alliance through Chiss space and on Csilla. It wasn't her fault that she'd been betrayed by a senior officer, whose orders she hadn't even thought to question. He could understand her wanting to fix the situation before word of her mistake spread.

The light flickered and died at the end of the tunnel. At some point, he knew, he was going to have to try to get closer. He could think of no actual way to hide along the dark and icy corridor so that Aabe and the other guards wouldn't see them, but he couldn't afford to hold back, either. The longer he left it, the farther away Wyn became.

"Come on, Commander. We're going to have to run to catch them."

"Are you sure you'll be able to? Running in these temperatures can be more draining than people realize."

"You just worry about keeping up."

He let the Force flow through him, guiding his footfalls and strengthening the muscles in his legs. His fatigue washed away, along with his concerns for Wyn and the others. He concentrated solely on running: a single, pure action that allowed him to focus his thoughts. What he would do when he caught up with Aabe, he didn't rightly know. Nor did it matter. Nothing did. He existed simply to cross this short stretch of ice that separated Wyn from himself, and while he remained focused on that solitary task, he was able to do it with an athletic ease.

Irolia matched his pace beside him, but with considerably more effort. By the time they reached the junction where the lit section had disappeared, her breathing was coming in long, deep gulps. She leaned against the nearest wall as Jacen peered around another corner. They seemed to be a lot closer now—so close, in fact, that Aabe was clearly distinguishable within the bubble of light ahead by virtue of the gleam off his scalp.

"Are you okay to continue?" he whispered to Irolia.

She nodded. "I am in perfect physical condition," she said, wiping sweat from her forehead. "I could run the same distance three times over and still fight at the end of it."

"That's good to hear," Jacen said, "because that's probably what you're going to have to do." He glanced around the icy corner again. "How far do you figure before they reach those carriages?"

"There are only two more junctions between here and the iceway terminus."

"Then I guess we'd better get moving. Are you sure you're ready?"

"You just worry about keeping up," she said.

He smiled at the commander's quip, then continued

with his pursuit. He was more cautious this time, because they were well within sight of Aabe's party. He didn't know how well sound carried through the fields keeping the heat in, but he couldn't afford to assume that their approach would be covered. He didn't even know if he'd be able to penetrate the field walls around the bubble. Another two corners would give him and Irolia time to catch up as Aabe and Wyn reached the terminus, when they would be distracted and out of the fields.

As Jacen drew closer, a faint hissing broke the silence. The sound came from the field walls as they swept over the icy surfaces around the bubble. Beneath the sound was a hint of voices, too low for him to catch anything more than broken fragments. From the handful of words he was able to make out, though, he knew that Wyn was starting to question Aabe's intentions, asking why her father was having her transported via the iceways rather than the barge. Aabe muttered something that went unheard, as did Wyn's response—although there was no mistaking the misgivings in the girl's tone.

They rounded one corner, then the second; all that lay between them and the iceway terminus now was a straight stretch of tunnel. Jacen and Irolia kept pace with the bubble, lurking just beyond the wash of light it cast. Jacen unclipped his lightsaber from his belt and held it ready, his thumb resting on the activation stud.

The bubble dissolved as Aabe, the guards, and Wyn left the tunnel. Beyond them was the terminus—a much smaller space than Jacen had imagined. Long and narrow, it had a series of sliding panels set into the far wall, which Jacen presumed to be air locks leading to the carriages.

Jacen and Irolia stopped at the end of the tunnel, watching quietly as Aabe and the others crossed the narrow room to one of the sliding doors. Only when one of these doors grated open did Wyn give in to the misgivings Jacen had heard in her voice.

"I'd like to talk to my father," she said, pulling away from the ex-Imperial and his Chiss sidekicks. "I want to know where he's sending me."

"It's a little late to ask that, don't you think?" Aabe's skull gleamed. His mouth, overshadowed by his large nose, curled into a menacing snarl.

She shook her head uneasily. "This isn't right," she said, taking another step back. "You're lying to me. My father wouldn't ask me to be taken down here!"

Aabe rounded on her in order to cut off her route to the exit. "And what possible reason would I have to lie to you, child? I am your father's trusted servant. You know that. Why do you dishonor me with such accusations?"

"*Trusted* servant?" she shot back, looking frightened but determined. "My father says he never even *heard* of you until you turned up on the Chiss border, looking for asylum. He thinks you're a deserter!"

Jacen could no longer see Aabe's face, but his posture noticeably stiffened. "Your accusations grow with your hysteria, child," he said frostily. "You should be mindful of the things you say."

"Do you deny it?" she continued, regardless of the obvious danger she was in.

"It is irrelevant," he replied, unclipping the holster at his waist. "You're coming with me whether you like it or not, and I'll hear no more said about your father. His time is over. The CEDF has better things to do than pander to neighbors who can't mind their own affairs. The sooner he and you are out of the way, the better it will be for all concerned."

Wyn backed away a few more steps, straight into the arms of one of the guards. Aabe drew his blaster and approached her.

Jacen had heard enough. Before, it might have just been possible that Aabe *was* following orders, but now there was no mistaking his intentions.

"I really think it's in your best interest to lower that weapon and let the girl go, Chief Navigator," Jacen said, activating his lightsaber as he stepped out from the shadowed corridor.

Aabe spun around, redirecting his blaster's aim at Jacen. Then, seeing Irolia with him, his face crumpled into a frown. "What is the meaning of this? I demand an explanation!"

"Funny, but I was about to say exactly the same thing," the commander said, drawing her own blaster.

"I need explain nothing to you, Commander," Aabe sneered. "I'm your superior officer. Remember? And I am ordering you to turn around and return to your normal duties."

"As an officer of the Expansionary Defense Force, I believe it is my duty to ensure the safety and security of the Chiss realm. That directive, as you are well aware, supersedes *all* others. It is my firm belief that I am following that directive right now." Irolia raised her blaster and sighted Aabe along the barrel. "So, if you wouldn't mind dropping your weapon, *sir* . . ."

"You fool!"

Jacen felt the Force rush through him an instant before Aabe fired. His instincts moved him forward, swinging his lightsaber up and across to intersect the bolt before it could hit Irolia. A split second later she, too, fired. Jacen didn't hesitate: his lightsaber came down again, deflecting that bolt also.

"What are you doing?" Irolia snapped.

Jacen didn't have time to explain to the commander that it was unnecessary for *anyone* to die; he was too busy advancing on Aabe as the chief navigator slowly retreated. The guards stood behind him, frozen with indecision.

"You cowards!" Aabe yelled back at them. "He's only a boy! *Take* him!"

But the guards took another step away from him,

making it clear to Jacen and Irolia that Aabe was on his own in this. When the commander indicated for them to lower their weapons, they did so without hesitation, laying them on the floor at their feet. Whether they had been part of the conspiracy or simply following orders was something that would have to be determined later.

Realizing his situation, Aabe grabbed Wyn and shoved her forcibly between himself and Jacen; then he turned to run for the open iceway carriage door, his only chance at obtaining freedom. Jacen took three long strides to bring himself within reach of the fleeing man, his lightsaber raised, tensed and ready to strike.

A single exertion of will, backed up by the Force, wrenched the carriage doors closed. Aabe crashed into them at full tilt, toppling back onto the ice at Jacen's feet, his blaster flying out of his stunned grasp and clattering across the floor. Wyn was quick to pick it up and point it at him.

"There's nowhere to run," Jacen said, the steady thrum of his lightsaber sounding in the cold air.

He felt Wyn watching in amazement as he stood over Aabe, willing the man to give up. Defiance lingered in Aabe's eyes, but then suddenly flickered and died. The man sagged back to the floor with a defeated sigh.

Jacen stepped back, lowering his lightsaber, glad that the crisis was over—and that nobody had been hurt.

He activated his comlink, and it bleeped immediately. It was his uncle.

"Jacen? Is everything all right?"

"It is now," he answered.

"And Wyn?"

"She's fine. I'll fill you in on all the details later."

"Well done, Jacen. You've defused a potentially difficult situation."

"Thanks, Uncle Luke," he returned, deactivating his

lightsaber and reattaching it to his belt. Irolia was already busy speaking into a wall communicator, calling for backup. "How's everything there?"

"Under control. We've heard from Tekli; someone made a halfhearted attempt to break through *Jade Shadow*'s air lock, but they failed and haven't come back. Port security is already looking into the incident. It looks like we've weathered the storm rather well, don't you think?"

As Jacen watched the guards hoist Aabe onto his feet, he found he could only nod in silent agreement. A failed attempt to put them out of the picture would almost certainly bring the Chiss more firmly behind them—as well as Fel. The real leaders behind the attempt—assuming Aabe wasn't as high up as they went—would no doubt lie low for a while, fearing reprisals from either Chiss loyal to the existing command structure, like Irolia, or the Galactic Federation of Free Alliances, which was bound to take an attack on peaceful diplomats poorly. It might also mean that the two-day deadline would be extended.

"How long do you think before you'll get back?" he asked his uncle.

"Probably within the hour," Luke said. "We'll resume our search, then."

Jacen nodded to himself again, glad to be able to put the incident behind them and get back to work.

"And Jacen?" Luke said. "Don't assume that everything that happened here has been unimportant. The smallest action can have the largest consequences. The good work we've done today may have far-reaching consequences—consequences we can only guess at right now."

"I know, Uncle Luke," Jacen said. "I'll see you when you get back, okay?"

"Take care, Jacen."

"You, too."

He closed the line and returned the comlink to his belt, reflecting upon the simple truth of his uncle's words. He couldn't help but wonder at what the consequences of this day would be. Perhaps saving Wyn would enable her to achieve her ambition of seeing Coruscant. One day, when the war was over, the girl could easily follow in her brother's footsteps and leave Chiss space in favor of the Galactic Alliance. He sensed strength and determination in her, as well as a keen intellect. If she wanted to do something badly enough, he had no doubt that she would find a way.

What will become of you, Wyn Fel? he wondered to himself. Only time would tell, he supposed—and if he could give her nothing else, he would do his best to give her that, at least. The time to realize her potential: her and the Chiss, as well as the galaxy itself.

He shrugged off the train of thought, forcing himself back to the present. Wyn was standing to one side, the blaster in her hand trembling slightly. She was staring at him with something approximating awe.

"Are you all right?" he asked her.

She nodded once. "A little shaken, but I'll be okay." She couldn't seem to take her eyes off him. "Thank you for coming when you did. You were amazing!"

He felt himself flush slightly, at the compliment as well as the girl's obvious admiration for him that had prompted it. But he forced himself to ignore it. There were much more important things to concern himself with. Bigger than Wyn or Aabe—bigger even than himself. The search for Zonama Sekot was of paramount importance. Everything else was just a distraction.

"All in a day's work," he told Wyn, with a smile that he hoped would hide his discomfort at her adoration. "The life of a Jedi is not a boring one."

* * *

Mom? Mom!

In the aftermath of the explosion, Jaina's mind was filled with psychic pain. She sent her mind out among the wounded and dying, searching for her mother. She found her mother and father down in the thick of it, fighting their way through the panicked crowd, trying to get to where help was needed the most.

Jaina sat up in the gloom of the room's emergency lighting. The locker was filled with dust, but it had remained intact—just as Harris had anticipated it would. Malinza was climbing to her feet, shaking her head groggily. Vyram and Goure were clambering upright, too, both coughing violently as the dust caught in their throats. Salkeli lay curled in a ball, looking up with a grin on his face, triumphant that their best efforts to stop the bomb had failed. Harris remained where Jaina had left him: out cold in the corner.

She collected the comlink from the floor where she'd dropped it and quickly activated it.

"Mom?" She opened the locker door to reduce the interference. "Mom, can you hear me?"

It took a few moments before Leia answered. "I hear you, Jaina." Relief rushed through her at the sound of her mother's voice. "Are you all right?"

"I'm okay. But, Mom—Tahiri!"

"I know; I felt it, too."

"Do you think she's okay?"

"I don't know, Jaina."

"I'll never forgive myself if she's—"

Leia didn't let her finish. "You aren't to blame for anything that has happened here, Jaina."

Jaina knew that wasn't true. If she hadn't been so closed off to the girl in the first place, if she'd tried to help her confront her problems earlier instead of . . .

She broke away from the guilt-ridden thought.

"How bad is it up there, Mom?"

"It's utter chaos. The blast took out the Prime Minister's stalls. Security is trying to clear the area now."

Jaina caught flashes from her mother: frightened faces, tangled wreckage, and blood—*lots* of blood.

Before she could ask if there was anything she could do, Salkeli took the opportunity to gloat. "You look a little concerned there, Jedi," the Rodian said with a half smile, half sneer. "Not so sure of yourself now, are—"

Vyram didn't ask this time; he just shut the Rodian up by stunning him with the butt of his blaster. "What do we do now?" he asked, stepping up to Jaina.

"We go topside to help," she answered. "Besides, security has to know about these two."

"I'll go," Malinza said.

Jaina shook her head. "They might not believe you."

"No," the girl said, "but they *will* listen."

"And I can stay here and keep an eye on these two, if you like," Vyram said.

Jaina thought about this for a moment, then nodded. "Okay, and I'll back you up when I get there."

"Wait a minute," Goure said. "Where are *you* going?"

"To find Tahiri."

"Then I'm coming, too," he said. The Ryn had a look in his eye that Jaina recognized from her father—the kind that said there was no point arguing.

Jaina shrugged helplessly and let him follow her out as they retraced Tahiri's steps through the damaged corridors, updating Leia as they went. The stadium's structure had held, but it was going to require an extensive overhaul. The closer they got to the center of the blast, the more damage there was. Ceilings had come down, ferrocrete had cracked, stanchions were twisted, and the air was full of dust.

"Through here, I think," she said, following the vague impressions she'd received from Tahiri's mind. Everything had looked so different then, with the smooth, clean corridors. Now they were in ruins, open to the sky. The cries of the wounded were very real from such close quarters, and the smell of smoke and dust was powerfully strong.

At the heart of the destruction, they found a clear space about two meters across. The blast had destroyed everything around the area, but nothing within it. And there at its center lay Tahiri, curled up like a child hiding from a nightmare.

Jaina came to a halt at the edge of the unaffected area, her heart pounding sickeningly fast in her chest. She tried reaching for the girl through the Force, but she still couldn't find her.

"What happened here?" Goure asked.

"She must have put a Force bubble around herself," Jaina said. She looked around, surveying the damage more closely. "Looks like it deflected the bulk of the blast away from above." She reached out cautiously with her hand, feeling for the bubble, and was surprised to find nothing there. "It must have closed when she passed out."

Goure moved to the girl's side and rolled her over. Tahiri turned without resistance and lay on her back with her eyes open. "Tahiri?" The Ryn felt for a pulse in her throat when there was no response. "She's alive."

Jaina tried to reach her through the Force one more time. *Tahiri?*

Nothing. Jaina had never felt anyone so empty before. The girl felt hollow in the Force, almost—

She stopped the thought, not wanting to introduce the idea into her mind. But it was too late.

Almost invisible, she thought. *Like the Yuuzhan Vong!*

Jaina's comlink beeped.

"Jaina?" Her mother's voice came again over the comlink.

She turned away from Tahiri and raised her comlink. "Yes, Mom?"

"Rescue teams have reached the epicenter of the blast."

Looking up, she could see movement through the hole. "We're directly below. Are you with them?"

"Yes. They've started pulling bodies out of the rubble."

A sickening sensation swept through her. If she'd only acted faster, not wasted time assuming the bomb could be defused . . .

"How many?" she asked.

"Four so far. And—"

Leia's hesitation told her there was worse to come.

"What is it, Mom?"

"It's Prime Minister Cundertol. He's dead."

Jaina looked down into Tahiri's empty, almost accusing eyes. The hollowness she exhibited was catching.

"Jaina? Did you hear me?"

"I heard you, Mom. I'm on my way up."

Goure took Tahiri into his arms and together they negotiated the rubble. As they reached the surface, Malinza's words about the Cosmic Balance came back to haunt her. *Good works lead to evil results.* Jaina had been trying to do the right thing, but it had all gone so terribly wrong. Salkeli had betrayed her; Zel and Jjorg were dead; Tahiri was unconscious; the Prime Minister had been murdered—all of this, despite her best efforts.

It wasn't just her, either. Uncle Luke had liberated the Bakurans from the Empire only to see them turn their backs on the Galactic Alliance. The New Republic had created the Bakuran Defense Fleet to protect the planet from the Ssi-ruuk, but half of it had been destroyed elsewhere in the galaxy, leaving Bakura vulnerable again. Bakura had never been the aggressor, yet bad things kept happening to it. No wonder its people were eager to look for alternatives.

And what if the treaty with the P'w'eck did turn out to be legitimate? she asked herself. What then? What evil might that reap farther down the track for the planet?

They clambered out into the daylight and saw the small knot of people gathered around the Prime Minister's body, looking down in shock and horror. The large man lay sprawled out on a repulsor gurney, the scorched remains of his ceremonial robes torn down the center, where a meditech had struggled unsuccessfully to revive him. Leia's attention was fixed on the Prime Minister's body and the activities taking place around it, but she looked up to acknowledge Jaina. She was pale beneath sooty smudges that covered her face. Her expression was one of abhorrence, and her eyes were filled with tears and pain.

Reports were garbled from below, but the sense of disaster was all too vivid for Jag's liking. Relayed from commentators and unofficial sources through *Selonia* to him, there was a lot of room for misinformation. There had been some sort of explosion during the consecration ceremony. Something had muffled the blast, though, according to commentators on the ground, and thankfully the damage to the intended target wasn't as extensive as it could have been.

Nevertheless, two Senators were dead, along with half a dozen guards and a couple of guests. Forty more had incurred wounds, with injuries ranging from hearing loss to loss of limbs. And, of course, there was Cundertol himself.

"*Ktah,*" he spat. The Chiss rarely expressed emotions vocally, but they did have words for it when the occasion arrived. Assassination was an ugly tactic, no matter who employed it, and if this turned out to be the work of terrorists hoping to disrupt the consecration ceremony, he was sure that retaliation would be swift and brutal.

It hadn't been terrorists, some of the uglier rumors said, *but the Deputy Prime Minister himself . . .*

Jaina's reappearance had brought some comfort, briefly. She had only confirmed everyone's worst fears: Blaine Harris had set the bomb, hoping to incriminate the Galactic Alliance and make a martyr out of Malinza Thanas as well as getting Cundertol out of the way.

The implications of this stunned Jag, and he shook his head at the thought. With Cundertol dead and Harris likely to face any number of charges, Bakura had effectively been stripped of its highest levels of command . . .

On the heels of that thought came an announcement from *Pride of Selonia*:

"We've just had word from *Sentinel*," Captain Mayn said. "General Panib has declared martial law. He's requested that, no matter what happens, we don't take any direct action. Word is filtering down the chains of command on both sides. He's not exactly sure what the Keeramak will make of this yet, but we're picking up activity on the Salis D'aar spaceport where the P'w'eck ships are parked. My guess is they're not going to sit around and do nothing while bombs go off around their precious leader."

Jag agreed. It made sense that they would pull out and try again later. There had been no mention that the ceremony had to be performed at a specific time, so presumably there'd be no problem with picking up and carrying on from where they left off later.

"What do you want us to do?" he asked Mayn.

"Just back off a little. This is a touchy time. Whatever this 'honor guard' is really about, we're just going to have to leave them to it for a while."

"Understood." He relayed the order to his pilots and changed the vector of his own wing, letting the trio they'd been following drift slowly away. Now more than ever, he wanted to ask for permission to land—not only to help out with things on the surface of the planet, but also, and more importantly, so that he could be with Jaina.

As soon as Tahiri was strapped safely onto a repulsor gurney, Goure joined the rescue effort. Han raised an eyebrow at the sight of the Ryn, but was too grateful for the extra set of hands to question his presence. Two people had been caught under the rubble and, with the help of hastily improvised repulsorsleds, their rescue was only slowly unfolding. Jaina lent her efforts where she could—using the Force to search the rubble pile for weak points, applying pressure where those on the outside couldn't reach, and shoring up the healing energies of the victims who couldn't be treated immediately—but it didn't feel enough. In the first minutes after the explosion, as panic prompted a mass evacuation of the area, chaos and confusion kept emergency services at a distance. The few who did get through, some of them dropping down from aircars with medpacs on their backs, worked harder than they probably had in their entire lives.

Beneath a foreboding sky, darkened further by a thick pall of smoke hanging over the stadium, the P'w'eck bodyguards had tightened their ranks around the Keeramak. The multicolored Ssi-ruuvi mutant watched on from the safety of this vantage point, its expression unreadable as it surveyed the carnage.

Jaina had barely had the chance to do more than hug her mother and father in relief at seeing them again. It was only later, when medical reinforcements arrived, that she had time to actually step back and take a proper look at the world around her. Everyone was covered in dust and splattered with blood; where the two met, they made a dirty red paste. The survivors had a shocked look in their eyes, even those who helped in the rescue. Senators and security guards were suddenly on the same level, united by the terrible tragedy that had taken place around them. No one paid any mind to the thunderstorm that was brewing overhead; it seemed almost irrelevant in the face of what had happened.

But there was something else that wasn't as easy to ignore—a sound that nagged at her from below the rumbling of the crowd. It was a strange and haunting wail, an ululation that seemed in search of a note of despair but couldn't quite find it.

Her father looked up, frowning. "You hear that, Leia?"

Leia turned in disbelief. "They've started again!"

Jaina followed her gaze to the heart of the stadium. Sure enough, the ceremony had recommenced. She could see lithe reptilian aliens dancing in a circle, and one multicolored shape prowling the center, uttering noises that sounded like the angry song of some mighty bird.

"What is this?" she asked.

"They're going to finish the job," Han said, the stubble on his chin flecked with dust. "You've got to admire their persistence, don't you?"

Admire them? Jaina thought. *Hardly.* If anything, it was incredibly insensitive. Even over the sound of rubble shifting and the moans of those in pain, the strange sounds coming from the P'w'eck set her teeth on edge.

"I don't understand," she said. "Why would the Keeramak finish it now when it would obviously be safer later?"

"They're aliens," a nearby meditech said. "Who's to say what goes on in their heads?"

"Threepio," Leia said, "translate for me, will you?"

The protocol droid stood up from where he'd been lifting chunks of rock and placing them into a hamper. He tilted his head to listen properly to the growing cacophony.

" 'The gulfs of space are not home to us,' " he translated, " 'and neither are the barren worlds. The worlds of fire and the worlds of ice are not home to us. Where oxygen burns and water flows, where carbon bonds and ozone protects—there we plant our roots. The seed of our species is fertile; all we require is the soil in which to plant it.' "

"More of the same, in other words," Han said. "But I still don't understand their urgency to get the ceremony finished with all this chaos around them!"

Jaina remembered what Harris had said earlier about the similarities between the Ssi-ruuk and the Yuuzhan Vong. The warriors of the Yuuzhan Vong wouldn't consider going into battle without making appropriate sacrifices to Yun-Yammka. The Ssi-ruuk in turn were loath to risk their souls on a world that hadn't been consecrated. Perhaps the sudden carnage around them made them want to get the ceremony finished as quickly as possible, just in case more attacks were to follow.

She found it hard to understand the logic that drove such notions. The Force didn't demand sacrifice, nor favor one location over another. It simply was, in and surrounding all things.

Jaina's thoughts came back to Malinza's words on the swinging of cosmic scales. She had to bring her parents up to speed on what had happened to the young activist, and she also wanted to ask Goure where he fit into everything. There were other, more pressing matters to consider, too—not the least of them being what the Bakuran government would do once things settled down. Would they put Malinza Thanas back behind bars? Or Jaina herself for having helped the girl escape? Without objective witnesses to Harris's treachery, an investigation could drag on for ages. And then there was Tahiri . . .

Good works lead to evil results.

Tahiri's brainwashing at the hands of the Yuuzhan Vong

shaper Mezhan Kwaad had been a terrible thing, but her rescue and apparent recovery had balanced that out. Anakin's growing love for her had been canceled out by his death. Where did that leave her now? The reemergence of the Riina Kwaad personality was only going to make things worse, surely. If there was balance in the galaxy, when was it going to swing again in Tahiri's favor?

Jaina's thoughts were distracted when the sound of engines whining joined the chanting. It was growing steadily louder. Jaina looked around, then up. Emerging smoothly from the clouds were three *D'kee*-class P'w'eck troopships. Bulbous around the middle and tapering to a fine point at the stern, they slowly descended toward the stadium. The huge canopy flag ripped beneath the landing struts of one of the ships. Its tattered remnants flapped chaotically in the wind.

"Reinforcements?" Han asked of no one in particular. Some of the stadium crowd had defied security after the explosion and spilled into the center space, waving placards angrily. Jaina wondered if they thought the P'w'eck were behind the crisis. The P'w'eck, armed with paddle beamers, were more than capable of keeping the crowd back, but they must have been aware that the crowd could easily grow larger and more hostile if provoked.

"A quick getaway, perhaps," Jaina suggested. "They might be keen enough to consecrate in the middle of all this, but I doubt that they'd want to stick around afterward."

"You could be right, honey," her father said. Jaina was struck by conflicting impressions of him: how old he was getting, and how much more alive he looked when the going got tough. He might sweat and fidget through diplomatic negotiations, but when things took a turn for the physical, he was often the first into the fray.

The alien vessels rotated in midair when they were over the stadium and descended at a safe distance from the ring of P'w'eck guards. The sound of engines had risen to an almost painful level, and the Bakurans below quickly scattered, shaking fists into the air as they ran. The noise drowned out any protest they made. *D'kee*-class ships were small as far as spacecraft went, but still four stories high from base to tip.

"Excuse me, Mistress," C-3PO said.

"Look," Han said, shouting over the growing din. "Three more!"

She shaded her eyes and looked where he was pointing. Another trio of ships was descending beyond the stadium walls, the same type of troopship as those that had just landed.

"What are they doing?" Leia asked. Jaina recognized the edge to her mother's tone. She, too, was starting to have misgivings about all this.

"If I might interrupt, Mistress," 3PO tried again, gesticulating off to one side. He was desperately trying to make himself heard, but the racket was smothering most of what he was saying.

Suddenly the engines from all three of the ships in the stadium below cut out, allowing a relative quiet to settle around the area. The chanting had ceased also, and the Keeramak was now standing in the middle of his enormous entourage, glinting as though wearing rainbow-tinted armor. The guards stood with their tails flat to the ground, paddle beamers held at the ready across their chests.

For a moment, everything was still. Then, with one eye on what was taking place with the P'w'eck, Jaina leaned toward C-3PO and muttered, "What was that you just said, Threepio?"

"The ceremony is complete, Mistress," the golden droid said.

"Thanks, Goldenrod," Han said. "But that seems pretty obvious from where I'm standing."

"But, sir, I've been trying to explain that the ceremony required the Keeramak to give Bakura a new name—Xwhee."

Leia faced him fully now. "Did he happen to mention this fact to the Bakurans before he did it?"

"I doubt that very much, Mistress," C-3PO said. "You see, the Keeramak has also dedicated Xwhee to the Ssi-ruuvi Imperium."

Han and Jaina also turned to look at C-3PO now. As if in response to the droid's words, a peal of thunder rumbled from the tropical sky. Fat raindrops began to splatter his metal cranium, turning what dust was there to a reddish mud.

"Threepio, are you sure about this?" Leia asked.

"Oh, quite certain. In fact, it was stated several times and in different ways: as the 'glorious Ssi-ruuvi Imperium,' the 'majestic Ssi-ruuvi Imperium,' the 'boundless and incomparable Ssi-ruuvi Imperium'—"

Han turned to Leia, speaking over the top of C-3PO. "Couldn't this just be part of the ceremony? Something carried over from the old ways? I mean, we still talk about the New Republic instead of the Galactic Alliance. Maybe their new Ssi-ruuvi Imperium has nothing at all to do with the old one."

"I don't think so," Leia said. "Look at the ships."

Rain began to fall in great sheets across the stadium as the sides of the troopships opened, issuing ramps. Jaina squinted to see through the rain, trying to make out what lay inside.

Dull brown paint was falling away in the rain, revealing golden scales, the sign of the Ssi-ruuvi priest caste. Relieved of the need for concealment, the priests' postures straightened, shrugging off the hunch of years of supposed servility and adopting the cold, straight-backed pride Jaina remembered from holos.

Realization struck her like a physical blow. Of course!

The treaty with the P'w'eck was a smokescreen for the real tactic: once Bakura belonged to the Ssi-ruuk, once it was consecrated, they could advance on it in force!

"This can't be good," Han said as columns of russet-scaled Ssi-ruuvi warriors began marching out of the nearest troopship.

Jag's frustration immediately increased when, at the peak of the consecration ceremony, the feed from the ground dissolved in a burst of static. All transmissions from the planet ceased, sending white noise blistering through his ears. He quickly checked his comm and ascertained that the problem wasn't onboard. It lay outside his clawcraft.

"*Selonia,* I seem to have a communications outage. Anything coming through from your end?"

"Negative, Twin One," came the reply, distorted but comprehensible. "We've lost our uplink, too. Hold on while we look into it."

Jag waited anxiously with only the persistent static to listen to. Then, amid the crackly hissing, he heard another noise. It was like a wailing, constantly fading in and out. It was unsettling—both haunting and hypnotic at the same time . . .

"I have launches!"

The voice of one of his pilots jolted him out of his reverie. A quick glance at his board confirmed the report: the nearest of the two P'w'eck carriers, *Errinung'ka,* was disgorging dozens of smaller vessels into the space around it. His computer instantly recognized and marked the familiar droid fighters, but that proved to be only half the complement of the new ships. The rest were of a type never before seen outside the borders of the Ssi-ruuk Imperium. They were *V'sett*-class fighters, and if his memory served him well they possessed twice the firepower of ordinary droid fighters, as well as a superior maneuverability. Most importantly, though, they carried flesh-and-blood pilots.

It took him only a moment to figure out what was going on. The P'w'eck's offer of peace had been completely bogus; the consecration of the planet had been nothing more than a means to clear the way for an invasion force! It didn't take a genius to know that things were about to get very nasty, very quickly.

"Twin Suns, full alert. *Selonia,* are you registering this?"

"We have it on our scopes now. Trying to raise General Panib . . . Communications are out down there, too." The transmission dissolved into static again. The voice returned briefly with ". . . be jammed somehow. Be on . . ."

The signal vanished beneath a howl of rising interference. Jag turned down the gain. What next? They had enemy ships pouring onto the scan and, as yet, no response from the local forces. Between himself and the enemy were the mixed flights comprising the Bakuran/P'w'eck "honor guard," now numbering in excess of two hundred. It seemed from the way they were still flying in formation that they hadn't received orders to engage or break away. This surprised Jag. Even if the messages were being jammed, surely *one* of the Bakuran honor guard pilots would have realized by now what was going on. And yet, there they all were, flying in perfect formation, completely unaffected by what was happening around them.

Clicking his wingmates, he brought his clawcraft around to match vectors with the nearest trio of honor guard fighters. Two droid ships flanked a Bakuran Y-wing in perfect synchrony, shadowing its every move as it swept around the planet.

He scanned the formation for energy emissions and soon discovered that "shadowing" was as far from the truth as it could get. The two droid ships had powerful tractor beams locked on the Y-wing and were forcing it to go where they wanted it.

He plotted its course. In two orbits, it would intersect with the carrier *Firrinree*. A cold chill ran through him. The droid ships were kidnapping the pilot!

A quick scan confirmed that the same was true of all the other honor guard flights. Powerless to resist the P'w'eck tractor beams, the Bakuran pilots were helpless in the trap sprung on them—and half of the Bakuran's Defense Fleet was about to be taken down with them.

There was no way he could warn Twin Suns, *Selonia,* or General Panib. However, he wasn't about to sit back and let those pilots be reeled in to be entched. He could only hope that others would understand his actions and follow his lead.

Arming his forward batteries, he thrust hard to cut off the droid fighters. A burst from his blaster cannon skittered off shields that were tougher than he'd expected. It weakened them slightly, but there was certainly no penetration. As soon as he'd swept past, one of them broke away to give chase. The first of his wingmates, Twin Six, met it with a hail of laserfire that forced it to change course. It ducked away, although not before sending a spray of energy at Twin Three as it did.

The second droid ship and its unwilling charge were making a break for it, abandoning all pretense of cooperation and changing course. Instead of arcing gradually around the planet, the pair headed directly for *Firrinree*. A quick glance at his scopes confirmed that the others were doing the same. The masquerade was over; there was no longer any mistaking the honor guard for what it was.

Jag lined up behind the fleeing droid fighter and sent a volley of lasers through its weakened shields, quickly reducing it into space dust. The liberated Y-wing instantly changed course, wiggling on its long axis in what Jag took as a gesture of thanks.

Twin Two dispatched the other droid fighter and swooped back to join formation. The Y-wing followed, emitting a series of clicks. Jag didn't need any more encouragement than that. Leading a diamond-shaped formation of mixed vessels, he targeted the next "honor guard" trio and closed in.

By then, his tactical scopes were full of new targets. The alien carriers had emptied their launching bays, and hundreds of fully fueled fighters were jockeying to protect the inbound captives. A rash of launches from *Sentinel* and *Defender* indicated that the Bakuran Defense Fleet had finally caught on. The sky around Bakura was soon boiling as the two forces clashed over the "honor guard" ships, one half fighting to save them, the other half doing everything in their power to repel the rescue attempt.

Jag flew as he hadn't flown in a long time. It felt good to be fighting an enemy who used a technology he was familiar with—even if that enemy easily outnumbered him and his squadron. In a strange way, it felt like he was back at the academy sitting through a simulation, riding out old melees with an instructor on his case. He was pleased that time away fighting the Yuuzhan Vong hadn't eroded the reflexes he'd honed as a child.

The manned V'sett fighters were tough kills, though. Flattened and slightly curved versions of the droid fighters the Ssi-ruuk usually sent into battle, these were equipped with shield generators and sensor arrays at every corner. Their engines flashed an eye-piercing violet when powering at max; their weapons burned a brilliant white. Each pilot hid behind an opaque hull and shields that turned mirror-bright every time a shot came too near.

It was an earlier version of those shields, Jag had learned in the academy, that the Emperor Palpatine had coveted. Hence his attempt to form a treaty with the Ssi-ruuk, just before the Rebels had beaten him at Endor. Jag dreaded to think what might have happened had the Emperor's dream come true. If he'd had these shields back then, the Rebellion would have undoubtedly been quashed and the outcome of the Battle of Endor would have been considerably different. Moreover, the Chiss, safe in the Unknown Regions, might not have been safe for much longer.

But the Chiss had fought the Ssi-ruuvi fighters before and, even after years of technical improvements, they were capable of doing so again now. V'sett fighters, Jag soon discovered, were vulnerable to multiple attacks. Converging in pairs from different angles was difficult to coordinate without the benefit of effective communications, but all the pilots read the situation similarly and they managed to struggle through. With a few multiple attacks under their belts, it got steadily easier, and in no time at all they were taking out V'sett fighters in sufficient quantities to make the Ssi-ruuk think twice. Soon the dense and volatile orbits surrounding Bakura were a mass of energy, dangerous for pilots on both sides to navigate through.

Seeing one of his squadron's X-wings trying to shake off the V'sett fighter riding its tail, Jag set off in pursuit. He got a lock on the fighter as it dog-tailed after the X-wing, and he fired when he thought he had a reasonable aim, but the fighter suddenly banked left after the X-wing and the shot went wide. Jag cursed under his breath as he brought the clawcraft back onto the fighter's tail. Before he could line up another shot, two more fighters came at him from his port side, weapons blazing angrily at him. He sucked air through clenched teeth sharply and nose-dived away from the incoming fire. Seconds later, when he had chance to look again for the X-wing, he saw it fall apart in a blaze of fire beneath the V'sett's blasters.

The two fighters he had just eluded were quickly back on his tail. With the rest of the squadron engaged in the battle elsewhere, he knew that help wouldn't be coming anytime soon. He was going to have to make his own luck . . .

Han was backing up, looking for the nearest exit. From below came the sound of screams as the crowd ran in a panic from the advancing aliens. Security guards opened fire on the Ssi-ruuvi warriors, who responded with blistering barrages from their paddle beamers. In leaps and bounds, propelled by powerful thigh and tail muscles, the Ssi-ruuk soon overwhelmed the Bakuran troops. The P'w'eck guards, who had originally protected the Keeramak from attack, turned out to be genuine P'w'eck, unlike the disguised priests; they protected their leader behind a tight huddle, beamers at the ready.

"A tactical retreat might be called for," Jaina suggested to her parents. "Now that Bakura has been consecrated, my guess is that these guys won't be afraid to fight anymore."

"If we get to the *Falcon*," Leia said, her Noghri bodyguards closing in around her, watching the Ssi-ruuvi warriors balefully, "we'll have a better chance of dealing with this."

"Does *Selonia* know?" Han asked.

Leia shook her head. "Jammed."

Jaina thought of Jag and hoped he was all right. There was no telling what was happening in orbit. If it was anything like what was happening down here on the ground, then it was going to get messy fast. She wished she were behind the controls of her X-wing, flying at his side, her only concern the enemy in her crosshairs. Things were a whole lot simpler in a dogfight.

But wishing wasn't going to get her or her family away from here. She needed to act—and quickly!

She turned to find Goure standing at Tahiri's side.

"We need a way out of here," she said.

He looked up at her, his face illuminated sharply by a flash of lightning. "The main exits are going to be blocked," he shouted over the thunder rolling from the sky.

Jaina looked around again. The rain was thickening, making it harder to see what was happening in the bowl of the stadium. Paddle beams sizzled through the air, weaving a dense and deadly fabric of energy below. The leading edge was coming rapidly closer.

She nodded after a moment. "I think it's safe to assume that that's what the other three ships were for: to keep us from getting out."

"The way we came, then." The Ryn pointed at the craterous hole in the stands. "It has to be safer than staying out in the open."

Jaina agreed, and together they began to gather up the confused rescue workers and spectators still milling about the area. She explained her intentions as best she could, asking them to trust her as she sent them down into the hole. There was little resistance from the people; in the absence of any other plan, most were more than happy to follow her instructions. Once everyone was in, Han and Leia were to go next, then wait for Goure to lower Tahiri into the hole on her gurney. Jaina and the Noghri guards would take up the rear to protect everyone's backs.

"What about the Prime Minister?" one of the women asked as she went past Jaina.

"What about him?" she shouted back over the rain. "He's dead!"

"We can't leave his body here for the Fluties!"

"But—" The protest died in her throat. "Okay, okay, I'll see what I can do!"

Leaving her parents to supervise the evacuation, she

looked around for the stretcher on which she'd last seen the body. She found it tucked away behind an outcrop, covered in a body bag. If she could slave it to Tahiri's repulsor gurney, maybe they'd be able to take both of them out in tandem. The moment it got in her way, she told herself, then she would cut it loose. The living had to take priority over—

Her thoughts stopped in midtrack as she went to move the stretcher. The body bag caught on a twisted seat and pulled away, revealing it to be empty.

Her puzzlement was short-lived. Someone else must have had the same concerns and already taken the body to safety; one of the guards or Senators, perhaps, who had made a break for it without the others. She didn't care. The problem was no longer hers; that was all that mattered.

She returned to the crater, where the last of the survivors was disappearing into the hole. Glad that they would soon be making a move, she looked over her shoulder at the battle taking place in the arena below. The rain was heavier than ever, but she could still make out figures moving in groups across the stadium bowl. The blasterfire was becoming increasingly sporadic as Bakuran resistance failed before the Ssi-ruuvi advance. It wouldn't be long now before the stadium belonged to the Ssi-ruuk. Soon after, she assumed with a shudder, the captives would be rounded up and taken to the carriers in orbit for entechment . . .

She turned when a hand touched her shoulder.

"Come on, Jaina," her father said. "There's nothing more we can do here."

Although it galled her to leave the battle, the odds were so overwhelming that she knew she didn't really have a choice.

Before she climbed back down into the hole, she cast her eyes up at the cloud-packed sky.

May the Force be with you, Jag, she thought. *Wherever you are.*

Catching sight of the nearer of Bakura's two moons, Jag pulled his clawcraft up and away, aiming with full throttle toward it. He didn't need to look back to know the fighters were following; the space ahead of him was puffing with bright explosions from their misfired shots.

He brought the clawcraft in steeply to the northernmost part of the moon, hoping to find some form of cover that might help him evade his pursuers. The closer he drew, the less likely this seemed. He brought his ship around from its almost perpendicular descent, speeding off across the surface of the moon. The ground was smooth and rolling, and looked to Jag to be made of an immense lava flow that had long since cooled. But it offered him no place to hide—and right now, that was all that mattered.

He jinked and swerved continuously in a bid to avoid both fire and tractor beams, but he knew he wouldn't be able to keep it up indefinitely. He cursed himself again; this little maneuver of his had put him in a worse situation than he'd been in before!

Without warning, the surface of the moon dipped sharply ahead of him, and the smooth ground he'd been following became a motionless waterfall that poured into a huge canyon easily fifty kilometers wide and at least a couple deep. Crags appeared out of the shadows, along with large rocky outcrops that jutted from the walls of the canyon like crimson fists. The V'sett fighters followed effortlessly, no longer trying to shoot him out of the sky. They were obviously intent on capturing him now. They must have realized that eventually they would get him; they just had to be patient.

He brought the clawcraft down, getting in as close as possible to the floor of the canyon, swerving frantically to avoid mineral deposits protruding from the canyon floor. Ten meters wide and at least three times that high, they looked like enormous petrified trees. And there were plenty of them, too, forcing Jag to bring all his flying experience to bear just to avoid hitting any. It was only when he inadvertently collected one with a shield that he realized it didn't matter whether he avoided them or not: the "tree" dissolved into a powder that silently washed over his viewport. After this he didn't even bother trying to fly his way between these bizarre-looking protrusions; he just flew in a straight line, bringing down whatever was in his path. Hopefully, he thought, the resulting dust would be enough to blind his pursuers— even if it afforded him only a moment or two, at least it would be *something*.

The canyon suddenly narrowed, though, and he knew he would have to climb out sooner rather than later, or wind up smashing straight into a wall. He brought his ship up, aiming for a rocky outcrop on the uppermost ridge of the canyon wall. Two bony fingers of rock stabbed out into the sky, as if pointing to the battle taking place overhead. If he could make it back up to the main battle, he might just be able to get help from the others in the squadron to get these fighters off his tail . . .

Realizing his intentions, the fighters opened fire again. Rock exploded from the canyon wall nearby; debris rattled against his shields. He aimed between the fingers of rock, but miscalculated the space between them and clipped one on the way through. He called out in alarm as the ship rolled out of control out into the space above the moon.

He emerged from the spin battered and barely in control. The two V'setts on his tail negotiated the hail of debris and kept coming. He jerked his clawcraft from side to side in a desperate attempt to avoid their grasping tractor beams, but his collision with the rocks had allowed them to gain on him. It would only be a matter of seconds now before—

A white blur streaked up past his viewport. His sensors barely had time to register the Y-wing as it flew within meters of him, torpedo ports firing. The enemy Ssi-ruuvi pilots didn't have time to deactivate their tractor beams before they sucked in the proton torpedoes. One instantly exploded; the second took a hit that sent it spiraling wildly back to the surface of the moon, where it flowered in a brief and silent explosion.

Jag's rear scopes were clear again, but his little jaunt to Bakura's moon hadn't come without a price. His damaged thruster complained with a stutter and a whine as he pulled hard around. The Y-wing swooped back to match vectors with him. The pilot—the same one Jag and his wingmates had rescued at the beginning of the battle—waved through her canopy. The gesture had little joy in it, though, and a quick scan told him why.

The Bakuran Defense Fleet was in bad shape. *Sentinel* had been hit by heavy bombing and its shields were down. *Defender* was standing defiant but without enough fighters to have any real effect on the battle. The Ssi-ruuvi forces rapidly mopped up any fighters it launched. Outnumbered and taken by surprise, Bakura lay open to attack.

In complete contrast, the two giant *Sh'ner*-class planetary assault carriers hung shining and impregnable above the battlefield. Their impenetrable shields had repelled everything thrown at them. Clusters of captured ships of all shapes hung nearby, waiting to be processed. Denied the basic dignity of dying in battle, hundreds of pilots trapped in durasteel coffins had only entechment to look forward to.

A triangular formation of seven V'sett fighters accelerated over the horizon of the small moon, coming up hard on Jag and the Y-wing. Jag urged his clawcraft to go faster, but it had given him everything it could. Seven fully armed ships against his damaged craft and the old Y-wing was a foregone conclusion.

The jamming ebbed long enough for him to check in on his squadron.

"Twin Suns, report!" He juked to avoid a crippling energy blast.

"Three here."

"Four."

"Six."

"Eight." There was a slight pause. "Jag, they've got me."

"And me," Six said.

"Looks like I'll have company, then," Three said. "They've got me, too."

Jag cursed. Apart from himself, that left just one pilot free—and he wasn't sure how long he would last!

He watched with dismay as the Y-wing tried to dodge the incoming vessels, only to be jerked back in the clutches of seven combined tractor beams. The pilot went without a sound. Either her comm was down or she was sparing him her despair.

Jag vowed then and there that he would not share a similar fate. He would sooner blow his engines than allow his soul to be sucked out and squeezed into a battle droid. But how could he do that when there was a chance he and his pilots could escape? While there was life, there was hope.

Jag was so frustrated he wanted to scream to get it out of his system. He almost didn't feel the tractor beams as they wrapped around his struggling clawcraft and started to drag it back into captivity.

Jaina watched from the rear of the column of survivors as they moved along the tunnels under the stadium with only the red glow of emergency lighting to guide them.

Despite the ferrocrete around them, she could hear the sound of paddle beamers and screams from up above. Although her lightsaber was still attached to her belt, she kept one hand on the weapon at all times. There was no evidence of immediate trouble, but she knew that pursuit wouldn't be far behind.

The Ryn led the way, retracing their steps quickly but carefully, with Tahiri's gurney never more than an arm's length away. Water trickled ahead of them in snake-like streams, washing dust and debris down into the depths of the building and making the floor slippery and treacherous.

"I don't think my circuits will stand another minute in this humidity, Mistress," C-3PO declared after slipping for the sixth time. The complaint was directed to Princess Leia, but he'd made sure it was loud enough for all to hear.

"Stop your complaining, Goldenrod." Han clapped the droid on the back, producing a metallic echo in the damp tunnel—as well as nearly causing the droid to stumble again. "You've been through worse than this and survived. Remember the incident with the stormtrooper uniform, last time we were here?"

If 3PO could have shuddered, Jaina was sure he would have done so from the top of his bronzed cranium to the base of his metal soles. "All too well, I'm afraid, sir," he said, his servomotors whirring with each step and his photoreceptor eyes glowing sharply in the gloom. "Mine is not the kind of memory that allows me to forget easily."

Jaina stopped listening when she heard a commotion ahead. Her lightsaber was out and ignited before she'd barely taken two steps through the stream of survivors in front of her.

"Princess Leia! Captain Solo! What are you doing here?"

Jaina knew that voice. "Malinza?" she said, pushing

forward. People made way for the buzzing, glowing blade. "You should've left long ago."

"The exit was blocked." The girl was at the front of the small group, blaster held down at her side. Vyram stood between her and their captives—a sullen Salkeli and a defiant Harris. Both were bound and gagged. "There are Ssi-ruuk everywhere out there!"

Jaina turned to Goure. "Is there another way out of here?"

"I'm not sure." The Ryn sounded calm and unflustered, but the lashing of his tail betrayed his nervousness. "But *he* might know," he said, pointing at Harris. "We followed him in here."

She indicated for Malinza to remove his gag. "Well?"

"Well what?" he said, eyes blazing with anger.

"*Is* there another way out of here?"

"Why should I tell you anything? To *help* you?" He laughed lightly as he shook his head. "Don't imagine that I'll be doing that in a hurry."

"In case you hadn't heard, your plan went horribly wrong. The P'w'eck were just a smokescreen for the Ssi-ruuk. You may have killed the Prime Minister, but it didn't stop the consecration. Once it was completed, the invasion force moved in."

Harris noticeably paled in the dim light of the tunnel. "Invasion?" He was at a loss for words, but not for long. "If Cundertol is dead, Bakura will need a strong leader. You might not like my methods, but I can get the job done. Set me free and—"

"It's too late for that," Jaina said. "There's a good chance you might not survive the next hour, let alone take the Prime Minister's job."

"So now *you're* in charge?" he sneered. "Is that the way it works, Solo?" He turned to Malinza and the other survivors. "Don't you think it's convenient that the

Galactic Alliance is here just in time to save us from a crisis we never knew we had? At a time when—"

"Save it, Harris," Jaina cut in. "No one's listening to you. There's no mistaking what we all saw out there. The Ssi-ruuk are on Bakuran soil, and it's partly your fault they're here. You should have made sure of your new allies before selling your soul to them."

"It wasn't him who sold his soul," said a new voice from the shadows farther along the corridor.

A tall figure stepped into the light. At first Jaina didn't recognize him. His blond hair had been burned away; bruises and scorch marks blackened his skin. He wore the remains of ceremonial robes around him like rags, concealing his hands.

"The market for politicians," Prime Minister Cundertol said, "is, perhaps unsurprisingly, quite small."

"You?" Leia couldn't keep the surprise out of her voice. "But you're—"

"Dead?" The big man smiled. "Not quite. Luckily, the blast only stunned me for a time. I woke up down here, disoriented and lost. I heard footsteps and saw Malinza, but I didn't want to reveal myself until I knew what she was up to—and what exactly she was doing with Blaine. I thought Freedom might have kidnapped him as well as set the bomb. But I guess I was wrong about you, Malinza—and for that I must apologize."

The girl nodded a wary acceptance. "It was Harris," she said. "He set us up."

"This is impossible," the accused man said. "That bomb was—I mean, they said you were dead!"

"Well, they were mistaken." Cundertol pulled his right hand from beneath his robes to reveal a blaster. "As I was mistaken to put my faith in you, Blaine. I can't believe that you're responsible for everything that's happening to us today."

Although the weapon pointed only at Harris, Jaina

instinctively tensed. Her lightsaber rose slightly. Leia's Noghri bodyguards also moved, hissing in warning as they placed themselves between Cundertol and the Princess. Something about the Prime Minister wasn't quite right. Jaina could sense it, even if she couldn't define it. When she deep-probed him to see if he was a Yuuzhan Vong spy, she encountered a strange texture. His presence was unlike any she'd felt before.

As if her instincts, and those of her mother's bodyguards, weren't enough, she could feel Goure's unease radiating palpably from him. He knew something, she was sure of it, but he couldn't say anything with Cundertol there. She decided to keep her lightsaber activated until she knew exactly what was going on.

"You must forgive our surprise, Prime Minister," Leia said. "But the last hour has been confusing, to say the least. You may have gathered that the P'w'eck peace plan was a sham for a Ssi-ruuvi attack—"

He nodded, keeping his eyes on Harris. "The Fluties have obviously been planning this a long time. I don't suppose you have any idea how we can force them back?"

Jaina winced at the racist reference to the aliens. She'd heard it before, but on the lips of the Prime Minister it sounded especially crass and offensive.

"No doubt the defense fleet and *Selonia* are working on something as we speak," Leia replied. "Unfortunately the comm channels are jammed, and there are Ssi-ruuk right behind us. We need to get out of here as quickly as possible. If we can get to the *Falcon*, that would be ideal."

The Prime Minister nodded. "A sensible plan," he said. "Blaine, you were about to tell us if you knew a way out of here, I believe, before I rudely interrupted."

"And I'll say to you what I said to her," the Deputy Prime Minister answered, inclining his head toward Jaina. "Why *should* I help? The way I see it, I have absolutely nothing to lose." He glared balefully at Cundertol as he raised his arms up in front of him and rattled his binders.

"You have your life to lose," Cundertol said simply. "Would you prefer entenchment with the rest of us when the Fluties finally catch up?"

Harris's glare intensified. "I can't help you, I'm afraid. You see, there *is* no exit. They're all blocked. Our only hope is to hide in one of the equipment lockers until the Ssi-ruuk are gone, and then try to sneak out."

"I'm not really one for hiding," Cundertol said, with a regretful shake of his head. The blaster in the Prime Minister's hand fired and Blaine Harris fell back onto the floor, dead before he hit. "Sorry, my friend. But that was the wrong answer."

Jaina stood, stunned, as the blaster came around. Harris had been guilty of mass murder, but she would never condone cold-blooded execution as punishment—and had never expected it from someone like Cundertol. Salkeli dropped to his knees in supplication, obviously anticipating a similar fate. Jaina stepped forward to prevent another travesty of justice.

However, Cundertol's interest lay not with the Rodian. Instead, in one smooth motion he pressed the blaster directly against Malinza's temple.

"Now, seeing as there are no other options available . . ."

Jaina froze. If she had thought she couldn't be more surprised than she already was, she was quickly proven wrong when the Bakuran Prime Minister opened his mouth as wide as it would go and called out in the Ssi-ruuvi language. It consisted of just three notes, but they were so loud even the echoes hurt her ears. An answering reply came almost immediately.

Her worst fears realized, Jaina cursed under her breath for allowing herself to be caught like this. She took a step forward, but stopped when Cundertol pushed the blaster even harder against Malinza's temple.

Cundertol grinned in triumph. He didn't have to move or say anything; he simply knew that Jaina wasn't about to risk Malinza's life. One squeeze of the trigger and the girl would be dead.

Jaina lowered the lightsaber and tried another tack. "Let her go." The mental command accompanying the words would have made an ordinary person instantly obey.

But the Prime Minister just shook his head. "I don't think so," he said, smiling.

"What *are* you?" Jaina asked.

The Prime Minister's smile widened, if that was possible.

"New," he said. "But we haven't got time for that right now. We need to go and meet your new masters."

Rapid footfalls came down the corridors behind and ahead of them. Deep, fluting calls passed back and forth between the two alien search parties as they converged on the maintenance area. The survivors drew closer together, moving instinctively into a corner. Jaina planted herself protectively between them and Cundertol, her eyes on both corridor entrances. Behind her, she felt her father and mother, Goure, and two security guards doing the same. If only they'd rushed Cundertol when they'd had the chance, she thought. If only—

She fought herself to stop such thoughts. They were nonproductive at best. There'd be time for regrets later. If there *was* a later, of course.

"You knew about the Ssi-ruuk," Malinza hissed, held tight in his grip. Her voice was steeped in disgust. "You betrayed Bakura. You're no better than Harris!"

"You're wrong on that score, I assure you," Cundertol said. "I am in every way better than Harris."

There was no time for Jaina to wonder what he meant. Six Ssi-ruuvi warriors burst out of the corridor to her left, running with long, bounding strides and flicks of their mighty tails, paddle beamers held before them in taloned hands. Their eyes and scales gleamed red in the emergency lighting. They came to a halt, hissing and screeching, at the sight of the fugitives before them.

The leader directed a series of piercing notes at Cundertol, who responded fluently in the same language.

"Threepio?" Han prompted the droid from the corner of his mouth.

"I believe it is a standard welcome," the droid said, looking from Cundertol to the Ssi-ruu. The giant saurian indicated the body of Harris and swished its tail. "Now it is reprimanding the Prime Minister that he has wasted this one."

The second party arrived before Cundertol could defend himself. At its head was the largest Ssi-ruu Jaina had yet seen—a beautiful red female warrior with pronounced ridges running back along her snout and across the top of her skull. She wore a black harness adorned with silver medals that jingled with each step she took, and her nostrils flared when her gaze fell upon Jaina and the others.

Behind her came five more warriors of ordinary size, protected by four golden priest-caste Ssi-ruuk as well as the Keeramak itself, its brighter colors subdued in the dim light. The large party concluded with a group of P'w'eck warriors that fanned out to cover the entrances.

The Keeramak moved forward with muscular grace, its massive jaws snapping as though at imaginary insects. Its gold-scaled servants eyed the Bakurans warily, daring them to speak. No one did.

A series of eerie, melodic notes then issued from the mutant Ssi-ruu's mouth.

" 'Surrender now,' " C-3PO translated, " 'and I will ensure that, once entenched, you will be put to productive tasks.' "

"We were told you no longer required entenchment,"

Leia said, not attempting to hide the disapproval from her voice. "I suppose that was just another lie."

The Keeramak executed a graceful bow. "One of many, Leia Organa Solo," it replied via C-3PO's translation. "The truth is, however, that we have indeed perfected the entenchment process. It is now possible to sustain life energy indefinitely, reducing the need for frequent replenishment. Some energies, such as your own, are too strong to resist. You will enrich us for centuries!"

Leia's lips tightened. From under her robes, she produced her own lightsaber—something she did only when all attempts at diplomacy had failed. It cast a red light across the face of the Keeramak.

"You shall never have my life energy," she said with menacing determination.

"Or mine," Jaina said, adding her voice—along with her blade—to her mother's vow.

The Keeramak backed away, fluting as the guards closed in.

"The Keeramak says, 'As you wish,' " C-3PO reported.

"Don't be fools," Cundertol said. "Don't you understand what you're being offered?"

"All too clearly," Han growled.

"You're hearing the words, but you're not *understanding* them! Entenchment isn't what you think it is. It's not the end; it's the beginning! It's liberation, not captivity!"

"You don't really believe that," Leia said.

Cundertol ignored her, addressing the others instead. "Imagine being the controller of your own droid ship, the heart of an interstellar drive, the overseer of an entire city! Imagine the freedom you will achieve when you've been cut loose from the shackles of flesh and blood. You'll be able to live forever!"

"Freedom?" Jaina echoed. "We'll be slaves!"

"Immortal slaves! What are a few years of servitude in

exchange for eternity? They will pass as though mere moments!"

Suddenly it became all too clear why Cundertol had betrayed Bakura to the Ssi-ruuk.

"Is that what they've promised you?" Leia asked. "Immortality? You sold out your planet and people for a promise of longer life?"

Cundertol's smile was wide and amused. "Actually, Princess, they didn't promise me anything. I worked it out for myself. They didn't come to me seeking a bargain; we met halfway. From there, it was just a matter of working out the details."

Jaina shook her head. "Surely you can't be that naive! If you think it's going to happen like—"

"Not *going* to happen—it's already happened! If you refuse to accept the truth of it, then I cannot help you. Your fate is already sealed."

The Keeramak clicked its claws, and half the P'w'eck moved forward through the ranks of Ssi-ruuvi guards. If there was going to be a fight, then clearly these were to be sacrificed first. Jaina felt sick to her stomach. As bad as it was to be facing captivity and entechment, it felt worse to know that her only hope of escaping would mean having to fight and possibly kill slaves.

Lwothin, even more fidgety than usual, led the contingent. He turned to the Keeramak and inclined his head in what Jaina took to be a gesture of respect and subservience. The mighty Ssi-ruu uttered a deep, powerful warble that she didn't require C-3PO to translate for her. As far as she was concerned, it could have meant only one thing: the Keeramak was ordering the P'w'eck guards to subdue the prisoners.

Lwothin nodded his long, reptilian head and raised himself to full height. Jaina tensed, her lightsaber igniting with a press of her thumb as she braced herself for the assault. With a cry that both surprised and terrified her in equal measures, Lwothin brought up his paddle beamer and fired point blank.

The engines of Jag's clawcraft were running hot. Despite that, it was still firmly tethered to the V'sett fighters that had captured him and being drawn inexorably toward a growing knot of captured Bakuran and Galactic Alliance vessels. Comprised of more than one hundred fighters, the knot was being drawn through a narrow hole in the shields of the massive carrier *Errinung'ka*. Two Fw'Sen picket ships accompanied them, making certain there was no trouble. The vast, curving sweep of the carrier's bow loomed over him, making him and his fate seem powerfully insignificant.

Clicks came over the comm as he joined the formation of captured fighters. Bound tight by powerful tractor beams, all he and his squadronmates could do was signal each other as they were dragged to their doom. Nearby he could make out the pilot of the Y-wing in her cockpit, hands visibly poised over her controls, a grim expression on her face. Jag had no doubt from the look in her eyes as she stared through her cockpit canopy at him that, given the opportunity, she would fight back—to the death if need be. Her eyes held the same dark determination he felt in his heart.

Not that such an opportunity would eventuate. Once they were on the other side of those shields, that would be it. There would be no hope of rescue then.

I'm sorry, Father, he thought, wishing there was some way that Baron Soontir Fel could hear him. And his mother. They'd had such hopes for him. All his life he had struggled to prove himself worthy in their eyes. The slow-maturing child of aliens in a fiercely competitive society, growing up in the shadow of Thrawn and his father's ambition. How could he ever have suspected that he would meet such a fate as this?

"This is Captain Mayn." The voice came clearly over the comm unit. "I'm addressing you on an open frequency. The jamming has been interrupted to let me relay orders from the ground. All fighters must stand down or planetary bombardment will begin immediately. They have paralysis weapons that can knock out an entire city. Salis D'aar will be the first target. Therefore, in the best interest of innocent civilians, I am asking for all resistance to cease."

Jag listened to the words with growing amazement. Could this really be Todra Mayn speaking? The thought of just giving in to the Ssi-ruuk turned his insides to water.

"If we stand down now, Captain, then they're as good as dead anyway," Jag said over the same frequency.

"We have an assurance from the Ssi-ruuk that, once the planet is under Imperium control, we shall be treated fairly."

Jag jerked the yoke of his ship to fight the dreadful tug of the tractor beams. "Like the P'w'eck were, you mean? As breeding stock for droid fighters?"

"Anything is better than dying."

He could tell by the way his engines were shrieking that they weren't going to last much longer at full throttle. If he was going to blow them, to end it quickly rather than in the mental cage of a droid fighter, then he was going to have to do it soon—while he still had engines to do it with!

"You have to trust me, Jag." Captain Mayn's voice was thick with tension. "They have Jaina."

So? he wanted to yell back at her. *Is one life worth more than that of an entire planet?*

But he couldn't say it. His heart tore at the idea that Jaina might be hurt. With numb fingers, he throttled back and let the alien shield slip over his craft. The shield itself was invisible to all but his instruments, but he imagined it as the maw of some mighty beast waiting to swallow him. Once ingested, fierce gastric juices would remove his soul and dispense with his useless carcass afterward . . .

Then the barrier slammed shut behind them, and they were inside. In the awkward stillness and silence, it felt like an entirely different universe. Outside, beyond the barrier, skirmishes lit up the starry backdrop as pockets of resistance still fought the Ssi-ruuvi invaders. The picket ships, once they had delivered their cargo, returned to patrolling the area. Inside the *Errinung'ka*'s shield there was only stillness. Caught in the web cast by droid and V'sett fighters, the captives could do little more than curse their misfortune. And wait.

Everything suddenly stopped as the Keeramak, without a single noise of complaint, crumpled to the floor.

There was a split second during which the Ssi-ruuk were so stunned by Lwothin's actions that they did nothing at all. They simply stood there gawping at the Keeramak lying on the ground, oozing a gray, viscous fluid from the paddle beamer wound in its chest. The P'w'eck were quick to take advantage of the Ssi-ruuk's confusion, and other paddle beamers began to flash in the dimly lit tunnel. For a moment, Jaina was confused, too, but that didn't last. It was obvious what was happening: Lwothin and the P'w'eck were rebelling against their Ssi-ruuvi masters!

The Ssi-ruuk were better trained and better equipped than the P'w'eck, though, and they soon regained the advantage, fighting back with frightening ferocity. Jaina had no doubt as to whose side she was on, and when a Ssi-ruuvi warrior leveled his beamer at Lwothin, she quickly slashed out with her lightsaber and knocked the weapon from the creature's hand. It swung around, attacking her with three raking claws, and she barely managed to duck a decapitating blow. The saurian was *huge*—but she had sparred with Saba Sebatyne enough times to know the kind of things a tail could do in combat. And there was still the Force, guiding her every move, tweaking her instincts. Fighting the Ssi-ruuk, thankfully, wasn't like fighting the Yuuzhan Vong, whose every intention was hidden from view.

She ducked and rolled, kicking up into the Ssi-ruu's midriff. It whuffed explosively and staggered backward. It used its tail to keep its balance, swiftly regaining its footing and lunging at her again. But she was out of the way before it could strike out, rolling under its sweeping talons once again. She came around its side, two-handedly slicing across the creature's neck. It fell to the floor with a shriek, spraying blood.

Another warrior howled and tried to skewer her with a shot from its beamer. Her lightsaber was unable to deflect the beam as effectively as it would a laser shot, but she did manage to bend it harmlessly into a wall. A P'w'eck leapt onto the warrior's back and brought it down. Jaina pulled the beamer from its grasp and threw it over to Vyram, who deftly snatched it from the air and aimed it at Cundertol's face.

He fixed the Prime Minister with an unflinching stare. "I won't hesitate to pull this trigger if that blaster so much as gives Malinza a bruise."

Neither moved as the fracas around them came to a surprisingly quick conclusion. The shock of their leader's death seemed to eat at the Ssi-ruuk's initial confidence. As the last of the surviving warriors allowed herself to be subdued, the Prime Minister lowered his weapon to his side.

"You ruined it," he said, looking emptily down at the Keeramak. "You ruined it for all of us!"

"Yeah?" Han said, looking around at the P'w'eck collecting weapons and distributing them among the Bakurans. The paddle beamers were awkward to handle, but having *something* to fight with was better than nothing at all. "I don't see anyone else complaining."

The advance leader of the P'w'eck Emancipation Movement spoke urgently in his lyrical voice.

"Lwothin asks that you contact our fighters immediately," C-3PO translated. "He says that the jamming has been interrupted to allow you to speak."

"What am I supposed to tell them?" Leia asked.

Lwothin sang again. "Oh, my," 3PO said. "He wants you to tell them to offer no resistance—to allow them to be captured!"

Leia opened her mouth, but her husband spoke his mind first. "No one's giving any such order!"

Lwothin explained his plan as best he could in the limited time. When he had finished, Jaina watched Leia glance down at the body of the Keeramak, the look in her eyes suspicious and dubious.

"How can I be sure that you're not asking me to send those fighters into a trap?"

"You cannot," the P'w'eck sang in reply via C-3PO. "But if you say nothing then those pilots are as good as dead anyway. This is their only hope." The P'w'eck's eyes were luminous behind their rapidly flickering triple eyelids. "The time for lies and traps has passed. We stand before you now as allies and equals. We will not betray you."

Every instinct in Jaina's body screamed out to believe him. For the first time, she felt as though they had reached the heart of the conspiracies surrounding Bakura. Leia clearly felt the same. With a brisk nod, she activated her comlink and called *Pride of Selonia*.

The conversation was brief and to the point. The next

message Jaina heard over the comlink was Captain Mayn's general broadcast to all the Galactic Alliance fighters.

"This is Captain Mayn. I'm addressing you on an open frequency."

When she was finished, Jag's voice came back with:

"If we stand down now, Captain, then they're as good as dead anyway."

At the sound of his voice, something inside Jaina suddenly relaxed. When Lwothin had described the fighting taking place in orbit above Bakura, her first thought had been of Jag, wondering whether he had been among those killed. Or worse, captured for entechment.

"I have an assurance from the Ssi-ruuk," Mayn went on, maintaining the pretense of surrender, "that, once the planet is under Imperium control, we shall be treated fairly."

"Like the P'w'eck were, you mean? As breeding stock for droid fighters?"

"Anything is better than dying."

There was a high-pitched groan over the open line as though of a fighter undergoing stresses it hadn't been designed for. Jaina waited for Jag's reply, but it didn't come. She could feel his uncertainty and desperation as though he were standing next to her. His concern for her burned like a small but intense star.

Captain Mayn clearly sensed it, too.

"You have to trust me, Jag," she said. "They have Jaina."

The lie cut Jaina deeply, but she knew immediately that it was the right thing to say. If anything could make Jag defy his deepest, most ingrained instincts, then that would be it. His concern for her ran deep—deeper than he had admitted aloud.

He didn't reply, but she knew that he had capitulated.

"I presume you know what you're doing, Princess," the voice of Captain Mayn added on a private channel.

Leia adjusted the comlink to reply on that same channel. "I do, Todra." She glanced at Lwothin with the threat of murder in her eyes. "Trust me on this."

Time seemed to have frozen. Caught in the web of the Ssi-ruuvi shields, Jag vibrated with tension. He had no way of knowing what was happening on the ground or elsewhere in orbit. The jamming had returned not long after the end of Mayn's transmission. He felt isolated and powerless, like all the other pilots trapped in their fighters around him, waiting for their captors to move in and take them . . .

Then something strange happened. His sensors registered a slight lessening of the tractor beams holding him in place. Suspecting that some of the Ssi-ruuvi escort may have dropped away now that they were safe within the shields, he checked his scope. Their escort hadn't moved.

A second later, the tractor beam readings dropped again. He flexed his controls and found that his clawcraft had retained a measure of mobility.

He sat for a moment, fighting the impulse to pull loose. What was the point? If he did break free, what was he supposed to do? The shields around the carrier would stop him from escaping anyway, so it seemed a pointless exercise.

But then there was yet another dip in the readings, and this time he couldn't help himself: he found his hopes rising. It couldn't just be him, surely. The grip of the Ssi-ruuk on their captives was slipping. A rush of excitement thrilled through him as he realized what must be going on.

The P'w'eck droid ships that had accompanied the Bakuran fighters on the "honor guard" flights were slowly redirecting their tractor beams. Having delivered an undamaged attack force behind the shields of the enemy, they were now setting them free—gradually, so the Ssi-ruuk wouldn't notice. The P'w'eck were rebelling against their masters—for real, this time—and using Bakuran firepower as their weapon!

Jag clicked three times in rapid succession to call for attention. The captured Twin Sun pilots clicked in immediately. There was a growing rustle over the comm indicating that others were noticing the change and wondering what was going on. He didn't have much time; he would have to act fast before the Ssi-ruuk noticed.

When the tractor beams dropped once more, he clicked twice, then twice again. It was the squadron's code for "attack," and the response was instantaneous. Jag and his pilots pushed their ships from a standing start to full throttle at virtually the same instant. Tearing free of the weakened forces binding them, they roared out of formation and swooped around to attack the unprepared Ssi-ruuk. The V'sett fighters were, much to their surprise, caught in the droid ships' tractor beams, reducing their maneuverability. Within seconds, it was over. The Ssi-ruuk were destroyed and the tractor beams holding the remainder of the captives fell away completely.

The formation immediately dissolved into chaos. Communications cleared. Jag opened his comm on all frequencies, hoping to regain order before the jamming returned.

"Stay calm, people!" he ordered. "Maintain your original formations! Do not fire on the droid ships! I repeat, do *not* fire on the droid ships. They're piloted by the P'w'eck, remember, and they're on our side. They were the ones who got us here."

"What's so good about *here*?" one of the Bakuran pilots returned.

"Here we have a target," Jag replied, turning his clawcraft in the direction of the alien carrier. "We're inside the shields, and their squadrons are outside. They can't call for reinforcements without opening themselves up for attack from *Selonia* or *Sentinel*." He grinned in anticipation of the battle ahead; it was so obvious, now that he saw it. "They've given us a chance, people, so let's not waste it!"

The dramatic triple reversal of the P'w'eck—from enemy to ally, then to enemy and now back to ally—left the Bakuran pilots understandably confused, but they obeyed Jag's orders and left the P'w'eck alone. Flights of threes and fives re-formed and swooped down from the inner edge of the shields to attack the carrier. Jag gathered the remnants of Twin Suns around him and did the same. The carrier bays weren't completely empty, and a dozen V'sett fighters soon rose to meet them. Six droid fighters came in close pursuit. Caught from behind, the Ssi-ruuk's defensive charge was soon scattered.

"Go for the tractor beam generators," Jag instructed the pilots swarming around him, searching for targets. "Then make strafing runs across the deflector-shield projectors. Try to keep structural damage to a minimum. We have friends in there, and I'd rather not lose a single one of them to friendly fire."

Then he was down in the maelstrom, finding targets and launching laser bolts as fast as he could. He made a couple of passes at the ion cannons that ringed the carrier's bulging waist and managed to destroy three. Others from his squadron cleaned up the rest.

The response from the carrier was sluggish, and he put that down to the P'w'eck who were revolting both inside and outside the ship. But he wasn't fool enough to believe that this advantage would last indefinitely. At 750 meters long, the carrier would have been a formidable opponent for even a hundred fighters.

Still, he thought, any amount of damage they could inflict upon the carrier would be something. The more they could do here, he figured, the less work there'd be for Jaina later . . .

*   *   *

Word of the breakout of the Galactic Alliance fighters came from *Selonia* within moments of the airwaves clearing. Jaina, however, had no time to hear the details. A sudden blur of motion caught her attention. Thinking that one of the Ssi-ruuvi captives had made a break for it, she whirled with her lightsaber at the ready, but instead all she saw was the back of the former Prime Minister sprinting off down the corridor. Vyram was lying on his back, rubbing his right forearm.

"I'm sorry," he said, clambering to her feet. "He moved so *quickly*!"

Jaina didn't wait; she immediately set off after Cundertol. They couldn't let him escape. If he got to a communicator, the plan would be exposed and Jag could be captured for real. She followed the rapid *pad-pad* of his footsteps along the dusty corridors as he looped around the others and headed up toward the hole Harris's bomb had blown in the stadium.

She soon realized what Vyram had meant about the Prime Minister being quick. Cundertol's speed was impressive.

The sound of his footsteps ahead veered off in a new direction. Two corners and fifty meters later, she understood why. A squadron of P'w'eck who had overthrown their masters came down the tunnel toward her, blocking the exit to the stadium. Cundertol hadn't wanted to run into them, so he had ducked down an alternate tunnel, probably heading for the exit Malinza and the others had tried before. Jaina didn't hesitate; she turned down into the tunnel, too, startling the P'w'eck squadron as she ran past but not stopping to explain herself.

Jaina could hear Cundertol running down stairs two floors below. His footfalls were heavy and, incredibly, unflagging. The source of his strength and endurance concerned her. Even she was beginning to tire, despite having the Force to augment her stamina.

A door slammed somewhere up ahead of her, and she knew that Cundertol had left the stairwell on the fifth basement level. She made herself run faster, hurling herself forcibly at the door when she reached it. The door had barely begun to swing back when something struck out at her from the gloom on the far side. She knocked it aside with a reflexive Force shove and rolled away. As she got to her feet and adopted a defensive stance, she had just enough time to make out Cundertol at the far end of a wide corridor. Something whizzed through the air toward her. She moved her head just as a small bolt ricocheted off the wall behind her, leaving a deep dent. Her first thought was that he was using a slingshot, but his hands were clearly empty. She didn't have time to dwell on it, though, as another bolt whizzed by her head, so close that she could feel it flick her hair.

He's throwing *them!* she thought, incredulous.

His strength might have been superior to his aim, but she wasn't about to give him a chance to practice. She sent a Force push that would have thrown an ordinary man off his feet. All it did to Cundertol, though, was make him stagger backward. It wasn't much, but it was enough. She ran across the open space before he recovered.

He had no intention of sticking around to fight. Instead he disappeared through yet another door with disconcerting speed. She followed, but more cautiously this time. What *was* he? Where was he getting his strength and speed from? Whatever was going on, it was obvious she wasn't going to be able to catch him with speed alone. She was going to have to try something else.

His footsteps receded down another corridor, then abruptly stopped.

Jaina hesitated at the corner, warily peering around it.

The dark corridor seemed empty, but she knew he was down there somewhere.

"You must know you're not going to get away with this, Cundertol," she called, hoping to get at least an estimate of his position from a reply.

"No?" he responded. His voice was muffled by something other than just distance. "And I suppose you're going to stop me, girl?"

"That's my intention, yes." She frowned, unable to place him.

"I'm afraid that the best intentions can often count for nothing," he said, suddenly dropping down behind her. "Not when survival is at stake."

She spun around to strike out at him, but he knocked her aside as if she were nothing more than a rag doll. His speed and strength were far beyond those of an ordinary man. She shoved off the wall and came back at him with a strike to the head, igniting her lightsaber with the other hand as she did so. He was under the blow before it could connect, punching up at her and knocking her off her feet. She flew five meters through the air, her lightsaber inscribing a wide, black arc on the floor as she fell— but she didn't let go of it.

Cundertol didn't want to waste time with talk. The twisted expression on his face told her that he was concerned with only one thing: escape. As long as she stood between him and that goal, she would have to be eliminated. She back-flipped onto her feet before he could reach her and warned him away with a swing of her lightsaber.

He feinted to her left, then came at her from her right, ducking under the blade and delivering a blow to her chest that felt as though she'd been hit by a force pike. She flew off her feet again and landed on her backside with a painful grunt. This time her grip on her lightsaber failed and the weapon went skittering across the floor. Before she could snatch it back with the Force, Cundertol had already stepped up to finish her off.

"You put up a good fight," he said, looking threateningly over her.

"It isn't over yet," she returned, summoning the lightsaber back toward her.

It shot through the air with a whine and a hiss. Hearing it coming, Cundertol rolled away to one side, but not before the sizzling blade connected. He fell back with a roar, clutching his injured arm. Jaina used the moment to climb back onto her feet, albeit with some difficulty. Her legs were weak from Cundertol's attack, and the world seemed to be swaying crazily around her. Nevertheless, she managed to hold her ground, directing her thoughts once again out to the lightsaber. This time it flew straight back into her hand.

Cundertol, however, had already taken flight. She could see him at the end of the corridor, nursing his arm as he rounded a corner and disappeared from sight. She was about to give chase again, when the sound of feet came clattering up behind her.

"Jaina!" Her mother was beside her, arms coming around her shoulders. "Are you all right?"

She nodded. "Cundertol," she said, waving vaguely in the direction he had taken. "He went that way!"

"Don't worry, kid. We'll get him." Her father's silhouette led a mixed group of humans and P'w'eck up the corridor after the former Prime Minister.

"Be careful!" she yelled after them as her mother's hands guided her down onto the floor, where the world was mercifully level. She crouched there for what felt like forever, fighting nausea. Cundertol had hit her harder than she'd suspected.

"You'll be okay," her mother was saying. "It'll be all right."

Jaina knew that it wasn't. Her thoughts were confused,

fragmentary. Something about her fight with Cundertol bothered her. What was it? She had wounded him, she knew that much. She'd cut his arm—

Then she saw it, lying in the shadows a few meters away from her. She wriggled from her mother's grasp and made her way over to it, staring at the thing with a mixture of satisfaction and puzzlement.

"What is it?" her mother asked from behind her.

"His arm," Jaina said, squinting at the limb. She hadn't just cut his arm, she'd completely severed it below the elbow! "At least the lower part, anyway."

But there was something distinctly not right about it. Apart from a small smattering and some minor seepage about the stump, there was no blood to be seen anywhere. Sometimes a lightsaber could cauterize veins as it cut and stop the bleeding, it was true, but it wasn't just the blood that piqued her suspicions—it was the *smell*. It stank of cooked synthflesh.

"It's okay, Jaina," her mother said, coming up beside her. "It's over now. They'll get him—especially if he's injured."

Her mother's words washed over her as she realized uneasily what it was she'd been fighting. Cundertol was a droid!

"No, they won't," she said, staring numbly at the artificial arm. "Even injured, he's going to get away."

Before she could explain, a barrage of fluting sounded from nearby.

"Excuse me, Mistress," C-3PO said, "but Lwothin reports that *Errinung'ka* has surrendered to the P'w'eck. *Firrinree* is expected to follow shortly."

That should make up for losing Watchkeeper *and* Intruder, *at least*, Jaina thought to herself.

"What about Jag?" she managed to ask her mother. "Has there been any word?"

"There has," she said, nodding. "He's leading the attack on *Firrinree* even as we speak."

Her mother's voice was soothing. Under the words, Jaina knew she was trying to say, *It's not your problem; let it go.*

Maybe she was right, but Jaina doubted she'd be able to relax fully until she knew for sure that Jag was nearby and they were both a long way from the threat of entenchment . . .

EPILOGUE

Jacen stared at the result in disbelief. He could feel the combined attention of everyone in the room as the data from Wyn's search through the library's records flowed down the holopad in front of him. Listed was every system that had gained a planet in the last sixty years. Saba and Danni had already examined most of them during their search of CEDF's files, and the rest had turned out to be either ordinary planetary acquisitions or fleeting encounters with the living planet. All told there were fifteen acquisitions and a further forty encounters. But unfortunately—and frustratingly—each of them could be ruled out.

Jacen shook his head in dismay. "It's not here."

"It *has* to be here," Mara said. "There's nowhere else it could have gone!"

"Unless it's hiding somewhere in the rest of the galaxy," Luke said, wearily.

"But we'd know about it if it was," Mara said.

"Perhaps we just haven't looked hard enough. It might be in one of the smaller backwaters—like the Minos Cluster, for instance."

"Or maybe it left the galaxy altogether." Danni's voice was heavy with gloom. "Or perhaps it just died."

"No," Jacen said. "It didn't die. We have holos of it around two of the systems it visited, remember?" Jacen was finding it hard to keep the frustration from his voice.

"And it can't have left the galaxy, either—not unless it knows something about hyperspace that we don't."

"Or it's found a way to exist without a sun," Luke put in.

Jacen shook his head. "I refuse to accept any of those possibilities."

"Then what are you going to do?" Fel's was the voice of cold reason. "If you've looked and you haven't found it, and you've ruled out every other possibility, then where does that leave you? Perhaps Zonama Sekot really is nothing but a legend."

"No," Jacen said firmly. "No, I can't believe that, either. Vergere wouldn't have lied to me."

"Can you be absolutely sure of that?"

"Yes." Jacen met the one-eyed stare of the assistant syndic with stubborn determination. "Yes, I can. Zonama Sekot *is* real. All we have to do is find it." He turned back to the hologram. "Somehow . . ."

"Well, you now have the support of the Houses if you want to continue looking in Chiss space," Fel said.

Jacen felt exhausted. His uncle's hand came to rest on his shoulder, reassuring him. Saba and Mara brushed minds with his to offer their support, too. He was grateful for the gestures, but he was unable to silence the doubt that Soontir Fel had given voice to. What if Vergere *had* lied to him? What if Zonama Sekot was just a dream?

From far away, almost a quarter rotation around the galaxy, he sensed Jaina's capitulation to exhaustion at the completion of her duty. He occasionally felt flashes of his twin sister, even from so far away. It felt good, he thought, and wished he could do the same. He'd barely slept since arriving on Csilla, and it was getting so that he couldn't think straight anymore. His body felt weak, hollow and fragile, and had it not been for the Force propping him up, he was sure he would have collapsed into himself hours ago.

But despite the aid of the Force, he knew he was going to have to rest eventually. Staring dully at the data—even if he did it forever and a day—wasn't going to surrender any answers.

"Right or wrong," he said, standing, "you're going to have to try to find it without me for a while, I'm afraid. I need to rest."

Without another word, he brushed past his aunt and left the room, ignoring the concerned look from Commander Irolia as he walked deep into the aisles of the library.

Danni came to him half an hour later. He had tucked himself in a corner at the library's uppermost level. It was peaceful there, uncomplicated—the perfect place to clear his head.

"Hey." She eased herself next to him and leaned against the wall. They sat side by side in silence, their legs gently touching. He felt he should say something, but he simply didn't know how to express what he was feeling.

"You know," she said after a long silence he barely noticed, "I had another thought."

He half turned to her. "About Zonama Sekot?"

She nodded. "What if it broke apart? The stress of all that jumping must have taken its toll. Worlds are pretty fragile, after all. One slipup could have cracked it wide open, and we never actually looked for new asteroid belts."

Jacen acknowledged her suggestion with a polite nod, but he didn't really credit it. He couldn't afford to. Zonama Sekot was out there; it had to be! There had to be something lurking in the data that he'd overlooked—or something he hadn't yet looked for . . .

"Are you angry with me?" Danni said hesitantly.

"Huh?" The question startled him from his thoughts. "Angry with you? Why would you think that?"

She shrugged. "You don't seem to want to talk to me, that's all."

"No, I'm not angry, Danni. I'm just tired. I haven't slept properly. I came up here to think things through."

"Things?" she prompted. "You mean Zonama Sekot kind of things?"

He nodded, grinning. "Zonama Sekot kind of things."

"I've been thinking about things, too," she said. "*Us* kind of things."

"Really?"

She nodded once, turning her gaze briefly on to the vast expanse of books spread out before them, as if searching for the words that might best convey her thoughts. "It's strange, you know. I can crack the biological secrets of the Yuuzhan Vong; I can plot the likelihood of a solar system capturing a new planet; but sometimes I can't even begin to guess what goes on inside your head, Jacen Solo."

He took her hand. "Danni, I—"

"No, let me finish. We've known each other for a few years, now—since the beginning of the war, when you rescued me from Helska Four. But it wasn't until that day on Mester Reef that I saw you for who you are. Not as one of the Solos, or a Jedi Knight, or Jaina's brother— but as *you*. And I liked what I saw."

Jacen remembered that day well: the variety of life in and around the coral; the green of Danni's eyes and the brownness of her skin; the promise in her smile . . .

"You're strong," she said. "It may surprise you to know that I think you're the strongest person in the entire Galactic Alliance. You're the only one with the courage to question what everyone else regards as a great privilege. Most people would happily accept the honor of being a Jedi Knight, but you don't. You look beneath the honor and try to understand what it means to be a Jedi. That sort of strength can't be taught, Jacen; it comes from within.

"And you're kind," she went on. "No, look at me," she said when he turned away, beginning to feel awkward. "This is stuff you need to hear. In the middle of a war, it's hard sometimes to remember the good things. People are rewarded for being great fighters, but rarely for exhibiting gentler strengths, such as kindness and compassion—or the kind of loyalty that questions rather than accepts. Your sister gets all the medals while you fade into the background."

"The medals don't interest me," he said. "And I certainly don't begrudge Jaina getting them—"

"I know that," she interrupted. "You would never resent anyone for her success. That's just another of your strengths." She paused, smiling. "Shall I go on?"

He shook his head, smiling also. "I think I get the idea."

"Jacen, I'm not saying this to embarrass you—or to prompt you into saying something similar in return. Don't ever think that. I'm saying it because I think you need to hear it."

"Why?"

"Because to you, success depends solely upon finding Zonama Sekot. I understand that, and I understand its importance in the greater scheme of things. But there's a smaller scheme, too—one that I feel you've already succeeded in. After years of crossing each other's paths like some wandering satellites, I'm glad that I'm finally close enough to you to be able to say that you've grown into a man I'd be proud to call a friend." Her gaze held his, its intensity matched only by the seriousness of what she was saying.

She stopped there, with a gentle squeeze of his hand that told him it was his turn to speak. He knew he had to say something in return, regardless of whether or not he felt comfortable doing so. He sensed that she was talking about more than friendship, and he wasn't sure how to define his feelings in return. He vividly remembered the day he had rescued her from Helska 4; she had seemed so beautiful to him, so much older and more mature, and utterly unobtainable. He may have rescued her from the Yuuzhan Vong, but at the end of that day, he had been just a boy and she was a woman. And he still carried a measure of that impression with him. Although he was with her now, talking as equals, the young boy in him remained at a distance, unable to believe that anything else could be true.

Like some wandering satellites . . .

He was about to try to explain his feelings to her when her phrase returned to him. The words were niggling at his thoughts, demanding attention. For some reason her use of the metaphor troubled him, but not because of what it meant to him. It made him think of the fruitless quest Vergere had sent him on—although it wasn't immediately apparent *why* her simple words caused this reaction in him. *Satellites?* As far as he was aware, Zonama Sekot didn't have any satellites. In fact, he doubted it could have even kept one with all the hyperspace jumps it had performed. Perhaps it had acquired one since—

Then the answer struck him in one blinding flash. It was so obvious he could have kicked himself!

Consumed by the inspiration, he completely forgot about Danni and their conversation. Afraid of losing any more time, of missing an opportunity, he abruptly stood up.

"Jacen?" Danni said, her expression puzzled as her hand fell back into her lap. "What—"

"I've got it!" The exclamation came out with a laugh. "Come on, Danni. Let's go!"

He hurried down the stairs, heading back to the ground level and the massive pile of books they had sorted through. He was vaguely aware of Danni running behind him, calling out for him to stop and asking what was wrong. But there simply wasn't enough time to stop and explain; she would have to hear what he had to say when he told the others.

Everyone looked up when he ran to the table. Danni was only a few seconds behind him, her look of confusion reflecting the expressions of the others.

"We need to run another search," he said breathlessly as he stepped up to Wyn.

His uncle was the first to respond. "*Another* search? But, Jacen, we've already searched every planet in the—"

"Not for planets," Jacen interrupted. "For *moons*."

Luke crinkled his brow at this. "Why would we do that?"

"Think about it," he said breathlessly. "If Zonama Sekot entered a system around a gas giant, it wouldn't show as a world, would it? It'd be registered as a satellite— just like Yavin Four. A habitable world in a habitable zone—but it would be listed as a moon! Don't you see? We would have missed it!"

"But Jacen," Danni said from behind him, "the tidal forces of entering such a configuration would be incredibly severe."

He dismissed her protest with a wave of his hand. "I'm sure Zonama Sekot could find a way around that—just as it always found a way to escape whenever it needed to. It's resourceful and determined." He faced his uncle, wanting the Jedi Master to believe him. "I know I'm right about this. We *have* to do the search."

His uncle thought about it for a long moment, and then turned to Wyn. "Will it take long?"

The girl looked nervous at being the sudden focus of such attention. "That depends on how many possible targets there are."

"There probably wouldn't be too many," Danni said. "System captures are scarce enough as it is, but the acquisition of extra-solar world-sized moons by gas giants would be extremely rare. I'd be amazed to find even one in the last hundred years. The odds of it happening in a system's habitable zone are minute."

"Could Jacen be right, then?" Mara asked.

Danni studied Jacen critically, then shrugged and smiled. "I guess there's only one way to find out."

Jacen sent a wave of warm gratitude in her direction.

The look of rage on Shimrra's face was the most satisfying thing Nom Anor had ever seen. Even from a distance and viewed through a villip beacon concealed in Ngaaluh's robes, it thrilled him to the core of his black heart.

"Tell me again," Shimrra said, in the tight, too-controlled manner that presaged an explosion of anger, "how your incompetence led to the fugitives' escape."

"Yes, Dread Lord." Taking a deep breath, the commander Hreven Karsh repeated almost word for word his explanation of how his warriors had allowed a small and relatively helpless party of Jedi and Imperials to slip through their fingers in the Unknown Regions. Nom Anor was coming into the story late, but it appeared as though this party, led by the Skywalkers, had been instrumental in foiling an operation that should have taken the insular but fiercely militaristic nation known as the Imperial Remnant out of the picture altogether. From there, they had moved into the Unknown Regions. Karsh, sent by the leader of the attack on the Imperial Remnant, had tracked the mission from a distance but lost them on the edge of Chiss space. The present whereabouts of the Skywalkers remained, much to Karsh's embarrassment and chagrin, unknown.

Hreven Karsh was an inexperienced commander. His relative, Komm Karsh, had died trying to obtain information from the abominable libraries on Obroa-skai, and he had slipped into the empty shoes with ambitious relish. His ritual modifications—vonduun crab armor plates inserted under his skin and coaxed to grow and overlap at odd angles so that his skin took on the appearance of a buckled, jagged crust—had been conducted in haste. The wounds, in fact, were still weeping. But the discomfort they would have caused was nothing compared to the indignity he must have felt at having to detail his failure to the Supreme Overlord—nor to the punishment that would inevitably follow.

"We are presently combing the fringes of the Chiss empire for any sign of the fugitives and—"

" 'Combing'?" the Supreme Overlord interrupted, descending with menace from his spiny, bloodred throne of yorik coral. His scarred, slashed, tattooed face twisted into a sneer. The mqaaq'it implants in his eye sockets burned with an all-too-familiar glare. "Did you say 'combing'?"

Karsh swallowed uneasily as the Supreme Overlord approached with careful, calculated steps. "I did, Great One." There was no mistaking it for anything but an apology.

"What are you, Karsh? The handmaiden of some infidel princess?" Shimrra snarled out his words barely centimeters from the commander's face.

"My Lord, no! I only meant—"

"We are the Yuuzhan Vong, Karsh. We do not *comb*. We *take*. This galaxy and everything in it belongs to us—including the worlds in the Unknown Regions! You will remind the Chiss of that fact. If they are harboring the fugitives you seek, then you will not let their borders hinder you. Nor will you pander to their delusions of grandeur. You will put them in their place—and you shall do so by *taking* what is rightfully ours, not by *combing* delicately through that which the Chiss mistakenly believe to be their own. Do I make myself clear?"

"Yes, Supreme One!" Karsh stiffened in resolve. "I assure you that the *Jeedai* will be found. I swear it on my domain's name."

His tone had lost its frightened edge. He sounded more relieved that the audience with Shimrra seemed to be drawing to a close. If he was lucky, he might yet walk away from this meeting unscathed. With the luxury of distance from Shimrra's wrath, Nom Anor knew better. By sending Karsh into the Unknown Regions, Shimrra had effectively sacrificed the commander in a gambit that would do nothing more than antagonize another enemy.

"Excellent, Karsh. Excellent." Returning to his throne, Shimrra sat and faced the commander one more time. "Now, come to me and give me your hand."

Karsh did so, climbing the steps nervously to Shimrra and extending one scarred, clawed hand. The Supreme Overlord looked the commander in the eye and smiled.

"No," he said, resting back in his black-and-gray robes. "Sever it and give it to me. I will keep it as a reminder of your promise. Should you fail me again, I shall sacrifice each and every member of your domain to the gods. Is that understood?"

Karsh nodded tensely, understanding all too well that Shimrra meant precisely what he said. Taking a sharp-edged coufee from the scabbard at his side, he raised it with one hand and, with a blank expression on his face, neatly sliced off the other. The severed limb fell with a heavy thud to the floor. A patter of light footsteps came as the bent, mutilated figure of Shimrra's familiar capered forward to collect it while Karsh stood rigidly to attention.

Shimrra waited a long moment as Karsh's lifeblood spilled out onto the ground, splashing his boots. Then he nodded his approval to the commander. "You may go."

Karsh walked stiffly to the exit. The view was perfectly clear in the villip. At last, Nom Anor had exactly what he needed: an insight into Shimrra's inner sanctuary, an ear to the Yuuzhan Vong leader's words and thoughts.

Things were clearly not going well for the Supreme Overlord. The lack of advancement since taking Yuuzhan'tar seemed to have afflicted the entire Yuuzhan Vong force. Resistance had formed where previously there was none, supply lines had been sabotaged, terraforming of the capital world was at a standstill, and the priests warned incessantly of the tightening hold of heresy on the lower ranks. This last part pleased Nom Anor the most. His efforts had sent a tide of dissent lapping at the walls of Shimrra's stronghold.

Nom Anor's satisfaction deepened as the conversation in Shimrra's throne room moved to other matters. He could hear every word perfectly. Attacking Ngaaluh had turned out to be the best thing he could have done. Far from making the priestess fear him, it seemed to have bolstered her resolve to defy the Supreme Overlord.

"I owe you my life, Master," Ngaaluh had gasped up at him from where she had lain on the floor, the day they had met under their new circumstances. She had been weak and pale, but gradually regaining her strength. The antidote Nom Anor had administered was slowly taking effect. "You are truly Yu'shaa, the compassionate one, and I am your humble servant."

Nom Anor recognized an opportunity when he saw one, and he had no reservations in exploiting one when it came his way.

"I have given you back your life," he had said to the priestess. "With what are you prepared to repay me?"

"I would repay you *with* my life, my Master."

"You would willingly risk it for me?"

"Without hesitation, my Master."

"And if I were to ask you to risk it for the Jedi?"

"If you were to ask me to risk it for a ghazakl worm, I would do so without question," Ngaaluh had said. "But for the *Jeedai* I would gladly offer my life in sacrifice, so that I might again become one with the Force."

Nom Anor remembered Ngaaluh's words distinctly. It was a conclusion that hadn't come from him or his followers, but rather something Ngaaluh had devised herself. Over subsequent days, as the priestess slowly regained her strength, Nom Anor had probed for the source of this and other conclusions Ngaaluh had come to before deciding to seek out the Prophet for herself. It transpired that Ngaaluh had had contact with the treacherous creature Vergere, who had sowed the seeds of doubt in her mind while in the safekeeping of the deception sect. Ngaaluh had been doubting the established pantheon for some time since, and had been seeking a way to incorporate the Jedi and the Force into the worldview she'd been brought up to accept. Some of the priestess's conclusions echoed Nom Anor's fictitious propositions—such as the idea of the Force being an echo of the spirit of Yun-Yuuzhan—but others were truly her own. The idea that death reunited the Yuuzhan Vong with the spirit of their creator was, in Nom Anor's opinion, an inspired one—and one that allowed him to offer the Shamed Ones an excuse to risk their lives in his service.

As someone well acquainted with deception and deceit, she had tracked the Prophet's Message to its source and, by virtue of her sincerity, had inveigled herself among the acolytes. Nom Anor was not so naive as to take the priestess's servitude at face value. He knew there was a possibility that Ngaaluh was a double agent, emptily spouting the words she knew Nom Anor wanted to hear. Nevertheless, the opportunity to send Ngaaluh back to Shimrra equipped with a villip beacon was one too perfect to turn down.

". . . marked downturn in the far-reaches destabilization program," a subaltern was saying. "The infiltration phase is complete in many rival communities, with conflict escalating to the point of open war in others. But in at least two major instances the infidels have intervened to halt our work. In both cases the work of our agents was not just undone but ultimately used to strengthen the infidels. I fear that this counteracts the successful work achieved in other areas."

"This was the program initiated by Nom Anor, was it not?" an aide asked. "If so—"

"Do not speak that name in my presence!" Shimrra interrupted sharply, standing. Then, with more composure but no humor at all, he smiled. "Not until I have his severed head before me and I wear his flayed skin as a cloak will I hear the traitor's name again." The Supreme Overlord's mqaaq'it implants burned like miniature suns. "You will do well to remember that. Otherwise it will be *your* head I shall have before me."

The aide backed away. "Yes, Most Potent and Powerful One. I simply wished to point out that the fact that this program is the work of—of a certain former executor might explain its failure. It was flawed to begin with, My Lord, and perhaps therefore should be abandoned."

"No," Shimrra said thoughtfully, descending the steps of his throne. "It was a good plan when it was proposed, and it is still a good plan. We will continue with the program for the time being. It is an effective use of resources in a region far from the main front. Any temporary alliances formed as a result of the incompetence of our agents will be corrected when the rest of the galaxy has fallen."

As the subaltern retreated into anonymity, Nom Anor told himself that he should be feeling satisfaction, not hurt. Shimrra's acknowledgment of his destabilization plan was the highest praise he had ever received from the Supreme Overlord. It was nice to know that, reviled as he was, his skills were at least appreciated. But to hear himself dismissed as a "certain former executor" was galling.

"What news of the heretics?" Shimrra asked.

High Priest Jakan glided reverently forward. "Our spies have failed to penetrate the inner command circle," he said. "Our lack of knowledge of their doctrine is too great, their loyalty too strong."

"Loyalty to *what*?"

"To their leader, Great Lord. He is the one from whom this heresy springs."

"And what is his name, this so-called leader of Shamed Ones?"

"He is called Yu'shaa, the Prophet."

"A prophet?" Shimrra offered a short, menacing laugh. "Does he see things, this prophet? Things that are to be?"

"So it is said, Great Lord."

"And does he see his own death, I wonder?" The high priest did not say anything to this, nor did Shimrra expect a response. The Supreme Overlord clenched one gnarled fist and raised it in the air for all to see. "I want him destroyed. Do you hear me? I want him found and destroyed. I want him crushed along with all of those who follow him!"

"It will not be easy," Ngaaluh announced evenly, disguising the voice of her heart behind an intelligence report. Claiming information gleaned through the work of her sect, she had persuaded the priest Harrar to allow her into the throne room with him. "Yu'shaa's followers grow steadily with each day. His message spreads farther. His voice, through them, is slowly building from a whisper into a shout that will soon be too loud to silence."

Shimrra turned on her, a mask of cold anger. From the steadiness of the image he was watching, Nom Anor knew that Ngaaluh neither flinched nor trembled as the Supreme Overlord approached her.

"And what is it they will be shouting, priestess?" he said. He was so close to her now that the seared and tattooed face of Nom Anor's former master seemed to fill the villip. "What is it they want?"

Ngaaluh didn't hesitate. "They want status, Highest One. To be un-Shamed. They want acceptance."

Shimrra's hideous visage creased in puzzlement. *Acceptance? Un-Shamed?* Nom Anor could barely repress a cackle. He could almost read the Supreme Overlord's mind. *What sort of infidel nonsense was this?*

The puzzlement faded. Shimrra pulled away. He was no fool. He would not mistake the ultimate goal of the heresy. The concept of redemption of the Shamed Ones struck at the very heart of Yuuzhan Vong hierarchy. It undermined the authority of those who stood at the top of that hierarchy. It gave a voice to those who were crushed at the bottom.

On the glorious day when Nom Anor walked into the Supreme Overlord's throne room as the un-Shamed leader of a rising tide of resentment, he would look in Shimrra's eyes and stand before him as an equal. Only then would Shimrra know just how thoroughly he had lost and how triumphant Nom Anor had been.

That a "certain former executor" could tunnel into the heart of the Supreme Overlord's ziggurat from its deepest basement would show everyone that he was someone to be reckoned with. His name would be accursed no longer.

In a high-pitched singsong voice, Onimi, the hideous familiar of the Supreme Overlord, spoke:

> *"Know, my Lord, they will not succeed*
> *In turning seditious dreams to deed."*

Shimrra turned his attention to his familiar. "I agree that it sounds preposterous, inconceivable—but if every Shamed One were to revolt, to take up arms . . ."

> *"Numbers alone will not suffice,*
> *nor any amount of sacrifice.*
> *Night and day you are protected by*
> *guards loyal to you, prepared to die."*

"Indeed," Shimrra said, scowling around the room at those attending. His thoughts, again, were obvious: on top of the shapers, intendants, and priests who were having increasing difficulties maintaining his realm, Hreven Karsh had failed him, a perfectly good plan set in place by a fugitive was beginning to fall apart, and a priestess had just delivered his death sentence. And these were the people who were supposed to protect him?

No, things most certainly were not going well for the Supreme Overlord.

Indeed, Nom Anor echoed with growing elation. *And if I have my way, Shimrra, things are going to get a whole lot worse for you yet!*

When she walked into the Bakuran infirmary ward, Leia couldn't help feel as if she'd done it all before. She'd been in enough med units in her time to know that they all pretty much looked the same, and this one was no exception. However, this wasn't the source of her déjà vu. What gave this moment such a strong sense of familiarity was the patient.

Tahiri lay unconscious on the room's sole bed, just as she had on Mon Calamari. The only difference was her eyes. This time they were wide open and saw nothing. She could have been resting peacefully, but for the fierce burning of her scars. The marks left on her forehead by the Yuuzhan Vong master shaper on Yavin 4 seemed to flare up in response to her psychological distress. Salis D'aar's meditechs had found no means of easing her internal suffering. The girl made no impression in the Force, giving Leia nothing to work with. All she could do was imagine what was going on inside the young woman's mind and body.

Jaina and Jag looked up from their position beside the bed. Jaina was still supposed to be confined to the hover-chair the medical droid had assigned to her, but in a typical show of independence, she had discarded it within minutes of getting out of bed. Jag hadn't left her side since she'd awoken, despite the fact that he must have been as exhausted as she was. Their hands stayed firmly clasped whenever they were in range, as though they were terrified to let go for fear of losing each other again.

Leia warmed at that thought. She had felt that way many times, and understood it all too well. What pleased her more than anything else was the fact that Jag was slowly abandoning his reservations about open displays of affection in public. It seemed that his close encounter with entechment had made him realize that time was simply too short to waste on worrying about what people thought.

"How's she doing?" Leia asked.

"The same." Jaina turned her attention back to Tahiri. "She's not responding to anything they try, and I can't get through to her. Perhaps Master Cilghal could do something, but . . ." She shrugged helplessly. "It's like she's not even there."

They stared at the injured girl for a long moment, the gloominess of their thoughts filling the room. Then Jaina made a visible effort to change the mood, straightening and stretching her arms.

"So, has the new treaty been ratified yet?"

"Signed and sealed." Leia was grateful for the change in topic. "The P'w'eck Emancipation Movement has formally allied with Bakura. Lwothin and Panib put their names to the papers half an hour ago. They've agreed to hold elections within the month, to share all Ssi-ruuvi assets seized in battle, and to initiate a liberation program for the P'w'eck who stayed behind. My guess is, once word spreads, they'll start seeing refugees from the Imperium within months, and some sort of retaliation within a year. I hope that by then Bakura will be strong enough to stand on its own. At least they know it's coming, so they can prepare."

"What about the Keeramak?" Jag asked.

"The body is already on its way back to Lwhekk. They figure returning the body of their Grand Shreeftut will temporarily appease the Ssi-ruuvi Conclave, even if it arouses the Elders' Council. The resulting conflict should keep them occupied for a while, at least."

Leia was still amazed at both the complexity and the audacity of the Keeramak's plan. Having risen to power ten years after the decimation of the Imperium at the hands of the New Republic, it had used its unique status to formulate a reprisal that very nearly worked. Faking a P'w'eck uprising wasn't hard; New Republic worlds responded to the idea of rebellion all too easily, so to the locals the story wasn't implausible. The nagging fear that the P'w'eck might be as bad as their former masters could only be assuaged by reassurances from the very pinnacle of Bakuran government, and the Keeramak had found an elegant way to solve that problem.

"The droid technicians have finished analyzing Cundertol's arm," she said.

Jaina's face hardened. "And?"

"It's as you thought. He was a human replica droid."

Jag hugged Jaina lightly around the shoulders when she shuddered. "He looked so *real*."

Leia nodded, understanding her daughter's revulsion. "The specs of his wrist and hand matched those of the droids made by Simonelle the Ingoian, over thirty years ago. The bones are poly-alloy; the muscles and other organs are made from biofiber; his skin was grown in a clone vat; and everything else is just synthflesh. Despite it being an abomination, it's actually an incredible piece of work."

"No wonder he didn't want to be examined on *Selonia*," Jaina said.

"I didn't think such things were possible," Jag said to Leia. "Imperial intelligence reported that Project Decoy failed."

"It did. We never managed to get the droid brains up to scratch—although Simonelle did by modifying an AA-1 verbobrain. They can be useful in certain circumstances, but by and large they tend to be clumsy and unconvincing."

"None of which applied to Cundertol," Jaina said, rubbing at her breastbone, which obviously still smarted from when the Prime Minister had attacked her.

"Someone on the black market must have made progress in the last twenty-five years. Someone prepared to charge for their efforts, too. Long before you were born, Jaina, HRDs used to cost over ten million credits. I can only imagine how much one would cost today."

"I'm sure we'll find that out once Vyram and Malinza have finished tracing the missing credits." As part of a "rehabilitation" scheme, the two ex-activists had been co-opted by the government to demonstrate that the information they'd found earlier was genuine. Although the kidnapping charges had been overturned, Freedom had still technically been an underground operation, and some sections of the interim government wanted an assurance that they would no longer pursue illegal activities.

Salkeli, on the other hand, had been sentenced on all manner of charges. The Rodian wasn't going to see daylight for a very long time indeed.

"So, let me get this straight," Jag said, frowning. "Cundertol covertly pays someone untold millions of credits to build a replica droid of himself. Right?"

Jaina nodded. "Then he books the *Jaunty Cavalier* to pick up the droid from the manufacturer and deliver it somewhere near here. We don't know where yet; maybe an abandoned base or a temporary station. It doesn't really matter, just as long as it's somewhere private."

"Then he fakes his own kidnapping," Leia went on. "This is the tricky part. He has to get offworld and back without raising suspicion. He can't take his bodyguards or his advisers. He has to be completely alone while the process is under way."

"And that process was entenchment." Jag's face was pale at the thought. "I can't believe he voluntarily turned himself in to the Ssi-ruuk so they could suck out his soul."

"Well, he must've had a good idea that they wouldn't just stick him in a droid ship and bleed him dry. He was their key to Bakura, after all. As long as they gave him what he wanted, he would reciprocate."

"You've got to admire them, really," Jaina said. "The plan was actually quite brilliant. They were going to get an entire world in exchange for making Cundertol immortal. And it almost worked."

"But *would* it have worked?" Jag asked. "I thought entenchment wasn't permanent—that the life energy of the subject gradually decayed."

Jaina nodded. "Lwothin explained when we met him that they'd made significant advances in the science of entenchment. That much was true, at least."

"There was a Jedi student named Nichos Marr," Leia explained, "who had a similar process performed on him for medical reasons. He died with the *Eye of Palpatine*, so we don't know how long he would have lasted."

"Cundertol wasn't a clunky droid like Nichos was,

though," Jaina protested. "He looked as real as you or I—and he smelled real, too, otherwise he wouldn't have fooled Meewalh and Cakhmain. Once the Ssi-ruuk had stuck him into the HRD and sent him back, all he had to do was avoid the invasion and get away. He could have dealt with any problems later, and no one would have been the wiser."

Jag shook his head. "You have to feel sorry for the crew of the *Jaunty Cavalier*. Cundertol sacrificed them all so that no one would contradict his story."

"That's the sign of an evil mastermind," Leia said, remembering her previous trip to Bakura and her first encounter with the spirit of her father. "No price is too great to pay to ensure his own survival."

Jaina looked down to Tahiri. The girl hadn't moved throughout the conversation. Her eyes were fixed on the ceiling, their only movement the occasional blink—the regularity of which they could have set a chronometer to. That and the slow rise and fall of her chest were the only signs that she was alive at all.

"You haven't found his body," Jaina said. It wasn't a question.

Leia replied anyway. "No."

There was movement in the doorway. Thinking it might be a meditech come to examine Tahiri, Leia stepped aside to let them through. But it was Goure, the Ryn whom Tahiri had befriended, and a Bakuran native, a Kurtzen dressed in a sand-colored, sleeveless gray robe with a wide leather belt around his waist. Numerous pouches adorned the belt, rattling as he walked.

"I apologize," the Ryn said, embarrassed. "I didn't mean to intrude."

"No, please. Come in." Jaina had told Leia the little she'd learned about the Ryn from Tahiri. "Han will be along later. I know he'll want to talk to you."

Goure looked uncertain about this. "Oh?"

"He has a friend he hasn't heard from for a while that he thought you might know of. A Ryn by the name of Droma."

"Droma?" He considered the name for a moment. "It doesn't sound familiar, I'm afraid. I could probably find him for you, if you like. The chances are good that one of my colleagues knows him."

"That's okay," Leia said. "It's no problem. I'm sure he's doing all right, wherever he is. Han was just curious, that's all." Goure's manner was pleasant and relaxed, perfectly likable. "He is blessed with the same talent as my husband."

Goure's smoky-colored forehead wrinkled at this. "Which is?"

"A knack for survival, of course." She matched his toothy smile, then looked away. The Kurtzen was standing patiently to one side, his ridged head gleaming in the harsh hospital light.

"This is Arrizza," Goure said, following her gaze. "I asked him to come."

"It's a pleasure," Leia said as she stepped up to the Kurtzen. She inclined her head in a slight bow of greeting. "This is my daughter, Lieutenant Colonel Jaina Solo, and Colonel Jagged Fel." Both nodded, and Arrizza bowed in return. "But you came to see Tahiri, I presume, not us," Leia added, once the introductions were over.

"We came to help her, yes," the Kurtzen said, exchanging a look with Goure.

"Help her in what way?" Jaina asked. "The meditechs and healers haven't been able to do anything for her. What makes you think you can?"

"They haven't been able to help her," Goure interrupted, "because they don't know what is wrong with her. They are looking for a physical ailment. They won't find one, because Tahiri is not fighting a disease. She is fighting herself."

Jaina glanced at Leia, then back to Goure. "She told you about her problem?"

"I saw enough to confirm what I had already heard. Everyone in the Ryn family knows the story of the Jedi-who-was-shaped. We know that the Yuuzhan Vong Shamed Ones tell it to each other as an epistle of hope. We also know that it is not encouraged outside certain circles of the Galactic Alliance. If word got out that a Jedi had been corrupted by the Yuuzhan Vong shapers—that such a thing was even possible—the growing support for the Jedi could be dramatically eroded."

There was no point denying anything that Goure said. "It's true," Leia admitted. "Mezhan Kwaad tried to turn Tahiri into a Yuuzhan Vong warrior by giving her a new persona—that of a Yuuzhan Vong warrior called Riina. My son Anakin rescued her and managed to break the programming. We believed the new persona had been erased, but it seems more likely now that Tahiri had simply buried it."

"Not 'it,' " said Goure. "*Her.* Riina of Domain Kwaad does not want to be buried. She wants to live, as does any intelligent being. Until she's allowed that, she will not lie easily."

"She's real?" Jag asked. "She's not just a figment of Tahiri's imagination?"

The Ryn shook his head. "In a manner of speaking, Riina is as real as Tahiri herself. You see, Tahiri wasn't simply brainwashed to think and act like a Yuuzhan Vong. Mezhan Kwaad designed Riina to be a person in her own right—with everything that entails. When Tahiri came back, she had more than just the knowledge of Yuuzhan Vong language and customs in her head; she had the makings of a new personality in there with her, wanting control of her body."

"But Tahiri got better," Jag said. "She was fine."

"Only until Anakin died," Leia pointed out. "Ever since then she's been struggling."

"But this Riina couldn't just have reappeared for no reason," Jag argued. "Something must have triggered her emergence."

"I agree," Goure said. "And I think that trigger was when the Galactic Alliance recently began making progress against the Yuuzhan Vong. Don't forget that when Riina came into being, her people were on the rise. She may have fallen, but so had Coruscant; so had the Senate. Her personal loss was overshadowed by the victories her compatriots were enjoying. Ultimately, I don't think she ever expected the Yuuzhan Vong to lose—as they very well might, now. In the face of defeat, the spirit of the Yuuzhan Vong is fighting back. Unfortunately for Tahiri, this is taking place within rather than without, as it is for the rest of us."

"So how do we get rid of her?" Jaina asked, her eyes shining with tears. Leia knew that Jaina felt responsible for Tahiri's breakdown and injuries on Bakura. She had suspected Riina's presence on Galantos, but hadn't known back then what to do.

"There's only one way to be sure of doing that," Goure said.

"And that is?" Jaina pressed.

The Ryn fixed her with an even and calculating stare. "To kill Tahiri, of course."

"*What?*" Jaina's voice was cold and angry. "Don't even *think* of joking about something like—"

"This is no joke, I assure you." The Ryn's tail quivered with repressed energy. "The basic mistake everyone in this room is making, is assuming Riina to be something that can be simply excised from Tahiri. However, Riina isn't some kind of tumor; she's as much a part of Tahiri as Tahiri is."

Jag shook his head. "I don't understand."

The Ryn looked apologetic. "I'm not entirely sure that I do, either, to be honest," he said. "Although I suspect that my species has a greater affinity for outcasts and refugees than most people, having spent most of our history being either or both. Since Yavin Four, Tahiri has been set apart from everyone else by virtue of her experience and her knowledge of the enemy. Anakin accepted her, but then he died, leaving her alone. We know that the idea of family is very strong among the Yuuzhan Vong, so she might have attempted to attach herself to you, Anakin's family. Ultimately, though, it wouldn't have been enough to keep her stable. What she needed, no one could give her, except herself."

The Ryn came to the side of Tahiri's bed and placed a hand on her forehead. If she registered his presence, she made no sign.

"The shapers know what they're doing. When they set out to turn Tahiri into a Yuuzhan Vong warrior, they did exactly that."

"But they failed to get rid of Tahiri," Leia said.

Goure nodded. "Thanks to Anakin, she was able to come back—only to find that her mind was now inhabited by someone else. And that someone had no intention of going away quietly, either. From Riina's point of view, Tahiri is the interloper. Tahiri has done little else but resist her ever since her reawakening. Unfortunately it's a battle that cannot be won, and it's taking a terrible toll on her mind."

"If it can't be won," Jaina said, "then what are you suggesting we do about her?"

"Simple," the Ryn said, turning to face her. "We have to help them learn to live together. We must teach them how to become one."

Jaina's incredulous laugh came out as a short, sharp bleat of defiance as she rose to her feet. "I don't think so."

Leia stepped forward to assuage her daughter's anger. "Jaina—"

"No, Mom," she said quickly. "Teach Tahiri to *accept* the Yuuzhan Vong in her? After what they did to her? After what they did to *Anakin*!" She shook her head firmly. "I won't let that happen. There has to be another way of removing Riina without harming Tahiri. There *has* to be."

Goure met her anger unflinchingly. "There isn't," he said soberly when her outburst had abated. "Just as Bakurans cannot integrate the P'w'eck and remain the same as they were before, so, too, is it with Tahiri and Riina. Moreover, there is a similar urgency. The P'w'eck and the Bakurans had to work together in order to save the planet from the Ssi-ruuk; now Tahiri must work with the personality of Riina Kwaad to save herself from madness."

Jaina opened her mouth to object, then shut it when her mother touched her arm. Leia could sympathize with her daughter. The idea that Tahiri couldn't be cured of the treatments the Yuuzhan Vong had inflicted on her did sound preposterous, but she also knew that everything they'd so far tried had failed miserably.

"Okay," Jag said, "assuming there is only one option, then how do we go about it, exactly?"

The Kurtzen stepped forward. "Like Riina," he said, "my people have been cast out and ostracized from the place in which we feel we belong. It almost killed us, but as have many others in such situations, we found our own way to survive. We believe that the power of life focuses in the objects we surround ourselves with. Either inadvertently or intentionally, the things we gather reinforce who we are, making us stronger or, at times, weaker. In a balanced life, the internal and external worlds reflect each other perfectly. When a life is imbalanced, internal and external aspects must be adjusted accordingly."

"That's all well and good," Jag said. "But again I have to ask: what do we have to do to help Tahiri?"

The Kurtzen native opened one of the pouches at his side. Reaching inside, he removed a small, wooden totem, its carved surface worn back by time. "We Kurtzen focus aspects of our lives' energies in items such as these. When our inner self lacks a particular aspect, we use these objects to bring ourselves into balance. Goure says that Tahiri had such an object in her possession. A silver totem that she produced at a time of crisis."

Leia reached into her robe and produced the pendant that Tahiri had taken from her and Han's bedroom that night, just before she'd fled.

"Is this what you're looking for?" She placed the silver pendant in Arrizza's callused hand. The tiny representation of Yun-Yammka glared up at her, as though vowing vengeance. "Tahiri blacked out when she found this on Galantos. She blacked out again when I confronted her with it the other night in our room. She was also holding it when they brought her in to the infirmary."

"This is it," Arrizza said. He folded the pendant in one hand and closed his eyes.

He seemed to collapse into himself for a moment then—his impression in the Force changing in a way Leia had never seen before. She couldn't help wonder just what he was doing, or what he was sensing. The pendant belonged to the Yuuzhan Vong and they were invisible to the Force, so there was no way they could have left any impression on the tiny statue.

Unless, of course, the "power of life" the Kurtzen had referred to was something else entirely.

With the attention of the room upon him, Arrizza stood silently as if in a trance. He muttered something unintelligible under his breath and clutched the pendant tightly in his grasp. In her life, Leia had experienced many strange traditions on many worlds. The Kurtzen's actions weren't surprising or outlandish, and they were meant well, but she didn't have the heart to tell him that they weren't likely to help.

Clearly, though, Jaina wasn't so willing to accept the gift in the spirit it was offered. She kept staring at Tahiri, shaking her head. As if reading her thoughts, Goure stepped up and placed a reassuring hand on Jaina's shoulder.

"I know how you must feel about this," he said. "But remember, while the personality of Riina is undeniably Yuuzhan Vong, she doesn't represent all that the Yuuzhan Vong have done these past years. If she can be accused of anything, it can only be of trying to survive."

"I don't care," Jaina said. "She's still Yuuzhan Vong."

"But she's a victim in all of this," Goure said. "Just as Tahiri is."

Jaina looked as if she was about to argue this, but the Ryn cut her off. "Tell me, was Tahiri herself when the bomb went off?"

"What? No, Riina had taken her over by then. Why?"

"So it was in fact Riina who created the Force bubble. Riina who saved the lives of those in the stands above by staying close in to the bomb where she knew she would have the greatest effect." The Ryn's stare was piercing, and beneath it Leia saw Jaina's stubbornness flag slightly. "Is that the work of someone who deserves our contempt? Someone who deserves to be put down?"

Jaina looked away from Goure, back to Tahiri's motionless body. "So what are we supposed to do? Sit back and let Riina take her over?"

"We have a choice to make. We can either help both of them, or we can watch them both die."

Leia felt the responsibility Goure was giving them like a heavy weight around her neck. He was asking them to do something potentially very dangerous. She knew about Anakin's vision of Riina as a dark force sweeping across the galaxy; and she also knew that the vision could well come to pass if Riina was released, with all Tahiri's knowledge of the Jedi to back her up. Cilghal had once described one of the Yuuzhan Vong's other hybrid creations—the voxyn—as "part of this galaxy and part of the Yuuzhan Vong's." If Goure was right, Tahiri would have to achieve the same state in order to survive, and there was no guarantee that she wouldn't end up as murderous and vicious as those creatures.

But in the end, Leia had to have faith in Tahiri's strength and resolve not to allow Anakin's vision to come to fruition.

Arrizza's silent mumbling ceased, and he opened his eyes. Goure stepped aside as the Kurtzen approached Tahiri's bed. No one spoke as Arrizza held the silver pendant with one hand and rested the other on Tahiri's forehead. His lips moved soundlessly. There was no response from Tahiri as the Kurtzen gently placed the pendant on her chest.

"Are you sure we should leave that there?" Jaina asked a little anxiously.

Arrizza nodded. "It is traditional. It will help cleanse her spiritually."

With that, Arrizza bowed reverently over her, holding the moment with an indrawn breath, then finally exhaling and backing away.

The sound of boots clomping along the corridor outside broke the sudden quiet of the room. Leia turned to see Han walk into the room, a look of some urgency on his face.

"We've just received word from Luke," he said, stepping up to Leia without acknowledging the others in the room. "He says . . ."

Han stopped, looking around the room, noting for the first time the people gathered by Tahiri's bed. "What's going on?"

Leia was about to explain the healing ceremony that Arrizza was trying to perform, but decided against it before she started. She didn't particularly feel like listening to her husband's cynical *sounds-like-mumbo-jumbo-to-me* speech.

"I'll explain later," she said instead, taking his hand in hers.

Han accepted this with a nod. "I heard the Ryn was here. Where'd he go?"

"He's right—" It was her turn to leave a sentence unfinished. "Well, he was."

"My friend had no intention of staying any longer than he was needed," Arrizza said, stepping forward. "Before we arrived, however, he did ask that I give you this."

The Kurtzen handed a sheet of flimsiplast to Leia. She unfolded it and read, with her husband reading it also over her shoulder.

My apologies for leaving so abruptly. I received word this morning that I am required elsewhere. Part of my instructions was to advise you to travel to Onadax at your earliest convenience. You will be met there.

When she awakens, please extend my heartfelt thanks to Tahiri for all she has done here.

With gratitude, Goure

"I am sorry," the Kurtzen said.

"Don't be," Han said. "It's not your fault. I was just hoping to ask him about Droma." He took the note from Leia and scanned it again. "We'll be met there," he paraphrased. "Does he mean by another Ryn, by the head of the family, or by someone else altogether?"

"It's not really made clear," Leia said. Despite—or because of—that, her interest was definitely piqued.

"Isn't Onadax in the Minos Cluster?" Jaina asked.

Leia nodded. "It's not all that far from Bakura."

Han looked concerned.

"What's wrong, Dad?"

"Well, it's not exactly the best of places to be visiting. It's a tough place, filled with all manner of lowlifes. I just don't want anyone getting their expectations up that this trip will be some sort of romantic holiday or something."

"Han, we had our first kiss in the belly of a space slug," Leia said. "Believe me when I say that my expectations of doing anything remotely romantic with you have never been particularly high."

She smiled at her husband, and was glad to see him lose his somberness and smile back. Then, placing an arm about her shoulder, he made to leave with her. "Come on, Your Worshipfulness," he said wryly. "You need to talk to Luke before he goes off to call Ben."

"Wait." She turned to Arrizza. "What about Tahiri?"

The Kurtzen shrugged again. "I do not know how long it will take for her to heal. It might be one hour; it might be a year. She might never heal at all. I'm sorry that I cannot give you a definite answer. All you can do is wait and see."

Leia looked at the girl on the bed once more. She hadn't moved the entire time they'd been in the room. No, wait—that wasn't quite true, Leia realized. She *had* changed: the young Jedi's eyes were now closed, as though she was sleeping. What that meant, exactly, Leia didn't know, but she hoped that it was a positive sign, at least.

Dream well, Tahiri, she sent into the quiet dark that was Tahiri's mind. *Dream well and come back strong.*

The small shuttle rattled out of hyperspace just on the border of the Ssi-ruuvi Imperium. Its holds were almost empty, as was its flight deck. In total, it carried eight passengers. Only one of them was alive.

Cundertol watched from the commander's station as the shuttle performed a cursory sweep of the space around it. He had changed its original settings shortly after leaving Bakura, immediately upon assuming control of the ship. This was a destination he had visited just once before. The event that had quite literally changed his life had taken place not far away, in a small research base left behind by the New Republic during its extended offensive against the Imperium. Abandoned for many years, it had been easy pickings for someone looking for a secret operations center.

The shuttle's scan picked up the station and a modified *Fw'Sen*-class picket ship parked nearby. He set the shuttle on an intercept vector for the latter, broadcasting a preplanned signal.

A response came within seconds. The picket ship extended docking grapnels and, once they were near enough, mated the two vessels together. A booming *clang* resounded through the ship around him, announcing contact.

Grunting in satisfaction, Cundertol climbed from the commander's chair and headed for the air lock, stepping over the bodies of the P'w'eck crew as he went. The stump of his severed arm had healed over perfectly, leaving a smooth patch of skin that was barely tender to the touch.

"I have been waiting," said the Ssi-ruuvi general whom Cundertol knew only as E'thinaa. His words came in the Ssi-ruuvi language, which the makers of Cundertol's body had preprogrammed him to understand.

"I came as soon as I could." Cundertol executed the smallest bow he could deliver without seriously offending the general. There were no guards in the bare stateroom, but he didn't doubt that he was being watched. "There were . . . complications."

The thick black ridge that was E'thinaa's eyebrows lifted in disapproval. "The Keeramak?"

"Is dead," Cundertol reported instantly and without

emotion. "I have its body onboard the shuttle as proof." He didn't mention that the shuttle had originally been intended to deliver the body to Lwhekk as a placatory gesture, or that he'd been forced to stow away on the craft in order to redirect it—and to survive.

The general nodded his approval, his scent-tongues tasting the air. "As long as this objective has been achieved, then everything else is unimportant."

"I must admit that I don't understand why you wanted this, above all else," Cundertol said. "Your people regard the Keeramak as some sort of god. Surely killing it will cause chaos and civil war—more disruption than the Imperium can possibly withstand. You've spent so long rebuilding things. Why destroy them now?"

The general's massive tail thumped the ground once, as if demanding silence. "You are not required to understand anything, human. You stink of lies."

Cundertol nodded, averting his gaze from the general's stare. He'd heard too many stories about the persuasive powers of the Ssi-ruuk to risk being caught now. His HRD body might be physically strong, but it couldn't protect him against the many traps that might befall his mind.

But . . .

His mind tripped on the general's words. How could E'thinaa have detected the scent of deception when the tissue comprising the outer layers of his new body had been specifically designed to release scents identical to a natural, nonstressed human, no matter what his state of mind or what lay beneath the facade? The general had to be bluffing, he told himself dismissively.

It wasn't, however, so easy to shake himself free of his sudden suspicions. The Ssi-ruuk didn't often bluff, after all. They were usually more direct in their approaches to and manipulations of what they regarded to be "lesser" species.

And now that he thought about it, the superior olfactory senses of his new body were picking up something odd about the *Ssi-ruu* . . .

He suddenly felt distinctly uncomfortable, wanting to leave there as soon as possible. Something wasn't quite right, and he didn't like it one bit.

"I've met my side of the bargain," he said, glad that he had retained his sabacc face, after the transfer. "Now, how about you?"

"You have your new body. What more do you want?"

"You know what I want. You said you'd refund half the money I paid for this body if I delivered you Bakura. I've done that, so now I'd like what you promised me."

The general began to pace the room with clicking strides, his tail sweeping menacingly. "It is my understanding that Xwhee is no longer part of the Imperium."

"It *has* been consecrated—"

"And the P'w'eck traitors have taken it for their own, no?"

"Yes, and you can fight for it now. You can send troops without fearing for their souls—"

The general cut him off with a chopping gesture of one mighty arm. "You have not delivered your side of the bargain, yet you expect me to keep mine!" he roared close to Cundertol's face, spraying him with spittle. Cundertol flinched, and the general straightened. "I am disappointed, but I can't say that I'm surprised. Your species is not known for its honor."

Cundertol could feel his control over the situation quickly slipping away. "Listen, we're both doing a job here, and as you know, sometimes it's not possible to meet every expectation. I've taken you halfway there—"

"As we have taken you halfway," the general interrupted. "You have your new body; you have your bottled soul. Surely that is enough."

And maybe it was, Cundertol thought. With his mind safely ensconced in its new HRD home, he was free from aging and disease. He really could live forever, if he was careful. With the right contacts, he could get his arm fixed, establish a new power base somewhere else, begin building himself up to where he had been. There were thousands of opportunities in a galaxy this large. All he had to do was—

Cundertol stopped the thought in its tracks. What was the point of dreams without money to bring them into reality? Without money, he would never be able to replace his missing limb or buy new contacts; he wouldn't even be able to refuel the shuttle after its next stop. There was no point being immortal if you couldn't do anything—or worse, if you ended up drifting through space, heading nowhere.

"I'm not leaving here without the payment I deserve," he said slowly and firmly, staring the big lizard right in the eyes.

"No?" The general squared off and flexed his powerful muscles. "Would you combat me for it?"

Cundertol felt the strength coursing through his artificial body. What were flesh and blood against poly-alloy bones and enhanced biofiber muscles? If he could outfight a Jedi, then a Ssi-ruu should be no trouble whatsoever.

Cundertol nodded. "I will," he said, "and I will crush you as I would an insect."

The general laughed. "The hatchmate returns to destroy his mother!"

"I'm serious." Cundertol clenched and unclenched his fists with a mix of anger and nervousness. "Give me my money."

The general took up the challenge unflinchingly as he stepped forward, pinning Cundertol with his stare. With lethal deliberation, he said: "The only thing you shall get from me is death."

Cundertol braced himself for the fight, and suddenly found that he was unable to move. He was rooted to the spot, every muscle of his body rigid as though he were nothing more than a statue. He couldn't move his eyes, his mouth—he couldn't even breathe! And then, in mid-stroke, the beating of his heart stopped.

The general's leering visage came so close that he could feel the alien's breath on his face. Twin scent-tongues tasted him, licking at the fear surely emanating from his synthflesh.

"You are a fool, human," E'thinaa said. The general's breath stank, but Cundertol couldn't turn away from it. "Did you honestly think that we wouldn't be ready for you? Do you believe us to be so stupid? We have learned much of your vile machines since coming to your galaxy. We know how to encourage your filthy technologists to perform for us, to build restraining bolts that activate on hearing a particular phrase. We are perfectly capable of stealing that which we require to reach our goals—goals you helped us attain. You sowed chaos; now we shall reap the rewards."

Cundertol yearned to pull away . . .

Since coming to your galaxy . . .

Panic flooded through him.

The alien's hideous face seemed to melt and peel away. The long snout folded back and rolled down the long neck, taking the triple-lidded eyes and scent-tongues with them.

Beneath lay a face more horrible than any Cundertol had ever imagined. A long, sloping forehead swept down to two gaunt, tattooed cheeks. Purple sacks bulged under cold, black eyes. Deep scars carved the gray flesh like the cracks of an ice moon, and sharp teeth grinned at him as he realized his mistake.

"You are nothing to me," hissed the voice of the imper-sonator. "Perhaps, had you remained alive, we might have taken you as a slave or a sacrifice; but as you are, you are worthless, unliving filth. We have destroyed the machine that made you and purified the hands that touched it with the blood of a thousand captives. We would never deign to deal with dead stuff such as you are now made of. Life is tissue; it is soil; it is blood." The creature paused, then, and smiled. "It is death."

The face that would be the last thing Cundertol ever saw pulled back out of range. So profoundly was he frozen by the restraining bolt, he couldn't even focus his eyes. Everything beyond a meter remained a blur—a blur that filled with dark shadows as more of the vile creatures entered the room. They swarmed around him, twisting and writhing in impossible shapes.

The only thing you shall get from me is death. So E'thinaa—or whatever the alien's real name was—had said, and with those words he had been condemned. The last thing Cundertol felt was the powerful sting of amphistaffs striking him and tearing his artificial body apart. He couldn't move, but the aliens had ensured that he could still feel pain. The agony was blinding, too much to truly comprehend.

When Cundertol's containment fields finally dissolved and his mind fell away, it came as pure relief.

In the end, there was just one.

Klasse Ephemora was an isolated system on the side of Chiss space opposite the galactic Core. Named after the explorer who had first charted the system, centuries ago, it had once housed a small gem-mining operation around its one gas giant, a bloated monster hovering just inside the star's habitable zone. Severe atmospheric disturbances had prevented the gem station from ever being profitable, however, so it had been abandoned more than fifty standard years earlier. Klasse Ephemora had lain fallow ever since: lacking terrestrial worlds that might have encouraged colonization; too remote to warrant commercial interest, and yet too far away from the Chiss border to justify even a token military presence. Every few decades, an automated probe would sweep through the system to update astronomical charts and ensure that the navigational anchor points left behind by the initial survey were still true. Beyond that, it was completely ignored.

And so it might have remained forever, had not the last probe to pass through some twenty-five years earlier happened to note that the sole gas giant in the system, Mobus, had acquired a new satellite. This satellite joined a family of seventeen other satellites around Mobus, but exceeded their combined mass more than ten times over. A world in its own right, it was shrouded in clouds that prevented a visual survey as the probe flew by. The presence of water vapor might have warranted further investigation, but the probe was not programmed to change course for something so nebulous. Had there been clear signs of intelligent life on the moon-world, the probe might have braked into an orbit around Klasse A and observed the new moon in more detail, then reported the findings back to its superiors in the CEDF. But the planet emitted nothing on the subspace channels, nor were there any transmissions on the electromagnetic spectrum. So the probe simply noted the moon's appearance, then continued on its way.

The fact of the moon's existence had languished in the Chiss Expeditionary Library ever since, filed with all the myriad other reports from thousands of identical probes. As rare as the orbital capture was, it wasn't startling enough to attract the attention of the astronomers who studied the data on the probe's return. There were countless more interesting discoveries waiting in the Unknown Regions. So what if an abandoned system acquired an extra moon or two?

Jacen stared at the pictures of the moon brought back by the probe with a feeling bordering on profound awe.

He saw a gray orb lit by the baleful light of a boiling red-yellow gas giant. The atmosphere soaked up infrared, but radar showed a hilly terrain around the equator, with several small flat spots that could have been seas scattered evenly across both hemispheres. There was evidence of recent eruptions and crust movement, as would be expected for a world that had endured capture not just by a sun, but also by a gas giant.

"That's it," he breathed, barely able to contain his enthusiasm. "That's Zonama Sekot."

"The charts list it as M-Eighteen," Wyn said.

"It's Zonama Sekot," Jacen repeated. "It has to be. What did you say the odds were, Danni?"

"Very much against something like this happening naturally, Jacen," she said. "But that doesn't mean it *couldn't* happen."

"I know," he replied easily. "But it didn't."

R2-D2 whistled cheerfully, as though backing him up.

"We should at least check it out," Mara said.

"We will," Luke agreed. "After all, it's the best lead we've had so far."

"If there's anything we can do to assist you," Soontir Fel said, "consider it done." He hesitated for barely a second before adding, "Within reason, of course."

Those weren't empty words. The Chiss had already provided detailed tactical maps of the Unknown Regions, revealing several torturous trade lanes through areas that previously had been thought impassable. More sinisterly, the data showed that the Yuuzhan Vong had been more active in the area than Galactic Alliance intelligence had known. As far back as the first attacks on New Republic systems, a Yuuzhan Vong task force had made an end run around Chiss space and made it into the Unknown Regions. That it had never been heard of since—or that no other task force had made it past the Chiss—was no cause for complacency. Further Chiss assistance might well prove welcome at some point.

Luke smiled genially. "Thank you," he said. "And I promise not to mention a treaty with the Galactic Alliance until the next time we pass through here."

"If there is a next time," Mara said.

Jacen nodded, thinking of the attack on the Imperial Remnant, the Krizlaws on Munlali Mafir, and Chief Navigator Aabe; and then, of course, the Yuuzhan Vong themselves, whose incursions into Chiss space were becoming more frequent every day.

It's been hard enough getting this far, he thought. *I doubt it's going to get any easier.*

He felt Danni's support and confidence nearby, and was warmed by it. At least, he added, there was no shortage of support—for him and the Galactic Federation of Free Alliances. All they had to do was follow their hearts, letting the Force guide their decisions, and eventually, he was sure, they'd get there.

What they would find when they arrived, however, remained to be seen . . .

"Begun, this Clone War has!"
—MASTER YODA

Turn the page
for an excerpt
from the very first Clone Wars novel,

STAR WARS: SHATTERPOINT
by Matthew Stover

an original Star Wars adventure
featuring Jedi Master Mace Windu.

ONE

CAPITAL CRIMES

The spaceport at Pelek Baw smelled clean. It wasn't. Typical backworld port: filthy, disorganized, half-choked with rusted remnants of disabled ships.

Mace stepped off the shuttle ramp and slung his kit bag by its strap. Smothering wet heat pricked sweat across his bare scalp. He raised his eyes from the ochre-scaled junk and discarded crumples of empty nutripacks scattered around the landing deck, up into the misty jade sky.

The white crown of Grandfather's Shoulder soared above the city: the tallest mountain on the Korunnal Highland, an active volcano with dozens of open calderae. Mace remembered the taste of the snow at the treeline, the thin cold air and the aromatic resins of the evergreen scrub below the summmit.

He had spent far too much of his life on Coruscant.

If only he could have come here for some other reason.

Any other reason.

A straw-colored shimmer in the air around him explained the clean smell: a surgical sterilization field. He'd expected it. The spaceport had always had a powered-up surgical field umbrella, to protect ships and equipment from the various native fungi that feed on metals and silicates; the field also wiped out the bacteria and molds that would otherwise have made the spaceport smell like an overloaded 'fresher.

Mace wore clothing appropriate to his cover: a stained

Corellian cat–leather vest over a loose shirt that used to be white, and skin-tight black pants with wear-patches of gray. His boots carried a hint of polish, but only above the ankle; the uppers were scuffed almost to suede. The only parts of his ensemble that were well-maintained were the supple holster belted to his right thigh, and the gleaming Merr-Sonn Power 5 it held. His lightsaber was stuffed into the kit bag, disguised as an old-fashioned glow rod. The kit bag also held what looked like a battered old datapad, most of which was actually a miniature subspace transmitter that was frequency-locked to the band monitored by the light cruiser *Halleck*, on station in the Ventran system.

The spaceport's probiotic showers were still in their long, low blockhouse of mold-stained duracrete, but their entrance had been expanded into a large temporary-looking office of injection-molded plastifoam, with a foam-slab door that hung askew on half-sprung hinges. The door was streaked with rusty stains that had dripped from the fungus-chewed durasteel sign above. The sign said CUSTOMS. Mace went in.

Sunlight leaked green through mold-tracked windows. Climate control wheezed a body-temp breeze from ceiling vents, and the smell loudly advertised that this place was well beyond the reach of the surgical field. The other passengers who'd gotten off the shuttle were inside already: two Kubaz who'd spent the de-orbit fluting excitedly about the culinary possibilities of pinch beetles and buzzworms, and a mismatched couple who seemed to be some kind of itinerant comedy act, a Kitonak and a Pho'pheahian whose canned banter had made Mace long for earplugs. Or hard vacuum. Even incurable deafness. The comedians must have been far down on their luck; Haruun Kal's capital city is a place lounge acts go to die.

Inside the customs office, enough flybuzz hummed to get

the two Kubaz chuckling and eagerly nudging each other. Mace didn't quite manage to ignore the Pho Ph'eahian broadly explaining to a bored-looking human that he'd just jumped in from Kashyyyk and boy were his legs tired. The agent seemed to find this about as tolerable as Mace did; he hurriedly passed the comedians along after the pair of Kubaz, and they all disappeared into the shower blockhouse.

Mace found a different customs agent: a Neimoidian female with pink-slitted eyes, cold-bloodedly sleepy in the heat. The Neimoidian looked over his identikit incuriously. "Corellian, hnh? Purpose of your visit?"

"Business."

She sighed tiredly. "You'll need a better answer than that. Corellia's no friend of the Confederacy."

"Which would be why I'm doing business *here*."

"Hnh. I scan you. Open your bag for inspection."

Mace thought about the "old-fashioned glow rod" stashed in his bag. He wasn't sure how convincing its shell would be to Neimoidian eyes, which can see deep into the infrared.

"I'd rather not."

"Do I care? Open it." She squinted dark pink up at him. "Hey, nice skinjob. You could almost pass for a Korun."

"Almost?"

"You're too tall. And they mostly have hair. And anyway, Korunnai are all Force freaks, yes? They have powers and stuff."

"I have powers."

"Yeah?"

"Sure." Mace hooked his thumbs behind his belt. "I have the power to make ten credits appear in your hand."

The Neimoidian looked thoughtful. "That's a pretty good power. Let's see it."

He passed his hand over the customs agent's desk, and

let fall a coin he'd palmed from his belt's slit pocket. The Neimoidian had powers of her own: she made the coin disappear. "Not bad." She turned up her empty hand. "Let's see it again."

"Let's see my identikit validated and my bag passed."

The Neimoidian shrugged and complied, and Mace did his trick again. "Power like yours, you'll get along fine in Pelek Baw," the Neimoidian said. "Pleasure doing business with you. Be sure to take your PB tabs. And see me on your way offworld. Ask for Pule."

"I'll do that."

Toward the back of the customs office, a large poster advised everyone entering Pelek Baw to use the probiotic showers before leaving the spaceport. The showers replaced beneficial skin flora that had been killed by the surgical field. This advice was supported with gruesomely graphic holos of the wide variety of fungal infections awaiting unshowered travelers. A dispenser beneath the poster offered half-credit doses of tablets guaranteed to restore intestinal flora as well. Mace bought a few, took one, then stepped into the shower blockhouse.

The blockhouse had a smell all its own: a dark musky funk, rich and organic. The showers themselves were simple autonozzles spraying bacteria-rich nutrient mist; they lined the walls of a thirty-meter walk-thru. He stripped off his clothes and stuffed them into his kit bag. There was a conveyor strip for possessions beside the walk-thru entrance, but he held on to the bag. A few germs wouldn't do it any harm.

At the far end of the showers, he walked into a situation.

The dressing station was loud with turbine-driven air-jet dryers. The two Kubaz and the comedy team, still naked, milled uncertainly in one corner. A large surly-looking human in sunbleached khakis and a military cap stood facing them, impressive arms folded across his equally impressive chest. He stared at the naked travelers with cold unspecific threat.

A smaller human in identical clothing rummaged through their bags, which were piled behind the large man's legs. The smaller man had a bag of his own, into which he dropped anything small and valuable. Both men had stun batons dangling from belt loops, and blasters secured in snap-flap holsters.

Mace nodded thoughtfully. The situation was clear enough. Based on who he was supposed to be, he should just ignore this. But, cover or not, he was still a Jedi.

The big one looked Mace over. Head to toe and back again. His stare had the open insolence that comes of being clothed and armed and facing someone who's naked and dripping wet. "Here's another. Smart guy carried his own bag."

The other rose and unlooped his stun baton. "Sure, smart guy. Let's have the bag. Inspection. Come on."

Mace went still. Pro-bi mist condensed to rivulets and trickled down his bare skin. "I can read your mind," he said darkly. "You only have three ideas, and all of them are wrong."

"Huh?"

Mace flipped up a thumb. "You think being armed and ruthless means you can do whatever you want." He folded his thumb and flipped up his forefinger. "You think nobody will stand up to you when they're naked." He folded that one again and flipped up the next. "And you think you're going to look inside my bag."

"Oh, he's a funny one." The smaller man spun his stun baton and stepped toward him. "He's not just smart, he's funny."

The big man moved to his flank. "Yeah, regular comedian."

"The comedians are over there." Mace inclined his

head toward the Pho Ph'eahian and his Kitonak partner, naked and shivering in the corner. "See the difference?"

"Yeah?" The big man flexed big hands. "What are you supposed to be, then?"

"I'm a prophet." Mace lowered his voice as though sharing a secret. "I can see the future . . ."

"Sure you can." He set his stubble-smeared jaw and showed jagged yellow teeth. "What do you see?"

"You," Mace said. "Bleeding."

His expression might have been a smile if there had been the faintest hint of warmth in his eyes.

The big man suddenly looked less confident.

In this he can perhaps be excused; like all successful predators, he was interested only in victims. Certainly not in *opponents*. Which was the purpose of his particular racket, after all: Members of any sapient species that are culturally accustomed to wearing clothes will feel hesitant, uncertain, and vulnerable when they're caught naked. Especially humans. Any normal man will stop to put on his pants before he throws a punch.

Mace Windu, by contrast, looked like he might know of uncertainty and vulnerability by reputation, but had never met either of them face to face.

One hundred and eighty-eight centimeters of muscle and bone. Absolutely still. Absolutely relaxed. From his attitude, the pro-bi mist that trickled down his naked skin might have been carbon fiber-reinforced ceramic body armor.

"Do you have a move to make?" Mace said. "I'm in a hurry."

The big man's gaze twitched sideways, and he said, "Uh—?" and Mace felt a pressure in the Force over his left kidney and heard the sizzle of a triggered stun baton. He spun and caught the wrist of the smaller man with both hands, shoving the baton's sparking corona well clear with a twist that levered his face into the path of

Mace's rising foot. The impact made a smack wet and meaty as the snap of bone. The big man bellowed and lunged and Mace stepped to one side and whipcracked the smaller man's arm to spin his slackening body. Mace caught the small man's head in the palm of one hand and shoved it crisply into the big man's nose.

The two men skidded in a tangle on the slippery damp floor and went down. The baton spat lightning as it skittered into a corner. The smaller man lay limp. The big man's eyes spurted tears and he sat on the floor, trying with both hands to massage his smashed nose into shape. Blood leaked through his fingers.

Mace stood over him. "Told you."

The big man didn't seem impressed. Mace shrugged. A prophet, it is said, receives no honor on his own world.

Mace dressed silently while the other travelers reclaimed their belongings. The big man made no attempt to stop them, or even to rise. Presently the smaller man stirred, moaned, and opened his eyes. As soon as they focused well enough to see Mace still in the dressing station, he cursed and clawed at his holster flap, struggling to free his blaster.

Mace looked at him.

The man decided his blaster was better off where it was.

"You don't know how much trouble you're in," he muttered sullenly as he settled back down on the floor, words blurred by his smashed mouth. He drew his knees up and wrapped his arms around them. "People who butch up with capital militia don't live long around—"

The big man interrupted him with a cuff on the back of his head. "Shut it."

"Capital militia?" Mace understood now. His face settled into a grim mask, and he finished buckling down his holster. "You're the police."

The Pho Ph'eahian mimed a pratfall. "You'd think they'd hire cops who aren't so *clumsy*, eh?"

"Oh, I dunno, Phootie," the Kitonak said in a characteristically slow, terminally relaxed voice. "They bounced *real* nice."

Both Kubaz whirred something about slippery floors, inapppropriate footwear and unfortunate accidents.

The cops scowled.

Mace squatted in front of them. His right hand rested on the Power 5's butt. "It'd be a shame if somebody had a blaster malfunction," he said. "A slip, a fall—sure, it's embarrassing. It hurts. But you'll get over it in a day or two. If somebody's blaster accidentally went off when you fell—?" He shrugged. "How long will it take you to get over being dead?"

The smaller cop started to spit back something venomous. The larger one interrupted him with another cuff. "We scan you," he growled. "Just go."

Mace stood. "I remember when this was a nice town."

He shouldered his kit bag and walked out into the blazing tropical afternoon. He passed under a dented, rusty sign without looking up.

The sign said: WELCOME TO PELEK BAW.

Faces—

Hard faces. Cold faces. Hungry, or drunk. Hopeful. Calculating. Desperate.

Street faces.

Mace walked a pace behind and to the right of the Republic Intelligence station boss, keeping his right hand near the Merr-Sonn's butt. Late at night, the streets were still crowded. Haruun Kal had no moon; the streets were lit with spill from taverns and outdoor cafes. Lightpoles—tall hexagonal pillars of duracrete with glowstrips running up each face—stood every twenty meters along both sides of the street. Their pools of yellow glow bordered black shadow; to pass into one of the alley mouths was to be wiped from existence.

The Intel station boss was a bulky, red-cheeked woman about Mace's age. She ran the Highland Green Washeteria, a thriving laundry and public refresher station on the capitol's north side. She never stopped talking. Mace hadn't started listening.

The Force nudged him with threat in all directions: from the rumble of wheeled groundcars that careened at random through crowded streets to the fan of death sticks in a teenager's fist. Uniformed militia swaggered or strutted or sometimes just posed, puffed up with the fake-dangerous attitude of armed amateurs. Holster flaps open. Blaster rifles propped against hipbones. He saw plenty of weapons waved, saw people shoved, saw lots of intimidation and threatening looks and crude street-gang horseplay; he didn't see much actual keeping of the peace. When a burst of blasterfire sang out a few blocks away, none of them even looked around.

But nearly all of them looked at Mace.

Militia faces: Human, or too close to call. Looking at Mace, seeing nothing but a Korun in offworld clothes, their eyes went dead cold. Blank. Measuring. After a while, hostile eyes all look alike.

Mace kept alert, and concentrated on projecting a powerful aura of Don't Mess With Me.

He would have felt safer in the jungle.

Street faces: drink-bloated moons of bust-outs mooching spare change. A Wookiee gone grey from nose to chest, exhaustedly straining against his harness as he pulled a two-wheeled taxicart, fending off street kids with one hand while the other held onto his money belt. Jungle prospector faces: fungus scars on their cheeks, weapons at their sides. Young faces: children, younger than Depa had been on the day she became his Padawan, offering their services to Mace at "special discounts" because they "liked his face."

Many of them were Korun.

A later entry in his journal records his thoughts verbatim:

> Sure. Come to the city. Life's easy in the city.
>
> No vine cats. No drillmites. No brassvines or death hollows. No shoveling grasser manure, no hauling water, no tending akk pups. Plenty of money in the city. All you have to do is sell this, or endure that. What you're really selling: your youth. Your hope. Your future.
>
> Anyone with sympathy for the Separatist Cause should spend a few days in Pelek Baw. Find out what the Confederacy is really fighting for.
>
> It's good that Jedi do not indulge in hate.

The station boss's chatter somehow wandered onto the subject of the Intel front she managed. The station boss's name was Phloremirlla Tenk, "but call me Flor, sweetie. Everybody does." Mace picked up the thread of her ramble.

"Hey, everybody needs a shower once in a while. Why not get your clothes spiffed at the same time? So everybody comes there. I get jups, kornos, you name it. I get militia and Seppie brass—well, used to, till the pullback. I get everybody. I got a pool. I got six different saunas. I got private showers—you can get water, alcohol, pro-bi, sonics, you name it—maybe a recorder or two to really get the dirt we need. Some of these militia officers, you'd be amazed what they fall to talking about, alone in a steam room. Know what I mean?"

She was the chattiest spy he'd ever met. When she eventually stopped for breath, Mace told her so.

"Yeah, funny, huh? How do you think I've survived this game for twenty-three years? Talk as much as I do, it takes people longer to notice you never really *say* anything."

Maybe she was nervous. Maybe she could smell the threat that smoked in those streets. Some people think they can hold danger at bay by pretending to be safe.

"I got thirty-seven employees. Only five are Intel. Everybody else just works there. Hah: I make twice the money off the Washeteria than I draw after twenty-three years in the service. Not that it's all that hard to do, if you know what I mean. You know what an RS-17 makes? Pathetic. Pathetic. What's a Jedi make these days? Do they even pay you? Not enough, I'll bet. They love that 'Service is it's own reward' junk, don't they? Especially when it's *other* people's service. I'll just bet."

She'd already assembled a team to take him upcountry. Six men with heavy weapons and an almost-new steam-crawler. "They look a little rough, but they're good boys, all of them. Freelancers, but solid. Years in the bush. Two of them are full-blood korno. Good with the natives, you know?"

For security reasons, she explained, she was taking him to meet them herself. "Sooner you're on your way, happier we'll both be. Right? Am I right? Taxis are hopeless this time of day. Mind the gutter cookie—that stuff'll chew right through your boots. Hey, *watch* it, creepo! Ever hear that peds have the right-of-way? Yeah? Well, *your* mother eats *Hutt* slime!" She stumped along the street, arms swinging. "Um, you know this Jedi of yours is wanted, right? You got a way to get her offworld?"

What Mace had was the *Halleck* on station in the Ventran system with twenty armed landers and a regiment of clone troopers. What he said was, "Yes."

A new round of blasterfire sang perhaps a block or two away, salted with staccato pops crisper than blaster hits. Flor instantly turned left and dodged away up the street.

"Whoops! *This* way—you want to keep clear of those little rumbles, you know? Might just be a food riot, but you never know. Those handclaps? Slugthrowers, or I'm a Dug. Could be action by some of these guerillas as your Jedi runs—lots of the kornos carry slugthrowers, and slugs *bounce*. Slugthrowers. I hate 'em. But they're easy to maintain. Day or two in the jungle and your blaster'll never fire again. A good slug rifle, keep 'em wiped and oiled, they last forever. The guerillas have pretty good luck with them, even though they take a *lot* of practice—slugs are ballistic, you know. You have to plot the trajectory in your head. Shee, gimme a blaster *any* time."

A new note joined the blasterfire: a deeper, throatier *thrummthrummmthrummthrumm*. Mace scowled over his shoulder. That was some kind of repeater: a T-21, or maybe a Merr-Sonn Thunderbolt.

Military hardware.

"It would be good," he said, "if we could get off the street."

While she assured him, "No, no, no, don't worry, these scuffles never add up to much," he tried to calculate how fast he could dig his lightsaber out of his kit bag.

The firing intensified. Voices joined in: shouts and screams. Anger and pain. It started to sound less like a riot, and more like a firefight.

Just beyond the corner ahead, whitehot bolts flared past along the right-of-way. More blasterfire zinged behind them. The firefight was overflowing, becoming a flood that might surround them at any second. Mace looked back: along this street he still could see only crowds and groundcars, but the militia were starting to take an interest: checking weapons, trotting toward alleys and cross streets. Flor said behind him, "See? Look at that. They're not even really *aiming* at anything. Now, we just nip across—"

She was interrupted by a splattering *thwop*. Mace had heard that sound too often: steam, superheated by a high-energy plasma bolt, exploding through living flesh. A deep-tissue blaster hit. He turned back to Flor and found her staggering in a drunken circle, painting the pavement with her blood. Where her left arm should have been was only a fist-sized mass of ragged tissue. Where the rest of her arm was, he couldn't see.

She said: "What? What?"

He dropped his kit bag and dove into the street. He rolled, coming up to slam her hip-joint with his shoulder. The impact folded her over him; he lifted her, turned, and sprang back for the corner. Bright flares of blaster bolts bracketed invisible sizzles and fingersnaps of hypersonic slugs. He reached the meager cover of the corner and lay her flat on the sidewalk, tucked close against the wall.

"This isn't supposed to happen." Her life was flooding out the shattered stump of her shoulder. Even dying, she kept talking. A blurry murmur: "This isn't *happening*. It *can't* be happening. My—my *arm*—"

In the Force, Mace could feel her shredded brachial artery; with the Force, he reached inside her shoulder to pinch it shut. The flood trickled to sluggish welling.

"Take it easy." He propped her legs on his kit bag to help maintain blood pressure to her brain. "Try to stay calm. You can live through this."

Boots clattered on permacrete behind him: a militia squad sprinting toward them. "Help is on the way." He leaned closer. "I need the meetpoint and the recognition code for the team."

"What? What are you talking about?"

"Listen to me. Try to focus. Before you go into shock. Tell me where I can find the upcountry team, and the recognition code so we'll know each other."

"You don't—you don't understand—this isn't *happening*—"

"Yes. It is. *Focus.* Lives depend on you. I need the meetpoint and the code."

"But—but—you don't *understand*—"

The militia behind him clattered to a stop. *"You! Korno! Stand away from that woman!"*

He glanced back. Six of them. Firing stance. The light-pole at their backs haloed black shadow across their faces. Plasma-charred muzzles stared at him. "This woman is wounded. Badly. Without medical attention, she will die."

"You're no doctor," one said, and shot him.

The *Star Wars* adventure doesn't end here!
Read *Star Wars: The New Jedi Order.*

THE COMPLETE NJO SERIES

VECTOR PRIME by R. A. Salvatore

DARK TIDE I: ONSLAUGHT by Michael Stackpole
DARK TIDE II: RUIN by Michael Stackpole

AGENTS OF CHAOS I: HERO'S TRIAL by James Luceno
AGENTS OF CHAOS II: JEDI ECLIPSE by James Luceno

BALANCE POINT by Kathy Tyers

RECOVERY by Troy Denning (eBook)

EDGE OF VICTORY I: CONQUEST by Greg Keyes
EDGE OF VICTORY II: REBIRTH by Greg Keyes

STAR BY STAR by Troy Denning

DARK JOURNEY by Elaine Cunningham

ENEMY LINES 1: REBEL DREAM by Aaron Allston
ENEMY LINES 2: REBEL STAND by Aaron Allston

TRAITOR by Matthew Stover

DESTINY'S WAY by Walter Jon Williams
YLESIA by Walter Jon Williams (eBook)

FORCE HERETIC I: REMNANT by Sean Williams & Shane Dix
FORCE HERETIC 2: REFUGEE by Sean Williams & Shane Dix
FORCE HERETIC 3: REUNION by Sean Williams & Shane Dix

THE FINAL PROPHECY by Greg Keyes

THE UNIFYING FORCE by James Luceno

WWW.READSTARWARS.COM

Published by Del Rey/LucasBooks • Available wherever books are sold